Praise for THE LAST KHAN

"Blockbuster plot . . . a heart-pounding thriller. Twisting and turning at every level. This story will keep you so riveted that you'll need to keep food and drink close by."

—STEPHEN JOSEPH KEELER, MEMBER OF THE COUNCIL FOR EMERGING NATIONAL SECURITY AFFAIRS

ଓଃ

"Amazingly powerful imagery about the world and intensely personal descriptions of the people in a gripping story. Fiction so real you wouldn't know it. Geoff Hammond's writing in this book makes him the new master of shock and awe."

—BOB WEINER, WHITE HOUSE AND CONGRESS NATIONAL COLUMNIST, FORMER WHITE HOUSE NATIONAL DRUG POLICY SPOKESMAN, FORMER SPOKESMAN FOR HOUSE GOVERNMENT OPERATIONS COMMITTEE, FORMER HOUSE AGING COMMITTEE CHIEF OF STAFF UNDER FLORIDA CONGRESSMAN PEPPER

ଓଃ

"This is a novel for those who think clearly and relish the thrill of plausible, orderly suspense. In *The Last Khan*, one is brought into the arcane world of Planckian atoms and, at the outset, might fear the mind will go hurl-a-whirl in contemplation. No worries are warranted, however, because the author writes with Saganesque clarity and allows one to glide over the physics. . . . It is not too much to say that one is left on razor's edge by the logic and skillful narrative until the final few paragraphs of the work."

—CHARLES L. COX, PH.D. IN EUROPEAN HISTORY

☙

THE LAST KHAN

GEOFF HAMMOND

HORIZON
PUBLISHING
FORT LAUDERDALE
FLORIDA

Horizon Publishing, LLC
6700 North Andrews Avenue, Suite 400
Fort Lauderdale, FL 33309

AUTHOR'S PHOTOGRAPH BY
Daniel Azoulay

EDITED BY
Carol Killman Rosenberg
COVER AND INTERIOR DESIGN BY
Gary A. Rosenberg
THE BOOK COUPLE • www.thebookcouple.com

Printed in the United States of America

*For Ava
and Rosemary*

PROLOGUE

Hebei Province, China 1995

As the elderly Ying Chek neared the riverbank to keep a closer watch over her only grandson, her dark eyes filled with horror at the sight of the dozens of grotesquely bloated bodies floating along the river's edge.

"Get away from the water!" she shouted in panic to the young boy. "Get away from the water!" she shouted again, moving as quickly as her thin legs would carry her.

Yao Chek turned to look up at his grandmother as the old woman rushed forward. Terror had etched itself upon his once angelic face, and he would never be the same again.

For many generations the river had been their benefactor. The crystal clear waters had beckoned invitingly to the villagers and had satisfied many of their daily needs. Its graceful turns and calm eddies had created idyllic pools for bathing and children's play. But recently, a catastrophe had occurred. A mysterious virulence had suddenly stricken the peaceful Chinese farming village, and it had changed everything.

It had happened without warning, as if the devil's hand had touched the waters. The once benevolent river had become a cauldron of witches' brew literally over night, contaminating everything it came in contact with—even the fields and the crops. Within twenty-four hours, it had spread its venom throughout the small community like an enormous poisonous serpent. Even some who hadn't ventured into the deadly river suffered agonizing muscle spasms, gut-wrenching nausea and vomiting, and blistering body-wide rashes before their bodies just gave out and expired. In desperation, some of the villagers immediately tried boiling the water to purify it, but to no avail. Its horrific effects persisted.

The village leaders were powerless to control the ongoing human devastation. Helplessly, they all became victims trapped in a horrifying scenario. Without the river there was no subsistence; within it lurked certain death. Trying to come to grips with the finality of their plight and overwhelmed by the circumstances, they had made numerous and frantic appeals to the local government. But nothing was done. The terrible crisis was ignored.

No one would acknowledge that farther to the east, deep inside the distant mountains, a toxic soup of virulence had been festering for a long time, waiting for its release. Something unearthly had caused a fracture in the bedrock directly above the huge aquifer from which the river was sourced. Toxic materials had quickly leeched into the aquifer—materials far more deadly than anything created by nature. The thin crack in the earth's crust had allowed the deadly flow to begin. Nothing stood in its way. Nothing could prevent its devastation. Nothing could tolerate its fiendish composition. Only the darkest imaginings of the worst nightmare described the terror of its life-destroying potency.

☙

"Oh, my dear God," the elderly Chek uttered slowly, recognizing her sister and daughter among the dead. She had little hope that the rest of her family had survived.

She and the boy hadn't been gone very long, but it was long enough to escape whatever evil had stricken their village. Unwilling to fall prey to the unknown scourge that had laid claim to all that she held dear, the feeble but fiercely determined Ying Chek carefully strapped her trembling grandson onto her back and hiked the long trek into the mountains and to a safe haven. Her heavy heart made the journey that much more difficult.

In the end, countless hundreds of lives were ravaged. For many years, the awful tragedy that had befallen the doomed village went unnoticed . . . and unaccounted for.

1

ANOMALY

Black Hills, South Dakota 2025

An explosion of power erupted beneath him.

His back was rammed up against the seat. A cool slipstream of air whipped across his tanned face, causing his eyes to water. His heart began to pound. The surge of momentum was building with every second. A deep-throated rumbling emanated from in front of him and quickly enveloped his body. He could feel the vibration travel upward, cell by cell. His adrenals were in full overload.

With perfect timing and precise movements, he executed his next move. As he sensed that the critical moment was upon him, his anticipation heightened. He deftly moved his right hand back and simultaneously slammed his foot down hard. The lever slipped firmly into place, and the energy pulsed up his arm. There was a split second before the jolt of acceleration overtook him. He was in heaven. His newly acquired vintage V-12 Jaguar XKE growled deeply in response to his urgings.

The powerful roadster rocketed along the winding ridge road. As the early morning sun crept over the Black Hills, prisms of light reflected through the windshield and the sun's rays warmed his face.

Handling this sleek vehicle had become his drug of choice, a rush of pure enjoyment and a way to clear his mind to meet the mental challenges of his detailed work.

An all-too-familiar sensation on his hip quickly brought him back to earth. His PDA was vibrating. *It's the office,* he grumbled, hitting the ignore button without looking, and downshifted through the next set of switchback curves. He skillfully maneuvered the powerful vehicle along a high-banked stretch of road toward the small store up ahead on the corner. Arriving there, he brought the Jaguar to a smooth stop, parked, and went inside.

Hardly bigger than a school bus, Williams General Store was an old post-and-beam building that was barely standing, but he stopped there nearly every day for coffee and a paper.

"Hey, Doc, just made a fresh pot of that Columbian blend you like. Got a slow start today, so you're my first customer," Ethel Williams said with a toothy smile. Her family had owned the little store for almost fifty years.

"Morning, Ethel. That sounds great," Dr. Jeremiah Xavier replied, glancing through the window toward the black sedan parked awkwardly across the street.

As Ethel poured the hot liquid into the tall cup, she noticed his glance. "No idea who that is, Doc. Been there since I arrived this morning and not a soul's emerged," she said with concern.

"Huh . . . you might want to call Earl down at the station. Have him drive by and check it out," Xavier suggested. Something about the sedan didn't feel right.

She nodded. "Think I will."

"See you tomorrow, Ethel," he said, tucking a copy of the *Wall Street Journal* under his arm and grabbing the cup of steaming coffee. "Have a great day."

As he slid into his Jaguar, he felt his PDA vibrate again. It was a text message this time: EMERGENCY ALARM INDICATION IN LAB.

Damn . . . not today, he cursed silently. He had a project-update meeting in fewer than three hours with important clients—a Saudi Arabian company that had invested close to two billion dollars in a highly experimental research project. *This'll be awkward,* he thought.

Backing out of the narrow parking space in front of the store, he noticed that the sedan had switched directions. It was now facing the way he was headed. He gave a quick glance as he rolled passed, but the sedan's blacked-out windows blocked any clear view inside. Meanwhile, a few of Ethel's routine customers began meandering into the store. Xavier looked at his watch—an old moonfaced Patek Philippe his grandfather had bequeathed to him.

Need to get to the office, now, he reminded himself. He eased off the clutch and headed toward the research facility, figuring whoever was in the sedan had chosen the store as a meeting place for some covert deal that was no business of his.

As he made his way down the winding ridge road reveling in the Jaguar's high performance, a sudden screech of tires from behind startled him. Glancing in the rearview mirror, he saw the dark sedan approaching fast. With some mild agitation, he tapped his brakes as a warning to the driver to slow down. Unexpectedly, the Jaguar was jarred violently from behind. His body lurched forward, and he thought for a moment about pulling over to confront the driver. The impact from the second jolt changed his mind. His agitation grew to anger.

"What the hell kind of game's this guy playing?!" he asked aloud, his mind racing for answers.

The road ahead was empty, and the fast-approaching caution signs gave him an idea. He accelerated the sports car and jetted into the first series of switchback curves. The sedan dropped back momentarily as the centrifugal force, which the Jaguar had handled in stride, had its effect on the larger vehicle. Keeping his right foot on the gas, he downshifted as he raced past the caution sign. The powerful roadster let out a redlined-rpm growl as its tires clawed for traction around the ninety-degree bend.

Checking the side mirror, Xavier saw the sedan swerving through the torturous curves. *The guy's good,* he thought. *But let's see how good.*

The entrance road to the facility was ahead on the left. A lush stand of hemlocks camouflaged the frontage of the facility, partially obscuring the road. Xavier punched the accelerator again. This time, he turned the wheel slightly and grabbed the hand brake. Jerking it upward, he yanked the heavy front end of the sports car abruptly to the left and straight toward the trees. The single-lane entrance roadway appeared seemingly out of nowhere. As the Jaguar got enough purchase on the macadam to straighten out, he turned the wheel back to the right, and the car hurtled toward a yellow-and-black-striped access gate.

A uniformed man appeared directly in the Jaguar's path. Xavier stomped on the brake, and the sleek sports car lurched to a skidded stop. Instinctively, he whipped around to look back at the intersection where the sedan had come to a stop. The rear window began to open, but then the dark vehicle quickly sped off.

"Good morning, Doctor. See you're exercising her," the stern-looking security guard said with just a hint of a smile as he admired the vintage car. "And who was that behind you?"

"No idea . . . followed me from Williams' store and tried to run me off the road," he replied, holding out his ID card, as was the protocol. It read:

DR. JEREMIAH XAVIER
DEPARTMENT HEAD—EXPERIMENTAL PHYSICS

"Are you serious, Doc?" The guard asked with a frown. "I'll send a report form to your office to complete. In the meantime, I'll have it checked out with the local cops."

"Thanks, Chuck," Xavier said, shaking his head. "Helluva way to start the day off," he mumbled to himself. But with the emergency situation inside the lab, he didn't have time to ponder the incident involving the dark sedan any further.

As the access gate arm rose, Xavier eased the Jaguar forward. He blended into the stream of cars flowing in from the other entrances toward the connected parking area. Quantum Physics Research

Corporation was housed in an enormous structure built of reflective bronze-tinted glass. With its backdrop of the hemlock-lined Black Hills, it was difficult to discern where the massive research facility began and nature ended.

The vast complex housed nearly 3,000 employees, most of whom were unaware of the current crisis in the lab. As Xavier hurried through the maze of biometric security devices on the way to his office, he wondered what had triggered the alarm.

"Good Morning, X. I've been trying to reach you for the past half hour," said his executive assistant Rachel Sinclair. "We've got a problem in the experimental caverns."

Xavier detected a note of urgency in Rachel's normally cool and calm demeanor. Intelligent and vivacious, the tall and alluring brunette was the rock of his office staff . . . not to mention very easy on the eyes.

"Hi, Rache. Sorry, I've been a little preoccupied," he replied, getting a tantalizing whiff of her fresh scent as he neared her desk. "So far I'd have to say it's not shaping up to be a very good morning. So where's Winston?" he demanded.

Elliot Winston was a senior project manager and the world's foremost scientist in his particular field of quantum physics, and Xavier needed him *now* to get this situation under control.

"I can't find him. He hasn't responded to any of my calls," Rachel replied, meeting Xavier's gaze for a moment longer than necessary. "But Hammerstein's been here all night. He's working at the super-computer," she continued, tilting her head ever so slightly.

Xavier shifted his weight. *She makes it hard for me to focus sometimes. And she knows it,* he thought. In the few years since the tragic death of his wife and their young daughter, Rachel had become much more than an assistant to him—a friend and confidant. His feelings for her had grown even beyond the close platonic relationship they shared, and he knew she felt the same for him. Still, neither had been willing to cross that delicate line between longing looks and something more in fear that it would spoil their friendship.

"Contact the Saudis immediately and cancel the meeting, Rache," Xavier instructed, as he headed toward the lab's biometric-security door. "I'm going back to see Hammerstein."

Xavier glanced back and caught Rachel eyeing him, which made him smile. Still extremely fit for someone in his early forties, he had maintained a strenuous daily exercise regimen since his days in the military. At almost six-foot-three, his muscular frame and boyish good looks belied a PhD in quantum mechanics and his definitively geeky job at QPR.

As soon as he had cleared the biometrics into the computer lab, he was assaulted by the blare of the alarm. Running past the myriad of partitioned workstations, Xavier found Elliot Winston's assistant, Gunter Hammerstein. The bespectacled Austrian scientist was pounding away at the keyboard of the supercomputer that controlled all functions in the underground experimental caverns. A huge complex of caverns carved out of the Precambrian granite of the Black Hills was located almost a half-mile directly below the research facility and housed a highly advanced atom smasher—a linear-plasma-particle accelerator—dubbed SOLA for Speed of Light Accelerator.

"Dr. . . . Dr. Hammerstein, what's happening?" Xavier yelled over the piercing din of the alarm.

Hammerstein appeared startled to see him. "I . . . *uh,* believe there's been a breach of SOLA's containment systems," he said, quickly turning his attention back to his keyboard and screen.

A breach? That can't be! Xavier thought. "When did it occur?" he asked the scientist.

"I'm not quite certain, Dr. Xavier. There seems to have been a malfunction in the proton-beam firing sequence. It eventually triggered the alarm when the containment systems failed."

"So, whatever caused the alarm probably happened much earlier," Xavier concluded.

Hammerstein hesitated. "That's more than likely the case because I haven't been able to reset the system for quite a while."

"Then, why didn't you notify me sooner?" Xavier asked with obvious annoyance.

The Austrian ignored the question. Instead, he hammered out more keystrokes, watching patiently as the screen flooded with streaming data. The supercomputer scrolled information on the screen at petabyte rates too quickly for Xavier to follow. Hammerstein never flinched. Then, with a quick move, he hit the stop key. "Dr. Winston's been working all hours and had been running a new series of experiments," he finally replied. "Until I was certain, I didn't want to speculate. However, it's clear now . . . there's been an event. Based on the preliminary data, there was an accidental burst of super-high energy, which somehow forced its way through the firing tunnel's containment system and into the lower cavern."

"How strong was the energy burst?" Xavier asked, seeing the uncertainty on his colleague's face.

Hammerstein pointed to a graph on the screen. "It's off the scales, and for reasons I can't explain, the automated systems are unresponsive. It's highly unusual that I can't identify the source of the problem. I'm trying to access the remote video feed in the lower cavern."

Xavier peered over Hammerstein's shoulder.

"The activity I'm observing is entirely different. There's no logical explanation for what's happening. This is highly, highly unusual," Hammerstein repeated.

Xavier remained calm. In a pure research environment such as in QPR, there was the occasional unusual happening, but he could tell that Hammerstein was perplexed. Then, something suddenly seemed to catch the Austrian scientist's attention. He pointed to one of the video monitors. "Look there!"

Xavier saw it immediately and recoiled. "What *is* that?"

Hammerstein seemed momentarily mesmerized by his disbelief. He finally glanced up from the startling image on the monitor and looked at Xavier. "I'm not particularly religious, Dr. Xavier, but I think we need to start praying."

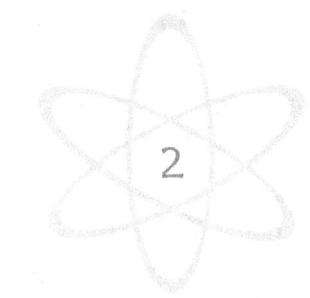

CREATION

Black Hills, South Dakota

The absolute darkness was overwhelming. The cold, dank space was filled with an eerie stillness until a subtle flutter of air was whipped into a cyclonic vortex. Moments prior, a strange blue-white flash had illuminated the depths of the lower cavern. Within seconds, the life-supporting atmosphere had been sucked away. The shrill sound of an alarm echoed hauntingly.

Elliot Winston pressed his gaunt figure against the heavy safety glass of the testing chamber. He began sweating profusely. "I can't believe what I'm seeing," he whispered excitedly inside his control lab deep within the granite-encased experimental caverns of QPR.

He had been working feverishly since the misfire of one of the world's most powerful atom smashers. Ignoring the blaring alarm, he prepared to manipulate the insulated-mechanical arms. An extremely volatile nuclear substance had been trapped. And although it appeared inert now, seconds before it had absorbed the energy from the intense laser, probing with such voracity that it had startled him.

"I didn't anticipate such radical molecular activity," he continued into the voice-actuated recorder, as he peered through the electron microscope. "The accidental super-high energy burst created a residual substance, a *hybrid,* having vastly different characteristics from the molecule it was split from, and evidencing significantly more instability. I need to contain its behavior so I can evaluate its potential. It would appear, from initial observations, that the substance may be capable of spontaneous-nuclear reaction. The only way to ascertain the cause of such dramatic activity is to initiate a series of controlled experiments . . . that damned alarm!"

He retracted his arms from inside the testing chamber and wondered how long it would be before maintenance shut down the support subsystems. *If that happens,* he thought, *I'll have lost all chances to continue the experiment. There must be a way.*

Winston scurried over to the keyboard directly below the enormous control screen. Quickly, he entered a series of complex commands. He waited . . . nothing. He frantically entered another set of commands. All at once, the video monitor located in the lower cavern flashed an image onto the screen. Instantly, he saw what had triggered the alarm. His eyes widened in disbelief as he studied the image: a massive energy anomaly that was rapidly expanding.

His mind worked quickly as he thought to himself, *I don't have much time. They'll have no choice. The entire underground experimental caverns will be isolated without power. I need to lock-out the control lab.*

He rifled through an adjacent file cabinet. There in the bottom drawer, he found what he had been looking for. He pulled out the large six-inch black binder and set it in on the desk. FAIL-SAFE PROCEDURES read the embossed bold lettering on the front of the binder. Referencing the index, he flipped the dividers and stopped midway through. It read: IN CASE OF A CATASTROPHIC EVENT, INITIATE THE FOLLOWING SEQUENCE ONLY IF THERE IS NO OTHER RECOURSE.

He paused briefly. Even his inexorable single-minded focus over his scientific obsession was momentarily interrupted as he fully comprehended the implications of what was about to follow. Slowly, he closed the binder after reading the specific instructions. It would all be compressed into the next few hours—the time he would need to complete his life's work.

Winston found the access key hanging from a small glass enclosed case located near the rear of the control lab. Opening the case, he hesitated briefly before inserting the key into the activation mechanism and punched in a code. The hissing sound of pressure locks indicated the sealing of the reinforced doors. Almost simultaneously, the lights inside the control lab flickered, and then went dark. Within a few moments, the standby generator began whirring. A soft-red glow filled the confines of the lab as the emergency power sprung to life. The control lab was in lock-out. He immediately checked the operating time for the generator. *Only two hours,* he complained silently. *Not nearly long enough to complete all the testing. But maybe time to complete the most critical aspect of the process. That should be indicative of the hybrid's capabilities.*

A slight smirk appeared on his face as he recalled how he was able to keep his research a secret at QPR. Even his closet colleagues were kept in the dark about the exact nature of his experiments. *And little does anyone suspect that the contract with Saudi Arabia is the perfect ruse to get the funding I need to complete my work,* he mused. *I'm so close . . . so close to a great discovery.*

Although the accidental-firing event had indeed surprised him, the terrifying force of the misfire had presented him with the potential solution for which he had searched. Within two hours, Winston completed his testing of the hybrid. He marveled at its capabilities. Next, he prepared to transmit the data files of his experimental findings to a remote server location for posterity's sake. The password for the encrypted files was known to only one other person. But hopefully, in time, his work would be appreciated by all who had explored the mysteries of the universe and had sought the elusive answers to some of humankind's greatest questions.

The secured, reinforced doors of the control lab shook violently under the influence of the anomaly. Winston realized he had but scant moments to send his data files and execute his plan. With one keystroke, the extensive files were almost instantaneously routed to the remote server via the petabyte-speed hard drive.

Turning toward the testing chamber where the sample hybrid molecule was contained, Winston opened the venting tubes. From his previous procedures, he knew that the hybrid would become very unstable when exposed to conditions other than the vacuum environment of the testing chamber. He had speculated that under the proper conditions and with further experimentation, the hybrid could become a force for good, maybe even capable of solving man's long-standing energy crisis. But he had also suspected that under certain situations, it possessed more omnipotent force than anything known in recorded science—something he was about to witness.

In the very next instant, the reinforced walls of the control lab imploded as the force of the anomaly tore its way through. Winston had but one fatal gasp to observe the confrontation between the anomaly force from the misfire and the nuclear hybrid it had created . . . waiting to be unleashed from its testing chamber.

The anomaly immediately encircled the hybrid's chamber as if somehow sensing another ominous presence. In an instantaneous clash of nature, the two monsters of highly charged particles collided and formed into a single band of pure energy stretching the entire length of the cavern. Within a nanosecond, the band expanded outward exponentially, completely filling the voluminous cavern in an explosion of blindingly brilliant light and searing heat intense enough to partially liquefy the Precambrian-granite walls before finally extinguishing.

The hybrid had exceeded his expectations. Winston's final thoughts flashed through his mind. *I've found it—the superparticle. My place in history alongside Einstein's and Newton's has been secured.*

3

MYSTERIES

Black Hills, South Dakota

"The automated fail-safe systems in SOLA's lower cavern have failed!" Xavier shouted, as he monitored the control panel from high above in the main facility.

Already assessing the tenuous situation, Hammerstein said, "Whatever it is hasn't moved up the tunnel that connects the lower with the main cavern. Consequently, the automatic closures haven't activated as yet. I'm trying to manually override the controls for the main cavern complex barriers."

After several moments, he let out a sigh of relief and smiled briefly. "It's done. The main cavern area is secured."

But Xavier wasn't convinced. "If this is what I suspect, we're dealing with much more than a breach of the containment systems."

The Austrian looked up at him quizzically. "What is it, then?"

He hesitated for a moment. "It's something Dr. Winston and I'd discussed in the past. Something that we know very little about but has the potential to cause chaos beyond anyone's imagination."

Hammerstein didn't react immediately. "I'd advised Dr. Winston against continuing to increase the power levels of the accelerator," he said slowly.

15

"What?!" Xavier asked with dread, glaring down at Winston's assistant. "Why would he be increasing the power levels of the accelerator? . . . I hope that whatever Winston's done, he didn't somehow—" He stopped midsentence as the images on the monitor gained his full attention. The lower cavern was crumbling into itself. The thick, steel-reinforced-concrete containment walls were disintegrating into a fine-powdered mist. The energy from the anomaly was pulling apart everything in its path.

This is my worst fear. Some type of quantum vacuum collapse. Consuming matter like a ravenous beast. It's only a matter of time before it envelops the entire complex and possibly beyond, he thought and, then without hesitation, said, "Shut down the experimental caverns, Dr. Hammerstein."

Hammerstein was so fixated by the mind-bending images that he didn't respond to Xavier's directive.

"Do it now!" Xavier yelled, picking up the receiver of the emergency phone. "This is Dr. Xavier. We have a crisis in the experimental caverns. Initiate a code-red emergency for the entire research facility," he said.

The building manager on the other end of the line knew that a code-red emergency called for the immediate evacuation of all personnel. He started to say something, but Xavier had no time to listen. He hung up abruptly and turned toward Hammerstein, who was cranking away on the keyboard, executing the shutdown commands.

"How long until you're finished?" Xavier said. "We've only got a short time before the facility's evacuation procedures go into effect."

"Go ahead, Doctor, I'll be right behind you . . . be done here shortly," Hammerstein replied, keeping his eyes focused on the data still streaming in on the supercomputer's screen.

As Xavier headed back to his office, the announcement to evacuate blared on the com system. But when he reached the office, he saw that Rachel was still there, apparently waiting for him.

"Get out of the building, *now,* Rachel," he said strongly, taking note of the surprise on her face. "I'll call you later. This is serious . . . *very* serious. Go!"

She shot him a worried look, then grabbed her purse and headed for the nearest exit.

Back at his desk, Xavier tried Hammerstein's extension. No answer. Looking outside, he observed the orderly egress process already in progress. Most of the employees were either technical types or experienced enough around research installations to know that emergency circumstances periodically occurred. . . . But not quite like this one.

Xavier grabbed his computer tablet and headed for the stairway exit. A code-red alert was the final warning for all occupants to immediately exit by the nearest method possible. Beneath the facility's bronze-mirrored chameleon skin, the QPR engineers had disguised an impregnable citadel. It wasn't only that getting in was so difficult—it was—but also the measures that were taken to prevent any biohazard or other contaminant from escaping due to errant experimentation were no less than extraordinary.

Within thirty minutes after the alert was issued, the facility began to automatically shut itself down—locking out every ingress and egress point from ground level to rooftop. Built with high-impact, reinforced, pressurized doors and venting louvers, the facility's connections to the outside world were systematically being shut down. Everything inside would be sealed off until all evidence of the emergency condition had disappeared.

About a half mile away, Xavier stopped his Jaguar on the ridge road overlooking the facility. Even from this distance, he could hear the faint echo of the emergency alarm bouncing off the Black Hills.

He checked his watch. It was a little past noon and nearly an hour had passed since the building was evacuated. The anomaly should have reached the main cavern level within the hour, based on his and Hammerstein's projections.

A few more moments passed, and he wasn't certain at first, but he thought he detected that something had changed. It had. The faint sound of the alarm had finally ceased. He peered through his binoculars to observe any other indications that something had occurred. Surprisingly, the bronze-mirrored facade of the massive research complex stood intact, gleaming in the bright afternoon sun. The anomaly must have dissipated inside the solid-granite experimental caverns. *Strange,* he puzzled, *based on the destructive power I saw, I'd expected it to have affected the upper research complex as well.*

As he pondered over the events that had so quickly transpired, his cell phone rang. It was Hammerstein. "Dr. Xavier, where are you?"

"I'm on the ridge road about a half mile from the facility . . . I tried reaching you before evacuating. Are you safe?"

"I'm close by. I couldn't stop to answer your call. But you'll understand when you see what I've found," the Austrian scientist replied. "I was downloading Dr. Winston's files as well as the data from his control-lab computer. . . . There's something—something else you need to see. Winston's made a startling discovery."

"Where do you want to meet?" Xavier asked.

"How about Williams' store . . . say twenty minutes?"

Xavier pulled up to the front of the small store. He noticed that the few parking spaces in front were filled and proceeded around to the rear. The sudden motion of the dark sedan behind him caught his attention. Too late, like a clap of thunder, he heard the sound of exploding glass. The bullet whizzed past the side of his head, slamming into the passenger seat and exiting through the windshield. The sedan had moved in very close along the back of the building, blocking any retreat. He was trapped. His mind moving quickly, he took note of an old dumpster located adjacent to the back of the store. He bolted out the door of the Jaguar, instinctively rolling for cover behind the refuse container.

He saw the barrel of a rifle poking out of the sedan's rear window just before the door opened and a stocky man stepped out. Taking aim, the man fired a burst of rounds that ricocheted off the dumpster, missing Xavier by mere inches. By this time, a couple of the store patrons had cautiously began making their way around back to check on the commotion. He watched as the gunman sighted his weapon again, but then abruptly turned and retreated to the back of the sedan, whose driver expertly reversed it away from the store.

"You alright?" asked an old codger who had slowly ambled over with a corncob pipe sticking halfway out of his mouth once the sedan was out of sight.

Xavier picked himself up off the ground. Still reeling from the rush of adrenaline, he replied somewhat breathlessly, "Yeah . . . I'm fine, thanks. Someone should call the police." He looked around for further danger, but sensed none.

"I think Ethel's on the phone to the chief now," the codger said. "But I gotta say that Chief Earl won't be too accommodating. He'd already been here earlier and was pissed it was a false alarm. Ole Earl's a fuddy duck . . . more interested in the politics than chasing down problems."

"Yeah, I know Earl has his days, but this is something else again. He certainly won't ignore someone trying to gun me down in broad daylight," Xavier replied, brushing the dust off his pants.

The old man squinted. "You recognize that fella . . . the one shooting at you?"

"Never saw them before this morning. I haven't the slightest idea what the hell's going on," Xavier replied, although he was beginning to think that there had to be some connection between the emergency at the lab and this attempt on his life.

The codger didn't respond for a moment. He moved closer to Xavier. The wisps from his corncob pipe did little to camouflage the pungent smell of garlic and foul body odor. "You real sure you wanna get Earl into this? 'Cause lately he's not up to investigating much. But he'll surely make you fill out plenty of paperwork and answer a bunch of questions till you can't stand it no more. Unless you got dead-solid reasons and proof, it won't amount to much. Seen it before. Besides, no one got hurt."

Xavier eyed the old man carefully and slowly shook his head. "You're saying that Earl doesn't care about this sort of thing?"

The codger stared back at him. "Oh . . . he cares all right, just not enough to make it worth his while," he said, before he turned and trudged casually back toward the store.

Xavier could tell by the looks on the few faces around that the old buzzard was probably right. *Small-town justice can be very quirky,* he thought. "Thanks for the advice," he called out, as he glanced over toward his car to survey the damage. There was a sickening feeling in his stomach as he saw his new acquisition so beaten up. The rear window was completely shattered by a high-powered round—a fact he had realized after he saw the size of the hole in the top of his passenger seat. As he struggled to comprehend the whole sequence of events, he heard a booming voice behind him.

"Sorry about your car, man. It's a real beauty. Don't know why anyone would want to do that," one of Ethel's burly-looking patrons said as he approached. "I reckon there're some folks around here who don't like you too much."

"Guess so," Xavier replied. "But nobody I know drives a dark sedan like that."

The big man had already started back toward the front of the store when he turned around. "Hey, man," he called out. "If it means anything, I saw that car pull up in front about twenty minutes ago. It was parked across the street . . . on the shoulder. Couldn't help but notice it."

Xavier nodded. "Thanks . . . appreciate the information."

How'd they know I'd be here now? he wondered, and suddenly, his thoughts shifted to Hammerstein. He looked around. *He was supposed to meet me here. Where is he?*

Xavier took out his PDA and tried calling the scientist. No answer.

4

MOGUL

Ten thousand miles to the east, at the base of the Taihang Mountain range in the western portion of Baoding Hebei province, resided the expansive empire of Zangshe Inc. Only eighty miles south of Beijing, the nearly two thousand square miles of uranium mines were owned by one man: Kongi Khan, the son of a Mongolian crime boss and the last descendant of the legendary warrior and conqueror Genghis Khan.

Proud of his infamous heritage and almost maniacally confident in his ability to lead, Kongi Khan had easily secured himself as the chairman of Zangshe Inc. almost twenty years earlier. Sturdily built with dark brooding eyes and a long braid of blue-black hair, the chiseled-faced, modern-day Mongolian despot had turned a corrupt and loosely run mining operation into a mega private enterprise even under the repressive Chinese regime. Zangshe's extensive uranium-ore mining operation became a preferred provider of high-grade uranium ore as well as refined uranium for nuclear fuel. Almost all of China's burgeoning number of nuclear reactors and those throughout Asia and

Europe became dependent on Zangshe's uranium—making Zangshe one of the world's most capitalized enterprises.

Utilizing his enormous wealth and unwavering force of will, Khan had ingratiated himself with almost every senior official in the Chinese national government. As a consequence, he had acquired a legendary reputation throughout all of Asia for operating with impunity. And his massive investments in most of the world's largest financial centers had assured Khan a position of intimidating influence elsewhere as well.

Contemplating his most recent project with smug appreciation for his own diabolical brilliance, Khan was interrupted by the buzzing of his intercom.

"Great One," his assistant said, using Khan's self-anointed salutation, "you have a call on line one."

Khan picked up the line.

"Hello, Mr. Chairman. I trust this is a good time for you," said the clear, accented voice on the other end.

Khan relaxed back into his leather chair. "Professor, it is always good to hear your voice," he said with sincerity. "The last time we spoke you sounded somewhat distressed. I sense you are feeling better."

"As well as can be expected. More importantly, I have good news to report. I've found the answer to the great mystery we have been seeking all of these years."

Khan's narrow eyes widened at this news and a wave of satisfaction rushed through him. "I never had any doubts about your commitment to our cause, Professor," he replied evenly. "I am most anxious to hear of this discovery. Let us meet and celebrate together, while we discuss the future."

"As much as that would please me, it is impossible now to do so," the professor replied.

"Are you concerned for your corporate obligations?" Khan asked with apparent displeasure. "What possible motive would you have to stay where you are? Your place is *here*, with us."

"Do not remind me how much I've missed being there. However, I've little time left to make certain that you receive all the necessary data regarding the latest discovery."

"Is there something wrong?" Khan asked, now concerned.

There was a brief hesitation. "Ironically, the fortuitous circumstance that allowed for the breakthrough discovery has caused a serious problem," the professor slowly explained. "There has been an accidental subatomic explosion of epic proportions that unleashed an anomalous energy force. Energy so intense that it split off a unique particle—one that may change the future of the world. While it has already proved to be a most powerful particle, it's somewhat unstable under certain conditions. However, in the process of the accidental event, the entire research facility will likely be shut down . . . and probably permanently evacuated. If my calculations are accurate, the energy released was overwhelming."

There was silence.

"Do others know of this discovery, Professor?" Khan finally asked.

"That is likely. As soon as this breakthrough became apparent, I immediately set into motion the plans as we'd discussed. Still, there were some complications."

Khan grew agitated but maintained a controlled voice as he insisted, "It *must* be completed. There *must* be no witnesses to the discovery."

"I understand, but I may need some assistance in that regard."

"Then I will proceed to make the arrangements," Khan replied. "You will need to identify those involved."

"I will transmit all the data on the experiment as well as information on those who have any knowledge of it. The communication lines throughout QPR's complex will soon be terminated. The encrypted-data device will shortly be useless."

Khan nodded. "Is there anything you wish me to do for you, Professor?"

"You have already rewarded me handsomely. The successful

application of this discovery will be more than enough. I trust it is in good hands," replied the professor.

"You can be assured that what I have in mind will change the world as we know it," Khan replied.

"Then, this may be our last contact, Mr. Chairman. Please accept my deepest gratitude and affections for all you've done."

There was a brief pause.

"Good-bye . . . Professor," Khan said, then hung up the receiver.

Sitting comfortably at his black lacquered desk, high above the expansive mining empire, a depthless smile emerged across his countenance. Even as he reflected over the professor's crisis, the Mongolian reveled in the news he had just received.

He typed a decryption code into his computer and watched in awe as the impressive flow of data filled his computer screen. He mused over how easily he had secured a position for the professor at QPR with his pervasive influence. He knew that with QPR's advanced technology there was no better venue for a breakthrough discovery of this magnitude, and it was now in his possession . . . as it should be.

The chairman of Zangshe Inc. opened the lacquered desk drawer and slowly withdrew a single piece of parchment and an Omas fountain pen. Setting the titanium utensil to paper, he wrote: *It is in this truly bittersweet moment that I must write this letter to inform you of some news—some very exciting news.*

Before he could continue, an e-mail message flashed on the bottom of his computer screen. It was a message he never would have expected.

5

BETRAYED

Black Hills, South Dakota

Xavier tried Hammerstein a few more times, but all his calls went direct to voice mail. It didn't take him long to conclude that whoever was after him had also gone after the researcher. He quickly got into his car and headed down the ridge road back toward the facility. His mind raced: *Who would want me dead and why?*

Maneuvering his wounded Jaguar through the switchback curves, he kept one eye on the rearview mirror and the other one searching for any signs of Hammerstein. He had fully anticipated seeing wreckage around each bend . . . but nothing. When he reached the deserted entrance to the facility, he stopped and looked around carefully for any signs of a struggle or accident. Seeing none, he dialed Hammerstein's cell once again. It rang a number of times. He was about to hang up.

"Hello, Dr. Xavier," a heavily inflected voice responded to the call. "I see you've survived. Your friend, on the other hand, was not as fortunate. I'd advise you to meet with us to discuss your alternatives. I can assure you that if you refuse, your continued safety will certainly be short lived."

Xavier quickly glanced around. He had guessed that whoever was on the line couldn't be very far away. "I'll need more assurances than that. It would appear you've already decided my fate," he replied.

"That may be so, Doctor, but your actions may yet save others."

What others? Who the hell are these people? he wondered, his mind racing for a plausible answer. He couldn't help but question if it had anything to do with what Hammerstein had discovered regarding Winston's experiment. "What is it you want from me?" he demanded.

"That is the purpose of our meeting, Dr. Xavier," replied the voice.

"I'll need time to think about what've you've said," Xavier replied, trying to stall awhile to figure things out.

"If I don't hear back from you very shortly, there will be serious repercussions."

The line went dead.

None of this made any sense to Xavier. It *was* obvious, however, that someone was after him and apparently others around him. Then, it hit him. *Rachel! They can't mean to harm her. She's done nothing*!

Reflexively, he punched in her number and prepared to hit SEND. *Don't do that!* his instincts yelled out. . . . *It's easy to trace. I need to find a way to contact her quickly without them knowing. Or do they already know?*

He made his decision. Regardless of the risk, he needed to warn Rachel in person. *Better to do something rather than let these bastards have their way without a fight,* he thought.

Xavier jammed the shifter of the Jaguar into first gear and headed away from the abandoned facility. He made a series of quick turns in and out of a neighboring community. Fairly certain he wasn't being followed, he took one of the secondary routes that paralleled the train tracks to a friend's house.

Pulling around behind the auto-repair shop that serviced his Jaguar, he parked in his usual spot and got out. He peered through the rear windows of the spotless garage but didn't see anyone. *Maybe he's upstairs in the apartment,* he hoped.

He walked up the narrow stairs and rapped on the door. A young, strapping man eating a sandwich greeted him.

"Mike, I need a favor," Xavier said. "I've had an accident with the Jaguar and left it outside the shop. I'm late for an important meeting and need to borrow your truck, if possible."

"Hey, Doc, no prob . . . whadda you do to the XKE?" the mechanic mumbled through a mouthful of bread and salami. He ruffled through his jean pocket and pulled out the key to the truck and handed it to Xavier.

"See for yourself," Xavier replied, grabbing the key. "You'll have some fun fixing her up." He shot down the stairs. "I'll call tomorrow after you've seen the damages!"

Xavier knew he'd be less conspicuous in the truck. Still, he kept on the back roads as he headed for Rachel's condo. Ten minutes later he had parked around the corner from her street. Walking quickly behind several old converted buildings, he found his way to her door.

"Rachel," he said, knocking quietly. "Rachel . . . let me in."

Slowly the door opened. Rachel stood there wearing a fitted T-shirt, leggings, and a pair of running shoes. "X, I'm glad you're here. I was beginning to worry. I tried calling. Where have you been?"

"Sorry, Rache, I saw your voice mail. You need to come with me, now!"

"What's wrong, X? I already received the emergency information notification over an hour ago, which said that although the crisis seems to have been contained, the facility would be shut down indefinitely pending a full investigation. All employees would be notified of any further change in status."

"It's something else. I don't have time to explain. Let's go. Please!" he urged.

"For how long and where?" she asked, her expression changing from confusion to concern.

"Rache, trust me. We've got to get out of here . . . now!"

She didn't hesitate any further and raced into her bedroom.

Moments later she came out with her purse and a sweater. "You're scaring me, X."

Without offering her any explanation, Xavier grabbed her hand and pulled her out the door. Outside, they ran quickly past the old buildings to Mike's truck.

"Whose truck is this, X? Where's the Jag?" she asked, as Xavier motioned for her to get inside.

"It belongs to a friend of mine," he replied, looking quickly in all directions.

"What's going on? Why are you acting like this?" Rachel asked, as she scrambled into the passenger seat. "Does it have to do anything with that guy from the CIA who called?"

"What guy?"

"He didn't leave his name, but he said it was important that he talk with you. I gave him your cell number."

Xavier turned quickly toward her. "I'm not sure what's going on. The last thing I heard from Hammerstein was that he'd found something in Winston's files."

"What was it?"

"It has to be related to whatever happened in the experimental labs," he replied. "Probably something Winston was working on . . . possibly having something to do with the Saudi contract. Whatever it is, somebody wants us out of the way—and permanently."

"Why?"

"I have no idea."

"How can that be, X? You're Winston's boss."

"According to Hammerstein, Winston was conducting some new experiments recently."

"They're that serious about this?" she asked.

"They tried to kill me, Rache, at the corner store," he said and then hesitated. "They've already killed Hammerstein."

She stared at him in disbelief. "So they intend to kill everyone who might know anything about Winston's experiment?" she asked anxiously.

"I know, it sounds crazy, but I've every reason to believe that's their intention."

"Who are these—" She was interrupted when Xavier's PDA buzzed.

He looked down. It was Hammerstein's number on the ID.

He answered. The voice on the phone was curt with a slight Asian accent.

"Dr. Xavier, that wasn't very smart of you. Let this be a lesson. Your friend at the auto-repair shop paid dearly for your transgression. You can't get away from us. For Ms. Sinclair's sake, I urge you to take the next turn off. We'll be waiting for your truck."

How the hell did they—? . . . Then it dawned on him. He cursed himself for not realizing that they had placed a GPS tracking device on the Jaguar. *Shit! It's my fault Mike's dead. I led them right to him.* "Rache, how far up is the turn off from this road?"

She looked around. "About a mile or so."

He stood on the brakes and jumped out of the pickup. "Get out, Rache, and take your stuff," he told her as he went to the back of the truck.

In the pickup's bed he found an eight-foot two-by-four board. It was bigger than he needed, but he hoped it would still work. Jamming the board against the cab roof, he managed to wedge it against the gas pedal. He took off his belt and tied the wheel firmly to the door handle. It was a dead-straight road. The rigged truck would probably get most of the way to the turn off.

He thrust the truck into gear. The engine raced past the rpm redline. It spewed up gravel, dust, and dirt, and then sped directly down the center of the road.

He figured they had ten minutes at most. "Let's go, Rache. I hope all that jogging you do pays off," he said, as they ran back toward the intersection. *How did they spot the truck?* he wondered. As he and

Rachel got closer to the intersection, he had the answer. Up ahead, there was a police cruiser with its flashers on. *They ran a DMV check on Mike . . .* was the first thought that came to him . . . *and identified the truck. They must've paid the cops off.*

Xavier heard the distant whistle of a train and grabbed Rachel, forcing her to the ground. "We've got to get to the railroad tracks," he whispered, pointing due east from where they were located. The whistle was growing louder, indicating that the train was getting closer.

The pair ran through the thick brambles alongside the track. Rachel's sweater got snagged on a branch, and she wrenched it free as Xavier urged her on. Minutes later, they were standing on the track bed facing the train—an old, restored chain of cars used for sightseeing—which had come to a dead stop. There was a passenger station only a few yards from the intersection. Xavier motioned to Rachel to keep running toward the train.

Rachel nodded.

"It's going to be close," he gasped. "We've got about a minute or so."

The loose gravel underfoot made traction difficult. Rachel slipped and fell. Xavier grabbed her arm and quickly lifted her to her feet. The train began moving slowly away from the station. He looked around. On the other side of the tracks, he noticed that the ground was almost four feet higher. *But just high enough,* he thought. He pulled Rachel across the tracks and waited for the train to reach them.

As planned, Mike's pickup truck had continued to barrel down the dirt road, finally veering off into a ditch several hundred yards from the intersection. Four men carrying automatic weapons fitted with silencers carefully approached. When they stopped, they aimed their laser sights on the cab. Spits of muffled sounds echoed softly as the cab was riddled with countless rounds. It didn't take long for the gunmen to realize that the truck was empty.

The old train made its way steadily toward the disheveled couple. Xavier estimated it was traveling approximately five to eight miles an hour. Faster than it looked, he knew it wouldn't be a simple task to get them both on the train. Although the ground was higher on their side of the tracks, they would still have to jump across the track bed and grab onto something to secure their position.

"Rache, listen to me very carefully. We have only one shot at this. We need to time our run and jump at the space between the cars." He saw that she was scared. He swung her around and looked directly into her eyes. "We can do this, Rache. Whatever you do, don't let go of my arm."

The train was almost upon them. He felt its heavy vibrations through his feet. As soon as it started to pass, he picked a spot immediately behind the second car. Giving Rachel a gentle nudge, they sprinted about twenty feet across the higher ground. He kept his eyes fixed on his target. As they both left the ground, their momentum carried them across the track bed, slamming their bodies hard against the side of the train. Xavier grabbed furiously for the bars that lined the sides of the steps. Gravity and the weight of both of their bodies tore at his grip. He struggled to get his legs underneath him. With one final, desperate motion, he swung his leg onto the step and pulled hard.

Rachel's body was dangling, her legs partly dragging along the track bed. He looked down at her, and her eyes locked with his as a look of resignation spread across her face. She wasn't able to hang on much longer. "Don't give up, Rache! Reach up and grab my arm! Do it now!" he yelled.

She blinked and glanced up at him. Desperation filled her eyes and fear distorted her features, as her left hand slipped out of his. Her head rolled back, and he felt the grip of her right hand begin to loosen as well. She started to fall.

Moving with lightning speed, Xavier wrapped his other leg around the railing, hanging precariously, and reached down to catch her right hand. He yanked her fiercely upward by her arm, and felt her shoulder joint pop. She let out an agonized scream, but he had gotten a tight hold of her. Together, they tumbled backward from the momentum and landed safely on the platform connecting the train cars.

6

INVASION

The ominous images in the satellite photos streaming in on his computer tablet surprised Agent Harry Carlyle. "Damn," he cursed aloud to himself, then quickly hit SPEED DIAL.

"Captain Boyd," he said when his call was answered, "how long have you been monitoring this activity?"

"It started late yesterday and has intensified over the past few hours," replied James Boyd, the officer in charge at SATCOM—Satellite Communication Command.

"Can you identify the exact nature of the forces involved and where they originated from?" Carlyle asked.

"No, we cannot, Agent. You'll need to deploy eyes-on-the-ground if you expect to verify that intel," replied Boyd.

"I can see from the images that this is no damn training exercise, Captain. What's your assessment?" Carlyle snapped.

There was a brief hesitation.

"Our preliminary assessment is that it's a large and fully integrated assault movement that appears to have been staged somewhere near the Iraq-Iran border. It has already transited through northern Kuwait.

Based upon the time-lapsed images, the progress of the assault appears headed south toward Saudi Arabia," Boyd replied stiffly.

"Now that wasn't so hard, was it?" Carlyle asked, his voice laced with sarcasm. He heard the phone line go dead and just shook his head. It surprised him that Boyd didn't seem even a bit nonplussed over the event. He figured it had to do with the circumstances over the past few years.

Harry Carlyle was a senior CIA agent and one of the Agency's most experienced operatives in the Middle East.

Where had this activity come from? Carlyle wondered.

Well into the second decade of the twenty-first century, the final collapse of the oil industry had occurred. The vast Saudi refineries and pipelines had been abandoned. And there were but a few strategic oil reserves left elsewhere in the world. As a consequence, over the past five years, there had been no significant disturbances throughout most of the Middle East. Carlyle was aware that well before the final collapse, the Saudi royal family had invested a large fortune in the desperate search for alternate energy platforms. He also knew that the new battles were being waged on technological fronts, rather than across the traditional geographic regions of strategic interest.

In fact, the Sandool Corporation, which was owned by the Saudi royal family, was working in collaboration with the American research company QPR from Black Hills, South Dakota. The secretive nature of the contract between the parties had put it on Carlyle's radar. He officially began investigating the secretive relationship when one of his sources inside Saudi Arabia informed him that the Saudis were involved in some highly advanced experimentation.

The Sandool Corporation had been formed almost twenty years earlier to research new methodologies of extracting oil from the depleting fields. When it became apparent that these efforts would never revitalize the Saudi oil industry, Sandool turned its attention to a more radical approach. The contract with QPR had culminated in the search for a new technology to put the royal family back in the energy business and reinstate them as world leaders.

Most recently, Carlyle had uncovered disturbing information concerning some of QPR's transactions. Founded by a group of brilliant scientists, QPR was involved in a number of projects that had attracted the attention of several federal agencies. It seemed that Peter McMillian, the chairman of QPR, was somewhat of a maverick entrepreneur who relished the opportunity to indiscriminately deploy his company's vast research resources for profit. Whether it was with South American dictators, the North Koreans, or the myriad of wealthy, behind-the-scenes kingmakers throughout the world, QPR openly entertained almost any idea or concept requiring solutions from technology—much like an ancient sorcerer dispensing potions. It was something that Carlyle began to speculate about regarding QPR's arrangement with Sandool.

Maybe there's a possible connection between the recent activity near the Kuwaiti border and whatever the Saudis are up to with QPR, he pondered. *Somebody might suspect that the balance of power will shift in the region.*

Acting under the aegis of the recently revised National Security Act, the veteran CIA agent had contacted QPR's corporate headquarters to discuss the exact nature of the contract between the two parties. After the company's corporate brass had exhausted their congressional influence, Carlyle had finally been directed to the head of QPR's experimental research division: Dr. Jeremiah Xavier.

7

HUNTED

Rapid City, South Dakota

Once Xavier and Rachel were safely onboard the tourist train, Xavier purchased two tickets to Rapid City from the conductor. If the conductor noticed the couple's disheveled appearance or the fact that Rachel could barely hold herself together, he didn't let on. The train had made its last local stop, and Rachel's pain from the dislocated shoulder was getting more intense. Xavier had been able to pop her shoulder back into place, but he knew that inflammation in the joint would continue to increase her discomfort.

"Rache, it shouldn't be too much longer before we can get you some pain medication." He knew that getting her to a hospital as soon as possible was important, but first he had to assess their situation and make sure he could get her out of harm's way.

"I'll be okay, X. It only hurts when I move," she replied with a weak smile, her face pale. "I'm just glad to be alive."

Xavier kissed her head, taking in the scent of her lavender shampoo. He was relieved they'd made it on to the train in one piece, but he knew they were far from safe. Whoever was after him wasn't about to give up. He had to assume that they had figured out that he and Rachel were on the train and that they would be waiting for them at Rapid City.

"There's a message notification on my phone, Rache. There's no signal here. I'm going out on the platform. Will you be okay for a few minutes?" he asked. He didn't want to leave her, but he knew he couldn't expect her to follow him out to the platform in her condition.

Rachel assured him she'd be okay, and Xavier moved toward the rear of the car and stepped outside. When he saw he had a faint signal, he hit RETURN CALL.

He didn't recognize the number that scrolled onto the screen. The answer came in the next instant. "You've reached the offices of the Central Intelligence Agency. Our normal hours of operation are . . ." *Of course, even the Feds have voicemail these days,* he mused. "This is Dr. Jeremiah Xavier. I'm returning your call," he said, then clicked OFF. He barely had time to wonder what the CIA had in mind for him when a return call came through. He answered.

"Dr. Xavier, this is Agent Harry Carlyle. Can we talk?"

"This may not be the best time, Agent. I have a situation," Xavier told him.

"What kind of situation?" Carlyle asked.

"Someone is after me and some of my associates with very serious intentions."

"And you know this, how?"

"They've already claimed to have killed one of my colleagues and another friend of mine and have threatened others if I don't meet with them."

"They did what?! What the hell do they want?" Carlyle asked.

"I have no idea," Xavier replied.

"Might it be related to your contract with the Sandool Corporation, Doctor?"

The question caught Xavier by surprise. "Why would you assume that?"

"On a hunch," Carlyle replied. "It's the reason I called you in the first place . . . to find out more about your company's relationship with Sandool. We need to meet, where are you?"

"I'm on a local tourist train heading for Rapid City. I have to find someplace safe," Xavier replied.

"How far from Rapid City are you?" the agent asked.

"I'm guessing about thirty minutes or so. But I'm not alone. One of my office staff is with me and she's been injured."

There was silence for a moment before Carlyle said, "Okay, I'll call you back in ten minutes. And, Doctor, be extremely careful. If whoever is after you has anything to do with Sandool, you're probably dealing with pros."

Xavier slipped his PDA into his pocket and went back to check on Rachel. A number of seats had emptied as some of the passengers began ambling into the club car for drinks. Waiting for them to move forward took a few minutes. As he approached Rachel's seat, he saw that she was gone. He hoped she had just gone to use the bathroom, but he had a sinking feeling.

He hurried toward the front of the car. Then he saw it: Rachel's sweater on the floor near the connecting door. He tried the restroom. It was locked. He knocked softly. No answer. *Maybe she's sick.* He was about to call the conductor when he heard the restroom door latch release.

Out stepped an elderly gentleman. "Sorry to hold you up, my good man. It's my prostate."

Xavier sneered at the man and looked around. *Damn, where is she?* he wondered. His military instincts began shouting an alarm that he couldn't subdue, and he rushed out onto the forward platform. Nothing. He had been gone for maybe five minutes. Someone would have had to board at the last stop and located them among the crowd almost immediately. Thinking they'd taken her to the club car, he started to move into the next car, but then stopped. The sweater was the key. They had wanted him to check the restroom. It was a trap.

No time for mistakes, he thought. *These people are pros. Rachel's life is at stake. I need to move.* But it was too late. He felt a presence behind him. He spun around quickly, but the blade of a knife had already made its arc. It came down on his left shoulder, but hit him with only a glancing blow. Xavier grimaced as the pain shot down his arm, but the surge of adrenaline coursing through his body had already begun doing its work. His body reacted reflexively. In a lighting-swift movement, the elbow of his muscled right arm arched viciously outward, landing on its target. He felt the soft-tissue impact as the assailant's larynx was severely crushed. The would-be killer lay in a heap, gagging his final breaths. Xavier looked down at the man in disgust, then took a few deep breaths and cleared his mind to continue his search for Rachel.

Moving forward toward the club car, Xavier felt blood trickling down his arm. He knew the wound wasn't that bad, but a bloody shirt would draw attention. He spotted a black sweat jacket hanging over the back of a seat and nonchalantly picked it up as he walked past. He easily slipped the roomy jacket on as he continued moving forward through the car. When he reached the club car's connecting door, he peered in carefully. A few dozen passengers were milling about enjoying their cocktails. Entering slowly, he spotted a squat, powerfully built Asian man sitting at the bar, his suspicious eyes darting back and forth.

Where is Rache?

Xavier eased over near the window next to a table with a plate of unfinished appetizers. He grabbed one of the serving forks and carefully approached the bar behind the wall of standing bar patrons. The man gave no indication that he had seen him. Xavier moved in closer, within two barstools of the Asian. It was then that he spotted the small-caliber weapon fitted with a silencer barely visible beneath the man's folded arms.

The bartender met his eyes and asked if he had wanted anything. Xavier nodded. "I'd like to buy a round for that gentleman," he replied, nodding in the direction of the gunman.

The bartender smiled. "He says he's not drinking, but I don't mind asking again."

Xavier watched the bartender lean over toward the man. With the gunman's attention diverted, Xavier reached across and jabbed the fork deep into his forearm.

"*Augh*!" the Asian grunted, immediately releasing his grip on the gun, which Xavier deftly grabbed and jabbed into the man's side. It all happened so quickly that the bartender didn't have time to question the odd looks crossing the Asian's features.

Xavier gave the bartender his best reassuring smile. "He's surprised to see me. Aren't you?" he said, nudging the barrel hard into his ribcage.

With the firmly embedded fork lodged against a nerve, the gunman just shook his head and gritted his teeth.

"We'll pass on that drink," Xavier told the bartender, who turned his attention back to the paying customers, and to the man, he whispered forcefully, "Move." He shoved the man off the stool toward the front of the club car and out of sight of the crowd.

"Where is she?" he asked, pushing his adversary into a bulkhead and jamming his forearm against his throat.

The man didn't blink. Xavier sensed that the guy wasn't about to be intimidated. Grasping the handle of the fork, he twisted it hard. A quick snort followed by a gurgle of spittle erupted from the man's mouth as the fork twisted the tendons in his upper forearm. Immediately, with his good hand, the Asian pointed shakily to a door directly behind him. Spinning his captive around, Xavier opened the door. It was a storage room for the bar. Rachel's body was partially obscured by the crates of liquor and other supplies. She was lying motionless in a pool of blood.

Xavier's emotions exploded violently. He raised the butt of the gun and smashed it down on the back of the Asian man's head. The gunman's body hit the floor with a smacking sound as Xavier rushed over to Rachel.

He felt her neck. There was a faint pulse. It looked like the bullet had gone through her upper chest and had exited out her back. A soft wheezing sound indicated that it had probably punctured her lung. In that moment, sitting on the floor cradling her head, he realized how important Rachel was in his life. She had been there for him ever since he'd lost his wife and daughter. And now when she had needed him most, he had failed her.

The call coming through on his PDA startled him.

"Dr. Xavier, I've been trying to reach you for the past fifteen minutes. Are you alright?" Carlyle asked.

"They were on the train . . . must've gotten on at the last stop. My friend's been shot. I'm not certain how much time she has left," Xavier uttered quickly.

"I've checked your ETA to Rapid City. You're about ten minutes out. I'll have an emergency vehicle waiting at the station. Where're you located on the train?"

"We're in a storage room at the front of the club car."

"Okay, Doctor. I've arranged for two federal marshals to meet you. They'll escort you to the hospital. I'll call you there."

"Thanks, Agent," Xavier said, as he looked down at Rachel. She gasped softly.

LEGACY

Beijing, China

"The information you've supplied regarding the ongoing activities of your country's largest and wealthiest corporation is *very* troublesome, minister. Are you *absolutely* certain of its accuracy?" the International Nuclear Agency representative asked.

"You can be assured that it was confirmed by a most reliable source . . . someone very closely aligned with my ministry," the minister of technology assured him.

"If what you have reported is true," began the representative, "then I'm confused by your unwillingness to issue a notice of noncompliance from your own offices."

There was a moment of hesitation before the minister explained, "There are many here who would rather overlook such transgressions than suffer the loss of certain favors or possible reprisals."

"So you are requesting that this agency act on an independent basis," the rep concluded.

The minister sighed. "I know that you have received many such requests. If you wish, I can arrange to have one of your inspectors accompany someone from my ministry to verify the circumstances of the violations."

"That will not be necessary at this stage of the process. If the violations are as severe as you've indicated, we will issue a notice to cease operations pending an inspection of the site."

"The sooner the better," the minister said.

"You do realize the significance of this action," the representative stressed. "Once the notice is issued, there will be substantial repercussions—quite possibly worldwide implications."

"It is exactly why I have initiated this request," replied the minister.

"May I ask why you have come forward at this time?"

There was a brief pause before the minister replied, "I have my reasons."

9

AMBUSHED

Rapid City, South Dakota

The tourist train pulled into the quaint station exactly ten minutes after Xavier hung up with the CIA agent. The waiting ambulance accompanied by a number of federal marshals and several Rapid City police cars created an imposing scene for the tourists.

Xavier was sitting with Rachel's head cradled in his lap when the door to the storage room was suddenly thrown open. He had tried to stem the bleeding from the wounds to her chest and back with the borrowed sweat jacket, but he feared that her internal injury would be fatal. He was relieved to see that help had arrived and hopeful that her life would be saved.

"Dr. Xavier, we're federal marshals. The EMTs are here," a rosy-cheeked man with a distinct Boston accent assured him.

Xavier waved them in. Within minutes, the paramedics had Rachel on a stretcher and she was already receiving oxygen and an intra-venous drip. Once the EMT's had carefully moved the stretcher off the train car, Xavier watched as the local cops gathered up the unconscious gunman. "You'll find another body on the rear platform of the next car," he told them, as one of the two marshals approached him.

"We have instructions to accompany you to the hospital, Doctor Xavier," the nattily dressed man said. "You can give your statement to the local cops there. . . . And have that wound on your shoulder treated."

Xavier nodded and followed the first marshal off the train, while the other marshal, the one with the Boston accent, followed closely behind.

The covered station in downtown Rapid City was a recently restored historic landmark. The large arched-glass-encased esplanade dated back to the turn of the century. As the men proceeded outside toward the street level, they passed under a porte cochere. The streets were alive with the noise of honking horns and moving traffic. The sound of the high-powered round that struck the lead federal marshal went unnoticed as it hit him squarely in the chest. He fell backward onto Xavier. The second round sent the other marshal scrambling for cover as it ricocheted inches from Xavier's head.

"Jesus Christ! Where'd that come from?" the marshal yelled.

Xavier didn't move. He was pinned beneath the first marshal. He could feel the wounded man's irregular breathing and knew that he didn't have long. He had no time to feel sorry for him. He suspected that when the two hit men on the train didn't report in, others were sent to wait for them at the station. Why no one had thought of that earlier irritated him.

Meanwhile, a small crowd had begun to gather around the fallen marshal. That irritated Xavier as well. If they had been aware that a sniper still had his sights on the area, they would have been screaming and running for cover. Xavier began to move, and the crowd gasped.

"Are you hit, Dr. Xavier?" asked the marshal from Boston from a short distance away.

"No," he replied.

"Can you make it back here?" the marshal asked.

Xavier looked up and over to his left. He nodded slowly feeling the heaviness of the wounded marshal's near-dead weight pinning him to the pavement.

"Get back . . . get back," the other marshal directed the crowd.

That seemed to spark some recognition of danger in the gawkers, and many started moving quickly away from the scene. As soon as they began to make room, Xavier arched his back and eased the marshal's body off him to the side. He quickly bolted back under the porte cochere.

The Boston marshal was already on his radio. "We need an EMT and fast. Sniper at the front of the train station. I have an officer down."

Within minutes, sirens blared in the near distance, followed closely by a helicopter circling overhead. This activity had most likely chased the sniper off.

"I'm not sure what the hell's going on, but I need to get you to the hospital," the marshal told Xavier. "As soon as my partner's attended to, we'll head out," he continued, watching with concern as the paramedics worked with fervor on his stricken friend.

"Sorry about your partner, Marshal. I wish I could give you a good explanation about who is after me, but I can't," Xavier said, frustrated and perplexed by the deadly situation.

Once the ambulance had loaded the wounded marshal, Xavier and the other marshal hustled into an awaiting vehicle and headed downtown toward the hospital. Xavier's thoughts quickly turned to Rachel's condition when his PDA buzzed.

"Dr. Xavier, you are most resourceful," said the familiar but dreaded voice on the other end. "However, your continued efforts to thwart us will only cause more deaths. I strongly urge you to reconsider your actions. As I had warned, you *cannot* escape us. You have forced us to consider other more appropriate options. I will give you one last chance to surrender yourself. After that, we will have no choice. I trust you understand our resolve. Your call will be expected within the hour."

Xavier turned to the marshal. "We need to get my friend to a different hospital, one that's under the radar."

The marshal stared back. "Who was that, Dr. Xavier? Was it the people who are after you?"

Xavier nodded.

"Let me make a call," the marshal said, retrieving his cell phone.

Xavier listened as the marshal explained the circumstances to whoever was on the line, and then took the phone when the marshal handed it to him. It was Agent Carlyle.

"Dr. Xavier," the agent began, "it seems as if you've got yourself a real pissing match. These people have some very serious motivations. We can't move your friend yet. I checked, and she's going into surgery as we speak. We're going to lock down the hospital for the time being and hope to catch these bastards—whoever they are."

"Let's do it quickly. I have the feeling that they may already be inside," Xavier warned.

Carlyle hesitated. "You're probably right," he said. "If that's their intention, they wouldn't have waited before threatening you. I'm on my way to Rapid City now. I'll be there in about three hours."

10

WARRIOR

Xiong Xian, China

Khan stared at the all-too-brief message on his computer screen in utter disbelief. Intense anger distorted his features and heat spread like a wave upward through his body. He felt ready to explode.

How dare these insolent bastards challenge me, he raged.

The notice—sent via the largest law firm in the UK, which had represented Zangshe for many years—read simply:

> *Effective immediately, Zangshe Inc. is hereby ordered to cease its mining operations based upon reported violations associated with the unsafe disposal of nuclear-waste materials.*

It had been issued by the International Nuclear Agency.

Khan pounded his meaty fist on the inlaid top of his enormous desk. "Send Yakubla to see me!" the chairman of Zangshe barked to his assistant through the intercom.

Gansukh Yakubla—Khan's closest friend and Zangshe's chief operating officer—was a direct descendant from an ancestral line of notorious Mongolian warriors. Khan found this fitting. Yakubla served the wishes of his chairman and master without question or compunction.

He was the epitome of the proverbial wolf in sheep's clothing, or in this case, a warrior dressed in Gucci clothing.

Yakubla walked proudly into Khan's office only moments after he had been summoned.

"I have just received a notice that is intended to threaten continuance of our mining operations," Khan told him, his voice steady and controlled. "It is but a feeble attempt made by the INA to exercise its authority. However, I am concerned that any inspections of our sites might interfere with our current plans. I will need to find the individual responsible for causing this notice to be issued and *convince* him of his misjudgment."

Yakubla bowed his head slightly. "I understand, Great One. I will see to it immediately."

Khan shook his head. "No, Yaku. The INA notice I will handle directly. There are two more urgent matters requiring your immediate attention," Khan told him. "As you well know, work has already commenced on QPR's data. Barring any interference, we will be ready to begin our new operations in the very near future."

A slight smile played on Yakubla's lips. "I have already seen much progress in that regard. Tell me, Great One, what you would have me do?" he asked expectantly.

Khan stood up from his desk and moved closer to his friend. "The details of the first one are in here," he said, handing his Mongolian friend a small white envelope.

Yakubla took the envelope and tucked it inside his suit pocket. "And the next?" he inquired.

"The scientists at Sandool have been reviewing with us the specifications for their uranium-encapsulation solution," Khan said. "There is a particular substance that is essential to their solution. And the substance is found in great abundance in only one place . . . the great Arabian Desert."

"I would be pleased to negotiate a most favorable arrangement to acquire this substance, Great One," Yakubla replied eagerly.

Khan turned toward his friend and held up his hand. "It is not your negotiating skills I require."

"Forgive my ignorance, Great One," Yakubla said with a slight, apologetic bow. "What is it that you are asking of me?"

"I wish to control access to the Great Desert," Khan replied.

11

FABLE

Rapid City, South Dakota

Xavier and the marshal arrived at the hospital without further incident. After a visit to the ER to treat his minor shoulder wound, Xavier was ushered up to the ICU to see Rachel. He had given his report to the local police while he was being treated, and now the only thing on his mind was Rachel's well-being. Her nearly three-hour surgery had been successful, but her vital signs were still very weak. The nurse who escorted him to the ICU advised him it would be touch and go for a while.

"She lost a lot of blood. The bullet severed an artery and passed through her left lung. We have her on a machine," the surgeon told him matter-of-factly.

"What are her chances?" Xavier asked, bracing himself for the worst.

The surgeon directed him to sit down. "She's fallen into a coma. I'm not certain yet if she'll come out of it. We'll have to wait."

Xavier dropped his head. There was an ache in his heart and a pit in his stomach that made him feel weak. "Thanks, Doctor. Please let me know if there are any changes. I'm the only one she has that's close to family. Here's my cell number."

The surgeon took the number, assured Xavier that he would call, and left him alone in the waiting room.

Xavier sat for a few minutes trying to collect himself. If Rachel didn't make it, he was to blame. His failure to keep closer tabs on Winston had allowed the situation at QPR's research facility to get out of control. Yet, he was still very much puzzled about the attack and how it all had related to QPR's research. As he contemplated Rachel's condition, he felt a comforting hand on his shoulder.

"Dr. Xavier . . . I'm Harry Carlyle. . . . I'm very sorry about your friend."

Looking up, Xavier's eyes rested on the strong chiseled features of the CIA agent. Close-cropped dark hair that was graying at the edges and a lean, muscular body not quite six feet tall completed the snapshot of the former Marine sniper.

"Thanks for coming, Agent Carlyle," Xavier said, shaking off the funk and tucking away his concerns for Rachel where they wouldn't interfere with his ability to respond to continued threats. "I appreciate your help. I guess your hunch was right."

"Believe me when I say that I had no idea to what extent," Carlyle replied. "So you know, perimeter security was established at each entrance of the hospital and SWAT teams have moved into position on the surrounding rooftops. Inside, there are plainclothes detectives and agents from our Rapid City office. I'm guessing that our actions chased them off. Is there anything you can tell me that might give a clue as to who's behind all this?"

"The caller had an Asian accent, with a peculiar, nasally tone," Xavier replied. "His English was clipped and grunted out. That's the only clue I have. Otherwise, I have no idea. When he last called, he said he'd have to consider other, more appropriate options and that he'd have no choice, whatever the hell that means."

Carlyle's brow furrowed. "From the note of urgency connoted by 'having no choice,' it's probably a contract job. The way you described the accent leads me to believe it might be Cambodian, possibly members of gangs who are throwbacks to the days of the Khmer Rouge."

That's a heinous name out of the past, Xavier reflected. *The Khmer Rouge had been some of the cruelest and most feared of all the communist factions as documented in the killing fields of Cambodia.* "How would they be involved?" he asked incredulously. "I'd thought that culture of violence was long out of existence."

Carlyle quickly explained, "A lot of the older gang members who had been hardened by their horrific experiences from the atrocities of the Khmer Rouge actually escaped to the U.S. seeking refuge. They settled in California and began forming gangs of their own to protect themselves from the local Mexican gangs. Because of a concerted crackdown on gang activities over the years, a lot of the younger members have been operating as contract mercenaries." Carlyle stopped to think for a moment. "As for their involvement here . . . if Sandool is somehow behind this, I'd expect another possibility—not the Cambodians."

"I'm not sure that Sandool even knows what's happened yet," Xavier said.

"What do you mean, 'what's happened'?" Carlyle asked, apparently realizing that there was more to this puzzle.

"There was a major accident at the research facility," Xavier told him. "I just assumed you knew. The facility has been shut down indefinitely."

"The accident was related to the Sandool contract?" Carlyle asked.

"I believe so. It was caused by the lead researcher on the project."

"Who else would know about the exact nature of the accident?"

"I'm not sure," Xavier replied. "I've been thinking about that as well, but I don't think the accident itself is the cause of the present situation."

"What then, Doctor?"

Xavier hesitated. "A particular experiment."

Carlyle moved to face him head-on. "Okay, Doc. You need to tell me *everything*. You've got to know that there's going to be an investigation anyway, but that may be too late."

Xavier shook his head. "I know and . . ." he paused for a second. "Presumably my colleague was working on an experiment for the Saudis, when something apparently went wrong."

"What did the Sandool contract entail?"

"Sandool had anticipated a molecular altering of the composition of uranium into a more adaptable resource for commercial applications," Xavier replied.

Carlyle smiled. "As I suspected. The Saudis want back in the energy business."

"That's correct, Agent Carlyle."

"Listen, Doc, I think we've gotten past the formalities of our relationship. Call me Harry."

Xavier knew that when people were on a first-name basis, it elicited more trust, and that Carlyle was playing him. Still, he liked the former sniper, and replied, "Okay, *Harry.*"

"Now then," the agent continued, "I have the feeling that there's something else you wanted to tell me."

"The truth is," Xavier replied hesitantly, "I'm not exactly certain what my colleague was doing, but apparently he'd made some kind of discovery. His assistant had found out something but unfortunately was killed before he could tell me."

"How can that be? I mean, your not knowing what happened in your own laboratory."

"It's a very good question, and one that might well come back to haunt me."

"What are you saying?" Carlyle asked.

"If the effects of what I witnessed in the underground experimental labs are any indication, we're dealing with extraordinary forces at work—forces that could have produced something very unusual and quite possibly unstable."

"That's way too cryptic for me, Doc. But you believe it might be dangerous, not simply another fuel source?"

Xavier nodded. "I do."

"I'm confused," Carlyle replied. "Why didn't you have a serious heart-to-heart with your colleague who made the discovery?"

"That wasn't possible.

"Why not?"

"We had to evacuate the research facility. He's most likely dead—killed by his own creation."

Carlyle looked surprised. "Jesus . . . so we may never know what it was. But it's obvious someone does. So we're back to the Saudis."

Xavier frowned. "I don't think so, Harry. They were already en route to our facility for an update on the project. The accident happened too quickly for any information to have reached them."

"Then your colleague was working with someone else," Carlyle concluded.

"Why would you assume that?"

"It has to do with my hunch, Doc, based on an old fable of sorts."

"An old fable?" Xavier asked curiously.

Carlyle smiled. "Care to hear it?"

"I'm not sure I'm up for any stories."

"It's short and to the point. You might enjoy it."

Xavier shrugged and smiled slightly. "Sounds like you are going to tell it whether I want to hear it or not."

"That's right," Carlyle chuckled and began, "There once was a king who ruled the world. Not through the power of his armies but with an unrelenting control over a most vital necessity. Everyone paid homage to the king for fear he would withhold such necessity from them. Over his long reign, the king amassed an enormous fortune and garnered great power for his large family and their families. Alas, one day, the king realized that the source of this vital necessity was dis appearing and so was his great power. Then, he found a sorcerer who claimed to have a magic potion that would help restore the king's vital

necessity and therefore his power. However, the king had many enemies who didn't want to see the king's power restored and were determined to take the power for themselves. So the king's enemies plotted
against the king and decided to capture the sorcerer."

There was a slight pause. It appeared that Carlyle had finished.
"That's quite a story, Harry. What's the point?" Xavier asked.

"It's kind of a metaphor that explains a lot of things in my world.
Most recently, we've had some unusual activity in the Middle East,"
Carlyle explained. "Only one thing over the past ten decades or so has
caused that much aggression . . . oil. However, with the decline of that
industry, it struck me that maybe the Saudis had cooked up something
to restore their energy kingdom. Then, I connected your company to
the Saudis. QPR has had somewhat of a checkered past supporting various undertakings under the guise of science. I thought it might be
worthwhile to follow up on my hunch."

"Interesting," Xavier said. "In your little fable, you think that
QPR's somehow going to help restore the Saudi royal family to prominence. And according to your tale, that would make QPR the
sorcerer."

Carlyle grinned. "It's a good story, isn't it? . . . And yes, I think that
more than ever, it applies. So, either someone's chasing you because
they think they can prevent the Saudis from getting the magic potion
or . . ."

"Or someone's chasing me because they already have it and don't
want to share it," Xavier interrupted.

"I couldn't have said it better, Doc."

12

NEGOTIATIONS

Ahvaz, Iran

On board Zangshe's black G-750 corporate jet, Yakubla squeezed the receiver of the air phone tightly with his powerful hand. "I was expecting to hear better news from you," he said. "You were well paid for the task. However, your report indicates that I may have over-estimated your abilities. When do you anticipate a satisfactory conclusion to our business?"

"The quarry is most resourceful," voiced the reply. "We were led to believe that he was a scientist with no skills at evasion. He has proven otherwise. I am certain we will prevail very soon, but the collateral damage may be more than incidental."

"I could care less what collateral damage you incur as long as none of it is traced back to us. You will have twenty-four hours in which to accomplish your objective. After which time, the contract shall be terminated and you will be replaced," Yakubla said calmly.

"That will not be necessary, Taiji Yakubla," the nervous voice on the line grunted, using a salutation of great respect. "You will have the news you desire by tonight's end."

A cruel smirk emerged on Yakubla's face as he put the receiver down, thinking, *Little do they know that their fate, as well, has already been sealed.*

The black jet landed in an unmarked airfield near the Iran-Iraqi border. Inside the perimeters of a local kabal, a meeting was convened with several of the heads of the mujahedin. Battle-hardened, treacherous, and ruthless to the core, these Muslim mercenaries and purveyors of terrorism were summoned for a report on the progress of their mission.

As he arose amidst them, Yakubla's sheer size was noteworthy. Well over six feet with a hulking frame, the foreigner looked very imposing. It was, however, his haunting and fearless countenance that riveted the terrorists' attention before he had even uttered a syllable.

"I have come today to meet with you in person. It has been nearly three weeks, and I am most anxious to learn of your progress," Yakubla said, looking around at the mercenaries.

Several moments passed. Then, in front of Yakubla, a wiry, scarred-faced mujahedin soldier slowly stood up. "You had requested that we gain control of the vast area of desert and seaports in a short time. Our forces have already moved close to the southern Kuwaiti border with Saudi Arabia. We are staged to launch the offensive along the Gulf coastline. But we have concerns—concerns that may involve more risks than were first apparent."

Yakubla glared at the mercenary, his arms folded against his chest. "You speak as if we have had no previous agreement on terms."

The rugged mujahedin stared back. "Things change. Your plan is very ambitious. There are other factors that may now affect our success."

"If you are interested in pursuing this course, you should be mindful of my intolerance for child's play," Yakubla said, well aware that renegotiations were most typical of mercenary behavior.

When the words left his mouth, Yakubla knew he had touched a chord. The knife was halfway to him even before he finished speaking. With lightning-quick reflexes, Yakubla expertly caught the blade firmly between his palms. In the next instant, he returned the knife at such speed that it caught the mercenary unaware and struck him in the shoulder, deeply embedding itself to the hilt. As the mercenary collapsed to the ground, several others around him charged at Yakubla. He never budged.

"Stop!" a loud voice bellowed from the rear. "We have made our point, but so has he. If he had wanted to kill, the knife would have found its mark. It is time for us to discuss our differences," the young but experienced mujahedin leader said.

Yakubla nodded. "I am listening."

13

PHENOMENON

Rapid City, South Dakota

Xavier's last conversation with his pursuers had occurred nearly three hours earlier. Apparently, the security measures Carlyle deployed had deterred any plans they had of getting to Rachel. The entire hospital was swept for bombs. Every person entering and exiting was thoroughly checked. But the hospital staff was growing impatient with the disturbance to their operations.

"I've told the hospital administrator that we'd be here for only another few hours," said Carlyle. "If nothing happens by then, it's probably safe to say, that for now, the worst is over."

"I hope you're right, Harry. It didn't sound to me like they'd give up so easily."

"I didn't say they'd give up, just that they'll choose another time and place. But I really think your friend's safe here. If you want, I can call an ex-CIA friend who's a private detective to look after her."

"I'd appreciate that," Xavier said.

"What are your plans, Doc?"

Xavier had been thinking about his next move. "I guess I'll stay here for a while, Harry, and then . . ."

"Let me suggest that you come back with me to Langley," Carlyle interrupted. "I have more resources there to try to fit the pieces of this puzzle together, but I'll need your help."

It's fine to collect pieces to the puzzle, but without knowing what that puzzle is . . . Xavier thought.

Carlyle took Xavier's silence as hesitation to leave Rachel and said, "If you stay here, you're going be out in the open. I can't protect you. Your friend's safety is secured. My buddy will be with her for as long as necessary. The best thing you can do for her right now is help me find who did this to her."

Xavier knew that Carlyle was right, and nodded. "Let's go then. But I'll need some things. I left in kind of a hurry."

"We can pick them up after we land at Andrews AFB," Carlyle replied.

Xavier could tell that the agent was glad he had acquiesced.

The three-hour flight to Langley and CIA headquarters had passed uneventfully. Xavier had slept most of the way.

"Doc, we're here. I didn't want to wake you. You've had a busy past few hours. How's that shoulder?" Carlyle said, as he motioned toward the airstairs of the Coast Guard Falcon jet aircraft.

"It's sore but nothing serious," he said, looking down at his watch and wondering how Rachel was doing.

Carlyle noticed the glance. "I just talked with my PI buddy. There's been no change in your friend's status. Everything's quiet at the hospital."

The men descended the stairs.

"I appreciate all your help, Harry. Feel like I've been in a rugby match and could really use a shower about now," Xavier said, as they walked toward Carlyle's agency-issued nondescript car parked near the hangar.

"We'll stop to get you some things first, and then we'll find you a shower and some coffee," Carlyle promised.

 C3

Up four floors, Carlyle's office was located on an outside wall, denoting his seniority at the Agency. Xavier couldn't help but notice that Carlyle's Marine assistant sat in an empty bullpen arrangement with only one other enlisted person. "You're operating a little lean here . . . new policy?"

"New budget constraints," Carlyle replied. "We've had a hiring moratorium on civilians for almost a year. With enlistment down, we've had trouble keeping military staff at the admin level. It's a whole different environment around here these days. A lot different, I'm sure, than when you were in, Doc."

"I've got to confess, I didn't spend much time in an office," Xavier replied.

"No, I'll bet you didn't. Although, I can't say for sure because your military file is buried somewhere. Mind telling me what you did?"

"Maybe someday, Harry. Most of it I've tried to forget."

"Well, apparently you remembered enough. I got an e-mail on the flight back from our offices in Rapid City. The two guys you took out on the train have been preliminarily identified. The one on the platform was killed from a blow to his throat. The other is now being interrogated by the local police. He's not given up much, but the body markings on both of them confirm that they're from a contracted Cambodian gang. We'll get our chance to find out more from him soon. And we have our ways, as I'm sure you know."

"It confirms your initial theory about the Cambodians, but it still makes no sense to me," Xavier said.

"That's why you are here, Doc. I've asked one of our tech types to do some background analysis on Sandool and what they've been involved in over the years. I'm hoping you can fill in some of the gaps."

"Show me to the showers and then we can get started," Xavier said, hoping that this would not be a total waste of time.

୦ଃ

Gregory Rudolph Riggins—or "Riggins" as he preferred to be called—was one of those human resources no one wanted to work with inside the CIA. He was obnoxious, condescending, and a downright pain in the ass. However, with an IQ of over two hundred, he was something of an intellectual phenomenon. And without question, he was indispensable in certain situations. His grasp of every form of math-based technology was astounding as was his ability to absorb large quantities of data and decipher it into cogent patterns in a short span of time. The CIA had tracked him down after he had trespassed his way through their newest and most secure hack-proof computer systems. It was ironic that someone so brilliant would make the simple mistake of leaving a tag identifier for the average geek to find. Or maybe it was just that Riggins wanted the recognition.

Instead of slapping him with Federal charges, which would have put his brilliant mind in prison for the remainder of his life, Riggins was given the opportunity to work for the Agency in return for a reduced sentence. Here he was ten years later, still the best tech spook in the industry.

"Riggins, I'd like you to meet Dr. Jeremiah Xavier from QPR," Carlyle said, directing the techie to take a seat at the conference table.

Xavier felt somewhat renewed after the shower and change of clothes. He extended his hand to greet the CIA technical genius.

Riggins had curly red hair, a bit long by Agency standards. A little on the portly side, he wore jeans, sandals, and an old sweatshirt with the letters AIC across the front. Casually holding a cup of coffee and clearly displaying his contrarian nature, he slowly ambled over to Xavier, looked him straight in the eyes, and shook his extended hand. "It's nice to meet you, Dr. Xavier," he said, then added, "Good to have someone else with a brain around."

Finally taking a seat as directed, Riggins slouched into the chair and shot a furtive glance at Carlyle.

"Cut the shit, Riggins," Carlyle said. "I've got little patience today for your attitude. I want you to brief us on your findings so far regarding the Sandool Corporation."

"When do you ever have any patience, Agent Carlyle?" Riggins muttered under his breath, then added clearly, "But I'd be glad to brief *you*, Dr. Xavier."

Xavier perceived the tension in the relationship between the two men and took note of Carlyle's obvious dislike of the techie.

"The Sandool Corporation was formed twenty years ago," Riggins began. "It was created by the Saudi royal family ostensibly as an environmental agency to implement greener methods of extracting and refining crude oil. However, as the sources of crude oil slowly dissipated, Sandool turned its sole focus toward new technologies to replace their vanishing black gold. Over the past two decades, their efforts had produced little if any noteworthy results. In fact, up until about five years ago, the royal family had all but abandoned their support of Sandool. Then, everything changed." Riggins stopped the briefing to take a sip of his coffee.

"I'm assuming that this is the point where they began their relationship with QPR," Carlyle said impatiently.

"Not so fast, Agent . . . there's a bit more to the story," the techie replied with a smile. Instead of continuing, however, he made a show of blowing on his coffee.

Although Xavier knew this brief history about Sandool, he was beginning to enjoy the repartee between the agent and the techie.

Carlyle gritted his teeth. "Let's get on with it, Riggins. We have other more important things to do."

"I'm sure that's the case," Riggins continued, "but you just might be interested to hear what I have to say next. As I'd indicated, almost five years ago, one of Sandool's scientists made an interesting discovery. Investigating some old French experiments, Sandool came across a previously unpublished study exploring the possibilities of altering the molecular structure of certain rare isotopes of uranium. The researcher in the French experiments apparently had been working on his own, because the results of his efforts were disregarded by the French as being too inconsistent and dangerous."

That's something I didn't know, Xavier mused, his curiosity piqued. "Mr. Riggins, mind if I ask a question?"

"I'd be pleased if you would, Doctor."

"Was there any documentation about the specific nature of these isotopes?"

Riggins paused for a moment. "I was only beginning to analyze that myself when Agent Carlyle asked that I provide a summary of my findings. However, the study did reflect the researcher's comments and frustration that the technology was not yet available to produce results on a reliable basis. I'm glad to continue my analysis in more detail, if you feel it might be meaningful."

Interesting, Xavier thought, as he glanced over at Carlyle.

"I have no objections, Riggins," Carlyle replied, "but I'd like you to stay in close contact with Dr. Xavier. I don't want anything going out of this office without my approval, even inquiries for clarification."

Riggins seem to acknowledge Carlyle's directive as he got up from the table and started for the door. "Dr. Xavier, may I ask *you* a question?" he asked, turning slowly around.

"Certainly," Xavier replied.

"I'm aware to some extent of QPR's advanced research experimentation. However, I'm a bit puzzled about this, and I'm curious to know if your corporation is aware that Sandool is currently working with the Chinese on something very similar?"

This question took the other two men by surprise and rendered them speechless for the moment. They just stared at the redheaded techie in disbelief.

14

CHIMERA

Xiong Xian, China

"I must see Chairman Khan right away," said Dr. Liang Wu, the head of Zangshe's experimental research, to Khan's diminutive assistant.

"The chairman is quite busy at the moment and cannot be disturbed," the slight woman replied.

Wu paced impatiently back and forth in front of her. "It is of the utmost urgency that I speak with the chairman. Please . . . please, I must insist that you inform him that I am waiting out here," Wu said, his voice growing louder with each word.

Acknowledging the urgency, the assistant hurriedly stood and bowed to Wu before she turned to the door of Khan's spacious office and opened it slowly. She entered quietly.

Khan's back was to her. ". . . and I have already assured you," he was saying into the handset of his private line, his voice biting and harsh, "that my plans do not conflict with your strategic interest. Our proposed agreement will provide you with the necessary resources to revitalize your economy. It is in your personal best interest as well as your country's to secure the necessary approvals." With that, Khan slammed the receiver into the base. Spinning around in his chair, he looked surprised to see his assistant bowing at the doorway of his office. "What are you doing there?" he barked, not liking to be caught off guard.

Raising her head slowly, she responded, "I apologize most profusely for my intrusion, Great One. But Doctor Wu is most anxious to speak with you. He insists it is a matter of extreme urgency."

"Send him in," Khan said with a dismissive wave of his hand.

The agitated scientist hurried into the office a moment later.

"What is so important that you would interrupt me, Wu?" Khan asked.

"I am sorry for my impertinence, Great One. I need to discuss with you my efforts to replicate the hybrid's molecular composition," Wu replied, bowing lowly.

Khan stood up and walked toward the scientist. "When can I expect the replication to be completed?"

Wu's nervousness grew more apparent. "The recent research data from QPR you sent me is very complex. The accidental splitting of the isotope molecule revealed a particle that was not known to exist. Its characteristics are highly unstable and require great care."

The chairman glared at him. "What are you telling me? I had thought the data was most precise and the process was well documented."

"Indeed, it is, Great One. It is only that . . ." the scientist hesitated.

"Only that *what?*" Khan shot out angrily.

"It is only that the particle accelerator at the University of Beijing is not quite as powerful as QPR's and the replication results may not be precisely the same. Using the data from the discovery of the superparticle, I may not be able to recreate identical results."

Khan's face contorted angrily. Rage resided just below the surface, as it always did, like a volcano waiting to erupt. "I will not be stopped now. Your incompetence will be severely dealt with."

Shaking visibly under Khan's disapproval, Wu stammered a

response, his mouth dry with anxiety. "I apologize for my excuses, Great One. Even if we had access to QPR's accelerator, I might not be able to do so. However, based on the data from my analysis, I believe I can develop something very similar, but it will take me some time. The resultant replicated hybrid maybe nearly as powerful . . . almost as unlimited in potential as the original."

Khan stood within inches of the trembling scientist and whispered harshly in his ear. "You *will* find a way to replicate the hybrid and *soon*. I will give you and your family no mercy for your failures."

Eighty miles to the north in the Chinese national government complex in Beijing, the determined minister of technology was strategizing. His plan was already in motion. The INA notice that he had initiated to halt Zangshe's mining operations was only the first manifestation of his obsession to seek justice—justice for a long-standing and horrible legacy.

15

CONUNDRUM

"I gather from your reaction that you didn't know about the Chinese involvement with Sandool, Dr. Xavier," Riggins said, barely trying to hide his smugness.

"That's fair to say, Mr. Riggins. How did you find that out?" Xavier asked.

"There're a couple of things about working in the CIA that have some benefit. One of them is hacking around anyone's data with impunity. In this case, I found a link while rummaging through Sandool's sandbox. It led me directly to their connection with the Chinese," Riggins said, grinning with pride.

"That's very clever," Carlyle snapped. "And what did you actually learn on Uncle Sam's dime?"

Xavier sensed that Riggins was on a roll, as if they were playing in *his* sandbox now.

"The relationship between Sandool and the Chinese goes back almost five years. It involved a partnership proposal from the Saudis. Apparently, the Saudis had already developed some type of advanced-encapsulating compound for uranium. It was purported to be a very efficient, safe, and adaptable method of utilizing uranium in a commercial environment as a fuel source," he said, stopping to look at Xavier and then at Carlyle.

"Okay, Riggins, enough of the theatrics. What's the bottom line?" Carlyle asked.

"Well, considering Agent Carlyle's attention span, I'll truncate my comments," Riggins said. "Since the Chinese had the uranium, the Saudis had proposed that, in exchange for the encapsulation technology, they would enter into a partnership for the production of a new type of nuclear fuel—a replacement for its failed oil business."

"And how does QPR fit into that scenario, Riggins?" Carlyle asked.

"I was getting to that, Agent Carlyle, but your predisposition toward impatience led me directly to the bottom line. If you'd like a full explanation, it'll take a bit longer."

Xavier could see that Carlyle was struggling to keep his temper in check.

"Okay, Riggins, in deference to Dr. Xavier, I'm going to give you some leeway, but hear me well. I've had enough of your bullshit."

"I can see I've already struck a chord with you, Agent Carlyle, and much faster than usual," Riggins chided. "Let me quickly paint the picture for you so that you can easily see the connections here. According to Sandool's scientists, in order for the uranium to be adaptable for commercial usage, it required some modification. The energy yield of refined-uranium fuel would be far too strong and dangerous. Instead, the Saudis had determined that the vast amounts of Chinese nuclear waste or depleted uranium would be an ideal starting point for their theory. If the depleted uranium could be modified or altered to produce sufficient energy under certain conditions, it might become a suitable and marketable fuel-replacement platform. Consequently, it led to the one place where research into advanced-molecular altering had proven to be highly successful . . . at QPR."

"That's correct," Xavier added quickly, before Carlyle dug in his heels. "When Sandool approached us a few years ago, they'd heard about the work that QPR had pioneered. They'd speculated that it might be effective for their purposes."

"And your company concurred?" Carlyle asked.

"One of our senior scientists believed it to be a worthwhile endeavor," Xavier replied. "The project was quickly approved by QPR's board of directors. We were actively conducting experiments on Sandool's initiative up until the recent accident."

Riggins smirked. "I can tell you, from their internal correspondence, that's what the Saudis were led to believe."

It was Xavier's turn to react to Riggins's comments. "What do you mean by that?"

"There was another agenda," Carlyle added.

"Bravo, Agent Carlyle. I'm impressed, and you're absolutely correct," Riggins added in short order to quell the look of disgust on Carlyle's face.

"What was it that you discovered, Mr. Riggins?" Xavier asked, trying to keep peace.

"The Chinese had already found a methodology to effectively alter the composition of uranium waste. However, they had convinced the Saudis to pay exorbitant sums of money to help fund a project for essentially the same results . . . all as part of the agreed-upon promise to allow the Saudis to participate with the Chinese in a partnership for the repackaging of uranium-based fuel for everyday use."

Like a wolf on the prowl, Carlyle began stalking around the conference table, staring intently at the techie. "Let me get this straight, Riggins. The Saudis hired QPR for research work on something that the Chinese had already developed?"

"That's about it, Agent Carlyle," Riggins said.

"It makes no sense to me. Why would the Chinese spend the time to do that if they already had a solution?" Carlyle asked.

Xavier watched Riggins closely. He was as surprised and puzzled as Carlyle, but he had a feeling that the technical genius had figured something out; although, it was clear that Riggins wasn't about to make it easy on Carlyle.

"Believe it or not, it had me perplexed as well, Agent Carlyle, until I was finally able to hack through the complex Chinese firewalls. Surprise of surprises. It turns out that the Chinese had another plan in mind—a plan that they didn't want anyone else to know about. That's why they used the Saudis to work with QPR. See where I'm going with this?" Riggins said.

Carlyle looked pissed. "Yeah . . . I can see that you're playing me along, Riggins. You might find this entertaining, but I don't. And if you don't make your point soon, I'll find a way to bury you in the IT sector so deeply you'll never resurface."

"Okay . . . okay, Agent Carlyle. Don't get all flustered," Riggins replied, realizing he had pushed way too far. "The Chinese had actually been involved in the same experiments with uranium isotopes as in the old French studies—the identical studies discovered by the Saudis. The difference was that the Chinese had known about it for at least ten years."

"Ten years!" Xavier said. *It's so typically Chinese,* he thought, *misdirection and deception wrapped around secrecy.* "Then, what *did* the Chinese expect to accomplish through the Saudi contract with QPR?"

"That's where it gets very interesting, Doctor," Riggins replied. "According to the information I could access off the Chinese computer servers, they're very familiar with the specific capabilities of your advanced-particle accelerator. Their scientists had speculated that under controlled conditions, using QPR's atom smasher, the earlier French experiments involving certain uranium isotopes could be performed on a consistent basis."

"How could the Chinese have possibly known about the specific capabilities of our accelerator? And what made them believe they could experiment on rare-uranium isotopes at QPR?" Xavier asked.

Riggins stared at Xavier. "They had been working with someone on your staff."

The words fell like an axe on Xavier. "Someone on my staff! Who?"

Riggins shook his head. "I really can't say, Doctor."

"Can't or won't?" Carlyle demanded.

"I don't know, Agent," Riggins replied. "The information I was able to uncover doesn't identify the person, just that he or she was in a senior capacity and had complete access to the experiment and the accelerator. Maybe Dr. Xavier has some ideas."

Elliot Winston . . . could it have been him? Xavier wondered, horribly dismayed by the thought. "The most likely possibility was the project manager," he said, "but I can't imagine he'd collaborate with the Chinese. He was obsessively driven by his work and he was a loner. I can't believe he was a traitor."

"Is he the same person who'd made some type of discovery in your lab, Doc?" Carlyle asked.

"He is."

"So, I guess it's a fair assumption that the Chinese might have the information regarding the discovery. Which might also explain who's after you," Carlyle said.

"I can't argue your conclusions, Harry. As much as I don't want to acknowledge the possibility of the connection, it seems to make some sense," Xavier replied slowly.

Riggins was listening attentively. "If I've heard correctly, there was a recent discovery at your laboratory facility. And that tracks with the data I saw in the Chinese files that indicated a 'breakthrough discovery in nuclear technology that would change everything.' However, that's where the information flow ended. They found out that I'd hacked into their server and changed protocols."

"Then we don't know what the Chinese intend to do," Carlyle said.

"I can speculate if you like, Agent," Riggins said, "but Dr. Xavier might be better equipped to do so."

What has Winston done? Xavier thought. "I'd like to hear your theory, Mr. Riggins," he said.

Riggins nodded his appreciation. "Based upon everything I've researched to date, I'd have to say that the Chinese are planning to broaden the spectrum of their nuclear business. The encapsulation process for depleted uranium waste will most likely be deployed as a replacement for carbon-based fuels. Separately, there may well be an initiative underway to take advantage of the recent discovery at QPR."

"And what could that be?" Carlyle asked warily.

Xavier watched the CIA geek. It was as if Riggins was directing an orchestral symphony and his grand finale was about to happen.

"There's been another event that occurred recently, Agent Carlyle, which might affect the timing of things for the Chinese."

"And?" Carlyle asked, holding his hands up in frustration.

"The INA has issued a notice to the Chinese to cease their mining operations pending investigation of charges associated with nuclear-waste storage practices," Riggins replied quickly. "Shutting down their uranium-mining business isn't something that the Chinese are likely to accept. Faced with that dilemma and given the alternatives, my assumption is that there's a high probability the new discovery will be used by the Chinese to somehow leverage completion of their nuclear plans."

Interesting deduction, Xavier thought.

Carlyle looked at Xavier. "Is that your sense as well, Doc?"

Xavier frowned. "What I know is that Elliot Winston's discovery in the wrong hands is a very dangerous prospect. Beyond that, I don't have any better theory at this point."

"Well, the only thing it doesn't explain is the current hostility near the Kuwaiti border. Any chance either of you think it's related to what we've been discussing?" Carlyle asked.

"It doesn't fit into any existing pattern," Riggins replied, "but with the urgency surrounding the energy crisis, it wouldn't surprise me if the Chinese were somehow involved there as well."

"It's hard to imagine why the Chinese government would have any current interest in the Middle East," Carlyle commented.

Riggins whipped his head toward the senior CIA agent. "Who said anything about the Chinese government?"

"I had assumed that's who we've been discussing," Carlyle fired back.

"Then you've misunderstood me, Agent. I never mentioned anything about a governmental agency."

"Then, who the hell were you referencing by *the Chinese*?"

"It's a private corporation and one big mother of one at that," Riggins replied. "It's called Zangshe Inc."

16

BAIT

Southern Kuwait

Colonel Chauncey Jackson had been receiving reports for the past few days regarding the advancing assault force coming down from the Iran-Iraqi border. His small Marine compound on the outskirts of Al Wafrah was part of the United World Federation, commissioned to monitor border activities.

"Colonel, we have a visual on the troops coming our way," said Sergeant Ducky Peterson, one of Jackson's best friends and the top sniper in the Corps. "It looks like every bit of two brigades with a full complement of armored vehicles. I'm estimating ETA in approximately one hour."

"Thanks, Ducky. Tell the guys to pack up everything. The plan's to go south and stay ahead of that movement until we know for sure what's going on."

"Hate running, but I have to agree, staying here's suicide," Peterson said, as an explosion nearly took the roof off the small-bunkered compound.

"What the . . . ?" Jackson yelled, as a second blast tore away the entire front section of the building.

"Incoming!" one of the Marines shouted, running for cover inside the rumble of the compound. The piercing sound of high-energy laser (HEL) weapon bursts confirmed the presence of the Russian-made vertical takeoff aircraft.

"Ducky, get to the roof and take out that aircraft!" Jackson ordered urgently.

"On it!" Peterson shouted in reply, scrambling toward what remained of the small stairs leading to the crumbling rooftop. He sighted up the target within moments. A small fighter jet hovered like a chopper directly overhead. Peterson could see the pilot through his high-powered scope. He assumed he was waiting for his HEL device to recharge. Wasting no time, the large-caliber sniper weapon let go a thunderous blast, firing its round into the jet's canopy, blasting off the top of the pilot's head. Almost instantly, the jet began to whirl uncontrollably with the pilot's body still strapped in the seat.

"One down," Peterson said aloud to himself, retreating to the bottom floor of the compound. "Let's move quickly before they regroup!" he shouted to the troops.

Twenty-two Marines piled into a half dozen Humvees and quickly sped away from the advancing brigade.

"This is Colonel Jackson calling base command . . . come in."

"Base command here . . . go ahead, Colonel."

"A large assault force moving southward toward the compound has engaged us. Currently, we're approximately ten clicks from the Saudi border. I'm requesting aerial support . . . over."

"Colonel, we've been advised to stand down. You'll need to take appropriate evasive maneuvers. I repeat . . . there will be no aerial support, over."

Jackson looked over at Peterson with disbelief plastered all over his dirty face.

"Did I hear that right? Telling us we're on our own. Jesus!" Peterson shouted.

"Base command . . . this is Colonel Jackson. I'm requesting the latest radar activity in our sector. Can you advise of any hostiles, over?"

There was no response.

"Base command, this is . . ."

The surrounding sand suddenly exploded, leaving giant chasms as the HEL bursts rocked the ground around the small convoy. Jackson's Humvee veered violently to the right and off the road.

"Get out of the vehicles, now!" Jackson shouted into his headset. Looking to his left, he saw two of the Humvees vaporize into thin air from the near speed of light velocity of the HEL bursts.

"Ducky, take positions! I've got two birds at three o'clock."

"I'm locked and loaded, Colonel. Ah, shit . . . there's another one coming up on our six!"

17

PIECES

avier held the cell phone close to his ear. He felt his heart rate increase as he waited for the update.

"There's no change in Ms. Sinclair's status, Dr. Xavier," the attending nurse told him. "She is stable for now."

Xavier thanked the nurse and ended the call. *C'mon, Rache, hang in there,* he prayed.

"Any news, Doc?" Carlyle asked.

"No change," he replied, looking back at the agent.

"She'll make it," Carlyle said. "I know it's hard to deal with . . . especially after losing your wife and daughter."

The remark caught him by surprise. "How did you know about that?" Xavier asked.

"We're the CIA, Doc. It's our job to know things," Carlyle responded.

The awkward silence that followed was interrupted by Carlyle's assistant: "Agent Carlyle, you have a call on line one. It's Agent Samuel Reynolds from the Rapid City office."

Carlyle picked up the line.

"Harry, I wanted to give you an update on the situation here," Reynolds said. "The local cops have turned over the train gunman to us. We'll find out what he knows, but there's something else. They found two other bodies in a slag mine today—identical body markings as the first two. Someone's cleaning up loose ends."

"Thanks, Sam, let me know what you learn from your interrogations," Carlyle said, putting down the phone. "Looks like our Chinese friends are busy, and they have enormous reach. Two more gang members with Khmer Rouge gang markings turned up in Rapid City. My bet is that since you neutralized the assailants on the train and foiled the contract hit on you, they're eliminating any trace of evidence."

But Xavier knew it was far from over. The intel from Riggins had confirmed his worst fears. Winston's accidental discovery was somehow in the hands of the Chinese. He also suspected that the Chinese had no way of knowing that he'd never received the information about the nature of the discovery and therefore he was still a target. "We'll need to somehow stop the Chinese company from developing their nuclear plans," Xavier said. "If they're able to replicate whatever was discovered, it could have devastating consequences."

"I've been thinking about that as well," Carlyle said. "We could try applying pressure through diplomatic channels and most likely, the Chinese will deny everything. But we could give it a shot, anyway."

That's not going to work. I've got to find another way, Xavier thought. "We need to try something else, Harry, and we probably don't have much time. If the information we've heard so far is any indication, the Chinese are on the brink of something big."

Carlyle met his eyes in confirmation. "Only two ways this can go, either through official channels or not."

Xavier knew the *or not* meant covert ops. "What resources do you have, Harry?"

"That's the rub, Doc, not many. Between budget cuts and retirements . . . not much to draw upon."

Xavier paused. "It's been a while, but my old network's still around. Can I get access to a clean phone line?"

Carlyle smiled. "Absolutely, and glad to have you on board," he said, turning to leave his office. "Let me brief the boss upstairs in case this goes down sideways."

"Anyway you could avoid doing that?" Xavier asked. "I'd prefer for this to stay between us for now. My experience is that the less said the better. Plausible deniability is usually preferred among the brass types."

"Beg forgiveness rather than ask permission . . . got it," Carlyle said, as his attention was suddenly diverted to an alert notice on his computer. "Hey, Doc, take a look at this," he said, focusing the satellite images on his screen.

Xavier watched what appeared to be a large force advancing along a desert road. In the next few frames, a smaller grouping of vehicles had pulled off on the side of the road. Carlyle toggled the image and zoomed in closer. Then, they both saw it. From out of nowhere, several small jet aircraft had descended and hovered over the vehicles. Within seconds, they watched as two of the Humvees were completely disintegrated.

"HEL bursts," Carlyle said. Then something caught his eye. He hit max zoom. "Holy shit . . . that's Chauncey Jackson," he exclaimed, pointing to a large African-American Marine huddled behind one of the four remaining vehicles.

Carlyle quickly grabbed the satellite phone on his desk and dialed. "Get me the Riyadh base commander, now!" he yelled into the receiver.

Within moments, a deeply toned Southern drawl resounded on the line. "This is Colonel Hodgkins. Who am I speaking with?"

"This is Special Agent Harry Carlyle. Are you monitoring your incoming satellite scans, Colonel?" Carlyle asked anxiously.

"Twenty-four-seven and who do you think you're talking to?"

"So, you know what's happening in sector eleven, just south of the Kuwaiti border?"

There was a brief pause in the transmission. "We've been following it for a while now, Agent."

"Why haven't you provided air support for that Marine contingent?"

There was another delay.

"We've been directed to stand down," the Colonel finally said.

"Stand down?" Carlyle yelled incredulously. "What the hell are you talking about?! Those guys are getting slaughtered in the open like that!"

"You think I like sitting here with my thumbs up my ass having to witness this bullshit?"

"Then for God sakes . . . scramble a couple of F-40's now. They'd be there in a matter of minutes."

"No can do, Agent. I've chased this all the way up the flagpole. My hands are tied."

"Who gave the order to stand down?"

"That's not your business," Hodgkins replied.

"Give me the name of the asshole who gave you the order, Colonel, or I'll personally make your life more miserable than it is at the moment."

"Don't threaten me, Agent. Besides, y'all should know where that order came from."

"What the hell does that mean?"

"The order came from the Director of the CIA . . . your f-ing boss!" Hodgkins blurted, and then clicked off the line.

18

CONSPIRACY

Carlyle's face was red with anger, but the emotion was quickly replaced by confusion and disbelief. "My boss gave the order? I'll be goddamned." He shook his head. "Get Director Cheskin on the line," he barked to his Marine assistant.

"Yes, sir," she replied, but after attempting to put the call through, she said, "He's in a meeting and can't be disturbed."

Carlyle glanced at Xavier. "Mind staying put for a while, Doc? I'm going up to see the old man myself. This is bullshit," he said, already in the process of downloading a few of the satellite images to his copier.

Xavier knew enough about government protocol to realize this situation was going to get very ugly.

"I'll work with Mr. Riggins on the data he's intercepted from the Chinese," he said as Carlyle headed out the door. "Maybe something in there will give us a clue where to start."

John Cheskin was a career bureaucrat who had served as director of the CIA for the past seven years. Extremely qualified and politically connected as well as anyone in D.C., Cheskin had maneuvered through the vagaries of party policies and the morass of omnipresent critics to accomplish the mission of his Agency: safeguarding the interests of the U.S. from its various detractors. Carlyle was determined to know what had changed.

"Sir, you need to see these," Carlyle said, barging into Cheskin's office through the previously closed doors. He wasn't surprised to see that the director wasn't actually in a meeting. He dropped the satellite printouts on the director's desk.

Cheskin looked at Carlyle and grinned, but there was no humor in it. "Still have those well-honed manners I see, Harry."

"Manners are for country clubs and churches. I dare say that this place is neither. Besides, pictures are worth a thousand apologies. Take a look at these images, sir. That's Colonel Jackson's squad getting massacred."

Cheskin glanced at the images and quickly turned away. Carlyle couldn't see his expression as he said, "I've seen them."

"And we're not doing anything to help, sir?" Carlyle demanded.

Cheskin hesitated and took a deep, measured breath before looking back at Carlyle. "Let me be perfectly clear, Agent Carlyle. I am not authorizing any action whatsoever to be taken in this matter. Colonel Jackson was appropriately advised of the risks involved in his mission."

Carlyle was dumbfounded. He had worked for Cheskin for a good number of years now and had always respected the director's judgment. Something was amiss here, and he didn't need to be a CIA operative to deduce that much. "What are you talking about, sir? We've got Marines in harm's way as we speak, and you gave the order to stand down!" Carlyle said, glaring intently at Cheskin.

The balding, blotchy-faced CIA director glared back. "Don't presume to be judgmental with me, Agent. You're unaware of a number of factors that take precedence at this time. If there's nothing else, you're dismissed," Cheskin barked, putting his glasses on and turning his attention back to his computer screen.

Carlyle backed up and exited the office. On the way out, he glanced over to the Marine staff sergeant who served as Cheskin's assistant.

"Couldn't help but overhear the conversation, sir," Sergeant Michael Strong said. "Things have recently changed around here. Not like the old days. The old man's been under a lot of pressure lately. Your story's not exactly news. I received some preliminary intel late yesterday. The assault force was identified as a faction of a mujahedin group from Iran. I was ordered not to pass it on."

"What?!" Carlyle snapped. "Cheskin has been sitting on this since yesterday?"

"There's more of that than you'd want to know, Agent. And if I didn't know better, I'd say we have a situation here."

"What kind of situation, Sarge?"

The staff sergeant looked away momentarily. "The kind you go to Leavenworth for, Agent," he replied, referring to the Department of Defense's maximum-security prison.

19

SIBLING

Andrew Wyncroft was a brilliant mechanical engineer. He had worked in the engine-manufacturing business for almost three decades. Starting out in the automotive industry, he had quickly risen through the ranks, becoming a vice president of General Motors at the young age of thirty-two. Recognized for his brash style and incisive managerial skills, Wyncroft was recruited into a senior position with the world's largest supplier of aircraft engines. Within three years, he had become its president.

That was more than fifteen years ago. However, it wasn't until Wyncroft was in his current role that he was able to fully exercise his considerable technical abilities. Now, as the CEO of Alternative Energy Technology Corporation, a consolidated energy-development company, Wyncroft employed more than a half million personnel in ten states. Headquartered in the defunct GM facilities, he had returned to the scene of his first job, bringing about an economic revival that gave hope to the once devastated region. Ever since the demise of oil, manufacturers of combustion engines had either gone out of business or desperately attempted to diversify into other forms of energy.

It was the vision of Wyncroft and his talented team that had leapfrogged the technology barrier and had developed a revolutionary replacement platform for all carbon-based, fuel-dependent power sources. In effect, Wyncroft had envisioned an adaptable, dependable, and safe energy source to fit every application from the largest power generation station to every mode of transportation. His uniquely innovative design had emerged from his belief in the one resource that had engendered continual controversy.

"The first installation of the nuclear-conversion energy system is completed, Mr. Wyncroft," the vice president of Propulsion Design reported. "Your changes regarding the ignition module made the prototype concept very adaptable in the new French jet. And once we receive the encapsulated-fuel samples from the Sandool Corporation, we can commence testing on it as the preferred fuel source. We should get confirmation shortly from the Saudis regarding delivery of the first samples."

"I want to see the latest revenue projections for each of our industry segments," Wyncroft said. "The installation of the prototype engine is more easily accomplished in all new assemblies. However, the assessment of the overall cost and effectiveness of installations across the entire *retrofit* market is of even more significance."

"Our rough estimates are easily in the tens of millions of units, including in the generating plant, automotive, aircraft, and marine segments," the vice president replied. "I'll have specific cost and revenue data to you by week's end. But it's fair to say that once we initiate deployment of our new energy system, we'll become the world's sole proprietor of this technology."

Wyncroft folded his arms across his chest. "I'd say it another way. In less than two years, AET will become the second-largest privately held business in the world, behind only our parent company . . . Zangshe Inc."

20

CODE

Xavier and Riggins were deeply engaged in conversation when Carlyle barged through the conference-room door.

"Son of a bitch," Carlyle said, as he sat down opposite the two. "The director knew about the situation in Kuwait and let it happen. Something's royally screwed up around here. I'll be damned if I'm going to ignore it."

Xavier waited for Carlyle to settle down. "Harry, Mr. Riggins and I found some information that might indicate what's so important in that region."

Carlyle was still visibly upset over his meeting with Cheskin. "Whatever it is isn't worth the lives of good Marines."

"I agree," Xavier said. "But it might help to explain all the commotion there."

"It better be the next coming of Christ," Carlyle replied.

Riggins shot a quick glance over to Xavier. It was clear Riggins knew now was *not* the time to goad the agent.

"It has to do with Sandool's uranium-encapsulation process. The primary component of the encapsulation solution is found in large abundance in only one place in the world—the Saudi Arabian desert."

Carlyle shook his head. "You're talking about sand?"

"It's not just your ordinary variety of sand," Xavier said. "The silica oxide or sand used by Sandool is almost ninety-seven percent pure. According to the Saudi specifications, it's the ideal main component in the development of an advanced generation of borosilicate-glass resin—a newer plastic-polymer-encapsulation compound."

Calmer now, Carlyle asked, "How much of the stuff do they need to make the encapsulation work, Doc?"

"A whole shit load of it," Riggins interjected, not able to remain mute for very long.

"I think Mr. Riggins's estimation's accurate," Xavier said with a smile. "It would require enormous quantities if the Saudis had intended to go into mass production of an encapsulating device. The silica oxide is used to develop a substance into which the uranium is immobilized through a process called vitrification. In this instance, a highly specialized variation of the substance was proposed by the Saudis. It would enable the end user to safely handle and efficiently utilize the depleted uranium. In short, the production process would utilize many millions of tons of silica oxide."

"So someone must know how important the sand is," Carlyle concluded. "Although, what good is the sand to them unless . . ."

"They controlled access to it," Riggins interjected. "In that instance, the Saudis would probably be extorted into paying huge sums for their own sand."

Carlyle nodded slowly. "Makes sense, Riggins, and it might explain the connection to the mujahedin mercenaries. The question is how did they get involved?"

Xavier looked at Carlyle. "As you said, Harry, someone's concerned about the balance of power in the region . . . or changing it."

Carlyle had been pacing around the conference table pondering the situation when he suddenly took off for his office. Xavier and Riggins quickly followed.

The satellite photos had continued to stream in showing the Marine squad's desperate situation. With only three of the Humvees intact, the remaining dozen or so Marines had hunkered down behind the vehicles.

Carlyle watched the series of firefight exchanges intently. One of the hovering aircraft had been disabled and left the scene. "Look there," he said. "I believe that's a sniper buddy of mine next to Colonel Jackson. If he can lock on to another bird, they might have a chance to make a fight out of this."

No sooner had Carlyle finished his last word, when another Humvee disintegrated into thin air leaving no trace of anything. In the process, it seemed that the pilot had guessed wrong about the location of the sniper, providing enough time for Ducky Peterson to target his adversary. They watched and waited anxiously. There was no immediate reaction from the aircraft. When the jet finally launched itself to level flight away from the scene, it was evident that Peterson's round must have found a soft spot. They could see the remaining group of Marines hastily piling into the remaining Humvees with their wounded and speeding southward again—hopefully toward safety.

Carlyle looked away from the computer screen and took a deep breath. "Well, for now, it looks like it won't be a complete massacre. If Jackson can make it another few clicks down the road, there's another Marine compound not too far away in the port city of Ra's Al Khafji. They have several antiaircraft frag launchers that are capable of providing some protective cover. However, based upon the size of that assault force, they'll need to evacuate as well," Carlyle said pensively.

"I'm beginning to appreciate your initial assessment, Harry," Xavier said. "It's an enormous geographic area to invade and control. There's certainly something of major interest involved."

"Yeah, and I'm not any closer to knowing what the hell it is," Carlyle replied. "Director Cheskin is somehow wired into the situation, and there's only one way I know to ferret out the truth . . . that's getting to the source. I'm betting I'll find some answers in Riyadh. You want to take a trip to Saudi Arabia, Doc?"

Xavier had other ideas. It was apparent to him that Carlyle was determined to pursue his own mission. "I think I'll find the answers I'm looking for elsewhere, Harry."

Carlyle smiled. "It didn't take you much time to get back into Agency mode."

"I wouldn't say I'm back . . . yet," Xavier replied.

Riggins had remained uncharacteristically quiet for a while. "I keep thinking about the French studies. Something I saw referenced there makes more sense now," he said. "The old studies discussed the possibilities associated with the rare uranium isotope's capabilities to change the current thinking about nuclear technology. I need to reexamine the studies more closely."

"What does that have to do with what we've been discussing, Riggins?" Carlyle asked.

"I'll bet it's related in someway to what the Chinese were working on and possibly, whatever was recently discovered at QPR," Riggins replied. "And maybe, just maybe, there's a much more significant reason for someone the likes of Iran to sponsor mercenary forces."

Carlyle didn't react to the response immediately. Then, slowly, he raised his eyes and stared at the techie. "I hesitate to say this, but I tend to agree with your speculation, Riggins."

Riggins seemed to puff up a bit, and added, "The Chinese made another deal, this time with the Iranians for their help in return for the promise of some new type of technology."

"It's the best motive so far for the aggression in the Middle East," Carlyle replied. "If it's true, then the Chinese don't intend to partner with the Saudis. Apparently, their plan is to seize the supply of encapsulation material by controlling access to its source."

"I think we've broken the code," Riggins said with a wide smile.

However, Carlyle looked far from convinced. The senior CIA agent was pacing around. "It doesn't explain a number of issues, Riggins," he said. "Like, why have we taken a laissez-faire role in the Middle East, and what do the Chinese actually have in mind?"

"Wait a minute," Riggins said. "We know more than we did before, Agent, and that should count for something."

Carlyle opened his mouth to speak but stopped. He looked at Riggins the way he might look at a small child, then said, "I'm sorry to say, Riggins, that this isn't one of your games. The truth is somewhere between what we think has happened and a whole bunch of other stuff that is just pure speculation. It's the difference between what you and I do. I need to find hard facts and soon."

21

WEB

Xiong Xian, China

"You were gone longer than I anticipated, Yaku," Khan said quizzically from his leather chair.

"Yes, Great One. The business of working with mercenaries is far from straightforward. They take much pleasure practicing intimidation and renegotiating their interests," Yakubla replied.

Khan let out a dismissive grunt. "I can think of no one more assured and capable than you in that situation."

Yakubla bowed his head in appreciation of the compliment. "They are but mere children when it comes to anticipating their motives. I do not trust their intentions, but for the time being, we have an understanding that will serve our purpose."

"It is a matter of timing that we need their services," Khan replied. "Once our production plans are fully in place, there will be no reason for further reliance on any outsiders. However, for now we must give the appearance of partnership."

"I understand clearly, Great One," Yakubla said. "When it comes to the mercenaries, I have made provisions for such future eventuality. However, currently, they have made much progress."

"Then tell me, Yaku, the results of your efforts," Khan said with anticipation.

"Let me show you, Great One," Yakubla replied, pointing a remote toward the rear wall of Khan's office where a large LED screen was disguised as a mural. The mural faded and was replaced by a satellite image of the Persian Gulf region with a map overlay. "Our entrance will be southward along the seaports of the great gulf. At each strategic location from the northern border all the way down to the southernmost point, we will establish permanent military compounds," he said, directing Khan's attention to the various targets marked in red with the remote's laser pointer. "Furthermore, these compounds will consist of integrated-force components capable of fending off land and sea or air attacks."

Khan studied the map carefully. "How quickly can these forces be in position?"

Yakubla looked intently at the deployment plan for a moment. "I believe with minimum resistance, we should have all of the permanent compounds in place in less than two months. The mercenary commander had indicated that already the UWF task forces are in complete disarray and have retreated as far south as possible."

Since the fall of the oil cartels, the Middle East held little, if any, strategic interest with any of the remaining superpowers. Khan had counted on that mind-set to continue, at least until he had solidified his presence in the region.

"We are on the precipice of a great moment in history," Khan said, his voice trembling with anticipation. "With the recent discovery from QPR, we will develop a deterrent against any future interference in our plans. It is more imperative than ever that control of the coastal areas from Kuwait to the U.A.E. be secured within the time frame as specified."

"It shall be done, Great One. However, I sense more urgency in your tone," Yakubla noted with concern.

The belligerent chairman turned toward his Mongolian friend.

"Someone with great influence is conspiring against me," Khan replied. He squinted as if seeing the perpetrator right there in front him and clenched his fist. "I will *not* tolerate being manipulated by the whims of some feckless international agency like the INA."

Yakubla replied reassuringly, "In that instance, I will proceed to accelerate our efforts, Great One."

Yakubla made ready to leave the office, but Khan's word stopped him. "There is something else, Yaku . . . the names in the envelope," he said.

Yakubla bowed. "It is with the utmost apologies that I must report to you that one of the names on the list has yet to be silenced. I was forced to remove any traces of our involvement before he could be terminated."

The truculent mogul tugged at his long braid in frustration. "Then you must see to the matter yourself, Yaku. There must be no witnesses to the data from QPR."

22

NETWORK

Langley, Virginia

Once Carlyle had departed for Andrews Air Force Base for his flight to Riyadh, Xavier planned to contact his old network. According to its own definition, his old network didn't officially exist, so getting in touch would be a challenge. Members of the Black Ops—one of the military's quintessential secret and perpetually deniable operations—had a code, an understanding that each member most often operated singularly with minimum contact. In an attempt to reconnect, Xavier could possibly violate the code. Once he had initiated the process, though, he would be back in—maybe for good. However, the stakes were too high now for any second thoughts.

"Mr. Riggins, can you arrange for me to get access to a clean line?" Xavier asked, calling down to Riggins's office.

"I can provide you a com link that'll defy any form of ID tracking. Give me fifteen minutes and you'll be ready to go," the techie replied.

Xavier shook his head. "I'm glad you're on our side."

"Tell Agent Carlyle that. Sometimes I wonder if he thinks I'm the enemy."

"You make him uncomfortable . . . you don't fit into any one of his boxes," Xavier shared.

That seemed to give the technical genius pause. "I get that. Thanks, Doctor. Call you back in a jiff."

Too bad his genius isn't fully appreciated . . . poor guy, stuck in a thankless job like this, Xavier thought, and before he knew it, Riggins was buzzing on the line.

"Okay, Doctor. Here's the setup. Use line two on Agent Carlyle's phone. Dial 000, wait for the confirming tone. Dial 999, wait five seconds. Then, dial whatever number you need."

"*Uh-huh* . . . routing it around the world and back?" Xavier chuckled.

"Further away than that. Try from the space station!"

Xavier smiled. "Thanks, and I apologize for not expecting as much, Mr. Riggins."

"No problem and good luck, Doctor."

Luck would be something he was going to need—that and a huge dose of persuasion. Getting in touch with the right operatives was complicated. Convincing them to help him might be stretching the possible.

There was never a contact list. Every number, name, or pseudonym was passed along verbally. Details regarding assignments, addresses, access, and data encryption codes as well as physical descriptions were all committed to memory. Loosely structured within the aegis of a quasi-military operation, most of the players were independent oper-ators, each highly skilled in various methods of assassination, inter-diction, fomenting, and insertion. There was no shortage of contracts for the clandestine talent pool. Abiding mostly by their own rules except within the context of the network, every member operated with impunity from any jurisdiction. It was the world in which he had once lived. Now, he would start where he had ended some ten years ago. Hopefully, that would lead him to someone who had knowledge to get him close enough to Zangshe Inc. After that, the hard work would commence.

He picked up the phone and dialed the sequences. Then recalling the series of numbers he had once used as if he'd only just committed them to memory, he punched them into the dial pad. The line rang once and went dead. He waited patiently, looked at his watch for exactly thirty seconds, and then redialed. This time, the line rang six times before a voice answered.

"X-man, long time . . . missed you. Heard you'd gone civilian."

"See you're still in," Xavier replied.

"No place for me anywhere else. What's up?"

"Need a favor—a contact in China."

"Why?"

"Matter of national security."

"Whose?"

"Everyone's"

"Sounds vague . . . but serious. Who're the players?"

"U. S., Saudis, and Chinese."

"Who stands to gain?"

"Not certain."

"Why the interest?"

Xavier paused. "It's personal."

"Wrong answer, X-man. You know the rules."

"Make an exception."

There was a lengthy delay. Xavier thought that the connection was over. He was about to hang up.

"Have anything to do with your wife and kid?" the contact said slowly.

The question surprised him. Xavier wasn't certain how to respond. "No, that was an accident," he replied. "I let something happen that's already caused a lot of pain. Not to mention what's likely to occur if I don't intercede."

"Who's the target?"

"Private enterprise—company by the name of Zangshe."

"See what I can do . . . terms?"

"Negotiable."

"Give me a few days. And X-man, don't overlook coincidences, particularly the seemingly unrelated ones."

The line went dead. He had no idea what the contact had meant by *coincidences*. The entire conversation was over in fewer than three minutes. After nearly ten years, the switch had been turned back on. It was as if he had never missed a beat. The network was like a good-old-boy's club without the social aspects—once a member, always a member. The word would go out. X-man was back in the game.

23

IDENTITY

Langley, Virginia

The phone in Carlyle's office rang, and Xavier picked it up. It was Riggins. "Doctor, can you come down to my lab? I want to show you something," he said, urgency in his voice. "I've just finished my analysis of the old French studies, and I found something very disturbing deeply embedded within the researcher's notations. If the Chinese intend to follow through on the concepts as proposed in the studies, there'll be no way to stop the chaos."

"I'm on my way, Mr. Riggins. Hang on," Xavier replied, already standing before hanging up the phone.

He stopped at Carlyle's assistant's desk. "Where's Mr. Riggins's lab?" he asked.

The attractive Marine lieutenant snickered. "Nobody here calls him *mister*," she said. "Quite frankly, I'm not exactly certain where his lab is located. It's in the sub-basement level somewhere."

Xavier took the elevator to the first floor, then found the service stairs and took them two at a time past the parking levels to reach the sub-basement. He wondered why the Agency had located the gifted techie in the bowels of the building. Making his way down, he was soon to understand the circumstances.

The lab space was carved out of the sub-basement's utilitarian functions. Sandwiched between enormous boilers and air-handling equipment was a large, bunkerlike room surrounded by thick concrete walls and abutments. Walking into the space was akin to entering a subway station control room minus the tile and sheetrock. Stacked into vertical configurations from the floor to the nearly twelve-foot-high ceiling was more computer hardware of every type and brand than he had ever seen. There was barely room enough to pass by. Fluorescent lighting was sporadically positioned overhead that cast shadows over the towering equipment, making it appear similar to the steel canyons of New York City at dusk.

As he weaved his way along the irregular aisles toward the center of the space, he heard a faint electronic beeping. He guessed that the more audible the noise grew, the closer he was to locating Riggins. Rounding another bank of blinking and flashing mini towers, he finally emerged into the center of the room . . . into Riggins's command center.

Riggins's back was turned; he was seated amidst an array of over-sized digital screens. The rhythmic beeping was coming from a zoom controller being manipulated by the techie. Each of the screens appeared to display pages of scientific notations. Xavier recognized several of the formulaic equations. Some of the notations were in French, but the characterizations were readily identifiable.

"Mr. Riggins, I was about to ask why you were banished into the depths here. But now I can appreciate your situation."

Riggins swiveled quickly in his chair. "Welcome to my humble world, Doctor. It's taken me a while to configure this place to suit my purposes."

"It's really quite something," Xavier marveled. "I've seen a lot of lab spaces and technical-support rooms. But yours is truly unique . . . very impressive."

"Thanks. If Agent Carlyle ever saw this, he'd freak out entirely."

"You mean he hasn't?"

"He's never as much as set foot down here. Just as well. He'd third-degree me on how I acquired all this gear."

"Enough to simulate a space shuttle launch," Xavier joked.

"What do you mean *simulate?*" Riggins replied with a quirky smile.

After getting to know Riggins, Xavier suspected he wasn't embellishing. "So tell me more about the French studies," he said, nodding up at the large screen of data.

"I didn't grasp the concept the first time I'd reviewed the data. After doing more research, I'm convinced that there's something far more sinister than what appeared on the surface. Here, take a look and tell me what you think," Riggins said, moving the zoom control into the middle of one of the detailed notations.

It took a few minutes for Xavier to evaluate the mathematical data. He looked away from the screen and down at Riggins. "They're equations for a new type of atomic activity. Based upon the formulaic expressions, the assumptions are indicative of completely unfamiliar molecular interactions."

Riggins nodded. "When I cross-referenced the results of my analysis with some later findings in the French study, it started to make more sense. The particular researcher involved in the study was experimenting on a very rare type of uranium isotope . . . a particle that he believed was capable of a specific kind of activity. Studying his assertions, it appeared to be some sort of self-initiating molecule—one requiring no external stimulation. Almost spontaneous."

"Huh," Xavier uttered. "According to the assumptions I'm looking at, it's capable of absorbing vast amounts of energy until its critical mass has reached a threshold. At that point, it can initiate its own internal nuclear reaction . . . apparently, over and over again."

"That's what piqued my curiosity," Riggins said. "I ran the math through some recognition software I've developed. It compared the level of energy released from a nuclear fusion reactor to the one proposed under the French research. They're nearly identical."

Xavier was astonished by the study's findings. "If these are anywhere close to being more than hypothetical, they're beyond an extraordinary evolutionary breakthrough—a self-sustaining, nonaccelerated nuclear-fusion reaction. It's incredible!"

"I'm guessing that's what your colleague at QPR was working on when something went out of control," Riggins said. "Apparently, in the process he discovered the missing particle. If so, we are now looking for a nuclear substance that has the capability of spontaneous activity. Do you realize what we're dealing with, Dr. Xavier?"

That's probably what Hammerstein found in Winston's files. And what absorbed the energy of the anomaly dissipating its force within QPR's experimental caverns, he thought, and aloud, he said, "Some form of nuclear hybrid and something almost impossible to control."

Riggins looked at him intently. "There would be no need to weaponize it: no missile-delivery system or fusing mechanisms. It's the perfect terrorist weapon."

"I'd like a copy of those notations, Mr. Riggins," Xavier said, his angst growing. "By the way, who was the researcher in the original French studies?"

"I don't recall offhand, but let me see if I can find it for you. Give me a few moments," Riggins said, as he rifled through the digitized pages. "Here it is. . . . The researcher's name was Elliot Winston."

WARNING

Riyadh, Saudi Arabia

The C-157 Cargo Master aircraft touched down smoothly on an airstrip just outside of Riyadh. Carlyle quickly disembarked and headed for a rusted hanger facility. He saw an old army jeep parked in front of the huge, closed bay doors.

"Aamir, thanks for meeting me here," Carlyle said, pulling himself into the passenger seat. "I hope this isn't a problem for you."

"It is never a problem to help an old friend, Harry. Besides, things are somewhat slow here at present. I appreciate the opportunity to do something other than perform my nighttime security job."

"How's your family, Aamir?"

The lean Saudi with deep-set, tired eyes turned toward his friend. "In truth, we have had difficult times since the demise of our oil industry. When your country finally pulled out, what remained of any employment disappeared. I'm very fortunate to have had the experience with you in the intelligence business. Otherwise, I would not have a job at Sandool."

"You were the best operative I had in Saudi, Aamir. I only hope your bosses at Sandool appreciate your talents."

"They have many more important things on their minds these days, Harry."

"And how's my old friend Prince Mohammed?"

"Did you not hear that he was killed in a helicopter crash?"

Carlyle turned toward Aamir with surprise. "I'm sorry to say that I haven't followed the situation here closely. When did this happen?"

"It was nearly five years ago, Harry. And the circumstances surrounding the accident were suspicious. But nothing was ever confirmed."

"Who'd have wanted the prince dead?" Carlyle asked.

"He had many enemies. There are many who blamed him for the overproduction of crude and the eventual collapse of the oil cartels."

Carlyle knew the prince had been a smart but ruthless businessman. In the waning days of the oil crisis, his control over world crude pricing had led to a buying spree that resulted in the hastening of the diminishing reserves. "Who's running Sandool these days, Aamir?"

"The prince's sister, Princess Almira bin Razul. She was still in business school at Wharton when her gravely ill father had asked her to return and take over as the president of Sandool—a most unusual move for the royal family. But as you might recall, she was the brightest, most ambitious, and, as it turned out, the shrewdest of all of King Abdul bin Razul's many children. And her role as its president has caused much controversy here."

"I would imagine that an Arabic woman in such a position of power poses some interesting cultural issues," Carlyle mused.

"That is the source of some of the problems but not the major one. It was her signing of the agreement with the Chinese that angered the royal family—the same agreement that the prince had continually rejected."

The timing of the prince's accident and the agreement with the Chinese seems too coincidental, Carlyle thought. "It's something I need to talk with the princess about. Is it possible I can meet with her?"

Aamir hesitated. "Since you first called me about meeting with someone in Sandool, I inquired with my contacts inside the company. The princess is not inclined to be hospitable: in fact, quite the opposite. There are numerous reports concerning her uncontrolled temper and her cruel, demeaning ways. I was informed that there is only one way to get access to her . . . through a mutual old friend of ours. Hopefully, you will be receiving a call shortly with instructions."

Carlyle smiled with appreciation for his friend's effort. "Things have changed here, but you have remained the same—always reliable."

"Old friends are irreplaceable. Take care, Harry. There are many around here who are very desperate and who are doing desperate things."

"Thanks for the advice, Aamir."

Aamir slowed the jeep at the intersection. He looked over at Carlyle. "I wish it was only advice, my friend. In these times, I would regard it more as a most serious warning."

25

CARGO

"Elliot Winston?! He was my colleague at QPR!" Xavier exclaimed incredulously. "I had no idea he was involved in this type of experimentation . . . and for such a long time. No idea at all."

"Well, he must have been one very clever scientist," Riggins said. "His notations were all well hidden in encrypted files. I was able to access them only after some effort; they're pretty advanced computing skills, even by today's standards."

"Brilliant, yes, but *clever,* I never saw," Xavier said, wondering how he could have missed it.

"Not only that," Riggins continued. "His experimental results were replete with numerous false trials. If one were looking for a specific finding, it'd be almost impossible to uncover."

"But you did, Mr. Riggins," Xavier said with an appreciative smile.

"Yes, and I have to admit that was partially by accident. The French nuclear research was very extensive. The volumes of documentation could fill the Library of Congress. However, I happened onto a particular aspect of the research through a quirk of luck. When

Agent Carlyle asked me to investigate the matter, I used a custom-designed search program to find anything related to QPR and Sandool. Interestingly, what appeared in one of the results was a reference to groundbreaking research in proton-beam splitting technology. Refining the search led me directly to your colleague's earlier French experiments."

"The same ones that he had obviously continued at QPR," Xavier added. "Connecting the dots is a science for you, Mr. Riggins. But there's a little luck involved. It's clearer now, the connection between Winston and the Chinese, but it's very hard for me to believe that it goes back that far."

Riggins ran his hands through his curly red hair. "Yeah, trust can be a bitch," he said. "I'm sorry it had to be someone you knew, Doctor."

Trust seemed to be an issue for Riggins, Xavier thought. "Me too . . . me too. But can I ask your help on another matter? I have to locate the whereabouts of Zangshe's laboratory."

Riggins smiled broadly. "I was expecting that request. I was able to track the IP address of the Zangshe server to a location deep in the Baoding Hebei province. I've accessed one of the Agency's satellites and programmed the coordinates. I can show you where the server's located. The lab can't be far away," Riggins said, as he projected a wide-view image of Zangshe's headquarters on the huge overhead screen.

Xavier studied the image and realized the challenge. *The area is expansive and extremely rugged. Getting close enough to survey it, much less infiltrate the lab, will be difficult,* he thought. "It's entirely possible that the lab may be underground, possibly adjacent to or located in an old mine shaft. Any chance you can identify anything that might give us a clue?"

Riggins keyed in some commands. "How about this," he said, highlighting a small corner near the side of the sprawling facility. "See the connecting link over toward the hillside slope? I'm almost positive that's where the lab is."

Xavier watched the movement of people inside the link. Most were dressed in lab coats. "The details of the satellite images are amazing. That's excellent work, Mr. Riggins. It'll give me a potential starting point in that huge complex."

"There's something else I noticed while snooping around Zangshe's operations. Take a gander at this," the techie said, snapping another set of images onto the screen.

"What am I looking at?" Xavier asked.

"It's Zangshe's shipping port in Tianjin on the East China Sea, from where they ship their uranium ore and refined uranium. Based on the data from the International Registry of Shipping, Zangshe has more than two hundred ships. They also have several dozen supercargo vessels, each capable of transporting upwards of a half-million metric tons of uranium."

"The port must be as large as those in Singapore and Rotterdam."

"It's larger," Riggins said. "In the past ten years, Zangshe has grown its fleet almost three times larger than any other commercial shipping line. The amount of cargo leaving the port everyday is staggering. Nuclear business is booming in China."

"Most of the ships are going to other Chinese ports?" Xavier asked.

"Also to Russia and parts of western Europe," Riggins added. "In that regard, I recently discovered something that seemed strange. Three of Zangshe's cargo vessels headed southeast into the South China Sea and through the Strait of Malacca," he continued, using a pointer to show the positioning of the vessels on the satellite image.

"Is that so unusual? Maybe they have new customers for their uranium."

"Zangshe has never filed for a shipping permit along that route," Riggins replied.

"Where do you think the vessels are headed?"

Riggins drew an imaginary line westward from the Strait of Malacca. "My guess is anywhere in this vicinity," he said, circling an area almost three thousand miles away.

Xavier studied the geography. He looked back at Riggins. "The Arabian Gulf ports? The Bushehr reactor in Iran is the only nuclear reactor in that region, to my knowledge. And they have their own sources for uranium."

"That's precisely what I was thinking. So, I went back and reviewed the sat-images from a week ago when they were still loading the vessels. Tell me what you see," Riggins said.

The magnified images scrolled onto the screen. Dozens of oversized dump trucks were lined up on the docks, waiting to disgorge their loads. Hundreds of workers with hazardous-material-protective clothing were milling about. Large containers were stacked on the vessels' enormous decks. It looked for all practical intent like normal uranium ore loading operations. Then Xavier saw them: the unmistakable markings. The INA had required that all nuclear material be specifically labeled. And there they were in bold symbols. "I'll be damned," Xavier said.

"My sentiments exactly, Doctor. It looks like Zangshe is trying to solve its current crisis with the INA."

Carlyle's instincts about the aggression in the Middle East were right. And it's the Saudis who are about to get royally screwed, Xavier thought, and then said aloud, "And I have a good idea where the vessels are going . . . where the Chinese intend to dump their nuclear waste."

26

THREAT

Beijing, China

"How soon do you anticipate the Zangshe site inspections to begin?" asked the respected Chinese Minister of Technology—Yao Chek.

There was a brief silence on the line before the INA official replied, "We have encountered a delay. It seems that Zangshe's attorneys have filed a counterclaim for cause and are seeking an appeal of the notice to cease mining operations."

Chek felt his face flush. "Surely your organization can expedite the process and commence site inspections," he said.

"In most situations that is not a problem, but Zangshe has very influential sources," the nuclear agency official replied. "They have forced us to convene a hearing on the matter and present evidence of noncompliance."

"Under the present circumstances, the delay is *entirely* unacceptable," Chek exhorted firmly.

The young minister's reputation among his Chinese peers and superiors was one of ruthless efficiency. Raised in an orphanage from the age of ten after the death of his devoted grandmother, Chek was selected to attend Beijing University when he displayed remarkable intellectual prowess. Graduating from university early and applying a relentless determination to succeed, the prodigy quickly rose through the ranks of the government. When the former minister died, it was inevitable that the ambitious Chek would fill the role. He was the logical choice for the position.

"I expected more from your agency," Chek continued, his grave disappointment evident in the tone of his voice. "The conditions I reported are *beyond* deplorable. There are pervasive leakages from improperly stored nuclear waste. The reckless detonations inside the mineshafts in a search for deeper veins of uranium ore have caused the continuous release of the radioactive toxins. The contamination is far more extensive than anything you have investigated to date."

There was a moment of silence before the INA official responded somewhat sternly, "I suggest, sir, that you convince your government to act accordingly and intervene in the interim."

Chek took a calming breath before responding. "I have already explained that the climate in our system is not conducive to an appropriate response at this time. If you are advising me that you are not prepared to act very soon, I *will* pursue other avenues. And if I do that, I hope you are aware that there will be political repercussions associated with your agency's noneffective response."

"I have heard of your reputation for getting things done at any cost," the official replied coldly. "However, your threats will not change the facts. We simply cannot proceed further on your report without a full hearing. The earliest we will be able to convene the parties is after ninety days. . . . And that is barring any further legal action from Zangshe."

"Allow me to be perfectly clear," Chek replied as coldly as the official had, "I am not *threatening* your agency. . . . I will, however, bring the wrath of public scrutiny down on your heads. *That* is a promise. You are as culpable as Zangshe for not acting expeditiously in this matter. You will come to regret what follows." And with that, Yao Chek hung up the phone.

27

LYNCHPIN

Langley, Virginia

With disturbing images of nuclear waste–laden Chinese super-cargo vessels swirling through his mind, Xavier left Riggins's basement command center. He knew that if anyone could follow the unfolding of this intricate plot, it would be the CIA techie. He also knew that the challenge of finding and somehow destroying the nuclear hybrid would be his problem to deal with—albeit, with some anticipated assistance.

As he passed the Marine assistant's desk on his way back to Agent Carlyle's office, the assistant announced that he had a call waiting for him on line two. It was Mac Cowan, Carlyle's PI buddy, the one who had been entrusted with Rachel's safety.

"I promised Harry I'd take care of things for you here and update you periodically," the private investigator told him after a brief introduction. "Glad to report your lady is holding her own. She's still in the coma, but her vitals are stable. And there are no signs of any disturbances around the hospital."

"Thanks, Mac," Xavier replied, although he detected a minor note of forced cheer in Mac's voice. "If anything changes, let me know right away."

"She's in good hands. I will be here until you get back. I owe Carlyle a lot, and this is a small price to pay for all he's done."

Xavier thanked him again, and the call ended. He thought again about the slight hint of insincerity in Mac's voice when he said that Rachel was holding her own. He knew that the longer she remained in a coma, the worse her chances for survival. He felt even more driven now that he felt responsible for allowing the Winston situation to get completely out of his control. Several people had already become victims of his lapse in judgment, including Rachel. *I need to make amends,* he reproached himself. Just then, his PDA vibrated. He read the text message:

HAVE LOCATED OPERATIVE IN CHINA. WILL CONTACT YOU IN
NEXT TWENTY-FOUR HOURS.

He knew that once contact had been made there would be no turning back. It was time to make his plans. He called Riggins.

"Mr. Riggins, I need another favor. Can we discuss it in Agent Carlyle's office?" he asked.

"Be there in a jiff," Riggins replied. "I've finished a projected tracking program on those vessels and have some new sat-images I think you'll find intriguing."

Xavier raised an eyebrow. *If the Chinese had intended to operate under the radar, they surely hadn't accounted for anyone the likes of Riggins,* he chuckled to himself.

Within moments, quicker than it seemed possible for Riggins to travel from the sub-basement level to Carlyle's floor, the techie was setting up his computer tablet on the agent's desk.

"How can I help you, Doctor?" he asked.

"I'm going to need some special equipment," Xavier replied, handing him a handwritten list. "Can you procure it?"

Riggins studied the list and slowly lifted his head. "Procure it . . . *no.* But if you're asking me if I can get access to it, the answer is yes. I'll need a day or so, if that's all right. Normally I could do this much quicker, but some of this stuff you've got here is pretty radical . . . even for the CIA."

Xavier nodded. "A few days will be fine. Thanks."

Riggins folded the paper and put it in his front pocket. He looked thoughtful for a moment and then said, "I can tell that you've done this before. . . ." He nodded to himself in confirmation, then continued, "Yes, you've got that look about you. But, Doctor, you can't be thinking about going it alone."

Xavier appreciated the techie's concern and gave him a warm smile. "That's usually how these operations are done, Mr. Riggins— *alone*."

"Ah. The fewer the players, the less collateral damage," Riggins surmised.

"Exactly," Xavier replied. "Now, what about those images you wanted me to see?"

Riggins turned the computer tablet toward him. "The tracking software narrowed down the possible destinations of the Chinese vessels," he said, overlaying an azimuth line to indicate probable course headings. "Although it's not certain yet, the most likely scenario still puts the three vessels in the Persian Gulf port region in two days' time. They're moving at over twenty knots, even fully loaded."

"That was your earlier assessment, Mr. Riggins. So what's new?"

"Have a look at this," the techie said, enlarging one of the satellite images. The grainy photo on the screen came into focus. It was the deck of one of the vessels.

"What am I looking at, Mr. Riggins?"

"An empty deck with no equipment, vehicles, or personnel in sight. Compare this to the other two vessels," he replied, snapping in two more images side by side.

Sure enough, Xavier thought. The decks of the other two vessels were jam-packed with what looked like excavating equipment and vehicles. "What do you make of that?" he asked.

"I'm not certain," said Riggins, "but the different pattern recognition among the vessels struck me as odd. And then, there's this . . ." He toggled the zoom control on one of the main-deck hatches.

Xavier peered intently at an isolated image of the hatch cover. He was about to give up and ask Riggins what he was supposed to be looking for when he noticed heavily scarred burn marks along the hatch edge. His eye followed them all the way around the entire hatch. The seam between the deck and the cover held the final clue—a small bead of metal. He stood back and said, "This entire hatch cover was welded closed. And I'm guessing every other hatch cover was as well."

Riggins grinned. "And if that's your guess, Doctor, you are absolutely correct!"

"It makes no sense why they would weld shut cargo that needs to be off-loaded. Unless—" Xavier paused.

"They never meant for it to be off-loaded," Riggins finished for him.

The two men continued to examine the images for several minutes. It was evident that the vessel with sealed cargo was somewhat smaller than the other two vessels. Riggins identified its particular classification as an older style cargo ship. Measuring more three hundred meters in length and capable of carrying more than three hundred thousand metric tons of cargo, the vessel was unlike its two nuclear-powered sister ships. Following the energy crisis, Zangshe had converted most its fleet to nuclear power, but this sealed ship was powered by diesel fuel.

"A fully loaded diesel-powered cargo vessel presumably filled with sealed cargo of nuclear-waste material. What are the possibilities?" Xavier wondered aloud.

"I don't like the implications, but I have no working theory for what the Chinese are planning," Riggins replied. "Maybe once we know exactly where it's going, we might have a better idea."

"If the Chinese intend to use the sealed vessel as some sort of nuclear threat, where would it be most effective?"

Riggins frowned. "Other than some defunct oil pipeline depots and abandoned shipping ports, there aren't many valued assets left in the Gulf region anymore. It just doesn't make much sense."

"On the surface, it might sound ludicrous to park a nuclear waste–laden vessel somewhere in the midst of a defunct kingdom, but it's apparently very significant to the Chinese," Xavier replied.

Riggins cocked his head. "Or maybe it's just a bluff. A ship loaded with nuclear waste is not the same as a nuclear device. The Chinese know it would only be a localized threat at worse but nothing worthy of major concern."

"You may know that, Mr. Riggins, but no one else does. Besides, I don't believe for a minute that the Chinese are bluffing. I think Agent Carlyle was right all along. It's all somehow connected to the aggression in Saudi Arabia. And that sealed cargo vessel could be the lynchpin of their entire plan."

"I'm sorry, Doctor, but I really don't see how they can leverage the use of that cargo vessel for any benefit, especially in the Gulf."

Xavier nodded. "Then we're missing something here. Zangshe isn't about to sacrifice one of its cargo vessels, even an older one, unless it's for maximum impact. We need to figure out what they have in mind."

"What do you mean *sacrifice*?" Riggins asked.

Xavier pointed to the image of the smaller cargo vessel's stern. "How much crude oil fuel does the vessel carry?"

Riggins thought for a moment. "The equivalent of maybe twenty thousand barrels, most of which they'll probably use by the time they arrive in the Gulf."

"But there should be enough left for what they need," Xavier said.

"You mean to detonate the vessel," Riggins deduced, "like a dirty bomb."

28

DECEIT

Riyadh, Saudi Arabia

The Sandool headquarters complex was located just outside the city. Situated in an oasis of meticulously manicured landscaping and lagoons, the large complex stood fifty stories above the desert. It had been constructed during the heyday of the Saudi kingdom and remained one of the last vestiges of great affluence and overstatement.

"We have completed our testing on the encapsulated fuel, and I am sending my chief scientist with the samples for your evaluation. I think you will find the results most satisfactory. I look forward to your comments," Princess Almira bin Razul told Andrew Wyncroft, the CEO of AET Corporation.

"I'm anxious to begin the final phase of our process, Your Highness," came his stern reply. "But I'm very disappointed by the delays in your schedule to deliver the samples. A prototype was already installed and is awaiting your fuel samples. Your contract with us was quite specific regarding the project criteria."

"Your tone with me is out of order, Mr. Wyncroft," the princess responded with indignation. "I understand very well the contractual language. There was a serious development with our research partners that was out of our control. Their lab in the States incurred an emergency shutdown accident. The experimental uranium samples were destroyed. Fortunately, we were able to successfully duplicate the formulations here. As I've indicated, I trust you'll find the results in total compliance with the agreed upon criteria."

"I apologize for any offense, Your Highness," the CEO said flatly. "I'll be in touch with you as soon as we've finished our assessment. Your final contract payment will be forthcoming at that time."

Almira paused anxiously. "There is the issue of our ongoing partnership regarding the production of the encapsulated fuel," she said. "I expect we will be discussing the terms of that relationship very soon, as promised."

A few moments of silence followed before Wyncroft said, "I've been advised by our parent company that those negotiations will be handled directly by the offices in China. I no longer have any authority to negotiate the matter with you."

The princess's sharp intake of air was audible across the phone line. "I am very surprised by this," she said, her voice a pitch higher than it had been previously. "I had thought the issue of our partnership in the fuel production was firmly established, predicated on our successful completion of the encapsulation solution. Your comments imply something entirely different."

"I don't know that to be the case, Your Highness," Wyncroft replied noncommittally. "I would expect that your understanding of the situation will be adequately addressed by Zangshe in the very near future."

"We will see about that, Mr. Wyncroft. In the meantime, I will await your comments on the final testing assessment," she said, then abruptly hung up the phone.

It is what I suspected, Princess Almira thought. *The Chinese think they can continue to use us for their purposes. . . . . It seems they still need something from us.* Suddenly, the recent activity occurring in the northern borders of her country now became much more troubling to her.

She called for her assistant. "Get me Hakim," she ordered.

"As you wish, Your Highness," replied the girl. "And if I may—" She waited for the princess's nod of approval before continuing, "Hakim indicated that there is a gentleman who is most insistent on seeing you. He said that you would know him."

"His name?" the princess asked impatiently.

"Agent Harry Carlyle of the CIA. He asked Hakim to tell you that he has some information that might be of significant interest to you."

29

FILE

Langley, Virginia

If there was any chance of getting inside the lab facilities at Zangshe, Xavier would need precise intel. Even then, he might be too late to stop the hybrid-replication process. His last contact with his old network had been almost twenty-four hours ago. As he considered the situation, he heard his PDA vibrate on Carlyle's desk.

The text message read:

> HAVE INTEL REQUESTED. MEET IN BEIJING TOMORROW.
> CONTACT AT NEWSSTAND KIOSK IMMEDIATELY INSIDE
> MAIN ENTRANCE OF AIRPORT AT 1400 HRS GMT.

There were no terms mentioned. *Unusual,* he thought, especially for independent operatives.

Aware that he was still a target of opportunity, Xavier had to be cautious about making his travel arrangements. Without direct access to network resources, he had limited ability to create a covert persona. But he did have another resource very close at hand. He dialed the extension to the CIA's answer to Star Wars.

"Mr. Riggins, hopefully you were able to *acquire* the implements I'd requested," Xavier said.

"You're leaving soon, I gather?" the wunderkind replied.

"Beijing tomorrow, and I'll need your assistance with a passport and other ID."

"No prob, Doctor. I guessed as much and already have something prepared for you. In fact, just in case, I've included a second set of credentials should you need them for any reason."

Xavier was becoming very fond of this guy. He wasn't certain whether Riggins reveled in the controversy that swirled around him or was simply mired in it. Riggins's history at the CIA had started under a cloud. Quite possibly, he had decided that he wouldn't be able to get out from underneath it. Or maybe his particular problems with Carlyle were related to authority figures—something that Xavier could understand from his own childhood and difficulty with his father. Even after he'd left home, Xavier struggled to reconcile his father's relentless discipline and abrasive behavior toward him. Whether it was because of Xavier's independent nature or his inquisitive tendencies, it seemed to bring out his father's forceful insistence to do things his way. Thus, Xavier's disdain for authority figures was indelibly imprinted on his mind when he'd decided to join the most covert of all CIA ops.

"Thanks, Mr. Riggins. With airport security being what it is these days, I'll need to be extra cautious."

"You won't need to worry about that either. I can arrange a direct flight for you from Andrews AFB. With the special gear you're carrying, it might be advisable for you to go in private."

"Even better," Xavier said. "It beats trying to smuggle that stuff through security. I'll need to leave at zero-four-thirty tomorrow."

"I'll commandeer you a flight. It'll be a real hoot utilizing Special Agent Carlyle's juice with the Coast Guard for use of one of their new jets," Riggins laughed.

"How will he feel about that?"

"Need you ask, Doctor? But by the time he gets the interagency charges for the flight, either the crisis will have been averted or all hell will have broken loose. In any instance, it won't be the most important thing on his mind."

Xavier found it admirable that despite the tensions, Riggins had maintained a good sense of humor—albeit often at Carlyle's expense.

"Speaking of important things, any updates on the location of the three Chinese cargo vessels?" he asked.

"They're already in the Persian Gulf. It appears their course puts them headed directly for the port city of Ad Damman in Saudi Arabia."

"What's there, Mr. Riggins?"

"The port itself contains extensive dock facilities and multiple large warehouses. Besides that, it's essentially abandoned."

"That's probably where the Chinese intend to stage they're off-loading operations for the nuclear waste. Are they all headed there?" Xavier asked.

"Even the vessel with the welded deck hatches appears to be following the same course," Riggins replied. "So far, it defies logic, but I'll keep looking for anything that might confirm your suspicions."

"If anyone can find it, it's you. Do you have any contacts in Saudi Arabia?"

"That's Agent Carlyle's territory. Having spent almost five years there on a special assignment setting up security for the royal family, he knows every source of credible information."

"Heard anything from him?"

"Nothing," Riggins replied. "But as you know, Doctor, he's not very communicative with me. You might check with his assistant. She's his first point of contact. In the meantime, I've got your requested equipment ready to go and will call back when I've confirmed your flight out of Andrews."

"Thanks, Mr. Riggins. Talk soon."

On his way out, Xavier stopped at the Marine assistant's desk. "I'll be traveling for a few days," he told her, knowing he didn't need to tell her more than that. "Have you had any news from Agent Carlyle?" he asked.

She looked up at him. "Oh, you're leaving?" She reached down into her bottom drawer as she spoke, " I don't expect to hear from Agent Carlyle unless there's a problem. Even then, it's not likely he'd call me. He's a loner." She resurfaced, holding something in her hand.

"I can relate to that, Lieutenant. . . . Did he indicate when he might be back?" he asked.

"Again, Doctor, it's not something he felt the necessity to tell me," she replied.

Xavier nodded and turned to leave.

"But wait."

He turned back.

The assistant handed him a large sealed file. "Agent Carlyle left this for you. He said I should give it to you when you completed your business here."

30

PROTOTYPE

Andrews Air Force Base, Maryland

It was five o'clock in the morning when Xavier reached the flight line at Andrews Air Force Base. The newest addition to the fleet was a gleaming Falcon 4000 XR jet, proudly displaying the markings of the U.S. Coast Guard. Xavier handed his gear bag containing the special equipment Riggins had acquired for him to a member of the flight crew.

"Welcome aboard, Doctor. This is our first official international flight, and we're pleased to have you aboard as our first passenger," the silver-haired Coast Guard pilot said. "Our flight time to Beijing is approximately five and half hours."

Xavier did a quick calculation. "That's more than Mach two!" he said.

The Coast Guard pilot smiled. "And that's against a strong headwind. This baby'll top out close to Mach three. It was built on a similar airframe as the old British Concorde but with a highly advanced propulsion system. It has some other unique capabilities for our mission profile, which was the reason we selected Dassault to build several of them for us."

"Dassault is a French company, isn't it?"

"That's correct, Doctor."

"Sounds like you know this aircraft very well," Xavier said.

"I should. I've recently returned from the Dassault flight test center in France where we completed an extensive evaluation of the aircraft. I actually participated in the first test flight. It wasn't until recently that the French were somehow able to leapfrog ahead of their competition with what they call a revolutionary nuclear-conversion energy system that gives the aircraft unlimited range and improved power performance. This is prototype number one. The Coast Guard has agreed to flight test the aircraft under actual conditions in exchange for buying the first fifty of them at substantial discounts."

Nuclear-conversion energy system. The phrase stuck in Xavier's head. "Are you familiar with the fuel-sourcing technology for the aircraft, Captain?"

The Coast Guard pilot frowned. "Not specifically. The French regard that as proprietary. But we were advised that one of their subcontractors was responsible for all maintenance on the fuel-source element."

"Would you happen to know the name of the subcontractor?" Xavier asked.

"You seem very interested in that aspect of the aircraft."

"Well, actually it's somewhat in my field of expertise."

"Propulsion technology?" the pilot asked.

"No . . . nuclear research," Xavier replied. "And I'm quite curious what methodology the French used to develop their revolutionary power system."

"Interesting," the pilot said, as he pulled out a large black briefcase with the graphic of a Falcon jet emblazoned on it. He rummaged through several manuals and found what he needed. "The name of the propulsion and fuel-source element subcontractor is a company called Alternative Energy Technology Corporation. It states here that they're located in Detroit, Michigan."

"*Hmm,*" Xavier murmured, "never heard of them. It's good to know that they're an American-based company. I appreciate the information."

"You're welcome. And glad to have you aboard. Buckle up and get ready for an exciting flight to China," the pilot said as he headed toward the cockpit.

Strapping himself into one of the jet's oversized jump seats, Xavier wondered if Zangshe was somehow connected to the French jet propulsion technology. If so, the encapsulated-fuel solution might become an alternative. It was another potential indication of why the Chinese were aggressively pursuing their nuclear plans. He would ask Riggins to investigate both Dassault and its Detroit-based subcontractor.

As the pilot slowly ramped up the power settings, Xavier could hear the roar of the massive turbine engines being fed superheated air from the plenum and nuclear core. With the brakes fully depressed, the big aircraft strained at the bit. When the sound level reached a high-pitched whine, he felt a jolting lurch forward as the jet blasted down the runway. The former test pilot rotated its nose straight up, obviously determined to challenge the aircraft under all conditions. Xavier's harness pulled tautly against his chest. A series of hydraulic sounds followed as the automatic-flap settings streamlined the aircraft for maximum climb speed. Within seconds after takeoff, Xavier could feel the G-forces bearing down on his body. *What a rush it would be to fly this thing,* he thought.

"Doctor, I trust everything is okay back there," the pilot said over the intercom. "We'll be leveling off in a few minutes. You'll be interested to know that our flight level puts us just inside the earth's atmosphere, almost twenty miles up. This is one of the first commercial-type jets to have that capability. It should be smooth sailing from that point on."

The future of commercial aviation is here, Xavier speculated. *With the new engine technology, it'll make every conventional aircraft outdated. But that's just the tip of the economic iceberg. Everything requiring power solutions would be on the table. Someone's about to make a ton of money.*

As he thought about the implications of a new energy solution, he couldn't help but consider again Zangshe's role from behind the scenes. If an encapsulated nuclear fuel was going into mass production, he would bet that the Chinese mega-corporation was also somehow involved in the new engine designs. It was the beginning of a new era of industrialization and possibly monopolies . . . or in Zangshe's case, maybe some new form of oligarchy. *Is that what Zangshe has in mind, to take absolute control of the marketplace for all aspects of nuclear energy?* he wondered. And with that thought, a shudder ran through his body.

Ten minutes after takeoff, the aircraft had reached its cruising altitude of nearly one hundred thousand feet. Essentially, it was flying on the fringes of outer space. Xavier noticed the absence of turbulence and found the smoothness of the flight restful. He relished the silence. He stretched out his legs and started to doze when he remembered the sealed file from Carlyle. Reaching inside his gear bag, he removed the file. He opened it, and began to read.

The file contained a confidential FBI report regarding the interrogation of the train assailant who had attacked him and Rachel. The agents in Black Hills had conducted a thorough investigation of the whereabouts of the contract gang killers and their exploits over the past few years. In an attempt to uncover the sources of their contracts, they had extracted and documented numerous occasions and dates that detailed the nature of the killers' targets. It was interesting reading, but Xavier had reviewed many of these types of files in the past. He wondered now why Carlyle had found it important for him to see this one.

Almost ready to doze off a bit in the quietness of the near-space ride, he turned to the next to last page of the report. His eyes scanned the words when suddenly he stopped. His heart skipped a beat and his body temperature rose uncomfortably. "It can't be true," he murmured aloud. "It just can't be."

STAGING

Xiong Xian, China

The acrid air from the continuous uranium ore–mining operations hung like a black cloud over Zangshe's headquarters. On a day with no breeze, plumes of ore dust hovered, trapped against the surrounding volcanic hillsides. Inside the vast complex, an intricate air-filtration system kept the noxious fumes out. Only the mine laborers were subjected to the onslaught of the life-sucking particles of uranium dust that coated everything and eventually became embedded in their lungs.

There were 24/7 work shifts until further notice: this order came down from Chairman Khan's office. Every one of Zangshe's multiple operations—including mining, refining, waste management, logistics, and shipping as well as research—were all in nonstop work mode. It was the first time in its history that the massive uranium-producing empire was loading its supercargo vessels from every one of its docks in the Port of Tianjin.

"Yaku, we must continue to accelerate the extraction process," Khan said with urgency. "Our attorneys have indicated that the appeal they filed will be reviewed in approximately ninety days. Once the inspections of our sites commence, we will be at the mercy of the INA and under the international microscope. I cannot afford for that to happen at this juncture."

Yakubla nodded. "We are currently extracting nearly one hundred thousand metric tons of waste material each day, Great One. At that rate, we will only have removed but a portion of the vast amounts stored in the old mines." He shifted his weight from one leg to the other, uncharacteristically revealing his discomfort over the situation, before returning to a balanced stance.

Khan noticed his comrade's brief show of concern. "We will need more time, Yaku," he said, tugging at his braid. "It would appear that we may have to implement our alternative strategy sooner than planned. Make your arrangements to meet the cargo vessels in Ad Damman."

"They should arrive late tomorrow," Yakubla said. "All has been readied to off-load the equipment and the material. The construction of the fuel-processing facilities will begin within the week."

Khan nodded his understanding. "I have recently received word from the CEO of AET that the initial prototype testing has gone very well," he said. "I expect mass production of all energy-system components to begin within three months."

"It shall be done, Great One. And now that the gulf ports are fully secured, I must attend to the issue of the mercenaries. They grow restless with little to do. Their usefulness to us is finished. I already began replacing security at the permanent compounds with our own personnel."

"I am confident you will see to an appropriate severance of that relationship, Yaku," Khan said with a smirk. "I do not want to have any further exposure for their actions."

The big Mongolian warrior smiled widely. "I have looked forward to this moment since I first dealt with them, Great One. You can be most assured that there will be no trace left of the mercenary involvement with us. Like a snake, when its head is cut off, the body slithers away and dies."

CONTACT

Beijing, China

Approximately five hours after leaving Andrews, the prototype Falcon jet made a steep descent into Beijing International Airport. As a government aircraft, the pilot had received clearance to a taxiway leading to a small cargo hangar and dispatching facility. Xavier watched carefully as two Chinese officials boarded the aircraft. The pilot met them at the top of the airstairs and after a few exchanges with the officials, the pilot walked back toward Xavier.

"I've cleared your documents with the Chinese officials, Dr. Christianson," the pilot said, handing over the credentials with the new identity Riggins had prepared for him. "Everything appears in order. Your entrance visa gives you forty-eight hours to conclude your business. I've orders to wait for you until then. Please be advised that wheels up after zero-nine-hundred GMT on Thursday involves a whole lot of additional red tape."

Xavier unbuckled himself from the jump seat and stood up. "Thanks. Hopefully, it's all the time I'll need. *If not, the ride back's the least of my worries*, he thought.

"There's a small jitney waiting to take you to the main terminal building, Doctor. See you back here soon," the pilot said, as he handed Xavier his gear bag.

Xavier walked down the airstairs and boarded the jitney parked just underneath the swept wing of the Falcon. He had to clear his mind for the task ahead. The information in Carlyle's file left him in emotional overload. Processing it would have to wait.

The short jitney operator greeted him with a scowl as a cold wind bit into his face. The open jitney was designed as a cargo hauler and afforded no protection from the elements. Xavier threw his gear bag on and jumped aboard. The jitney quickly jerked away, heading around the cargo hangar and onto a loop road toward the main airport terminal. Within five minutes he could see the sprawling terminal complex directly in front of him.

The driver stopped a short distance from the long line of vehicles that had formed near the main entrance. He motioned brusquely for Xavier to get off and pointed toward the entrance. The flurry of human traffic trying to squeeze through the terminal doors was something to behold. He reminded himself that this was China after all, still the most populous country in the world.

Xavier pulled a dark hooded sweatshirt from his gear bag and put it on. Bending over slightly in an attempt to conceal his height, he joined the melee at the main entrance. Once herded into the immense airport terminal building, he gradually pushed his way clear and quickly identified the location of the kiosk. Approaching cautiously, he glanced at the large overhead clock: he had fifteen minutes to spare. Arriving early worked to his disadvantage. He didn't want to appear eager or obvious by his lingering presence. He decided to circle around the back of the kiosk while keeping a watchful eye on the flow of humanity. Within a few minutes, he noticed something—something his past experience had imbedded in his sixth sense. It was no more than a slight movement of the head that caught his attention. A slightly built person wearing a ball cap had edged carefully toward the kiosk and made an almost unperceivable yet distinctive nodding gesture. His contact had arrived.

Xavier eased over toward the kiosk stand.

"Hao jiu bu jian," his contact said in a soft whisper.

His Mandarin was a bit rusty, but he immediately recognized the voice. *I can't believe it,* Xavier thought. "Is it really you?" he asked, stunned. "I'd heard you'd been killed in Palestine."

"It was part of my deep cover to infiltrate the Hamas. I'd honestly believed someone would've eventually told you," Elena Dupre said, moving her well-toned and curvaceous body closer to him.

Elena was an independent operative who had learned her craft from her double-agent father. Xavier had worked with her on several missions. They'd had a relationship before he'd met his wife, but it ended abruptly when Elena had accepted the high-risk assignment in Palestine. It became apparent to him now that his grief over her reported death was part of the ruse she had used to assume a new identity. "I was very upset," was all he could manage to say at the moment.

"It would've never worked out, X. You and I had little in common. And I couldn't bring myself to say it was over. I'm sorry you got hurt."

There was an uncomfortable pause between them. Thoughts of Rachel came flooding into his brain.

"It's over, Elena," he said, after a few moments. "We've got other more important business between us. What can you tell me about getting into Zangshe?"

She didn't look directly at him. "The security is beyond anything I've encountered in a corporate environment, or anywhere else for that matter. The place is a virtual vault. Even the extensive mining operations venues are carefully monitored with the latest video and biometrics technology. Getting into the main facility and the research laboratory are nearly impossible."

"I didn't come all this way to confirm how difficult it would be to gain access. I'd already suspected as much," he responded, with a little more agitation than he had intended.

"I said, *nearly impossible,* not entirely so," she replied softly with a slight French accent. "The main facility has all the biometrics you'd suspect plus full-body scanning and tracking mechanisms."

"What sort of tracking mechanisms?"

"It's a very sophisticated GPS system embedded into all employee ID badges."

"And the research lab?" he asked.

"The research lab is connected to the main facility via a walkway, which is additionally protected by laser biometrics. All movements to, from, and within the lab complex are tracked continuously and recorded."

"Hmm . . . so you have a plan to break into this citadel, Elena?"

A brief smile emerged on her face. "Not break into, X, but walk directly through the front doors."

33

MOTIVES

There was a sudden commotion outside the airport's terminal building. A minor fender bender between two taxis waiting at the main entrance had resulted in a skirmish that was quickly escalating into something more serious. Security personnel from everywhere descended onto the scene. Xavier was surprised by the number of uniforms.

Elena motioned for him to follow her. "We need to leave. My Fiat is parked on the lower level," she said, as the pair moved casually toward the elevator bank. "Ever since the last failed hijacking incident, security here has increased tenfold."

"I didn't hear anything about it," Xavier replied with a query to his tone.

"You wouldn't have. A typical Chinese blackout. Two weeks ago, a group of dissident students tried to take over a fully loaded aircraft. They might have succeeded had it not been for a mechanical failure that delayed the plane's departure. Since the attempt, the government has been cracking down on all vehicular and pedestrian traffic into and out of the airport."

Xavier's brow furrowed. "Then why did you select this as a meeting place?"

The elevator doors opened and the pair stepped in unaccompanied, as Elena explained, "For all the reasons you're familiar with: milling crowds, plenty of foreigners, and the usual assortment of distracting incidents."

"But what about the increased security?" he asked, as the doors closed.

"It would normally be a concern. But I don't have to worry about security," she replied, looking away.

"Your cover here's that good?" Xavier asked suspiciously.

"I'm almost invisible, X."

Xavier reached for her slender but muscular arm and pulled her toward him. "What are you talking about, Elena?"

Elena looked up at him with dark, almond-shaped eyes—a genetic gift from her Chinese mother. Her father had been a French double agent. "I work for them . . . for the Chinese government," she said, slowly placing a delicate hand on his chest.

Xavier was too surprised to react to her forward touch. "What's going on, Elena?" he asked, all of his senses going into high alert.

The elevator doors opened to the parking level, and Elena walked out before him.

"Let's get in the car, X. I'll tell you everything once we're on the road," she said. "I'm over there." She pointed to her black Fiat, which was parked in a reserved spot.

Elena weaved the car through the parking garage to the exit gate where a parking attendant and a security guard waited. She lowered her window and showed her credentials. The guard leaned in, gave Xavier a long, piercing look, and took her credentials. Within moments, he returned the credentials, smiled at the couple, and hastily directed the attendant to raise the gate arm.

As the Fiat cleared the garage and entered the bustling side street,

Xavier turned to her. "That was easy. Almost too easy. *What* do you do, Elena?" he demanded.

"It's not *what* I do that matters, X. It's who I work for. Several years ago, the Agency wanted to find a way inside the Chinese nuclear program. I was a logical choice. Fluent in Mandarin and familiar with the culture, I was able to move quickly through the bureaucracy," she explained, deftly swerving in and out of the endless maze of traffic.

"And that gives you the access you seem to have?" he asked.

"My current position affords me some flexibility," she responded.

"Enough flexibility to get us access into Zangshe?" he asked dubiously.

She glanced over at him. "Have you ever known me to exaggerate, X?"

He didn't respond. *She is full of surprises,* he thought. "We have to move fast, Elena. What I'm looking for has the capacity to unleash chaos and destruction in ways we've never experienced."

"Then we have much to talk about," she replied as the Fiat came to an abrupt stop in front of a nondescript apartment building. "Let's go inside."

Xavier followed her up the long stairway to a small alcove, noticing how well her curvaceous body filled out her clothing. Old feelings of desire came flooding back. As hard as he tried, he couldn't get the images of Elena's supple and eager body the last time they'd made love out of his mind. *This is not the time or place. The last thing I need now is a distraction.* He could smell her sweet aroma as he stood close to her while she looked for her keys.

"I just moved here recently," she said. "The previous tenant was obsessed with security. The locks are state of the art. I'd thought of replacing them, but it would require replacing the entire doorframe."

"I hope you have the only set of keys," he said once she'd found them. He helped her push the heavy reinforced door open.

"It keeps me in shape," she replied with a slight smile.

They entered the loft. "Besides, the tenant died suddenly. I'm fairly certain that no one has another key."

It occurred to him that her explanation seemed a little odd. But he decided not to press the issue. He suspected that Elena must have facilitated the previous tenant's demise . . . nothing dissuaded her when she wanted something.

The apartment, which had an unobstructed view of the crowded city, was spacious by Chinese standards. If there were any question that Elena was being truthful about living there, it was immediately quelled when Xavier looked around. Touches of her were everywhere—from the plum blossoms in the porcelain vase to the ornate oriental tapestries covering the walls. Her appreciation for texture and movement imbued the space. Even the parts of the walls that were not covered by tapestries revealed artful plasterwork in pastel swirls.

Soft and alluring, Elena exuded sensuality from every pore of her taut body. But underneath that veil, Xavier knew she was cunning and ruthless to the core . . . a veritable femme fatale. That, he had learned the hard way. During their last mission together, she had manipulated him and left his cover exposed to take on a lucrative high-profile assignment. He barely managed to escape the clutches of the Hamas. Not to mention she turned his insides into mush. Elena was the perfect Black Ops operative. He knew that working with her again would be complicated . . . and risky.

"I need to shower, X," she said, removing her outer garments where they stood. "There's coffee or something stronger in the kitchen. Help yourself." Making her way toward the bathroom, she removed her top, revealing her smooth bare back; he knew that she knew he was watching intently.

His mind was a flurry of emotions. He had long since reconciled his life without her—or so he thought. Unexpectedly, focusing on the mission at hand had become complicated. *There's too much at stake. I can't get tangled up in her web,* he reminded himself harshly, as she disappeared into the bathroom.

The vibration of his PDA interrupted his thoughts. He was glad for it. It was a text message from Riggins:

THE CHINESE CARGO VESSELS ARE AT DOCK. TWO OF THE LARGER ONES ARE AT THE PORT OF AD DAMMAN. THE THIRD VESSEL IS DOCKED AT THE PORT OF JEBEL ALI IN THE U.A.E. STILL TRYING TO ASSESS THE SITUATION.

Xavier suspected that the Chinese plan was quickly moving into place. How far along it was and whether or not it could be stopped was very uncertain. But he realized that Elena might be part of the solution. He had to immediately put his past with her to rest if there was any chance of preventing the hybrid from being replicated. He would do whatever it took to make certain that the mission was successful—whatever it took.

The door to the bathroom was ajar. He heard the shower running and could see the steam filling the small room. He rifled through his bag before moving quickly to the bathroom. Once inside, he whipped the curtain aside. Elena turned toward him, an expectant smile on her face. She licked her lips.

Xavier drank in the sight of her amber body glistening in the cascading water in the dim overhead light. He held back a smile as she raised her hands to her full breasts. Her brown nipples hardened under her own nimble caresses, as she stared into Xavier's eyes. His gaze dropped from her breasts to her perfectly sculpted abdomen. Noticing this, Elena slowly glided one hand down her body to reach between her glistening thighs. Slightly widening the stance of her long muscular legs, she let out a deep sigh.

"You've always enjoyed watching me, X. Watch me now. It gives me so much pleasure," she purred, manipulating her slender fingers to gently open the soft folds of her triangle. Her eyes lowered, and she began pleasing herself.

Xavier reached down near the buckle of his belt and stepped closer to the shower. His hand moved up to the tip of her rock-hard left nipple. She let out a deep, throaty moan. Her head back and her eyes closed, she began undulating, nearing climax. He waited for the critical moment.

The pressure of Xavier's cold, silenced Glock pistol against her bare chest startled her. Her eyes flew open and her spasmodic moans became gasps as she tried to regain control of her trembling body.

Xavier smiled. "Now that I have your attention, Elena, tell me what I need to know—now."

34

AGREEMENTS

Riyadh, Saudi Arabia

Carlyle woke up in his hotel room to a series of telephone rings. He looked at his watch. It was 4:00 AM.

"Agent Carlyle, Her Royal Highness Princess Almira bin Razul requests your presence at her office in two hours. Can you confirm your attendance?" a curt voice asked.

"I'll be there," Carlyle answered, shaking the sleep from his head.

"I trust a man with your experience can find his way to the Sandool office complex," the caller said, then hung up without waiting for a response.

Carlyle just looked at the phone askance.

The city was quiet in the early hours of the morning. Carlyle parked in the rear of the complex. He had been there numerous times in the past when he was involved with security for King Abdul bin Razul, the princess's father. Walking across the tiled parking area, he recalled the location of the access control station. Looking up, he saw the video monitor tracking his movement, as expected. He stopped at the entrance. "Harry Carlyle to see Princess Almira," he announced into the intercom.

"Proceed to the first elevator bank and enter the open one," the security attendant instructed as the door buzzed open.

Carlyle hurried toward the elevators through the long, vacant hallway. The lower floors of the complex had been designed to withstand an explosion. They could be safely isolated and locked down in the event of any unwarranted intrusion. Carlyle had recommended this feature during the early phases of construction. There were no manned guard stations at this level in case poisonous gas needed to be emitted through the lower air vents. The building was virtually terrorist-proof.

He walked into the open elevator. It was automatically programmed to stop at the fiftieth floor. When he stepped off the elevator, he felt like he had gone back in time. His assignment almost two decades earlier had lasted five years. During that time, he had befriended most of the royal family. His recollection of the princess was that of a little girl sitting at her father's knee. Today, he was certain, that image would change.

Carlyle was quickly ushered into an adjoining conference room next to the princess's office.

"Her Royal Highness will join you shortly. May I offer you a beverage?" the young assistant asked.

"Black coffee would be fine," he replied, looking out over the vast desert landscape from atop Sandool's headquarters.

Within minutes, a refined and beautifully coiffed woman walked swiftly into the room wearing a perfectly tailored black silk suit and immediately sat down at the head of the glass conference table. "My father had always spoken well of you, Agent Carlyle. Unfortunately, I was far too young to recall having made your acquaintance, so you must forgive my directness. What is it you wish to tell me that is worth my time?" she asked stiffly.

The princess motioned for Carlyle to take a seat; a moment of silence past as he did so. Then he responded, "You are indeed your father's daughter, Your Highness. You don't mince words. I won't either. We have intelligence that indicates the Chinese are most likely behind the aggression in your port cities."

There was a slight hesitation in her response. "It is something I had already suspected, Agent. I have my chief of security trying to confirm the reports. The Chinese are not good at honoring their agreements."

"That would be for production of the encapsulated fuel, Your Highness?"

He could tell by her reaction that she was surprised.

"Your information comes from what source, Agent Carlyle?"

Interesting response, he thought. "With all due respect, Your Highness, we are the CIA. We're very familiar with your new technology and your intent to partner with the Chinese. And we also know about your contract with QPR. One of their lead scientists was consulting with us on this matter. In fact, we've recently learned about a nuclear discovery that most likely has been passed along to the Chinese by one of QPR's scientists. It could have significant implications for you and everyone else."

The princess jotted down a quick note and then looked straight at Carlyle. "Your Agency obviously does not communicate internally. Were you not advised about the nature of our arrangement?"

"With the Chinese?"

"No, Agent, with your country."

It was Carlyle's turn to be surprised. "You have an agreement with my government?"

"I am sorry, Agent Carlyle. In deference to your past relationship with my father, I will not insist that you speak with my security personnel. But I will request that you leave immediately and return to your country. Your involvement in this situation may pose grave danger for you. I would advise against any further actions on your part."

"Your concerns for my safety are appreciated, Your Highness, but I came here looking for some answers."

"And I had thought you had come here to tell me something of significance," the princess retorted.

He had but one card left to play if he was going to get her to tell him what he wanted to know. "There's something else, Your Highness, which may have serious consequences for your country and may explain your own doubts about the Chinese intentions."

"I can see, Agent, that you are not easily put off. If I understand your proposition, you will tell me this piece of information in exchange for some answers."

"It's what your father called, 'trading on intellectual currency.'"

She looked away for a moment and then looked back at him. "Tell me what you have to say and I will determine its value to me."

Carlyle smiled. "Fair enough, Your Highness. We have recently confirmed that the Chinese intend to use the land near several of your major port cities to dump their nuclear waste."

The impact of his comments had an immediate reaction. Almira's eyes widened. "You must be mistaken, Agent. Even the Chinese would not be so brazen."

"I have the proof here, Your Highness," he said, holding a file of the satellite images Riggins had downloaded.

Almira took the file, opened it, and spread the images on her desk. After a few minutes, she raised her head. "Who else in your agency knows of this?"

"At this point, only the one who had downloaded the images for me, Your Highness."

"That is good news," she said, gathering up the images and quickly putting them back into the file. "Ask me your questions, Agent Carlyle."

He was somewhat confused by her comments and reactions. "What is the nature of your agreement with my country, Your Highness?"

She looked at him with the eyes of someone far more experienced and concerned than a young woman of twenty-eight. "I can tell that you will not accept anything but the truth and will not stop until you have found it. But I must warn you once again, your efforts in that regard may put you at considerable risk."

"You've made me quite aware of that, Your Highness," he replied. "I might as well know why."

Almira looked away. "The toll that the energy crisis has taken around the world, as well in your own country, is no secret. Because of the disastrous long-term consequences of the Deepwater Horizon rig oil spill in the Gulf of Mexico and its ecological backlash, almost all offshore drilling was eventually abandoned. As a consequence, the ensuing restrictions in such environments exacerbated the rapid depletion of our own oil reserves and those worldwide. My father predicted this eventuality. It is why he insisted that the OPEC nations contribute expertise and investments to promote offshore explorations and drilling around the world. Most people were not aware of this; instead they looked upon his efforts as entirely self-serving."

"I was aware of your father's efforts in that regard. We'd spoken about it several times. He was always mindful of your own diminishing resource but also of the rapid escalation in carbon-based fuel consumption, particularly from China."

"It was foremost on his mind," the princess replied. "In part, it was the reason why both he and my brother refused to deal with the Chinese. They believed the Chinese to be duplicitous in their efforts to work toward mutual solutions for new sources of energy. But since that time, things have become even more desperate for my country. I concluded that the only solution for our own survival would be to work with the Chinese."

"As I'm guessing was the decision made by my country as well," Carlyle said.

"Yes," she replied haltingly, "and it was one of your senior officials who had helped to broker the entire deal with the Chinese . . . much of which I was not made privy to."

"Tell me what you do know, Your Highness," he persisted.

Almira folded her hands in front of her. "There are some in your government who do not want the details of the agreement with the Chinese fully disclosed. And the warnings I have given you are based upon the strict nature of the confidentiality imposed by the agreements."

Carlyle stared at Almira. "With all due respect, Your Highness, so far you have told me nothing. All I've heard are your warnings and advice regarding confidentiality. I'm anxious to learn specifics, something that will help me to understand why my country would choose not to defend its troops when they are in harm's way."

Almira stood up from behind her desk and moved closer to him. She was tall like her father, with fine features and coal-black eyes. "My father said that you were a most insistent person. He was right," she replied, lowering her voice. "As part of the arrangement, we had to agree to several conditions that may at some point have an impact on your national security."

Carlyle began to have a very uneasy feeling. "I had my suspicions, Your Highness, when friends of mine were recently attacked near your northern borders with no response from my country in their defense."

"Yes, I was made aware of the incident, Agent. And you are correct. As part of our arrangement with the Chinese, we had agreed not to foster any further U.S. assistance within this region. We are working with your State Department to remove your few remaining military encampments."

Carlyle frowned. "While it incenses me to see our troops unprotected, I don't think random attacks on our security outposts would constitute a threat to our national security."

"There is one final condition of the agreement, Agent Carlyle. I am almost reluctant to tell you. However, given your willingness to share your recent intelligence, I feel somewhat obligated."

"My curiosity quotient's already exceeded, Your Highness."

The princess hesitated briefly before continuing. "The Chinese requested from us all of your most strategic domestic locations."

Carlyle was stunned. "But your country would not have had access to that information, Your Highness."

"It is why I made a personal appeal to a high-ranking official in your government. And why I no longer consider myself a friend of your country."

"Because we most certainly had to refuse your request?"

Almira turned her head away again. "No, Agent Carlyle, because I was successful in convincing him to comply with the request."

35

PLANS

Beijing, China

Xavier reached into the shower and turned off the water. He had already gotten as wet as he intended to get. Then, he pressed Elena against the back of the shower wall, the gun still against her bare chest. She glared at him like a caged tiger.

"You find it necessary to treat me this way, X?" she spat out, still a bit breathless.

"I'm in no mood to deal with your games, Elena. There's little time left for me to get into that lab. And frankly, I don't trust you," he told her.

"If you expect me to cooperate, you'll have to be more accommodating," she replied. "I'm not expecting financial compensation for this assignment. I'm helping you because I owe you for what happened last time. I simply wanted us to be on friendly terms."

"I'm not interested in your friendship . . . only your help. Tell me how and when we're getting into Zangshe's lab," he demanded.

With her back against the shower wall, her naked body still glistening and trembling slightly from her orgasmic interlude, she responded, "I work for the minister of technology. He's one of the most powerful of all the senior officials in the government and possibly the only one who is not on Zangshe's payroll."

"And that means what?"

She glared at him. "He is most interested in doing what needs to be done to insure compliance with Chinese laws."

"Zangshe has broken laws?"

"Almost every one associated with the safe disposal of nuclear waste."

"How does that help me get into the lab, Elena?"

"Recently, the INA issued a notice to cease mining operations pending further site inspections. Although Zangshe filed an appeal that delayed the inspections for ninety days, my ministry's office has the prerogative to conduct its own investigation. The minister has decided to proceed with such an investigation and has assigned me the responsibility of initiating the process with Zangshe."

"I gather your minister is unafraid of reprisals from his superiors."

Elena shivered slightly. She was getting cold. "Please hand me my robe, X. I know you enjoy seeing me like this, but I'd appreciate being able to get dressed."

He looked over at the plush white robe hanging on a hook within arm's reach. He grabbed it with his free hand and made as if to give it to her, but then held it away. "Answer my questions first, Elena."

She rolled her eyes, and said with exasperation. "Yes, the minister is unafraid and eager to pursue action against Zangshe. He has very strong personal motivations in that regard."

"What motivations?"

Elena bit her lip in an attempt to control her rising temper. "His entire family and most of his village died horrible deaths from radiation poisoning caused by Zangshe's operations."

Finally, Xavier lowered the Glock and handed the robe to her. She grabbed it and pushed his hand away when he tried to help her out of the shower.

"You are much more truthful and informative with your clothes off," he said with a slight smirk, before growing very serious. "But I warn you, Elena, if *anything* goes wrong, I will give you up the same way you tried to do to me."

"I know you'll never understand what I did and why," Elena said, putting on the robe. "And I know you were hurt. I am truly sorry. But back then, in the emotional place I was in, it could have ended much worse." She wrapped her hair in a towel, and the pair left the small bathroom. "Let's try to work together with some trust this time."

Xavier mused over how she always seemed to know the right thing to say and wondered about her level of sincerity. "It couldn't have ended much worse for me," he reminded her. "But in the interest of what's at stake here, I'll have to trust you. How do we begin?"

"I have a plan in mind," Elena replied. "It involves a bit of misdirection. Something, I'm sure you'll agree, I'm very good at. I've already contacted Zangshe and informed them that in preparation for the INA inspections, the minister wants to have his representative meet with their senior executives for a preliminary briefing. They have yet to respond. But we anticipated that and gave them twenty-four hours to comply."

"After which?" he asked.

"The minister will facilitate the meeting by force if necessary."

"He can do that?"

"X, this is China. Any senior government official has the authority to act in the best interest of the Republic. And Minister Chek doesn't need any convincing. He immediately accepted my suggestion and is prepared to escort me into Zangshe's headquarters whenever I'm ready."

"How do you plan to get me into the lab?" he asked, noting to himself that she'd been busy on his behalf.

Elena smiled. Her robe slipped off her shoulder as she mixed herself a drink at the long kitchen bar: vodka with just a splash of tomato juice for color. "You're going as my technical assistant. I've requested that full access be granted to all operational areas including the research lab. While I'm busy with Zangshe's senior management, you'll have an unfettered opportunity to investigate anything in there. What exactly are you looking for, X?"

"It's a superparticle that was accidentally discovered in my laboratory back in the States. Unfortunately, one of my colleagues—who had apparently been working undercover—transmitted the data to Zangshe."

"So you feel responsible?"

Xavier nodded. "I never saw it coming. I'd worked with him for over ten years, and I thought we were friends."

"You are an easy mark, X, when it comes to trust. That's the double-edged sword in the Black Ops business. . . ." With those words, Xavier shifted uncomfortably, and Elena refocused the subject on the experiment. "So, what does this thing do, this thing you're looking for?"

"It's a nuclear hybrid molecule . . . most likely very aggressive and very unpredictable. It could potentially be the most powerful substance yet discovered."

Elena paused for a moment, then said, "*If* you can locate it, how do you intend to contain it?"

"If it's already been replicated, we will be in *very* deep trouble. Assuming that's not the case, I just need to locate where the data resides and run an extraction program. It's the only way to prevent any further threats."

"That won't be easy. The lab is enormous, with over five hundred scientists. Is there any way to narrow down who might be working on that formula?" she asked.

"I have an IP address. But it likely has already been uploaded to the main server."

Elena pulled out her computer tablet and opened a file. A detailed diagrammatic floor plan was quickly displayed. "This is a layout of the lab. The main server complex is located here, in the south side of the facility," she said, pointing to a large raised floor area. "The control room is directly in the center of the space surrounded by soundproof-glass enclosures. I'm guessing you know your way around computer systems."

"You've surveilled the area?" Xavier asked, surprised.

She smiled. "Not personally. But the minister has his own spies, someone inside whose family was from his devastated village. He can be helpful once you're in the lab. How much time do you think you'll need?"

"It won't take long, maybe twenty minutes. Once I get into their system, I'll run the extraction program. But there's a chance the program might trigger some alarms."

"So we won't have twenty minutes. I'd prefer that we don't set off alarms while we're there. Zangshe will not be in a friendly mood, and they have their own hard-core security. I'm hoping to avoid any direct confrontation. The minister is extremely methodical. And he would definitely frown on an overt incident that might impede his ongoing investigation. Is there any other way of doing this?"

"There is, but it's not as clean or effective. . . . But it may buy us time to get in and out without incident."

"Collateral damage?" she asked.

"Limited and mostly property damage . . . if it happens at night," he replied.

"Good, let's plan on that course. Accidents happen all the time in laboratories as you know, X," she said. "I'll make the arrangements to leave for Zangshe first thing in the morning." She handed him a glass of wine. "In the meantime, we have a few hours to catch up on our lives."

36

TREACHERY

Port Ad Damman, Saudi Arabia

The two Chinese supercargo vessels were off-loaded at the huge docks of Port Ad Damman, and more would soon follow. What had once been the third-largest city in Saudi Arabia and a thriving port community of nearly one million inhabitants had become an impoverished desert slum following the demise of the oil-refining industry. It would now serve as Zangshe's uranium-repackaging hub.

Yakubla's midday meeting on the outskirts of Ad Damman City was punctuated by the constant roar of heavy equipment. Truckloads of containers carrying nearly one million metric tons of nuclear-waste material were transported to several holding areas awaiting final disposition. Massive earth-moving and excavation equipment had already completed forming the multitude of storage areas deeply gouged out from the Arabian Desert. In the midst of what appeared to be hundreds of enormous gravesites, welded alloy-shielded partitions were arranged in uniformed stacks ready to be installed. Several dozen large concrete trucks were being filled with specially formulated high-density and quick-drying material for pouring foundation slabs and weight-bearing footing columns.

CS

"When do you expect to complete the fuel production facility?" Yakubla demanded of his senior construction manager.

The small but powerfully built man bowed. "Taiji, we will have the foundation poured and the tilt-up partitions in place within a week. The entire structure will be closed within a month and ready for the installation of the preassembled laboratory modules. If I may be so bold, I would say that you should expect to begin preliminary work inside the laboratory well within the schedule."

Yakubla nodded his approval. "Chairman Khan will reward you well."

The manager stiffened at the chairman's name. It was almost imperceptible, but Yakubla had noticed. "And the waste-storage areas?" he asked.

The construction manager unrolled a large construction plan detailing the exact location and dimension of each of the nuclear-waste storage locations. "You can see by this drawing, Taiji, that every location has a designated completion date dependent on its proximity to the production facility. The storage sites nearest the facility will be finished in the same timeframe as the new transfer systems to insure the most efficient handling and reuse of the uranium waste materials. The sites farthest removed from the facility will be completed as quickly as needed to accommodate the cargo from the incoming ships. When completely finished, the entire site will cover ten square kilometers with an initial capacity to retain almost twenty million metric tons of spent uranium, almost double the existing storage capacity of the Xiong Xian mines."

Yakubla looked out over the expanse of desert and the array of equipment moving in every direction. "Very well, keep me informed of your progress," he said, as his satellite phone began to buzz. The construction manager returned to his tasks, and Yakubla answered the call.

"You will be pleased to know that all is well here in Jebel Ali, Taiji," the mujahedin commander said on the line.

"What is the status of the cargo vessel?" Yakubla asked.

"The big ship is securely docked in place next to the facility. I have left several of my men on board the ship to make certain that everything remains calm. The captain informed me that there are adequate provisions to last approximately six months, if necessary," the commander replied.

"Your work there is finished. Make plans to return to Ad Damman immediately. I have another task for you."

"May I inquire as to the nature of this task, Taiji?"

"It is a matter of utmost urgency and requires your special skills."

"Then surely it warrants additional consideration from you," the commander replied.

Yakubla gripped the satellite phone tighter. "We shall discuss the arrangements when you have arrived."

"No, Taiji. It is time for us discuss our immediate future together. We have done what you have requested. Your plans for this region are apparently far reaching and extend much beyond our original agreement."

"You speak as if we have not had this discussion in the past," Yakubla said, irritated.

"Things change, Taiji. There is soon to be another regime in Iran. An associate of mine intends to be the new ruling ayatollah. His people have requested that I return to assist in this movement."

"So you are telling me that you must leave to help your friend."

"You are also my friend, Taiji. I would not abandon you without proper cause."

"And what would compel you to continue to honor your agreement with me?"

The mujahedin commander paused. "I can see that once you have completed your installation in Ad Damman, there will be little need for our services."

"Then you must naively believe that our activity here will continue to go unnoticed," Yakubla replied.

"Your initiative is already well established. There is no one who will care enough to threaten you, Taiji. And I can see that you have many powerful relationships."

"If that is so, then why is it that I require your assistance?" Yakubla asked.

"There still is apparently some particular task you wish for me to accomplish. I know your kind, Taiji. You will utilize whatever resources you can to achieve your goals. If this is likely to be our last business, I must insist on one final condition."

"What is it that you have in mind?"

"Prior to any further decisions, we would need to have access to your most recent nuclear technology."

"I know of no such technology," Yakubla replied.

"Do not toy with me, Taiji. We are not unaware of your agreement with the current ruling powers in Iran for the promise of the new technology in return for our assistance. You cannot manipulate us as you please," the savvy commander replied.

It was Yakubla who paused. "You are very enterprising, and I may have underestimated you. Your request is most unexpected. I will take it under consideration and give you my answer soon," the Mongolian replied, his mind already working quickly.

"I understand, Taiji. In the meantime, I will remain in Jebel Ali. If you should decide for any reason not to grant my request, your ship will remain here under my control."

Yakubla heard the satellite phone go dead. As the Mongolian looked out over the panorama of activity across the desert horizon, a scowl fixed itself across his hardened face.

37

EMOTIONS

Beijing, China

"You're not built for this business, X," Elena said. "You're much too fair, too reasonable, and you have too much conscience. This is why I couldn't stay with you. I would have kept on hurting you." She took a sip of her drink.

Elena had changed into a silk pajama set and now sat at the opposite end of the couch from Xavier, looking quite alluring. Even though he didn't trust her fully and probably never would, he was glad to have this time with her to catch up on all that had transpired since their last encounter. He thought about what she had just said and knew that she was right. He was too discerning for this lifestyle. He'd left the agency shortly after being led to believe that she had died. Not because of her, per se, but because of what she had just said. He didn't have effective transference. He wasn't able to switch his emotions on and off like other operatives . . . like her.

"I'd thought that moving into civilian life was the right thing to do," he replied. "For a while, it worked very well. I had a great career that sated my competitive drive and intellectual pursuits. And when I married Samantha and we had Megan, my entire focus changed. My priorities reordered themselves."

Elena leaned over to the coffee table and poured more red wine into Xavier's empty glass. She looked into her own empty glass and reached for the bottle of vodka.

"I need more fortification than wine can provide tonight," she said, pouring a healthy portion of the clear liquid into her glass. "I was very sorry to hear about their death, X . . . So sorry. It must be hard to live with such a terrible loss."

He looked at her with surprise. "You knew?"

She nodded. "An auto accident, wasn't it?"

Once in the Agency, never completely out—especially Black Ops operatives, he thought to himself. Clearly, everything there was to know about him and his life was available in his file. "That's what I'd thought until a few hours ago."

Elena's eyes grew wide. "What do you mean, 'until a few hours ago'?"

Xavier got up from the couch and walked over to the window. He looked out at the panorama of the bustling city's flickering night lights. "It was no accident. They were killed . . . assassinated because of me."

"What are you talking about, X? Since when does a research scientist get mixed up in assassination plots?" she asked.

"When someone wants you out of the way. In this case, my old colleague," he replied.

"That makes no sense. Don't corporations have a more civilized process for dealing with that sort of thing?" she asked. "There is a variety of ways for them to force people out the door . . . they don't usually resort to murder."

Xavier nodded in agreement, then said, "But when you're part of one of the world's foremost research facilities, there's a lot at risk and often, very strange occurrences can take place."

"Murder, assassinations . . . I'll say. But how did you wife and child get involved in this mess?"

He stared at her for a few moments. "It was a screw-up . . . from the other end. I'd taken my wife's car to drop it off for repairs. She needed mine to take our daughter to dance practice. The brake lines had been cut. When she came down the ridge road in the Black Hills, she couldn't slow down. The car went through the guardrail and . . ." He stopped short and looked away. "By the time they'd reached the wreckage, there wasn't much to identify. They were able to lift a VIN number from part of the dash and apparently enough of a brake line to know what'd happened."

"How did you finally learn about this?"

"As I left to come here, I was given a file from a friend in the Agency," he replied. "It identified the killers as being part of a Cambodian gang contracted by the Chinese. Apparently, they had paid the local cops off and the information about the brake lines never ended up in the original accident report. It wasn't until a week ago that the CIA in South Dakota uncovered the missing information after interrogating a contract killer who recently came after me and some of my associates."

"What happened to your family is tragic, X. And I guess it doesn't surprise me that the Chinese are involved. Based on my experiences in the ministry, they'll do anything to advance their nuclear technology."

"And I'm intent on making certain they don't use the hybrid," he said.

"You certainly have more reasons now to want to stop them— maybe try to get even. You know that could be dangerous."

Xavier looked over at her. "There's no way I could ever get even. But you're right. I do want someone to pay for what they did to my family. If that means more collateral damage, then so be it."

Elena moved closer to him. "Listen, X, I'm behind you on this mission. And now I better understand your sense of urgency. But if we're going to be successful, you need to keep your anger under control. As I said before, the job requires you to focus on results, not emotions," she said, as she reached up to stroke her long fingers through his hair.

He turned toward her. He could feel the heat from her body as she pressed into him. She reached her mouth close to his lips. He cradled her face in his hands and . . . gently pushed it slightly away.

"You're still upset with me?" she said.

"Not anymore, Elena," he said gently. "But there's someone else in my life now."

At that moment, thoughts of Rachel flooded his consciousness. He couldn't help but hope with all his heart that Rachel *would* still be in his life after all this was over.

Elena lowered her eyes and smiled. "Too much conscience. You have way too much conscience, X." And she walked away.

CHALLENGE

Khan was livid. He had just received word from his government liaison that the Ministry of Technology would be conducting an impromptu investigation at the facility.

"I had instructed you to ignore the ministry's request for access," Khan bellowed at the liaison officer.

"I have done as you had requested, Great One," the officer replied. "But Minister Chek is not one to be ignored. He is sending a contingent today."

"Our attorneys filed an appeal to the INA notice. We were given a ninety-day stay pending review of specific charges," Khan blustered.

"The minister intends to conduct his own investigation," the liaison officer told him. "We were advised to expect a preliminary team to arrive tomorrow to outline the requirements of the process."

Khan exploded off his chair. "The requirements! Who does this minister think he is? Does he not realize that his superiors are in my debt?"

"I have heard that Minister Chek is regarded by most within the government as fearless and brilliant. He has no respect for bureaucratic power. Furthermore, he enjoys the favor of the premier, who views Chek almost as his protégé," the liaison officer explained.

"I intend to speak with the premier directly on this matter," Khan said. "I will remind him of our previous understandings."

"In the meantime, Great One, should I prepare for the arrival of the minister's contingent in the morning?"

Khan hesitated, then replied, "Do what is required. Until I have the opportunity to determine this minister's motivations and quell the investigation, I do not want to cause any more attention than is necessary on the matter. Besides, there is enough for them to see on the first visit to allay concerns about our process. If they request a tour of the operations, make certain they are directed *only* to the designated areas that have already been evacuated."

"It shall be done, Great One. Also, they have requested access to the research laboratory on today's visit."

Khan hesitated. "Most curious. There is nothing of relevance regarding waste management in that facility. Make certain they are *not* granted access to that area."

The liaison officer swallowed hard. "I will advise them accordingly, Great One."

39

EXPOSURE

Xiong Xian, China

Elena arranged for a contingent of the ministry's security to accompany them to Zangshe's headquarters, which was a two-hour drive south from Beijing. She had advised Zangshe's government-liaison officer to expect them at 9:00 AM. If the reaction from the officer was any indication of events to follow, the visit would not be well received.

"I'm not certain what to anticipate, X," she said, as they approached the entrance to the massive mining empire. "Zangshe's contact was most uncooperative and threatened legal reprisals against the ministry for the unauthorized investigation. I know that the chairman of Zangshe carries a lot of sway inside the government structure. However, they have little choice but to accede to our demands for access to their facility."

"And if they don't?" Xavier asked.

"Then we'll move to plan B."

"Which is?"

Elena pointed toward the trunk of their vehicle. "I don't plan to go back empty-handed. I've brought some convincing arguments," she said with a smile.

Xavier was well aware of Elena's appetite for violence. When required, she never shied away from a fight. "I thought you wanted to keep this first visit very low-key," he said.

"I did. But I realized how important this is to you . . . to the world, if what you say is true . . . and if it means that I might blow my cover, then let's have some fun. Hopefully, we won't need to go that route."

Looking out across the adjacent landscape as they approached Zangshe's main entrance, Xavier was surprised by the lack of any visible signs of extensive mining equipment. The immensity of Zangshe's enterprise was evident from Riggins's sat-images. But, for as far as he could see against the backdrop of the Taihang Mountain range, there was little indication of any activity, much less the presence of a world-class mining operation.

"Why am I not seeing any evidence of Zangshe's mining activities?" he asked. "I'd thought there'd be large conveying systems as well as excavation equipment."

"Zangshe is a not an open-pit mining operation, X," Elena replied. "An unusually rich vein of high-grade uranium ore was discovered in the Taihang Mountains almost twenty years ago. It is so extraordinary that some estimates have it exceeding Australia's remaining supply. But unlike mining companies in Australia, Zangshe is exclusively involved in underground mining operations. Although generally considered more expensive than open-pit mining, the Chinese have apparently developed an efficient way to excavate the ore from deep within the mines using innovative blasting and extraction techniques. That's why you're not seeing the obvious signs of a large-scale mining operation."

"Leave it to the Chinese to find a way to revitalize an industrialized business," he said.

"But not without devastating repercussions. Deep-mining operations are plagued by groundwater buildup. To keep the water out of the mines, huge pumps are constantly working to extract the contaminated, radioactive groundwater."

"And dumping it into the surrounding aquifers, which pollutes the water supply," he added.

"Zangshe has been doing that for many years with impunity. It is why Minister Chek is so determined to bring them to an accounting for their actions," Elena said.

The small convoy of ministry vehicles soon arrived at Zangshe's main gate. Several armed Zangshe security personnel appeared in front of the heavy steel access gate. One of the guards instructed the driver to stop and lower the window.

"I have orders from the offices of the Ministry of Technology to pass through the gate," Elena said, handing the guard their papers.

The security guard leaned into the window and looked them over carefully. "I'll be right back," he replied with an accent Xavier didn't recognize. The guard walked away and toward a small hut-like station.

"It's Khalkha . . . a Mongolian dialect. Zangshe's security personnel are all Mongolians," Elena whispered in response to the puzzled look on Xavier's face.

"All Mongolians?" Xavier said.

"Zangshe's chairman comes from a storied Mongolian ancestry and trusts no one else. But the mine workers are all Chinese. Their life expectancy is only about forty years because of the mine conditions."

"Interesting," he said, "a subjugated subgroup within a subjugated culture."

"You have no idea, X, how bad living conditions are in general for most of the Chinese. Minister Chek has been working very hard to change all that, but it's an uphill battle. The government here is interested in only one thing—world domination, not individual empowerment."

"You sound surprisingly empathetic, Elena. Your Minister Chek has influenced you."

"He's very impressive, X. And it has worked well for me to become part of Chek's movement. But there are many threatening forces at work inside the structure that are attempting to bring him down. His future is tenuous.

"Speaking of which," he said, "here comes the guard."

Elena watched carefully as the Mongolian guard approached the vehicle. She slowly slipped her hand inside her purse. The guard had motioned for the vehicle to move forward as the heavy gate swung back. As soon as their vehicle was inside, the gate closed immediately, blocking out the other two ministry vehicles. Xavier and Elena glanced at each other. They both knew what the guard had done.

"Clever," she said, "access granted but not for everyone."

"You didn't think this would be a cakewalk, did you?"

"Actually, I'm surprised we're in so quickly," she said. "I'd fully anticipated more of a challenge, especially to your papers. The guard looked you over closely. You don't exactly fit the mold here, X."

Sure enough, as soon as Elena had finished, the guard instructed Xavier to step out of the vehicle. Leaving his small gear bag on the floor of the car, Xavier stepped out and stood directly in front of the guard. The Mongolian was large but not quite as tall as Xavier. The men stared at each other for several moments, and finally the guard directed Xavier to move toward the security hut.

Once inside the hut, the guard pushed him into a chair. Xavier recognized the small biometric scanning device on the table beside him. Grabbing Xavier's index finger, the guard firmly placed it over the reader.

Meanwhile, Elena waited anxiously outside in the vehicle. She knew that Zangshe was very thorough and would uncover any inconsistencies in the ministry's authorizations. She had taken precautions and had provided Xavier with another covert identity. Still, the passing minutes seemed interminable and her concerns mounted. Finally, the door to the small hut opened, and Xavier was escorted back to the vehicle and climbed in. The guard instructed the vehicle driver to follow him.

Xavier leaned over to Elena. "The cover ID checked out for the time being. But they're suspicious and will keep digging."

"Then let's hope we're done before they figure out who you are," she said with some relief.

They followed close behind the Zangshe security vehicle as it wound its way toward the heart of the massive uranium-ore empire. The expansive, flat, open landscape with partially overgrown fields evidenced the once agrarian nature of this region. Prior to the discovery of the uranium-ore vein, most of the area in the Baoding Hebei province had been actively cultivated farmland. Now laid barren by the grossly tainted aquifers, the vacant land stretched westward toward the base of the Taihang Mountains and Zangshe's massive headquarters complex.

The Zangshe security vehicle made an abrupt left turn. The road began to slope gradually downward as a wall of stacked, massive stone blocks began to appear on both sides. Within five minutes, they were completely entombed in a large, dark tunnel; the security vehicle quickly circled behind them, blocking their exit.

Xavier could barely make out the two figures approaching their vehicle from a doorway in the tunnel wall. He glanced quickly over at Elena. "I don't like the looks of this," he said, as one of the figures moved into the headlights and aimed an automatic weapon at the vehicle.

The security guard motioned for them to get out.

"We've got a situation, Elena. And it doesn't appear to be a welcoming party."

Elena already had the backseat compartment open and reached through to the trunk. "Grab this, X," she ordered, handing him a heavy case. "I assume you still know how to use one of these," she grinned. "It's an RPG. If they find what's back here, we'll be shot where we stand. Looks like it's plan B after all."

Xavier and Elena slowly exited the rear door on the side farthest from the security vehicle. The glare of the headlights in the near-pitch darkness was blinding, and the guards had yet to detect their movement. Elena was first to go. She slinked like a cat under both cars and came up alongside the driver's door of the security vehicle; the window was open. She placed the barrel of her silenced weapon against the back of the big Mongolian guard's head and pulled the trigger. The muffled pop of the shot was barely heard as the guard's head exploded forward and then recoiled backward against the headrest.

The other guards had moved quickly to surround the ministry

vehicle. Xavier spied one of them moving behind the car with a flashlight. He signaled to Elena to move around to the front of their vehicle. He slung the RPG over his shoulder and waited for the guard to round the rear of the vehicle. In a quick lunging move, Xavier caught the guard with a short chop to the front of his neck. The guard went down quickly in a heap, grasping at this throat. At the same time, Elena had sighted the final guard, who stood in the headlights, and dropped him with another muffled round.

They looked around. No one else was there. "What's the plan now, Elena?"

She ran back to the car. "I have the diagrams of Zangshe's facility with me," she said, pulling out a large printout of the floor plan. "Here's where we are." She pointed to a spot on the site plan. "It's a blast tunnel probably used to test explosive charges."

"How much time do you figure we have before all hell breaks loose?" he asked, grabbing his gear bag.

"About twenty minutes, X. Just enough time for you to do your thing inside the lab."

"That was when I was already inside," he replied.

"No problem," Elena said. "There's a ventilation shaft running all the way back under the main facility. It's at the end of this tunnel . . . maybe a quarter of a mile or so."

"There must be a faster way to get there. Let's see what's behind that door on the side of the tunnel," he said as he walked over and pulled opened the reinforced blast door. An electric golf cart was parked inside.

"Get in, Elena. We need to find that terminal room quickly."

Xavier was fairly certain that if the guards didn't report in soon, more would be dispatched to check on the status of the visitors. He knew they could probably reach the terminal room . . . but getting out would be almost impossible without some help.

"Elena, anyway to notify your inside contact? We could use some sort of distraction."

Elena picked up on his logic. She tried her cell phone. No luck. "I've got to find an open area to get a signal. Stop here, X," she said as they neared a vent door in the passageway.

As she left the golf cart, he grabbed her hand. "Be careful, Elena."

She smiled at him. "Do what you came here to do, X. Don't worry. I'll be fine. Meet you back here," she said.

He watched as she opened the vent door and hopped onto a metal ladder that led up. It occurred to him that he might never see her again, but he didn't have time to dwell on the implications. He needed to find the terminal room. The tiny headlights of the golf cart barely showed the way as he felt the close walls of the claustrophobic passageway whiz by. Looking ahead, he faintly saw what looked to be a dead end. He slowed the cart as he got close: it was a solid concrete wall.

Elena had said that the ventilation shaft ran all the way under the facility. *There must be an access door somewhere,* he thought. He pulled a flashlight out of his gear bag. Shining it about, he saw that the passageway turned to the right and widened enough to turn the cart around. A small door was located at the rear of the turnaround area.

He grabbed his bag and headed toward the door. Once through the door, he saw another passageway. This one, however, was less than a few feet in width, but it was lighted. He estimated that it continued for at least several hundred yards. With the RPG slung over one shoulder and gear bag over the other, he jogged quickly to the end.

Reaching a junction point, he took out the floor plans and located the direction of the main facility's lab. The overhead maze of plumbing lines and heavy conduits were helpful in guiding him along. When his footing became slippery from groundwater seepage, he realized that he was very near the base of the mountain and the main facility.

The passageway soon split off again. He stopped. Looking up, he recognized large filtered traps commonly associated with laboratory usage. He knew he was close. But finding the exact spot would take more time, and time was quickly running out.

40

TRESPASSERS

Xiong Xian, China

"Where are the minister's representatives?" Zangshe's liaison officer demanded of the head of security.

"My guards suspected an irregularity in one of the party's credentials. We are running a deeper security check," the liaison spat out, clearly agitated by the non-Mongolian officer's harsh tone. "In the meantime, we have moved their vehicle into the blast tunnel to inspect for any unusual items."

"You have the minister's representatives inside the tunnel now?" the officer asked incredulously. "Did you not clearly understand my instructions to you? They were to be escorted immediately to the visiting area for a meeting with me."

"I have my duties to perform. And the security of this facility is my responsibility. As soon as their credentials are verified, I personally assure their expeditious passage to you."

The liaison officer slammed the phone down. His job of attempting to maintain some semblance of a harmonious working relationship with the government structure was difficult enough. If Minister Chek filed a formal complaint with Chairman Khan over the treatment of his representatives, the liaison officer's future was in serious jeopardy.

❧

Xavier had identified the laboratory wing. He was now carefully searching for the raised floor area, specifically looking for the location of the main servers. The extensive power-grid feeds supplying both regular and backup support for the computer systems was an easy trail to follow. Once he identified where the feeds turned upward into the space, he knew he had located his target.

He had hoped for a surgical approach to this mission. It would have been more conclusive to have confirmed the precise location where the replication data resided and the progress to date of the replication process. Since that opportunity has been preempted, he would have to use the broadest sword required to insure the destruction of the hybrid's formulation and any replicated samples.

Referencing Elena's floor plans again, he marked out the approximate dimensions of the entire raised floor area. Reaching inside his gear bag, he removed a dozen foot-long packages wrapped in a hard waxy, protective coating. Beneath the coating was a high-density and extremely powerful explosive. Called EG-1, it had been developed for use in blasting extremely dense and reinforced structures—such as the one he was about to use it on.

Although more powerful and infinitely more effective than its older cousin C-4, EG-1 was also much more sensitive, particularly to heat and moisture. Hence, safe handling of it necessitated awareness of the integrity of its waxy coating as well as its short shelf life.

It took only a few minutes for Xavier to affix the charges and timers to strategic locations under the raised floor space. And then he squeezed a black mastic-like material from a tube and applied it to the bundled network of conduits. Once the mastic made contact with air, it began its work melting through the heavily insulated cables and would eventually find the bare wires. Developed as an interruptive molecular compound, the mastic was designed to change the polarity of electrical connections, including computer circuitry. In effect, it mimicked the workings of a massive computer virus, creating chaos in the software for all connected operating systems.

Xavier estimated that it would take approximately two hours for the mastic compound to fully infect the Zangshe network. He checked his watch. It was almost 10:00 AM. By noon, the entire facility would be aware of the insidious crisis that had befallen them.

Fearing rather catastrophic consequences to innocent scientists in the laboratory, but unaware of the current twenty-four hour Zangshe work schedule, Xavier had set the explosive timing devices for 11:00 PM. *A safe margin,* he thought, *to insure minimum casualties.*

He closed his gear bag and was about to head back toward the passageway when he heard it: the sound of an alarm—a ringing sound, like a fire alarm. It must have been Elena's contact creating a diversion. He didn't stop to speculate further. Instead, he ran as fast as he could down the narrow corridor toward the blast tunnel access door. It had been over thirty minutes since he had left Elena at the vent door. *Surely she's had enough time to make it safely back to the car,* he thought.

Reaching the access door, he pushed it open and jumped into the golf cart. Racing full speed through the passageway, the cart banged against the sidewalls of the darkened alley. He almost didn't see the end of the passageway, stopping inches before the heavy stone block of the blast tunnel. He pushed the reinforced door wide open, hoping to see Elena waiting for him. But all he saw was the driver leaning against the hood of the car looking about anxiously.

"Where's Ms. Dupre?" Xavier asked, exercising his Mandarin.

The driver raised his arms with palms extended upward and shook his head.

"Shit," he said. "See anyone else?"

The driver pointed to the front of the tunnel. "One vehicle stopped. A guard got out but quickly got back in and sped off toward the main gate."

"They've got to know something's wrong. Where the hell's Elena?"

No sooner were the words out of his mouth than his PDA vibrated. He moved closer to the tunnel's opening to get a better signal. It was a text message from Elena:

DON'T WAIT FOR ME. SAFE, BUT CAN'T MAKE IT BACK TO TUNNEL. NOTIFIED ESCORT VEHICLES TO TAKE CONTROL OF MAIN GATE. WISH YOU LUCK. E.

That's probably why the guard took off so quickly toward the main entrance, he thought. "Let's go," he told the driver, barely managing to push down his concern for Elena.

"And Ms. Dupre?" the driver inquired.

Xavier looked down for a moment, then back at the driver and replied in his most convincing tone, "She said not to wait for her. But that she's safe."

For now, he added to himself.

41

ESCAPE

Xiong Xian, China

Xavier sat next to the driver with the RPG resting on the side-view mirror. As they approached the main entrance, he peered through his binoculars to see the Zangshe security vehicle on fire and the heavy access gate destroyed. One of the ministry escort cars was also ablaze. He instructed the driver to pull up within two hundred yards of the entrance. The second escort vehicle had moved around behind the guard hut, and the two remaining ministry employees had jumped out into a nearby ditch. Xavier immediately saw why. The last of the Zangshe guards had his RPG leveled at the second escort vehicle.

"Back up and turn to the right," Xavier instructed the driver while he loaded the RPG. He watched through the sight as the guard leaned against the hut to get a better aim at the escort vehicle. But the guard hadn't yet seen anyone behind him. As Xavier squeezed the trigger, the guard turned slowly around, just in time to watch in horror as the RPG projectile slammed into the small hut.

"Move," Xavier shouted, realizing that they needed to quickly put some distance between them and any retaliatory action from Zangshe.

The driver accelerated through the blown-away entrance gate. He stopped briefly, waiting for the remaining two ministry employees to jump into their car. Within seconds, they were speeding away from Zangshe's headquarters and back toward Beijing. Xavier's eyes darted from the road to the sky and back again as they sped along; he watched for the retaliation, which he was certain would come, from a chase vehicle or chopper.

Xavier called Elena's cell several times but received no answer. He glanced at his watch. There were four hours left before his clearance would expire: enough time to get to the airport and out of the country. He realized that there was nothing he could do to help Elena. She would be on her own. Not necessarily a strange place for her. And being a relatively high-ranking employee within the ministry, he knew she would somehow try to leverage that for her safe release. *Hopefully, before this evening,* he thought.

With less than an hour from Beijing, it appeared that no retaliation from Zangshe would occur. Maybe it was because the main-gate guards had been taken by surprise or more than likely, because of the disruption caused by the virus, that nothing had followed.

After some convincing, the ministry driver agreed to take Xavier directly to the one of Beijing airport's auxiliary hangars where the Coast Guard jet was waiting. As he boarded the aircraft, Xavier knew there would be a full inquiry by the minister's staff. The driver and his associates were on their own to explain the implausible happenings. And without Elena, Xavier realized that their story would seem suspect. But he had no choice. He was thinking of Elena. To stay meant further complications, especially for her—*if* she had survived.

"Wheels up in ten minutes, Doctor. Anything I can get you?" the pilot asked.

Xavier forced a smile. "An uneventful ride home."

42

VIRUS

Xiong Xian, China

"It would seem that your visitors had other intentions when they came here," Zangshe's top security chief informed the liaison officer over the phone. "I have just learned that there was an attempt to breach our security. In the process, several of my guards were killed. Explain yourself."

The liaison officer was stunned. "I can assure you," he stammered, "the ministry's request for access was quite specific and very much in order."

"For your sake, I hope you can convince Chairman Khan of that. I am about to meet with him to advise him of the situation."

"Where are they . . . the ministry's representatives?" the liaison officer asked.

"That is not your concern at this juncture. This is now a matter of the utmost urgency."

The liaison officer heard the line go dead. Before he had a chance to contemplate his fate, he received an indication on his computer warning of imminent disc failure. Within moments, the entire office staff was clamoring over the loss of data.

Khan listened to the security officer's report. "And you have not apprehended them yet?" he asked with mock wonderment.

"Not yet, Great One. It appears that two vehicles may have escaped from the main entrance. The guards destroyed one of them outside the gate."

"So you are not certain what actually transpired?" Khan asked, more calmly than was normal.

The head of security cleared his throat nervously. "We were rechecking their credentials. Until we can retrace their movements, it is difficult to say if anything happened at all."

"Something happened!" Khan thundered, erupting from his chair, startling the officer. "You have allowed someone to take advantage of your men and quite possible this facility! You will be held personally accountable for this breach."

The security officer felt mortal fear rising from the pit of his stomach. "There is something else, Great One," he said hesitantly. "Although it is most likely unrelated, a fire alarm went off near the laboratory. After careful checking, it appears to have been a false alarm."

"There are no coincidences," Khan said, settling back in his chair. "Do you have the identifications of everyone who entered through the main gate?"

"Yes, Great One. The first person was a senior aide to the minister. Her name is Elena Dupre. The second was her technical assistant. His credentials required more careful review. He was not Chinese."

"Then we must assume that the alarm was somehow connected to the intrusion today. Find out what transpired immediately," Khan demanded. "If you fail me further—" His threat was cut short as a critical-warning notice popped open on his computer screen.

After a moment, he gravely looked up from his monitor and gazed intently at his head of security. "We are about to lose our entire operating system. Make certain that all exits are blocked off and that all personnel stay in place."

The black mastic–induced virus spread rapidly though the main server terminal to all linked devices. Simultaneously, electrical power from the grid network shut down, and backup power failed to activate. Zangshe's headquarters went completely dark and silent. In fewer than two hours, the virus had completed its work. Without power of any sort in the main building, Khan established a temporary office in a testing facility adjacent to one of the working mines.

"You will find out what has happened to our main facility immediately," an enraged Khan bellowed to the head of technology.

"Yes, Great One. Until we can reestablish power, I have no way of determining what has happened. It may take us a while to identify the source of the problem. I will need to find a way to bypass the automatic switching and start the auxiliary generators to begin running diagnostic software. Until then, I am most sorry to say that there is nothing that can be done to restore our operating systems and—"

Khan clenched his fist and interrupted his underling. "I do not want your excuses. I expect an assessment of damages soon," he shouted.

"I will do my best, Great One."

Below the laboratory wing and directly beneath the massive raised floor area, something unexpected began to transpire. Within three hours of the power outage, moisture from the rising humidity levels in the raised floor space and from the groundwater in the basement had formed on Xavier's carefully positioned charges. The waxy protective coatings around the dozen or so charges had softened. As the waxy substance liquefied, portions of the explosive were exposed, and the effects of the moisture on the surface of the unprotected charges nullified most of the timing devices. Randomly, a series of intense explosions occurred. Continuing over several hours, the raised floor space was intermittently rocked by the blasts.

After several hours of calm, rescue workers from the mines were dispatched to the laboratory space. As they attempted to enter the obliterated area, they were surprised to find that most of the raised floor space had disintegrated. There was little trace left of anyone or anything.

Making certain that the environment was safe, and well after the explosions had stopped, the Mongolian head of Zangshe's security finally joined the rescue workers to assess the damage. Shaking his head as he surveyed the devastation, he reached down to pick up an untouched hard drive when the final explosive charges detonated at precisely 11:00 PM.

In the ensuing confusion, Elena had tried to mingle with the crowd of Zangshe employees who gathered outside in the great courtyard. But very soon afterward, all of the employees were directed to return to their offices. Her chance of remaining undetected and escaping was dwindling. Her cell phone appeared to have just enough battery power remaining for one more call. She punched in the number.

"I do not know what went wrong, Minister. Our papers were very much in order. The Zangshe security personnel became belligerent and refused us access. I fully expect to be restrained from leaving or from making any further contact," Elena said.

"We will see about that, Ms. Dupre," Minister Chek replied. "I will look into the matter personally."

43

ENEMIES

Langley, Virginia

The Coast Guard Falcon jet aircraft made a picture-perfect landing at Andrews Air Force Base. Xavier slept restlessly most of the way. Thoughts of Elena's welfare and his concern over Rachel's condition took turns nagging at him. Although his mission had been successful, he hardly felt vindicated. He would not allow himself a chance to relax until he knew for certain that Rachel was on the road to recovery, and as for Elena, well, he knew she'd get herself out of whatever jam she was in, assuming she was still alive to do so.

Once back in his rental car and on his way to CIA headquarters, he called Riggins.

"Doctor, it's good to hear your voice. I can tell from your tone that things must have gone well," Riggins said.

"As well as could be expected," Xavier replied. "I think that at the very least, we've contained the development of the hybrid. Although with more collateral damage than I'd hoped for. And I imagine it will be darker and quieter around the Zangshe facility for a while."

"It may be," Riggins replied, "but I can tell you that Zangshe's very busy elsewhere. They continue to send a steady stream of supercargo vessels to the Port of Ad Damman. And you'll remember the sealed cargo vessel we were tracking. It finally docked at Jebel Ali."

"Why there?" Xavier asked.

"I haven't figured it out, but that's not all. They've sent two more conventionally powered vessels on different routes."

"Where?"

"Still tracking their progress," Riggins replied. "But from every indication, their current courses put them headed toward entirely separate continents."

"What? That makes no sense at all," Xavier said, squelching a yawn.

"It confounds me as well. The only difference is that those vessels are traveling alone."

Xavier frowned. "There's got to be some commonality in all this. We're just not seeing it. I'll be there in twenty minutes," he said, pulling into a convenience store.

He barely heard Riggins's attempt to keep him on the phone a moment more before he clicked it off. Whatever it was, he figured the techie would fill him in when he arrived at the office. In the meantime, he desperately needed the jolt of caffeine he'd get from a cup of coffee. As he entered the store, his attention was immediately diverted to the plasma screen mounted from the ceiling behind the cash register. The headline crawl announced a recent accident at China's largest uranium-mining company. The reporter went on to say that the cause of the accident was unknown but seemed to be isolated to the company's research laboratory facility.

Xavier wondered if Elena had gotten out in time, as he placed the steaming liquid on the counter. After fishing a few dollars from his wallet to pay for the coffee he looked up at the screen again. Another update was streaming across the screen:

THE CAUSE OF THE TRAGIC CHINESE ACCIDENT IS STILL
UNKNOWN. BUT THE DEATH TOLL HAS NOW RISEN TO
OVER TWO HUNDRED SCIENTISTS AND RESCUE WORKERS.

Upon reading this, Xavier's breathing became labored. *What had happened? Surely, most of the laboratory employees had left by that hour.* He would be the first to admit that he sought justice for his family's murder and Rachel's condition, but a death toll of over two hundred . . . that was catastrophic and was not his intention.

Driving back to Langley, he was a bit overwhelmed with the news out of Zangshe. The victory was bittersweet; the report of the human carnage deeply disturbed him. Although the devastation was extensive, it didn't appear to initiate any type of nuclear reaction, which meant, in all likelihood, that no replicated hybrid samples had been developed. But this was a graphic reminder of why he'd left his former life. As Elena had put it, he wasn't built for this type of work.

As soon as he cleared security at the main entrance of the CIA building, Xavier headed for Carlyle's office. He was met by a flurry of activity as he exited the elevator. Carlyle's assistant spotted him and immediately rushed over.

"Director Cheskin's clearing out Special Agent Carlyle's office," she said.

"Something happened to him?"

"Not that I'm aware of," she replied. "When I came in this morning, I got a call from upstairs to gather up all his files and any personal effects. They've been rooting around in there for almost an hour."

"What about you?" he asked.

"I've been reassigned to Quantico," she said.

"Do you know if Mr. Riggins is involved in this process?"

"I'm not sure. I called to give him a heads-up, but no answer."

If anyone knows what's going on here, it'll be Riggins, he thought, and it occurred to him that Riggins had attempted to fill him in earlier. "Good luck to you. If you hear from Agent Carlyle, please have him call me," he said to the assistant, heading back toward the elevator and downstairs to find Riggins.

Winding his way through the lower basement, Xavier found Riggins at his command station.

"Greetings, Doctor," Riggins said, as Xavier approach. "Guess you want to know what's happening upstairs?"

Xavier nodded. "Looks like a full-scale Agency investigation."

"It's a whole lot more serious than that. It seems as if Agent Carlyle went off the ranch, so to speak. Word around here is that he royally pissed off the director. But that's not all. Apparently, Agent Carlyle didn't stop there. Now the White House is involved."

"Got any insight as to why?"

"I'm still piecing it together. I got a message from Carlyle yesterday. He was in Riyadh investigating something and wanted to verify some information he'd received recently. It had to do with the relationship between the Saudis, the Chinese, and our government."

"Harry's been busy. What did he uncover?" Xavier asked.

"Here's what I've found out so far," Riggins said as he snapped up an image on his big screen.

Xavier studied the image. It was marked, WHITE HOUSE DOCUMENTS—HIGHLY CONFIDENTIAL, and was from the office of the Secretary of State. It outlined the proposed arrangements between the Saudis and the Chinese under the terms of the new International Economic Development Act.

"Oh shit," Xavier muttered after reading for a while. "I can see why there's more than a little stir around here."

"That's only the half of it. Take a look at this," said Riggins, bringing up another document. "It's related to some very specific conditions of the agreement with the Chinese."

The document on the screen outlined the stipulations for the Saudi's participation in a partnership with the Chinese in very clear language: " . . . and in return for such an arrangement, there are required comprehensive strategic disclosures concerning the United States as defined in the attached Exhibit A and hereby made part of this agreement."

"Does this mean what I think it does?" Xavier asked.

"It means the release of strategic disclosures of some type. I'm guessing it's not the location of military country clubs. Unfortunately, I can't find Exhibit A."

"It's missing?"

Riggins frowned. "Along with some other documents. While I was researching the data files, someone else was also rummaging around."

"What are you thinking, Mr. Riggins?"

"I'm thinking that there's a hacker inside the Agency who's trying to erase tracks. I know all the signs. And if I'm right, he knows I exist as well."

"A cover up?" Xavier wondered out loud.

"And they've targeted Agent Carlyle. If the White House is involved, there must be something really screwy going on at the top. The deeper I dig into this, the more I don't like where it's leading," Riggins said.

"And Harry's trying to knock down the house of cards," Xavier said.

"In a manner of speaking, Doctor. I've been around here too long to ignore the obvious. They're trying to handcuff anyone who might intervene and spill the beans. Trust me when I say that Agent Carlyle and I've had our moments, but I've never doubted his loyalty and patriotism to this country. He's onto something, and other folks with extreme prejudice know it."

Again, Xavier appreciated the complexity of Riggins's persona—contentious, egocentric, but extraordinarily insightful when it came to logical thought process. Based on what Riggins had deduced, there was little doubt Carlyle was in harm's way—more than likely from some of his closest "friends."

44

FOREBODING

Langley, Virginia

"Mr. Riggins, you're not safe here either," Xavier warned. "If you're correct and the Agency hacker is aware of you, how long do you think it'll be before they find you?"

Riggins looked up from his keyboard. "Don't worry, Doctor. I'm always a step ahead. The good thing about being a supernerd is that I've got no associations. But just in case, I've erased all record of any correspondence between Agent Carlyle and myself."

Xavier shook his head. "If I know anything about the Agency, the walls talk around here. You need to be very careful," he replied, but doubted that Riggins would heed his advice.

"I appreciate the concern. But I'm as safe here as anywhere. And besides, if I can be of any help to Agent Carlyle, I'll need access to my equipment."

Xavier nodded. "Yeah, I figured you'd say that. But just in case, do you have a contingency?"

Riggins smiled. "Always, Doctor . . . always."

As Xavier was about to leave, he looked up at Riggins's large screen. "What's that?" he asked, pointing to the satellite image.

"It's the Chinese cargo vessel leaving the Suez Canal," Riggins replied, zooming in. "One of the benefits of the older, smaller cargo vessel is its ability to use the canal. Once it clears the island of Sardinia, we'll have a better idea of where it's headed. But my guess at this point is somewhere in the Mediterranean."

"Wouldn't that be outside Zangshe's normal shipping pattern?"

"I've checked with the International Registry of Shipping, and Zangshe has never filed for shipping route clearance anywhere close to that region," Riggins said.

"And what about the other vessel?" Xavier asked.

"It stopped briefly in Cape Town, South Africa. I discovered that there's some remaining crude oil reserves there, and they've most likely refueled and are moving again. After that, the vessel could be going anywhere," Riggins finished.

Xavier stared at him. "What's its range?" he asked.

"If the vessel proceeds at its current speed, almost ten thousand miles," Riggins replied hesitantly with a hint of apprehension in his voice.

"Enough to get here—to the U.S.," Xavier said, clenching his jaw at the prospect.

45

STRATEGIES

Xiong Xian, China

Plumes of smoke continued to rise from Zangshe's crippled laboratory. While most of the physical damage was limited to the massive computer complex, other disruptive effects were also experienced. Logistical support for the shipping operations ceased, and mining operations had ground to a halt due to the lack of lighting and ventilation.

Khan received a report that many of his top scientists had been killed or seriously injured in the blasts. And due to the extent of the computer virus, all but a few of the testing laboratories were inoperable. Effectively, most of Zangshe's daily operations had come to an abrupt halt.

Khan was livid both at the notion that someone could have done this to him as well as by the prospect of being effectively out of business at a most critical time. Preliminary estimates indicated that it would take several days, at the very least, to fully assess the extent of the damages and to begin restoring some of the operations.

The new head of security also reported that there was no sign of the whereabouts of the intruders. Apparently they were able to successfully escape after ravaging the facility and rampaging security.

After the ruthless decimation of his security staff and the bloody slaying of his liaison officer, Khan issued a diabolical ultimatum to his entire management that he would render even more brutality for any slippage in the mining extraction and shipping schedules.

Once Khan had exorcized his demons for the moment, he began to coldly assess the situation. He knew he had many enemies—most of them within his own government. But the recent attack on his facility didn't make sense in the context of the current environment. Minister Chek clearly had the upper hand, and his investigation into Zangshe's nuclear-waste practices might have serious consequences for its ongoing operations. Instead, the bombing of the research laboratory wing was a specific target that had nothing to do with the impending nuclear-waste investigations.

As Khan continued to consider the circumstances, it dawned on him *why* it had happened and *who* was behind it. He pressed a button on his call director. It took a few seconds for Khan's call to be routed through.

"Mr. Chairman, your call is quite unexpected," the voice answered.

"There was a development that necessitates a change in strategy," said Khan vehemently.

"I heard about the accident in your facility. I'm sorry for the loss of lives."

"It was no accident and your condolences are not required," Khan fired back. "But I have initiated actions that are intended to prevent any further threats to my plans."

"Are you suggesting that we may have had something to do with what occurred at your facility?" the voice on the other end said with a tone of surprise.

"I am not *suggesting*. I *know* that such action could only be carried out with the assistance of one of your agencies."

"You must be mistaken, Mr. Chairman. There would be no reason for such action on our part."

"Maybe not directly, but certainly it has come from your country," Khan said. "And as such, I am holding you accountable for your ineffectiveness to keep our arrangements confidential."

"The information regarding that matter is held in the strictest of confidence. I can assure you that there was no breach on our part," the tentative voice attempted to convince him.

"Your assurances are meaningless to me. What follows next are the consequences of your own making. However, I would advise you not to attempt to intervene in any way. It would be unwise for you to further test my resolve," Khan replied, then abruptly ended the call.

The Mongolian mogul looked outside with venom in his veins toward the desecrated remnants of his crippled and burning laboratory facility. He turned slowly away from the window and back toward his computer. He typed a brief message and, with fiendish determination, hit SEND.

46

REPRISAL

Jebel Ali, U.A.E.

The Zangshe cargo vessel sat eerily still at the dock, enveloped in the mist of the very early morning, a mist caused by the cool desert breeze as it blew over the warm harbor waters. Aboard the vessel, the captain and his crew were still entertaining their mercenary companions as they had been doing for the past few hours. Finally, the ship grew quiet as the last of the mujahedin, including their bold commander, were overcome by the alcohol.

Several figures emerged from the shadows on the long dock and moved silently toward the vessel. With the precision of a drill team, they split off into two groups. One group boarded the vessel's huge deck, while the other continued toward the ship's stern. Each group had a well-rehearsed task to carry out, and in less than an hour, they had reassembled on the dock.

"Everyone is below and the crew access doors have been welded shut. The explosive charges are in place as directed," the leader reported into his communicator.

"You and your men have done well," Yakubla replied. He went on to instruct the leader of the Mongolian operatives to move the team back across the harbor and up onto the enormous old cargo-hoisting equipment. Within ten minutes, the entire team had joined Yakubla on top of the cargo hoist. From there, they would have an unobstructed view of the Zangshe vessel.

Yakubla glanced at his watch, a twisted sneer creeping across his face. "It begins," he said to the leader of his assault team. "Unfortunately, the mujahedin commander will never know the full measure of my intolerance for his treachery. You may now ignite the fuel-tank charges."

Two high-explosives charges were positioned directly in the middle of the cargo vessel's massive fuel cells; each was almost half full of the equivalent of ten thousand barrels of oil. The percussive force of the charges alongside the ship's hull was quickly followed by a deafening roar. Almost a million gallons of highly flammable diesel-fuel ignited, sending a fiery plume three hundred feet in the air and setting the moonless sky ablaze in an orange cast.

The vibrations from the ruptured fuel tanks traveled instantly through the water and could be felt across the harbor by Yakubla and his team. The huge ship sat motionless for several seconds as if unaffected by the assault. Almost imperceptibly, the vessel shuddered, then began listing, first to starboard and then back to port. Straining against its large mooring lines, the enormous mass of the vessel slowly began to settle lower in the water. Then, in a dying groan, its hull gave way to an onrush of seawater from gaping holes below its waterline. A series of whiplike popping sounds indicated the final separation from its docking restraints. Angry flames and black smoke rose from the vessel, as it continued to sink.

⁂

In the forward cargo bays, the impact of the explosion had blown apart the shielded doors, exposing over two hundred thousand metric tons of uranium waste. The mangled ship came to rest on the harbor floor some twenty feet below. Slowly, a highly radioactive soup of nuclear waste and seawater began to leach from the fatally wounded hull of the Zangshe vessel and toward the extensive intake systems of the adjacent industrial complex.

&

Yakubla looked on as the once proud cargo vessel now sat firmly fixed on the sandy harbor bed, its hulking, burning superstructure sticking a hundred feet out of the water. The fuel fire would continue to burn for days until the ship's metal fully melted into a deformed carcass. But the environmental impact from the spent uranium waste would last far longer—almost five hundred years, rendering the area surrounding the entire adjacent industrial complex useless and uninhabitable. Yakubla folded his massive arms across his chest and smiled diabolically at his handiwork. He knew that Khan would be most pleased with this dramatic display of devastation.

Shortly following the explosions, workers on the early-morning shift from the industrial complex rushed out to witness the spectacle. Little did they suspect what was lurking below the waters around the dying vessel.

"Yakubla, if I may ask, what is the nature of the industrial complex near the ship?" the team leader inquired.

Yakubla continued to watch the confusion of activity near the stricken vessel. "It is an extremely important facility in this part of the world. An intricate network of piping from here carries a vital resource to millions of people throughout the Middle East," he replied, not taking his eyes from the gathering crowd of mystified plant workers.

The team leader seemed confused. "I can see that it is no oil refinery. Besides, there is no oil left in any case. What other resource is it that you speak of?"

Yakubla slowly turned away from the chaos below and faced his fellow Mongolian. "It is the most essential of all resources for human existence and infinitely more valuable than oil."

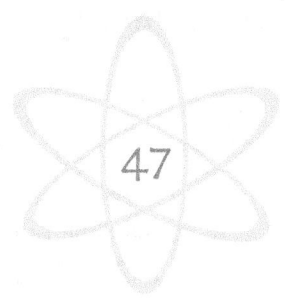

47

HIDING

Langley, Virginia

K nowing it would only be a matter of time before he got caught up in the Agency's investigation, Xavier quickly left Riggins's techno-world domain. He made a hasty retreat to the apartment Carlyle had set up for him, twenty-five minutes outside of Langley.

As he started to make the turn toward the apartment building, Xavier noticed several black SUVs parked directly across the street. His antennae went up. *Agency vehicles. They've connected me to Carlyle,* he thought. Straightening out his Ford rental, he proceeded to the next block over behind the building. Parking far enough down the street to stay out of the agents' line of sight, he looked around and quickly exited the car.

Xavier wasn't interested in returning to the apartment. He knew he couldn't stay there. But he was interested in the Agency's intentions. *If they continued to wait in their cars,* he thought, *that probably means they want to talk. On the other hand, if they're inclined to break into the apartment, that's something else entirely.* He had his answer within minutes of edging his way around the corner of the units and behind the hedgerows. He saw clearly inside the vehicles. They were all empty.

Hustling back to his car, he knew he had no reason to stay around. The Agency was determined to corral everyone involved. And the last thing he wanted was to be detained and implicated in whatever fiasco was going on. He thought of Riggins. The noose was tightening. As he accelerated slowly down the backstreet, he dialed the techie's cell. It immediately went to voicemail, so he hung up. *Riggins is probably being cautious about his communications,* he thought.

Driving through the maze of D.C. suburbs, it occurred to him that he had no place to run. And the stakes were too high for the Agency to stop chasing him. His recent association with Carlyle and his job at QPR made him a person of extreme interest. His only hope of extricating himself from the situation and making sense of all this was to somehow piece together the Chinese plot and expose it.

But staying off the Agency's radar would require some careful planning. The good news was that with all of the budget cuts, there might be fewer agents looking. And he was well trained in the art of becoming invisible. The bad news was that by now the Agency was, most likely, well aware of his background. As he thought about the situation, his PDA vibrated. It was a text from Riggins.

STILL HIDING IN PLAIN SIGHT. SETTING UP NEW COM-LINK
FOR COMMUNICATIONS. WILL NOTIFY WHEN DONE.

Xavier smiled. *The guy's good,* he thought. And with his skills, Riggins might effectively be able to mask any attempts to trace his signals. Hopefully, his techie friend would be safe for now.

48

IMPACT

Jebel Ali, U.A.E.

The effects of the explosion in the harbor were felt several miles away. The impact of the event garnered worldwide attention in a matter of hours.

"Great One, it is done," Yakubla said into the sat-phone. "You may be assured that the pictures and reports from the scene here will doubtless bring much exposure."

"You have done well, as always, Yaku," Khan replied. "We must proceed quickly if our strategy is to be most effective."

"The ships are currently in route and I am in contact with the captains. We will be prepared in less than a week's time."

Across the harbor on the Arabian Peninsula outside of Dubai, the remnants of Colonel Chauncey Jackson's Marine squad were encamped. Agent Harry Carlyle had joined his friends two days earlier. The repercussion from the explosion alarmed them, and Jackson directed Ducky Petersen to take a few men to investigate. They returned after two hours.

"It was a cargo vessel," said Ducky, "the big one that had docked a week ago. Fire and smoke everywhere. Looks like it's sitting on the bottom of the harbor. I talked with a few workers from the nearby industrial complex who were on the scene. They said it was an older vessel. And must've have had some sort of fuel-tank explosion. Lots of burning diesel oil in the water. It's a real mess."

Carlyle had been listening. "See any markings on the ship, Ducky?"

"Not much of it left when I got there. But the workers thought it was Chinese."

"Chinese?!" Carlyle said, his senses now on full alert.

"That's what they thought, Harry. But I didn't want to stay around much longer to ask more questions. The alarm at the industrial complex began blaring so loud it sent the workers scrambling. I heard someone mention something about trying to close the intake valves around the complex."

Carlyle looked at Ducky and then over to Jackson. "We need to find out what's in that industrial complex."

"What are you thinking, Harry?" Jackson asked.

"Just a hunch," Carlyle replied. "Everything we're talking about the past few days circles back to the Chinese. I don't believe that this was some random event."

"You think someone blew up that ship on purpose?" Ducky asked.

Carlyle nodded.

"Who?"

"The Chinese," Carlyle replied.

AGENDAS

C IA Director John Cheskin was in a foul mood. The White House was all over him. Ever since the call from Princess Almira, the president's senior staff had peppered the director with questions and requests for an explanation about the breach in confidentiality.

"The last thing we need at this time is for information to leak to the press about our agreement with the Saudis," the White House's chief council shouted at Cheskin. "You'd better make it your only priority to get control of the situation, no matter what it takes. Or else we'll have no other option but to replace you," he threatened before ending the call.

Over the past few years, Cheskin had been forced to work with limited resources. And every attempt to recruit more agents was declined. His already tenuous relationship with the current administration's views and politics had long reached the boiling point. The latest issue, he realized, could be the final nail in his coffin. On top of everything, he had an experienced rogue special agent determined to exercise his well-documented self-righteousness.

"Find out who else Carlyle's been in contact with," Cheskin said to his deputy director.

"We've got the word out all over," the deputy replied. "The questioning of his Marine assistant was a useless exercise. She knew nothing and had no files whatsoever related to the matter. There's someone else Agent Carlyle had met with recently and we're attempting to locate him. He's employed as a scientist with QPR."

"How hard can it be to find a damn scientist?"

"Normally, it wouldn't be. But this guy's also former Black Ops."

"Ah, Christ, just what the situation needs. I don't care what you have to do. Find him and fast," Cheskin snapped.

"What about Agent Carlyle?" the deputy director asked.

"I've already sent two of our best agents after him," Cheskin replied.

☙

Meanwhile, some seven stories immediately below Cheskin's office complex, Riggins was maneuvering to stay under the radar. He had rerouted all his incoming and outgoing data lines through a private network he had set up. There were very few people on the planet who would have the capability to intercept his communications even if they knew where he was located. He had double bolted the access gates to his basement command center and disguised them with copious amounts of storage materials. In case a wayward search happened to stray his way, he wanted to camouflage any obvious indications of his location.

He'd already sent Xavier a contact message regarding the com-link when he saw something pop up on his large screen—something that surprised even him. The sat-image of the dock at Jebel Ali, which he was monitoring, came alive with the pictures of the cargo vessel fully enveloped in flames and sitting on the bottom of the harbor. "Holy shit," he uttered, as he watched the scene unfold.

From the satellite's angle directly above the stricken vessel, Riggins clearly saw the swirls of fuel-oil effluent flowing out from the sunken hull. He picked up the phone and dialed his contact at the INA.

"There's been some type of vessel explosion in Jebel Ali. You may want to get one of your birds over there and drop some probes," Riggins said to Wayne Schuster of the INA.

Schuster was a slow-to-act but thorough technician. He was the epitome of an international agency bureaucrat. Everything was by the book and according to strict protocol. "Why would I be interested in a ship exploding near Dubai?"

"If it happened to be loaded with nuclear waste," Riggins said.

Schuster hesitated. "You can verify that?"

"I tracked the vessel from China and saw it being loaded with nuclear waste in the Port of Tianjin. I have the images here. I'll shoot them across to you."

"Okay, Riggins, I'll take a look. Thanks for the heads-up. Once I get authorization to launch the aircraft, and if we drop probes, I'll call you with any results."

Riggins shook his head. *I'm not holding my breath,* he thought, as he toggled the zoom control on the image to get a closer view of the scene at Jebel Ali. The harbor water was so crystal clear in front of the advancing effluent that Riggins could see the large intake valves below the surface. Workers outside the industrial complex were struggling to deploy a boom to keep the effluent away. *The water must be used for cooling purposes. Could be some type of manufacturing facility,* he thought. He zoomed in again. Looking more closely at the complex, he moved back reflexively in his chair. "How could I've missed this?" he mumbled. "Jesus, it's frigging Machiavellian. I know what the Chinese are planning!"

50

NIGHTMARE

Quebec City, Quebec

Xavier decided to get out of town. He knew that the Agency would make an all-out effort to locate him. The next twenty-four to forty-eight hours were critical. After that, they would realize that he had gone underground and that finding him would be infinitely more difficult.

Although he wanted to go back to the Black Hills to check on Rachel in person, he resisted the temptation. As much as he wanted to see her familiar face and assure himself that she was going to make it, it was the next place they would look for him.

Instead, Xavier put another plan into action. Using the Canadian credentials Riggins had prepared for him, he flew to Chicago and then on to Quebec. He landed at Jean Lesage International Airport, rented a car, and drove twenty minutes into the quaint European-like community of Old Quebec City, arriving around midnight.

More French than Canadian and decidedly less English-speaking, Quebec seemed a good place to stay out of reach for a while. A busy tourist location, it was fairly easy to remain incognito without the concern of constant vigilance from authorities. There was a history of limited reciprocity, in general, between Canada and the United States. And that political environment was even more in evidence in Quebec City.

Xavier checked into the Chateau Frontenac, one of Quebec City's oldest hotels and well known for its European ambiance. Late arrivals were graciously welcomed by an alert and competent staff.

"Bonsoir, monsieur," the night concierge greeted him.

He had always been grateful to Elena for motivating him to learn French. "Bonsoir, la reservations pour Michael Christianson," he replied.

"Oui, monsieur. Combien de temps vous ira faire rester avec nous?" the concierge asked.

Xavier wasn't certain yet how long he would be staying. Long enough to keep under the radar but that depended on events elsewhere. And longer reservations were best. That way, if he had to leave early, it made it harder for anyone to locate him.

"Peut-etre une semaine," he said, paying in cash for a week in advance.

"Vous remercier monsieur. Votre cle," the night concierge replied, handing him the room key.

Xavier put the key in his pocket and left his bag for the bellhop. There was an all-night Internet café down the block. He needed to check in with Riggins, but using the hotel Wi-Fi services was an easy way to leave tracks.

He walked out into the brisk night air coming off the St. Lawrence River and proceeded down the stone-lined motor court of the hotel. At the corner of rue des Carrieres, he turned left. Tucked away in a niche, set back from the cobblestone way, was a little pastry shop. The aroma of freshly baked croissants permeated the air as he entered. In the dim light, he saw two small cubicles with computer terminals. Sitting down at one, he entered the routing information that Riggins had given him. It took a few minutes for the system to connect. Then it came up: Riggins's virtual private network. He hesitated to guess where the signal had been routed. But he knew it would impossible for most mortals to trace.

WHAT'S YOUR STATUS? he typed.

He waited.

EVERYTHING'S COPASETIC HERE, came Riggins's reply.

NEWS ABOUT CARLYLE?

NOTHING. BUT I HEAR THE PRESSURE'S ON TO LOCATE YOU. HOPE YOU'RE SECURE.

USED TO DO THIS FOR A LIVING, Xavier typed back. SHOULD BE BACK IN CIRCULATION IN A FEW DAYS OR SO.

GOOD, NEED YOUR HELP ON SOMETHING. THE SHIP AT JEBEL ALI RECENTLY EXPLODED AT THE DOCK. I FIGURED OUT THE CHINESE PUZZLE. WE HAVE TO FIND A WAY TO STOP THE ONE IN THE MEDITERRANEAN SOON. IT'LL BE IN PORT IN FOUR DAYS.

When Xavier read the words, *ship* and *exploded,* his worst fears were realized. THEY'VE SET OFF A DIRTY BOMB, he typed. THE CHINESE ARE WILLING TO USE THEIR NUCLEAR WASTE TO GET WHAT THEY WANT.

WORSE THAN THAT. THEY INTEND TO CRIPPLE POPULATION CENTERS, responded Riggins.

Xavier had a sickening notion what Riggins was referring to. HOW DO THEY INTEND TO DO THAT?

There was a delay. It grew longer. He checked the connection. It was good on his end.

BEEN COMPROMISED. WILL NOTIFY YOU WHEN COAST IS CLEAR.

Somehow, someone must have tapped into Riggins's network. He recalled Riggins's suspicions about a hacker inside the Agency. If Xavier had learned anything about Riggins, his hubris at anyone challenging his expertise was his worst enemy. The supertechie's pride had already proved self-detrimental. It had once led to his own exposure by the Agency. He hoped Riggins had matured and would find a more strategic way around the problem.

As he considered Riggins's predicament, his curiosity grew. *What had Riggins meant by crippling population centers?* he wondered as he entered JEBEL ALI in the search engine. A general information website displayed the history of the Middle Eastern port town. It was located about thirty miles southwest of Dubai. Construction of its extensive port facilities began in the late 1970s. When it was finished, Jebel Ali became the world's largest man-made harbor and the biggest port in the Middle East. Spanning over fifty-two square miles, the huge harbor had deep, clear water that was constantly being fed from the Persian Gulf.

Xavier continued to read about more recent developments in Jebel Ali, especially after the fall of the oil industry and the disappearance of the U.S. Navy ships from the region. In a separate article, mention was made about a new construction project that was underway for a number of years. It had taken almost a decade to complete due to the extensive nature of the network of piping from the facility. He read further. When he discovered the specific purpose of the facility, he hurriedly browsed down the page and found a locator map. *It can't be,* he thought. *Not there. Riggins wasn't exaggerating. The impact of the explosion and the resultant fallout would be devastating. It would have international repercussions.*

Xavier dropped his head for a moment. The news unnerved him. If the Chinese were willing to do something like this, they would stop at nothing to accomplish their ultimate objective. Solemnly, Xavier disconnected from the terminal and walked slowly out of the pastry shop.

51

LINES

Quebec City, Quebec

Everything had changed. The explosion at Jebel Ali was about to ignite a firestorm of international outrage. The stakes involved in Zangshe's quest to capture the alternative nuclear-fuel market had now escalated well beyond any reason. And the agreements between the United States, Saudi Arabia, and China were destined to implode. The tragedy that followed in the wake of the Jebel Ali incident would forever change the status quo.

In the midst of the turmoil swirling through his head, Xavier thought of Riggins's request for help. The ship headed into the Mediterranean was on a death mission. He needed to find a way to stop it before another incident occurred. Without Riggins's support, he would have to rely on another source for intel. There was only one immediate option, and with no way to arrange for a clean phone line, he had purchased several prepaid phones at one of the street kiosks. Dialing a series of numbers emblazoned in his memory, he listened to the routing sounds. Then it went silent.

"Not certain the line's clean," Xavier said quietly as he slowly walked along the cobblestone street not far from the small pastry shop.

"Hello, X-man. Good to hear from you. Wondered how the mission went."

"Mixed results. Target's still operational."

"Sorry to hear that. By the way, Elixir's off the grid. Hasn't checked in as yet."

Elena's gone dark. Maybe even more serious than that, he thought. "She's still in. Things went a bit sideways. I'm hoping for the best," Xavier replied.

No response. There would be no help. SOP for Black Ops.

"What can I do for you, X-man?"

"I need some intel related to Jebel Ali."

"Just heard the news. Don't know any of the facts."

"It's not why I called. Need to locate another similar facility in the Mediterranean."

There was a brief pause. "Jebel Ali's the largest one of its kind in the world. The next biggest facility is a new one in a place called Punta Sabbioni on the northern Adriatic Sea near Venice."

That was the information he needed. He was about to hang up, when his contact continued, "X-man, word's out that you're on the run. Had some inquiries from the top. Watch your back."

It surprised him, not that he got the heads-up, but that someone with enough juice had reached out to his contact. "Thanks," he said, ending the call, and tossed the phone in the nearest receptacle outside of an all-night cafe.

If there was any question before about how badly the Agency wanted him, it was now answered. The message had been sent and delivered. He was burned. No one would go near him or attempt to help him. He was on his own. And the problem of trying to stop the Zangshe ship in the Mediterranean just became much more difficult.

According to Riggins, he had only four days to implement a solution. If the Chinese were willing to explode the ship in Jebel Ali, it was very likely that their intention was to do the same or threaten to do the same thing in Venice. He needed to convince someone else of that possibility. But who?

Sifting through his memory banks, he recalled an old friend—someone he had worked with very closely in his previous life. Not one of the Agency types, more of an independent contractor and definitely *not* in the loop. He recalled that the last time they had spoken many years ago, his friend was living just outside of Venice. He still had that number tucked away in his memory; he hoped it still worked.

Using another of the prepaid phones, Xavier made the call. The call connected and a beep sounded. There was no way to know if the number was good. He didn't leave a message. Within moments, the prepaid phone rang back. He answered.

"Did you call me?" asked a voice with a heavy Italian accent.

"I did," Xavier said. "I can tell your English hasn't improved much."

"A lot better than your Italian," Paolo Venuchi responded with a laugh. "Where have you been, X?"

"In the real world trying to make a living," Xavier quipped.

"How has that worked for you?" Venuchi asked with light-hearted sarcasm.

Xavier let out a heavy sigh. "Okay, up until a short while ago, and then it all went to shit."

"What doesn't?" Venuchi responded, his tone becoming more serious. "What's the purpose of this call, X?"

"I need a favor, Venuchi. Do you still have your contact in the Italian Ministry?"

"Maybe, but that depends. . . . What do you have in mind?"

"I need to have a cargo vessel intercepted by your Navy."

"Oh, is that all?" Venuchi asked with more than a hint of sarcasm.

"Actually, no," Xavier replied, "It's imperative that it is intercepted very soon."

Chuckling, the Italian man asked, "How *soon* is soon, my friend?"

"In the next few days," Xavier replied, imagining the surprise on his old friend's face.

"Are you outta your fottuto mind?" Venuchi exclaimed.

"Not yet, Venuchi," Xavier replied in all seriousness, "But soon, if I can't stop that vessel."

"I'll humor you, X. What's so urgent about stopping the vessel?"

"Did you hear the news recently about a cargo vessel exploding?"

"Yeah, it was in a port in the Middle East somewhere."

"Jebel Ali," Xavier said.

"That's it. So what does that have to do with stopping the vessel here in Italy?"

"It's owned by the same company, and they plan to blow it up near your port facilities."

"I've never known you to exaggerate, X. You're dead serious, aren't you?" Venuchi said.

"Unfortunately, I am."

"What's the motive behind the explosions?"

"Intimidation and compliance."

"By whom and for what purpose?" Venuchi asked.

"Zangshe, a Chinese company, wants to dominate the nuclear-energy marketplace and has decided the only way to accomplish that is through the use of threatening tactics."

"Why not do it the old-fashioned way? Create a monopoly and dictate terms?"

"Apparently, they don't control all the necessary parts yet. And the INA is trying to shut down their mining operations for nuclear-waste storage violations."

"So what's the big deal if they blow up a few of their own ships?" Venuchi asked.

"They're full of nuclear waste."

There was dead silence.

"Nuclear waste?!" Venuchi finally uttered. "Do they intend to try to contaminate an entire port basin?"

"Do you know what's in Jebel Ali?" Xavier asked.

"Other than a large port facility, I don't."

"I didn't either until last night. And that's when the whole picture became clear—crystal clear."

"What do you mean?"

"Jebel Ali has a larger facility than the one at Punta Sabbioni."

Venuchi was quiet again for a moment. "You can't be serious. Not the new one we have recently completed? You're telling me that the ship in Jebel Ali exploded next to the same type of facility?"

"Yes."

"Jesus, Maria!" Venuchi exclaimed. "If that were to happen here almost all of Europe would be affected."

"And suffer the same fate soon to be experienced in the Middle East," Xavier said gravely. He could hear Venuchi's intake of breathe.

"I'll make the call to my contact in the Ministry. He's a raving bureaucrat, but he's not an asshole. If your information checks out and he is able to verify the vessel's origin, he'll authorize the Navy to intercede."

"Thanks, old friend," Xavier said, then added, "Feel free to tell your contact that this intel came from a reliable source at the Agency. Just don't say who."

"Sounds as if you're operating outside the lines, X," Venuchi noted.

"I'm not certain where the lines are anymore," Xavier replied.

RESOLVES

Beijing, China

Minister Chek was surprised when he saw the reports of the damage to the Zangshe laboratory. But he was very pleased to hear that despite the devastating accident at the facility, the INA had decided to proceed with its formal investigations into Zangshe's operations. He wondered if his threats to bring public scrutiny down on the INA had any bearing on that decision. And there was the recent phone call from his senior aide, Elena Dupre. Her plea seemed rather well controlled and nondescriptive of the events that had led to her plight at Zangshe.

When he had hired Ms. Dupre, her résumé had been perfectly matched for the work in his ministry. She had an excellent grasp of technology as well as a strong sense of independence and self-confidence—all things he had needed in his dealings with the other departments within the national governmental structure.

Chek hadn't been certain at the time, but there also appeared to be a kind of aloofness, a very secretive side of her—more than simple inscrutableness. It was that aspect of her makeup that he had decided to exploit. Giving her more challenging assignments, he was pleasantly surprised by her performance. In some cases, her performance was quite remarkable—almost too remarkable. His curiosity about her continued to grow until it was finally satisfied by a methodical and very thorough evaluation of her background, which revealed that she worked for the CIA.

When Dupre had requested from Minister Chek the opportunity to spearhead the preliminary investigation into Zangshe's nuclear-waste abuses, he had agreed without hesitation. It was an interesting side play in his ultimate plan to bring Zangshe to its corporate knees. It was a no-lose scenario. And it appeared to him from all reported accounts that the damage assessed at Zangshe had all the elements of a covert CIA operation.

But Chek knew how very powerful Khan was and that it would take far more than an attack on his research laboratory to dismantle his empire. He had to admit, however, it was a very good start. And with regard to Ms. Dupre's predicament, he decided that he would definitely miss having her on his staff. As he contemplated his next move against Zangshe, his musings were interrupted by his assistant.

"Excuse me, Minister Chek, you have a call waiting. It is from Zangshe. Chairman Khan would like to speak with you," she said.

Chek was slightly taken aback. He had never actually spoken to his self-proclaimed archenemy and was surprised by his own sense of foreboding at the notion of Khan on the waiting call. "Mr. Chairman," Chek said, adeptly taking the initiative. "I am sorry we have not had the opportunity to meet one another, and I hope to rectify that in the very near future. I have heard about the terrible accident to your facility. I offer my sincere condolences on the loss of your valued employees."

Without responding to Chek's niceties, Khan said curtly, "I have a grievous matter to discuss with you, Mr. Minister. You authorized an investigation of Zangshe's operations despite the impending INA notification. I strongly suggest you give serious thought to the *conse-*

quences of that decision in light of the damages and deaths your representatives caused on our property."

Chek had been prepared for the accusation. "I intend to fully support the INA investigation into the abuses of your nuclear-waste program," Chek replied sternly. "However, I have no knowledge of anyone from my ministry either requesting or having been granted access to your company's property. And be assured, Chairman Khan, I have duly noted your threat against this ministry, and it will be dealt with in time."

"Then we have an understanding, Mr. Minister," Khan said, not backing down. "I did want to be certain that you understand firsthand my resolve to resist your unwarranted meddling in my affairs and in the affairs of my company. I *will* see an end to it."

Chek's jaw tightened. All pretenses aside now, he responded, "Mr. Chairman, hear me well and mark my words. It is not merely my intent to meddle in your affairs. I intend to hold you *fully* accountable for your abuses and atrocities against humanity. And if that means bringing your entire operation to a permanent halt, then so be it. . . . And be advised, Mr. Chairman, you have no concept of how deeply *my* resolve runs. I *will* see an end to your reign of destruction."

53

DETAILS

Quebec City, Quebec

Xavier was keenly aware of little things. Anything that appeared out of the norm would trigger a flurry of instinctive responses. This ability was most certainly enhanced by his military training and his years of detailed research work, but he had always thought that his penchant for details began as a genetic thing. His father, an aeronautical engineer and hobbyist model maker, had insisted that Xavier help in the meticulous design and assembly of the most complicated replicas. His innate ability to recognize the specific patterns of little things had always served him well.

So when Xavier returned to his hotel room, the several large footprints in the recently vacuumed carpet didn't go unnoticed. They were too large for the housekeeping maids he had seen bustling down the hallways. Someone else had definitely been in the room, very recently. He picked up the hotel extension. The concierge confirmed that other than the assigned housekeeper, no one else from the hotel staff had access to his room.

Looking around, he detected other telltale signs of intrusion: the zippers on his bag facing a different direction on the luggage stand, his toiletries bag slightly askew where it rested on the bathroom counter, and the drawer on the nightstand open ever so slightly.

It had only been two days since he had arrived in Quebec, but somehow his cover was blown. He wasn't certain how that was possible. He concluded that whoever compromised Riggins had found him as well. Clearly the Agency had another supertechie snoop on their team.

Xavier surveyed the corridor outside the room and determined that it was safe. There was no time to check his belongings for tracking devices, so he left everything behind. He figured his rental car would likely have been tampered with as well, so when he reached the lobby he asked the doorman to hail him a cab. He knew he was an easy target waiting there for a ride, but the cab pulled up within moments without incident.

Once inside, Xavier directed the driver to head toward the airport. Watching through the back window, he waited for evidence that he was being followed. His instincts told him that he was. It also hadn't taken long for it to occur to him that if it had been the Agency who had located his whereabouts, they would have grabbed him in the room. They wouldn't have given him the chance to make a run for it again. He realized that his belongings and his car had more likely been rigged with explosives or something equally as deadly. He was glad he had followed his gut and not touched anything. He needed a plan. He knew he would be better off in a crowded area—somewhere he could lure his pursuers into a trap.

"Turn around here and go back into the old city," he directed the driver in his best French, pointing to an off-ramp that had come upon them quickly.

The cab driver made the tight turn and reached the bottom of the off-ramp. Seconds later, the screeching of tires confirmed his suspicions. It seemed his pursuers had tried to negotiate the turn at the top a little too quickly.

The cab driver glanced in his rearview mirror at the small two-door coupe, which had steadied itself and was now barreling down on them. "Monsieur, what do wish me to do?" the driver asked nervously.

"Drive . . . drive faster," Xavier replied, handing him a hundred-dollar bill. "Lose them." He knew the chances of that would be slim, but he thought there might be a chance the driver would rise to the challenge.

The cab rocketed away from the red light and narrowly missed the rush of traffic from the adjoining road. They quickly blended into the steady flow of cars heading toward the old city. Xavier looked behind, keeping his pursuers in sight.

"Turn there," he said to the driver, directing him to a sign for the downtown area. They were almost back to the Chateau Frontenac. The driver made a series of weaving maneuvers, nearly hitting several vehicles. He ignored the rain of hand salutes as he skidded his way to the exit. Driving as if possessed, the cabbie ignored the stop sign at the intersection. The cab glanced off an oncoming pickup, causing the truck to spin around and block the road behind. Fully committed to his mission, the driver never looked back and pressed the accelerator harder.

Nearing the center of the old city, Xavier tapped the driver on the shoulder. "Let me off here. Great job, my friend," he said, handing him another hundred-dollar bill. "This one is to fix the dents."

The driver eagerly took the second hundred. His face flush with excitement and his breath labored, he said, "Thank you, monsieur, it has been most exhilarating."

As he exited the cab, Xavier spotted the coupe. The accident had slowed them down, but they had managed to maneuver along the shoulder and were coming quickly toward him. He needed them to follow him into the downtown tourist area where he could set up an opportunity to take them by surprise Whoever they were, his pursuers were very determined and patient. His instincts were on full alert. This was a killing team after all . . . not sent to bring him home.

54

ASSAILANTS

Quebec City, Quebec

Hoping Riggins would contact him, Xavier turned on his PDA. There was no sense trying to avoid the obvious. He was already made. Moving efficiently but not too fast, he made his way into the heart of the old city square. Surrounding the streetscape, the scenery and ambiance of the old walled city truly reflected its European heritage here. Cobblestone pavers weaving among quaint shops displaying crafts and small eateries created timeless images of life in a simpler world.

Xavier had selected a location that would serve his interest. Directly below the Chateau Frontenac and next to the St. Lawrence River was a place called Basse-Ville. The oldest quarter in the city, it was the location of renovated seventeenth- and eighteenth-century buildings. But more importantly from Xavier's perspective, it was known for its funicular railway—an outside passenger elevator that traversed the two hundred-foot cliff between the upper town at Haute-Ville and the lower town of Basse-Ville. It was an ideal place for him to isolate his quarry and to neutralize their intent.

Xavier's plan was simple. Assuming that his pursuers were not as

215

familiar as he was with the area, he would entice them to follow him down to the lower town where he would employ the railway as part of his plan. Built in 1879, the funicular originally used a water ballast system for propulsion. In 1907, it was converted to electrical operation and was in almost continuous operation for well over a century and a half. In a city marked by its steep hillsides, the funicular was a popular and convenient people-moving method to travel the almost two hundred feet of street elevation change within the old city. However, it had its history of accidents, most notably back in the 1990s when more than a dozen people were killed when its cabling broke.

But now, the confinement of the small cable car provided the necessary element of surprise for Xavier to get the upper hand. He soon spotted two men walking briskly toward the city square looking for him. They were only several hundred yards from his location when he made certain that they saw him. Gauging their closing distance, he looked at his old moon-faced watch, paid his fare, and jumped aboard a descending car. The waiting time between cars was no more than one minute. Several cars traversed the rails before the pursuers reached the tollgate. It would be enough time for him to arrange a welcoming trap.

Getting off the cable car, Xavier waited patiently at the bottom. As the car carrying his pursuers neared, he clearly saw their faces: Asian. It had occurred to him that besides Riggins and Elena, the only ones who could have made the connection to his Canadian identity were the Chinese. Zangshe's deeper security check must have debunked the identity Elena had set up for him and uncovered his second-level false ID that he had used at the hotel. Once they knew his cover, it would be relatively easy to follow his trail. And they had come for retribution.

The two men kept their eyes fixed on the bottom of the hill. One of them reached inside his coat. In a situation with overwhelming odds, Xavier knew the best tactic was to force his attackers into a confined space where their movements would be limited. That way he could take full advantage of the element of surprise and improve his chances of survival.

The two henchmen were alone in the car. And, fortunately for Xavier's plan, there were no passengers waiting at the bottom for a return car either. Moving quickly, Xavier hid himself atop the cable-car return-housing mechanism, which was located out of sight, directly above where the car doors open and passengers disembark. Seconds later, the car came to a stop and the automatic doors opened. Without warning, Xavier swung down from his perch and into the open car, knocking both men backward with a swinging kick to their chests. He followed up with a spot-on kick to the nearest man's head, rendering him unconscious. The second attacker struggled to get to his feet, trying to withdraw his weapon from inside his coat. Xavier quickly pounced on him, ramming his fist into the man's groin. Doubled over in agony, the second would-be attacker dropped his weapon. Xavier scooped it up and did a double take; it was a Taser.

He pointed the weapon at the second assailant and pulled the trigger. Two dart-like electrodes buried themselves into the attacker's back, sending enough voltage through his body to cause him to shudder violently and collapse on the floor—effective and painful but nonlethal.

Realizing the Asians hadn't intended to kill him after all, he wondered why they had come after him. However, at the moment, he didn't have time to sort out their rationale. As the cable car readied to make its turn to head back up the cliff side to the small upper town, the doors closed slowly with the two unconscious men on the floor of the car. When the car arrived at the top where several passengers had already gathered, the operator there would shut down the railway to investigate the problem.

Xavier walked out of the lower-rail station. No one took any notice of his casual departure. He continued along the riverbank walkway up to the next street where he hailed a cab.

INTERCEPTION

The ports in Venice had enjoyed a resurgence of business in the later decades of the twentieth century. Much of the revival, particularly in the Venetian port in the Marittima basin, was due to the prolific increase of cruise ships. But like the other vestiges of infrastructures that were dependent on fossil fuels, the cruise-ship industry had crumbled with the decline of oil. The large port facilities all along the Mediterranean coastline, including the two in the Venezia Terminal Passeggeri located very near the old historic city, had long since been quieted. But it was here that the Italian Navy had docked some of its ships.

Venuchi was able to convince his contact in the Italian Ministry that there was an impending threat from the approaching Chinese cargo vessel. It wasn't easy, however. The information Xavier had provided was accurate but somewhat sketchy. Although the approaching cargo vessel's origin was verified, the news regarding the explosion of the vessel at Jebel Ali was not as definitive. Early reports from the scene of the explosion stated that there was an unfortunate accident involving a welder's torch that led to the ignition of the vessel's fuel tanks.

And while the authorities suspected the cargo on board was nuclear-waste material, the manifest was not yet available. To further complicate matters, the INA was still in the process of completing its investigation of the incident.

After calling in one of his many favors, Venuchi's machinations led to the launching of one of the Italian Navy's cruisers into the Adriatic; the intent was to intercept the Chinese cargo vessel. In the early morning light, Comandante Vittorio Lesio maneuvered his ship through the Venetian Lagoon and into the Giudecca Canal. Turning southeast, the swift cruiser headed for the coastal waters off the Venetian isles where the strong currents from the Adriatic moved some of the earth's purist seawater toward the Punta Sabbioni isles.

Once in open waters, Comandante Lesio requested a radar fix on the approaching Chinese vessel. Within moments, the screen displayed the large radar image of the vessel. The radar officer called out the target's range of one hundred fifty miles to the southeast with a bearing of three-forty-five degrees, which put the vessel on a course heading toward Venice and Punta Sabbioni. The average depth of the water where the cargo vessel was located was approximately fifteen hundred feet. The comandante's orders were to intercept and board the vessel to verify its manifest and destination. In the event of any improprieties or if they incurred any resistance, the comandante wanted to be certain to have the intercept occur as far out into the Adriatic as possible. He directed the helmsman to proceed at full speed.

After two hours at sea, the swift Italian cruiser cut the distance to the oncoming cargo vessel to fifty miles. The comandante broke radio silence and ordered contact with the Chinese vessel. Several attempts met with no response. Finally, after repeated threats directly from the comandante, the Chinese captain replied.

"What is the meaning of your intended interception and threats, Comandante? These are international waters," the irate Chinese captain said.

"You are ordered to bring your vessel to a stop. We have reason to believe you are carrying hazardous materials and may be in violation of current INA regulations," replied the comandante.

"Your information is inaccurate. The cargo on board complies with all international shipping guidelines, and I am requesting that you not impede our progress."

"This is your final warning, Captain. Bring your vessel to a full stop immediately," the Italian commander bellowed. "Or else we will be forced to take appropriate measures."

Several minutes passed with no response from the Chinese captain.

"Comandante, it appears the cargo vessel is slowing," the radar officer said. "It will take several miles for it to come to a full stop."

The Italian Navy cruiser moved swiftly into position for boarding. Dwarfed by the sheer volume of the cargo vessel, the Italian cruiser laid several hundred yards off the stern of the Chinese vessel. A small pilot boat was winched over the side of the cruiser with several of the Italian crew on board, including Comandante Vittorio Lesio.

56

PLOTS

Quebec City, Quebec

With both the Agency and Zangshe after him, Xavier was running out of options. His plan to expose the Chinese had rested on limited resources and intel. Even if he was able to pull back the curtain on the international conspiracy in play, he began to wonder if it would mean anything and to whom. At that moment, he had no clear path to take; more importantly, he had no place to get out of harm's way.

Xavier's decision to take a cab to the airport was more out of reflex than any specific plan. Staying in Quebec didn't make sense anymore. When the Asian assailants reported their failed attempt, more serious efforts would follow. Even if the Asians' backup plan wasn't successful, the Agency was close behind—if they weren't already onto him. And Riggins's fate was unclear. His friend's communications appeared compromised and his location possibly identified. Losing access to Riggins created an enormous deficit in Xavier's efforts to stay ahead of the oncoming collision of events. For the first time in his life, he was undecided about what to do next.

His prepaid cell phone rang, giving him a chance to refocus his thinking. Only one person had the number: Venuchi.

"I've just heard from my contact in the ministry here. I can't begin to describe to you the ration of shit I've endured on your behalf," Venuchi said angrily.

"What happened, Venuchi?"

"The Navy intercepted the Chinese vessel about one hundred miles south of Venice. You were right about its origin. It was identified as a Zangshe-flagged vessel. The Chinese captain invoked his rights under international maritime law and requested not to be impeded. However, the Italian commander of the Navy cruiser was most persistent in his threats. The Chinese vessel was eventually boarded and searched as requested."

"I'm pleased and impressed you're able to pull that off, Venuchi. No matter the abuse you had to endure; it's worth every moment of it."

"You have not heard the reasons why I was not only subjected to the wrath of my contact at the ministry, but why I was also requested to appear before the Magistrate General to account for my actions and reveal my source inside the Agency," Venuchi said irately.

Xavier was perplexed. "What are you talking about? The ship contained nuclear materials, didn't it?"

"That's a fact. It did contain a full cargo load of nuclear materials—over three hundred thousand metric tons to be precise," Venuchi replied.

"And that wasn't proof enough of what I'd indicated might happen?"

"Not quite. You see, when the Italian commander asked for the manifest, the Chinese reluctantly accommodated his request after filing a complaint for illegal stoppage and boarding on the high seas. The ship's manifest clearly and specifically described the nature of the nuclear materials and its destination."

"What did it say?" Xavier asked impatiently.

"The nuclear materials on board the cargo vessel were verified as high-grade uranium ore bound for the Croatian port of Piran in Slovenia. It seems that there's a nuclear facility there that recently contracted with Zangshe for the uranium."

Xavier was flummoxed. He was so convinced that he and Riggins were correct that Zangshe had intended to hold most of Europe hostage to its demands. Instead, what had transpired was a serious breach of international law, and because of him, his friend was smack in the middle of it.

Xavier knew that Piran was only eighty miles almost due east of Venice and barely a few degrees difference in course that far out in the Adriatic Sea. And now it appeared that the Chinese had pulled off the perfect deception. Their timing was impeccable. Zangshe must have realized that after the explosion at Jebel Ali, someone might suspect their complicity and reveal their strategy too early. But when the notice of an incident such as the one involving Venuchi was filed with the International Maritime Organization, it would create a monumental distraction. The ensuing investigations by the IMO and the Italian Ministry of Foreign Affairs at the behest of the Chinese government on behalf of Zangshe could result in very severe penalties and rebukes. Zangshe could effectively have unfettered immunity going forward on all their shipping routes.

But none of this was of any import to Venuchi. He had far more immediate problems to face. "I'm sorry to have to tell you this, my old friend. But I have no choice but to disclose your identity in the upcoming investigations. In most normal circumstances, you know that I would never burn a friend or jeopardize his future. But this is not a normal matter. The entire Italian government and several international agencies are screaming for my head. My family will be harassed unmercifully if I don't comply, not to mention I'll be rotting in some godforsaken prison over here."

Xavier's guilt weighed heavily on his shoulders. "I'm sorry for the situation I've put you in. Do whatever you need to do to extricate yourself. If there's anything I can do to help, let me know."

"I may be asked to have you testify on my behalf. But I'll understand if that's not possible. I'll let you know. *Arrivederci, X.*"

As if things weren't complicated enough, this news from Venuchi had all but dashed any hope Xavier had held out for turning the tide against Zangshe anytime soon. It appeared that rather than uncovering the Chinese scheme, he may have opened a Pandora's box. It would be difficult to shine the light of any investigation onto Zangshe in the wake of the international hearings on the illegal actions taken by the Italian Navy. Zangshe would have free reign to pursue their plans for worldwide nuclear domination.

Xavier arrived at the airport in Quebec still pondering all the possibilities when something came to him . . . and where he had to go. He purchased a few necessities and other items he thought might come in handy as well as a change of clothing. The second set of credentials, which Riggins had prepared for him, had his cover as a press photographer. He was confident that neither the Chinese nor the Agency would be on to that one. In need of equipment to complete his cover, he found a small camera shop inside the terminal and purchased the highest-end Nikon they had with impressive-looking lenses and a pair of binoculars. He then boarded a flight to the one place where he thought he might find some answers to Carlyle's story about the king and the sorcerer. He smiled crookedly as he recalled Carlyle's expression when he had told Xavier the story. The agent's eyes had shone as he described the king's desperate need for something valuable to restore his great power and how he had discovered a sorcerer who had a magic potion to restore it—only the king's enemies were determined to prevent his return to glory.

How ironic, he thought, *that my future and the future of the world may very well rest on the interpretation of the message in Carlyle's fairytale.*

57

SURVEILLANCE

Jebel Ali, U.A.E.

During the nearly fourteen-hour flight to Dubai International Airport, Xavier fitfully struggled with the rationale for continuing the effort to thwart Zangshe's plan. The outcome seemed all but certain. His thoughts drifted back to Rachel's well-being and the hapless end to the QPR facility in Black Hills. The events that had followed only served to further convince him of the futility of his efforts. Maybe, just maybe, going to Dubai might lead him to some answers. But first he had to find Carlyle.

As Xavier deplaned, the sultry desert heat blasted him. He rented a compact car and tossed his small duffle bag with camera equipment and spare clothing in the backseat. As he drove from the airport through the city streets, he noticed how Dubai had deteriorated since his last visit almost ten years earlier. He remembered the unchecked construction activity fueled by the seemingly unending Arab opulence; once that had subsided, there remained a gluttonous supply of vacant high-end real estate. After the oil revenues dissipated, the omnipresent, hulking, empty edifices throughout the city were a testament to the former greed-driven excesses of the oil-cartel days.

Xavier noticed bands of marauding vagrants still picking the buildings clean. He couldn't imagine that much was left. As he neared the port areas, the scenery didn't change much. Here, alongside the huge docks, hundreds of people were encamped in makeshift homes trying to eke out an existence near the waters of the Persian Gulf.

Riggins had mentioned that Carlyle was headed to the U.A.E. Xavier needed to figure out a way to locate Carlyle. He didn't want to alert anyone to his whereabouts by turning his PDA back on. He figured Riggins had told Carlyle about the Chinese cargo vessel docked at Jebel Ali. Also, there was a good chance that Carlyle was close by during the explosion. And if that were the case, Xavier suspected the former Marine sniper would be investigating the scene. Therefore, to locate him, Xavier would stake out the dock where the vessel had gone down.

It didn't take long for Xavier to realize that finding Carlyle near the explosion site wouldn't be easy. As he approached the area, the blaring alarms from the industrial complex grew deafeningly loud. He parked his rental car behind a nearby vacant building and grabbed the binoculars from his duffle bag along with some other miscellaneous items including a small flashlight and a lighter and stuffed them in his zippered pants pocket.

Almost forty-eight hours had passed since the cargo vessel had ignited. Since that time, hoards of onlookers, the worldwide press corps, and INA investigators had been swarming the area. Active vestiges of the incident were still apparent. Black smoke continued to pour from the vessel's burned-out hull. The water around the site was covered in a thick, greasy film of crude oil. Crews from various response units, including the nearby industrial complex, had secured containment booms around the sunken vessel.

As Xavier surveyed the area from atop a vacant building, it occurred to him that all the activity and attention were a welcomed event for Zangshe. What better way for them to advertise to the world the devastating potential of their threats—although, officially, the explosion was still being called an unfortunate accident. Pending the completion of a full investigation by the INA, which might take months, Zangshe could take complete advantage of the situation. He grudgingly admitted to himself that it was a brilliant strategy with very few flaws.

Through his powerful tactical binoculars, Xavier could clearly make out the individuals in the small crowd that had gathered near the police line at the entrance to the crippled vessel's dock. He watched as a tall, powerfully built man presented his credentials to the officers and was quickly granted access to the area near the vessel. Xavier refocused his binoculars on the man and noticed a peculiar long purple scar running from his ear down the length of his jaw.

Xavier watched the man walk slowly along the dock, carefully studying the wreckage. Twenty minutes later, he crossed back over the police line, nodding his appreciation to the officers, and strode off to an awaiting Humvee. Whoever the man was, Xavier noted that he didn't appear to be connected to the formal investigation. In fact, Xavier had seen this type of behavior many times when he was an operative. The man's demeanor and efficiency clearly marked him as a high-security special agent of some kind.

Xavier turned his attention to the nearby industrial complex where workers were spread out over the extensive network of piping and pump stations. They were working feverishly to shut off valves and divert the action of the huge pumps.

After two hours of surveillance, Xavier thought about moving closer to the scene. But he knew the danger in doing so. By now, no doubt the Agency had dispatched agents to the scene to assess the situation. If Riggins had knowledge of Carlyle's whereabouts, it was more than likely that the Agency did too.

As he was about to move from his perch, Xavier noticed the arrival of a small car a block from the industrial complex. Two nondescript men wearing plain khakis and ball caps exited the car quickly and moved deftly toward the complex. His attention was riveted on their movements, which were too well practiced to be those of the average gawker. The men proceeded swiftly through the cover of the back-streets, observing everything around them. Once they reached an open area, however, they adopted a more casual pace and attempted to blend into the locale. *These guys have had training of some sort,* Xavier noted to himself. As he watched a little closer, he realized that there was something familiar about one of them . . . *Hmmm. That measured gait. . . .*

Xavier refocused his binoculars. He could only see the backs of their heads. One of the men was carrying a side arm. He had a thinner, lankier body than the other man and seemed to know where he was going. His partner, who appeared somewhat older, had a sat-phone in his hand, and as he surveyed his surroundings, his head moved efficiently from side to side. When they were within several hundred feet of the industrial complex, the younger man stopped and pointed to something ahead. Xavier saw that it was an access gate at the rear of the complex. The two men began to move forward slowly.

Xavier was watching them so intently that the sound of an approaching helicopter overhead startled him. He swung his binoculars in the chopper's direction. Arabic lettering on the chopper's side and a cameraman hanging from the passenger's position clearly indicated that it belonged to the local news station. Xavier swung his binoculars back down toward the men, who had quickly glanced up at the chopper. He could finally see their faces. He felt a surge of relief when he saw that one of the men was Carlyle.

The chopper continued to hover about fifty feet off the ground. Apparently having assessed that it was no danger to him, Carlyle continued on through the access gate toward the complex. Xavier watched as the agent directed his younger partner to remain in position while he headed for the large pumping station. Arriving there, he went in. A few minutes later, the agent emerged, and both men hurried back through the access gate toward their awaiting car.

Xavier kept his binoculars sighted on Carlyle and his partner as they got into their car and headed slowly toward Dubai City. He knew that once they were back in the city, he would have little opportunity to locate Carlyle. He tried to focus ahead of them to determine their route, but Carlyle had opted to stay on the local roads, which weaved back and forth. Just when Xavier thought he'd lost them, the car stopped in an alley next to a mid-rise apartment building. The two men got out of the car and entered the building.

Xavier could hardly believe his luck. He memorized the location of the apartment building and headed for his own car. It only took about five minutes to reach the building. Carlyle's car was still in the alley, and Xavier parked behind it. He looked around, then walked slowly to the front of the building. The door was open. As he stepped through, a hand grabbed his shoulder from behind.

"Hello, Doc. Good to see you," Carlyle said cheerfully, turning him around by the shoulders. "Saw you pull up. I was going to ask how you found us, but then I remembered you're no stranger to this lifestyle. What the hell are you doing here?"

Xavier smiled. "Couldn't leave you alone for too long, Harry. You might find trouble."

"Well, you're way too late . . . trouble's already found me."

"I heard. You've managed to attract almost everyone's attention back in the States."

"Apparently, here as well," Carlyle replied, leading him upstairs. "It's why we moved into this dump from the Marine encampment near Dubai City."

They had reached the top of the stairs. Carlyle knocked twice at a decrepit door in the small alcove and walked in. Inside were the remnants of what had once been a three-bedroom apartment. Now it looked more like a gutted shelter. Seated at an old wooden table in the middle of the main room were two men dressed in well-worn khakis. He could hear the sounds of others in one of the back rooms.

"Hey, Doc, meet some good buddies of mine—Colonel Chauncey Jackson and Staff Sergeant Ducky Petersen," Carlyle said.

The men stood.

"Nice to meet you," said Xavier. "I'm sorry about what happened to your squad in Kuwait."

"You heard?" Jackson asked, reaching out to shake Xavier's hand.

Xavier shook his head and replied solemnly, "I saw it . . . from Harry's office on the sat-link."

"Some very strange shit going on," Jackson said. "Harry and I've been discussing the situation with the Saudis. I understand your company had a contract with them."

"And still does as far as I know. But then again, things are changing quickly."

"Speaking of which," Carlyle said. "I understand from Riggins that you made quite an impression in China."

"I'm afraid not enough to change much. As you've seen here in Jebel Ali, Zangshe has continued to advance their agenda," Xavier said.

"And in a very dramatic way," Carlyle replied. "I guess you know the purpose of that facility next to where their ship exploded? It's going to create a crisis around here for a while."

"Not just around here, Harry, but across most of the Middle East. In fact, according to Riggins, as many as a half-billion people could be affected by Zangshe's actions."

"How's that possible?" Ducky Petersen piped in.

Xavier glanced at all three Marines. "Jebel Ali is the world's largest desalination plant. Its piping network and pumping stations extend throughout the Middle East as far north as Turkey and even to the east into parts of Asia."

58

ANSWERS

Jebel Ali, U.A.E

"It never occurred to me that a desalination plant would be a primary target," Carlyle said, his doubt lingering in the air.

Xavier clarified, "Due to the increasing number of droughts over the past decade, approximately two-thirds of the world's population now relies on desalinated water. Zangshe is using the last of the world's most precious resources as part of its blackmail scheme."

"Harry has briefed us on the arrangement between the Saudis and Zangshe. But how does blowing up one of their own ships near a desalination plant help the Chinese cause?" Ducky asked.

"Leverage. I have a theory that it's all about leverage with them," Xavier said. "Zangshe desperately needs both the space to dump their nuclear waste and the sand for their new encapsulated nuclear fuel. But, I think they realize that their control and occupation of the Saudi desert ports may be tenuous at best. To insure that the West doesn't wake up one day and thwart their efforts, I now believe that they've embarked on a plan that invokes essentially the same principles as in the Cold War—namely brinksmanship. In this case, the weapon is nuclear waste and the targets are water-supply facilities."

"That's very interesting, Doc," Jackson piped in. "But if my history serves correctly, brinksmanship required a certain buildup of weaponry to assure a convincing outcome. How does Zangshe intend to expand their strategy?"

"Their strategy is essentially the same, but it's not identical," Xavier replied. "They've incorporated some wrinkles. By exploding the ship at Jebel Ali, they've already demonstrated their resolve. That explosion was orchestrated to serve as a notice of their intentions; they knew it would be well publicized because of the disastrous consequences. Even the threat of that occurring again somewhere else is a very effective deterrent."

Carlyle smiled despite the bleak report. "I told you the doc was smart," he said to the Marines. "So, do you think there actually may be another one of these cargo vessels out there?" he asked Xavier.

"I was pretty certain that there was another one headed for the desalination plant near Venice. It turned out to be a false alarm. And now the Chinese have filed a complaint contending illegal stoppage and boarding of one of their vessels."

"Son of a bitch," Carlyle said. "The old bait-and-switch routine. Now I bet they'll have carte blanche."

Xavier nodded. "Exactly."

"But the question is, carte blanche to do what?" Carlyle asked, somewhat rhetorically.

"That's a good question. I haven't pieced all that together yet. I was hoping I'd find some answers by coming here," Xavier replied.

"How's that?" Jackson asked.

"Harry told me a story about a king and his sorcerer," Xavier said, winking at Carlyle.

"Yeah, Harry's good at telling stories," Jackson said. "But how does that relate to what's going on with the Chinese?"

"Well, it took me a while to figure some things out. Initially when Harry told me his tale, he had envisioned QPR as the sorcerer, the maker of magic potions . . . the nuclear-hybrid discovery. In Harry's story, once the king possessed the magic potion, his power would be restored. But one of the king's enemies had stolen the potion. Only the sorcerer knew of its whereabouts and how to get it back. And so, he became who the king's enemies feared the most. But it wasn't until Harry's techie, Riggins, pointed something out to me that it all made sense."

"I almost can't wait for this," Carlyle said, sitting down on one of the rickety chairs.

"When I was in Quebec City recently trying to stay off the radar," continued Xavier, "something happened that got me thinking. I thought that the Agency had found me. But it was actually the Chinese. I thought they intended to kill me, but now I realize that their intent was to restrain me. I didn't put it together until I recalled what Riggins had said about Harry."

"And you're about to share that with my best friends," Carlyle said half-jokingly.

Xavier smirked. "You might be surprised, Harry. According to Riggins, among your many attributes are patriotism and extreme loyalty. And you knew something was not right about the situation and were determined to fix it."

"Sounds like the guy we all know and love," Ducky chuckled.

Carlyle smiled sheepishly. "Ah . . . cut the shit. Okay, Doc, tell me, how does what you're saying square with the message in my story?"

Xavier moved toward Carlyle. "Who knows the situation best? Both the king and his enemies. And who has the knowledge of vital information?"

"I'm not sure I'm following you, Doc," Carlyle said hesitantly.

"I think you are, Harry. You said yourself that you had attracted the attention of almost everyone. You knew something was not right in the kingdom from the very beginning. And the enemies of the king are concerned that if certain things are revealed, the king might return to power," Xavier said, keeping his eyes on Carlyle. "*You* have the vital information, Harry, and the information is the magic potion—the potion that can restore the king's power. And the king's enemies are not about to let that happen. It's why they came after me—to find you. In the words of our beloved techie, 'There are folks of extreme prejudice who are aware of your intent.'"

"You've twisted my story a bit, Doc," Carlyle replied with a wry smile.

Xavier chortled. "That's the thing about fables, Harry; there are many interpretations. In my version, the king isn't in Saudi Arabia but in the U.S., and the sorcerer isn't QPR, but you!"

59

TARGET

Jebel Ali, U.A.E.

"You came all this way to tell me that, Doc?" Carlyle asked with some incredulity. "Hell, I'm the least important person in this scenario. Besides, I don't believe that anyone wants to hear what I have to say. I'm a nonfactor in the equation, as you might say."

"You're mistaken, Harry," said Xavier. "You're the only one who can connect the dots. It's why they've tried to isolate you. And you have little to lose. That makes you plenty dangerous to them."

"I think Doc's got something there, Harry," Jackson added. "That's exactly why someone wants you out of the way. You don't give a shit what anyone says. You're the type who can topple empires because you don't care much about your own well-being—that, and you are so dammed self-righteous. I hate to say this ol' buddy, but putting you out of commission sounds more and more like a simple solution for the bad guys."

Carlyle got up from his seat with his back to the men. He slowly turned around to face them. With a grin, he said, "Alright, so how do we make that work for us?"

"The first thing we need to do is to somehow convince the *king* he's in danger," Xavier said. "And based upon everything we know, that won't be easy. Although the agreement between the U.S. and Saudi Arabia has compromised our security, it appears to be mutually beneficial. The Chinese are double-dealing the Saudis who are too desperate to admit it. And someone in the White House has painted all this with a skillful brush."

Carlyle frowned. "Interesting you say that. It tracks somewhat with what Princess Almira had alluded to. Maybe the president doesn't know all the details."

"I know the president," Jackson said. "He's a former general, and there's no way he'd sell out the U.S."

"And there's no way that he could possibly know the full implications of what Zangshe has in mind," Xavier said.

"Do you, Doc?" Carlyle asked warily.

"More than I did before, Harry. And certainly as it relates to the hybrid issue, I do. If Zangshe's still capable of replicating the QPR technology, the Chinese must think that they have all the leverage they need."

"How does that technology you referenced provide the Chinese with such leverage?" Jackson asked.

"Zangshe, in concert with the Saudis, has already developed a solution for encapsulating depleted uranium into an alternative fuel source to replace oil," Xavier replied. "However, that technology would be relatively easy for the U.S. to adopt over time. That's why Zangshe is moving so quickly to control market share. But to control market share they need something else—a trump card."

"And you're saying that trump card is the hybrid technology?" Jackson asked.

"Not simply the technology but the willingness to use it," Xavier explained. "Eventually, the notion of sending vessels laden with nuclear waste as a deterrent becomes less effective. I'm convinced that their intentions are to develop some sort of nuclear device that will serve like a sword of Damocles."

"Like one of the old nuclear ICBMs," Carlyle piped in.

"Similar in concept but with a much more elegant delivery methodology," added Xavier. "The hybrid device would not need a missile system—or for that matter, any complex fusing mechanism."

The three Marines exchanged confused looks. "If it doesn't need a missile platform or some type of fuse, how would the Chinese intend to deploy and activate it?" Carlyle asked.

Xavier frowned. "That's another very troublesome aspect of a hybrid-nuclear device. It can be placed inside almost anything."

"So it could easily be carried," Carlyle concluded.

"Or even mailed," Xavier added.

"If it's that compact, what kind of explosive power and damage could be expected?" Jackson asked.

Xavier paused for a moment, then responded, "I believe that once activated, the hybrid has the potential to create devastation beyond anything we've ever seen. It absorbs all surrounding energy and releases it once it reaches its critical mass. At that point, the chain reaction is similar to a series of nuclear blasts. In effect, the hybrid has the ability to continue absorbing energy until its effective critical mass become negligible."

"If I understand what you've said, it sounds like some type of rechargeable nuclear device," Jackson said, looking for confirmation.

Xavier nodded slowly. "Pretty much, Colonel."

"And I'm almost hesitant to ask how the device is activated, Doc," Carlyle said, moving away from the window and turning toward Xavier.

"I'm not exactly certain. But based on some data I saw recently, it's very unstable and it doesn't take much to activate. Even exposure to oxygen can do it."

"You mean simply exposing it to the—" Ducky began, but his voice was choked away.

An instant later, the men realized that a sniper's bullet had pierced the Marine's throat.

60

OPTIONS

Riyadh, Saudi Arabia

At the still-opulent Sandool headquarters, Princess Almira bin Razul was busily assessing her options. She had come to the realization that Zangshe did not intend to partner with her for the production of the encapsulated fuel. Without that agreement, her slowly dying country would surely perish. She had confirmed Agent Carlyle's information regarding Zangshe's invasive use of her kingdom's port cities. But there was little she could do to resist the actions of the mercenaries. Her fate as well as that of her country would depend on what she did next. And she was determined not to fail as her father and brother had before her.

"Mr. Chairman, I appreciate your taking my call," said Almira. "There is a matter of utmost importance that I would like to discuss."

"Of importance to whom?" Khan asked dismissively.

"I believe to both of us," the princess replied.

"Our business has been concluded. Your contract for the encapsulation was satisfied. What else would matter to me?"

"The future of your plans, Mr. Chairman."

Khan huffed. "You have nothing of significance to say or to do with my plans," he replied brusquely.

"But someone else in a position of some influence might," Almira said very resolutely.

Khan paused. "And you have specific knowledge of this person?"

Sensing that she had gained some advantage, the princess replied in a measured tone, "I have recently spoken with him and can assure you that he knows of things that could prove very troublesome to you."

"There is little, if anything, that could be done to stop what I have put into motion," Khan said arrogantly. "Your attempt to bargain with me is futile." He let out a snort, then added, "As is your fate and that of your make-believe kingdom."

The princess quelled her feeling of surging rage. "I would not be so quick to dismiss my information, Mr. Chairman," she said with controlled calm. "I have heard the reports of the recent *accident* at your research facility. I do not believe that what happened there was a mere twist of fate or that certain vital information I have is unrelated."

The line went quiet for a moment before Khan replied, "What is it that you are proposing?"

61

SACRIFICE

Riyadh, Saudi Arabia

"I want to be certain that I understand your strategy, Your Royal Highness," said Hakim Khalid, the Saudi director of intelligence.

"My orders were quite specific, Hakim," Princess Almira replied firmly.

"They were indeed, Your Highness. It is only that they are so at odds with our current policy that I felt it important to clarify," the man responded.

"What is your confusion, Hakim?" she asked with impatience.

Hakim hesitated, then said, "The target has been a friend of our country for a long time. I remember how fondly your father spoke of him."

The princess stood up from her desk and spoke with cold authority, "My father is no longer here. And things have changed greatly. The *target* knows too much information about us and our arrangements with his agency. He can present many problems. Besides, the information we have about him and others has been bartered for the future of our country. I had little choice but to make the bargain."

Hakim's hesitation wasn't lost on the princess, her ire rising, as he said, "Begging your indulgence, Your Highness, is there not another way of dealing with this matter? I know him well. He is a man of good reason. He may listen to me."

The princess walked to the door of her office, her hand on the doorknob. "If you cannot follow my wishes in this regard, you must step aside, Hakim. Otherwise, I expect you will send your most reliable person to assist in the positive identification—that must be someone who knows him."

She raised one eyebrow to indicate that she was awaiting his decision.

He let out a deep sigh, and responded, "I will do as you have requested, Your Highness. But I do not trust the Chinese. How do we know they will honor their end of the bargain?"

"We do not, Hakim. But without it, we have nothing to hope for."

Hakim shook his head. "If you will pardon my saying so, Your Highness, this is a fool's bargain with the life of a good friend."

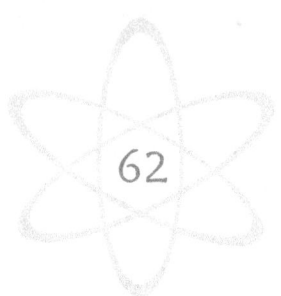

62

FRIEND

Jebel Ali, U.A.E.

With horror and disbelief, Jackson and Carlyle watched their friend crumple to the floor, blood spurting from the gaping hole in his throat. The death rattle of air from Ducky's fatal wound sounded his final breaths. Seconds later, a hail of bullets from the sniper's rifle sent all of the men scrambling for cover.

Xavier quickly glanced over at Carlyle crouched low next to Ducky's body. "Nothing more you can do for him, Harry. We need to get out of here. Those rounds are going through these walls like butter," he urged.

Carlyle nodded slowly and began to rise.

"Only one place to go," Jackson replied, pointing upwards. "Grab Ducky's rifle, Harry, and let's move."

The three men bolted for the door. The first grenade hit the center of the rear bedroom, instantly killing the three Marines there. The second one followed in rapid succession and exploded directly behind Jackson. The force of the blast violently catapulted Carlyle into Xavier, sending the pair crashing through the door and into the hallway.

Stunned but otherwise unharmed, Xavier crawled over to Carlyle, who was laying motionless a few feet away. He was unconscious but still breathing. Looking back, Xavier saw the room they'd previously occupied engulfed in flames. Jackson hadn't made it out, and all that was left of him was his upper body sticking partially into the hall. Xavier knew he had to move. A reconnaissance crew would be following shortly.

He staggered to his feet, dragging Carlyle out of the alcove and across the hall into another room. Making a split-second decision, he hoisted the agent over his shoulder, grabbed Ducky's rifle, and headed for the stairs to the roof.

If the carnage below wasn't convincing enough and the attackers came searching for survivors, he would have a far better vantage point from the rooftop. And it would also allow him to surveil the surrounding buildings. However, getting to the fifth floor was no easy effort. His legs were wobbly from the grenade's concussion, and Carlyle's dead weight was taxing. He was relieved to find the door to the roof unlocked. He placed Carlyle near the edge of the parapet. Looking through the rifle sight, he scanned in the general direction of the sniper shots. He soon spotted the assailants.

On the opposite rooftop, one story below Xavier's position, the gunmen peered through binoculars from behind some air-venting equipment. Obviously in no hurry, they appeared to be making certain that all targets were incapacitated. They were both dressed in traditional Arabian garments with their heads covered by turbans. Seemingly satisfied that they could detect no movement in the room, the assailants turned toward the roof access door directly behind them; the spot was just out of Xavier's range.

He sighted his rifle on the door in the front of the building. He knew they would come across the street. The door opened slowly, but only one man stepped outside. It was then that Xavier saw it—a long purplish scar running down the length of the man's jaw. Unmistakably, it was the same man he had seen earlier in the day at the docks.

Xavier didn't hesitate. He gently squeezed the trigger of Ducky's sniper rifle. The bullet struck the assailant in the chest, knocking him backward into the building. Xavier tried to see into the doorway but couldn't get an angle. He looked over at Carlyle, who was beginning to stir.

"Harry, can you hear me?"

"Yeah . . . but just barely. It feels like I'm inside a bell tower," Carlyle replied, trying to raise himself up on his elbows.

"Take it easy, Harry. You've probably got a concussion. Just stay put while I check out what's going on. And I might take this as well," Xavier said, shoving Carlyle's hunting knife in his belt as he headed for the roof-access door. .

Carlyle indicated to him that he would be all right, and Xavier headed downstairs to find the second assailant.

The lower door was wide open, and he could see into the opposite building. *Nobody.* He walked across the street, carefully watching all around him, and moved toward the open door. *No blood.* As stealthily as possible, he moved through the doorway and down a narrow corridor, where a faint trail of blood became apparent. *The assailant must have worn a bulletproof vest,* he noted to himself. Even so, the powerful projectile from the sniper rifle would have surely passed through the vest. It was not a clean-kill shot. The man with the scar was wounded, maybe mortally and possibly still alive. *But where was the second assailant?* he asked himself.

Xavier heard the shuffle of feet ahead of him. He grasped for the long hunting knife tucked in his belt. The corridor ran from the front of the building to the rear with apartments off each side. In the dim lighting, he could barely make out a lone figure hunched over and struggling toward the rear exit. Xavier hurried down the corridor. Ready to swing his rifle into action, he watched as the tall man reached the rear door. With a burst of waning strength, the man pushed the door wide open and fell outside onto his face.

Xavier reached the opened door and quickly scanned outside for the other gunman. Seeing none, he was quickly on the fallen one. The man had no weapon and offered no resistance. Xavier turned him over with the butt of his rifle. Blood hemorrhaged from his mouth and nose. His tunic was torn, revealing a penetrating hole in the vest. The hole was large enough for Xavier to see clearly through to the entry point in the center of the man's chest, where it was deeply lodged immediately above his heart.

Eyes wide open and glazed over, the man wheezed and gasped for air, as he motioned for Xavier to come closer.

Xavier leaned in.

"Is Harry dead?" the man gurgled.

The question took Xavier by surprise, and he answered honestly. "He'll be okay."

"Good," replied the dying man. "Harry is a friend. Tell him, tell him that I am sorry." He coughed and blood spurted from his mouth, but he managed to continue, "I was trying to warn him. I killed the two snipers when they came down from the roof." He was fading fast. "Others will come." He let out a final grunt and then was gone.

63

DISCLOSURE

Langley, Virginia

Furiously trying to block the hacker's attempts to invade his domain, Riggins's agitation was growing. Everything he threw at the hacker was repelled and countered. In another setting, Riggins would have admired the intruder—even applauded him. But this was a life-or-death struggle. Whoever was involved meant serious harm to him and everyone around him. Over the past few days, he had found tracking cookies on every communiqué he had sent and received. The Agency had turned against Carlyle and would stop at nothing to find or eliminate him. But for Riggins, exposure was not an option. He had to evade the slowly tightening net. With yet another lightning-quick reaction, he decided on another tack.

"Director Cheskin, there's a call for you on line one."

"Who is it?" Cheskin barked.

"The party won't identify himself. But says it's a matter of national security. I have someone running a trace on the line now," the Marine staff sergeant replied.

Cheskin waited a few moments before answering. "This is Director Cheskin. How can I help you?"

"You're chasing after the wrong person," Riggins said, his normal grating tone distorted by a voice changer. "Agent Carlyle isn't the only one who knows the facts. There are others who are prepared to disclose the nature of recent agreements that intend to harm this country."

"Who are you? And what do you know about Agent Carlyle's information?"

"It doesn't matter who I am. Suffice to say, I'm aware of the Saudi's involvement with the Chinese and the U.S. attempts to foster an arrangement involving the transfer of proprietary technology to our enemies," Riggins replied.

"That's preposterous! But it's apparent you were able to gain access into our systems. It's a Federal offense to trespass as such. I can assure you that we *will* find and prosecute you to the fullest extent."

"I have proof of my assertions and am prepared to go to the press with it."

Cheskin paused. "What is it you want?"

"A meeting with you, and you alone."

"Where and when?"

"I'll contact you soon," Riggins said, hanging up.

"Did you get the trace?" Cheskin asked.

"We got something, but it doesn't make sense," the staff sergeant replied.

"Where did the call come from?"

"The International Space Station!"

64

IRONY

Jebel Ali, U.A.E.

Once he had returned to the rooftop, Xavier was relieved to see that Carlyle was fully alert. His eyes appeared clear, and he suspected that his friend had suffered only a mild concussion.

"We have to move and fast," he said, helping the agent to his feet.

"What about Jackson?" Carlyle asked, steadying himself against the door.

Xavier lowered his eyes and shook his head solemnly. He knew that the bond between soldiers was very tight and that Carlyle would take the news hard.

"Goddamnit," the agent spat out. "Goddamnit."

"I'm sorry, Harry." He paused a moment, then added, "There's been another death. I shot who I thought was one of the snipers. He told me that he was your friend, just before he died."

"What the hell?! Who was he?"

"I don't know. He had a scar, a long purple scar running along his jaw line."

Carlyle almost tripped in his effort to face Xavier. "Hakim? It can't be. Why would he be involved?"

"He said he had no choice and had come to warn you. He killed the assailants. Who was he?"

"Head of security for Princess Almira bin Razul and a very good friend," Carlyle replied remorsefully.

"He said others would be coming. We need to get invisible and let you recover a bit," Xavier said, as the pair began making their way carefully down the stairs.

"I'll be fine, Doc," Carlyle said, letting go of Xavier and finding his own footing. "And we don't have time to hide. Apparently Princess Almira thinks I'm a serious threat to her. I've underestimated her cunning."

"And her desperation," Xavier added, as the pair emerged onto the street. He pointed in the direction of his car. "You've seen the state of things over here. The future of her country rests on making some sort of deal, and most likely it's with the Chinese. Like I said, you're the one who can connect the dots. We have to find a way to make that work."

"Got any bright ideas?" Carlyle asked.

The men stayed close to the buildings as they made their way to Xavier's car.

"I've been thinking about that. You need to reach out to Director Cheskin. You said you've known him to be a standup guy," Xavier replied.

Carlyle shook his head. "He's so entrenched in the system that he can't see the forest. I don't think he'll listen to what I have to say."

"I don't think you have a choice. You can't keep running from everyone. Eventually someone *will* catch up with you."

"How do I convince him that our country's on the wrong track?" Carlyle asked.

"Tell him something he doesn't know. Tell him about the hybrid technology and its potential. If he has any spark of Agency responsibility left, the consequences of that technology ending up in someone else's hands should make for a compelling conversation."

"I'm not qualified to explain the details, Doc. You should come."

"I've got a better idea. Take Riggins. He knows enough to be credible."

"At least brief Riggins with me. Your insights would be helpful and he respects you," Carlyle said.

"I was telling the truth before, Harry. Riggins has real feelings for you. What I mean is . . . he thinks you're one of the good guys. But I'd be happy to talk with him."

Carlyle cracked a little smile. "Ironic, isn't it? Turns out Riggins may be one of my only real friends left."

"Count me in as well. But if we don't get out of here, we'll both be minus one friend," Xavier replied, as the pair climbed into his car. "We should have a few hours head start."

∞

A few blocks away on the rooftop of another building, two more pairs of eyes followed Xavier's rental car as it headed away from the port town and back toward Dubai City.

"This scientist continues to be more resourceful than I had thought," Yakubla muttered in anger at the leader of his assassin team. "You have failed me and our great chairman."

The assassin team leader looked sheepishly down. "My men were very thorough, Taiji. The man called Hakim conspired against us."

Yakubla pointed forcefully in the direction of Xavier's moving car. "I will give you one final chance to kill them both and leave no mistake as to who is responsible," he grunted.

65

STANDOFF

U.S. Embassy, Dubai City

Xavier stopped the rental car around the corner from the old U.S. embassy building, which Carlyle had suggested would be a good place to take refuge for a while. Abandoned almost a decade earlier once the United States' strategic interests in the region had vanished, the complex was in disrepair.

Having visited the embassy several times during his tour with the Agency, Carlyle was somewhat familiar with the building's layout

"This place is built like a bunker," he said, scanning the spacious lobby. "It also served as a safe house for Arab royalty in the event of a terrorist uprising. The com center is located in the basement, but I'm betting most of the equipment was either removed or stolen over the years."

"Let's take a look downstairs anyway," Xavier said. "Maybe there's something they left behind that we can use to contact Riggins."

"Doesn't hurt to have a look," Carlyle agreed, leading the way through a door adjacent to the elevator.

The light in the stairwell was almost nonexistent, but Xavier could still see that the walls had been made with poured concrete rather than concrete block and were probably steel-reinforced. He wouldn't be able to get a clear signal in the basement, so even if he found what he needed, they'd have to return to the lobby or maybe even head up to the roof to get a signal. He pulled a flashlight out of his pocket that he'd stashed there earlier and handed it to Carlyle. The men proceed slowly down the concrete stairs following the narrow beam of light. At the bottom, Carlyle scanned the room with the light. Amid the shadows, Xavier saw what appeared to be old equipment racking lining the perimeter of the walls; it was empty. Carlyle pointed the tiny light farther into the room. There was another smaller area off to one side.

"That's where the server room was located," Carlyle said, walking toward a closed door.

As he opened the door, both men recoiled from the overwhelming stench of decomposing bodies.

"Shit," Carlyle said, trying to cover his nose. "What the hell—"

At the end of the narrow beam of light were two bodies lying in a heap face down. Xavier and Carlyle reluctantly moved closer to inspect.

Carlyle rolled one of the decomposing bodies over with his foot. "Son of a bitch! I know this guy," he said with alarm. "They're agents!"

"They've been gutted," Xavier said, wanting to look away from the grotesque image in front of him. He assessed that both men had been sliced open from the lower ribcage to the pelvis, exposing their entrails.

"Mujahedin," Carlyle said.

"I don't think so," Xavier replied slowly, as he looked at the wounds more carefully. These cuts were made by daggers. The mujahedin are more ritualistic in their killings and tend to behead their victims. Their weapon of choice is usually the sword. No, I think this is the handiwork of someone else," he continued, as he bent down to take a scrap of cloth from one of the dead men's hands.

"Who then, Doc?" Carlyle asked, as Xavier pried the fingers away.

He didn't respond right away. Turning the bloodied remnant of cloth over in his hand, he finally looked up at Carlyle, who hadn't yet torn his gaze away from the mutilated bodies. "This is part of a uniform, Harry. The agent must have grabbed it in the struggle. It confirms my suspicion. I recognize part of Zangshe's corporate logo on it. I saw it recently on their security guards and vehicles. The killers were definitely Mongolian."

Shaking his head in lament for his deceased colleagues, Carlyle said, "I guess it's clear why the Agency hasn't caught up with me yet."

"Based on the condition of the bodies, this happened about two or three days ago," Xavier said, looking around the small room.

"About the time of the explosion at Jebel Ali," Carlyle said, bending over to remove the agents' IDs. "Why would the Chinese do this?"

"I think it's partly retaliation, Harry—for what I did in China."

Carlyle stared at Xavier. "What the hell did you do there, Doc?"

"Let's just say that Zangshe's research efforts are off-line for a while."

"How did they make the connection?"

"My cover was blown. When another operative and I attempted to clear security, the Chinese suspected something. They ran a deeper security check. We were fortunate to have been able to complete the mission . . . but . . ."

"But . . . ?" Carlyle asked.

"We weren't both able to get out. The other operative had an inside contact at Zangshe and was connected to one of the ministry departments in the government. She'd arranged for the official visit, but things went bad. We needed to create a distraction to keep them off balance until I could do my thing. She found a way to do that."

"She was killed in the process?"

"No, she sent me a message that she was safe but couldn't escape. There wasn't time to reconsider options."

"Sorry about the operative. A friend?"

"She is . . . and extremely capable. But I can't shake this gnawing feeling I have about leaving her there."

Carlyle nodded understandingly. "I know how you feel. But you know the game and so did she. Same as Jackson and Ducky and the others. There's nothing more you can do now."

"You're right, of course," Xavier said, briefly thinking of Rachel. He pushed her out of his mind as he spotted something in the corner of the small room. "Shine the light over here, Harry."

Carlyle pointed the flashlight in the direction Xavier indicated. Stacked against one of the walls was a pile of equipment. Xavier removed several items from the top, as Carlyle approached to give him more light. Removing the cover from one of the server modules, he reached in and removed a tiny chipboard.

"I think I've found what we need. Let's get out of here," he said, tucking the board into his pocket.

The men moved quickly back up the darkened stairs to the lobby access door. Carlyle stopped in his tracks at the door. "I hear something," he whispered, putting his ear closer to the door. He signaled to Xavier that at least two men were talking in the lobby. He cracked the door open slightly and peered through. "They're splitting off in different directions," Carlyle whispered. "Looks like your Mongolian friends, Doc."

Xavier handed Carlyle the rifle. He kept the hunting knife in his belt. The two men moved cautiously through the door and into the elevator vestibule. Xavier spotted the two Mongolians, armed with automatic weapons. One headed for the rear of the lobby while the other remained slightly hidden near the front entrance door. Xavier recognized it as a classic two-man search pattern: one hunted while the other stayed just out of line of sight but in a controlling position to pick off the prey once flushed out. And Xavier knew it was impossible for him and Carlyle to move without being detected.

He looked over at Carlyle, who nodded in recognition of the situation. They knew they had to risk taking out the lobby guard first and hope that the second Mongolian wouldn't immediately identify their position.

Carlyle put his arm expertly through the rifle sling and tucked the rifle tightly against his shoulder. He sighted the weapon on the guard whose head was barely visible along the side of the large revolving entrance door. The former Marine sniper stood motionless without any hint of breathing. He slowly squeezed the trigger. The echo of the powerful weapon filled the expansive lobby seemingly from all directions. The top of the Mongolian's head exploded, sending shards of bone and brain tissue through the plate glass door that shattered behind him.

Xavier looked toward the rear of the lobby, hoping to see the second guard. There was no movement. Minutes felt like hours as they held their ground. *The Mongolian's smart,* he thought. *He's expecting us to make a break for the door.* He glanced at Carlyle. They both knew it was a Mexican standoff. The first one to move was dead.

66

PAYMENT

Port Ad Damman, Saudi Arabia

The mercenaries were in disarray after the death of their commander. Yakubla convened a meeting with them to try to quell the rising distrust. Every one of the sectional leaders had been requested to attend the meeting, which was held inside one of the recently constructed nuclear-waste storage facilities.

"You say our commander died in an accidental explosion," said the scar-faced second in command. "How do we know this to be true?" He made no attempt to camouflage his accusatory tone.

"I say it is true," Yakubla replied stiffly. "After all, some of my own people died in the same accident. What is your meaning?"

"It is no secret that you had differences with our commander. And we are aware of his most recent demand," the commander said. "It appears to us that your answer to his demand lies at the bottom of the waters in Jebel Ali."

Yakubla stared hard at the rugged mercenary. "You have a most vivid imagination. But I have no further need of your services. Final payment for your men has been arranged. You will find the amount very generous."

The new commander eyed Yakubla carefully. "Since we have no relationship with the current regime in Iran, we have no interest in your new technology. However, our knowledge of your intentions here must be quite valuable."

Yakubla remained stone-faced. In response to a slight gesture of his hand, the large bay doors to the facility began to close. Armed Mongolian guards wearing gas masks entered from the rear. Yakubla calmly stepped backward and out through an access door behind him.

The mercenaries reacted immediately when they heard the closing of the gear-driven bay doors. They rushed wildly for the large exit bays as canisters of gas were dispersed into the large concrete room. Within a matter of moments, the mujahedin began clutching at their throats and collapsed on top of each other in heaps. Those not overcome by the gas were swiftly mowed down by the Mongolian guards brandishing automatic weapons. The entire contingent of nearly one hundred of the mujahedin leaders lay exterminated across the rough concrete floor of the waste disposal vault.

Outside the facility, Yakubla sported a satisfied grin as he contacted Khan on his sat-phone.

"Great One," he said when the chairman answered, "things go well here. The construction of the facilities is complete. We are in readiness for the production process to commence. We are also rid of the infidels. Our guards have replaced the leaders in each of the permanent military compounds, and we have wrested control over the remaining mercenary forces."

"I am pleased with your progress, Yaku," Khan said with subdued enthusiasm. "But I have need of your services here. While your men pursue the ones responsible for the damage to our research facility, we are pursued by the minister of technology. He wishes to see our operations halted."

"I will leave immediately, Great One," Yakubla said without hesitation. "I have the utmost confidence that we will find those responsible for the bombing of our facility. As for the minister, his time in office will soon come to an end. We must exploit his weaknesses."

"In that regard," Khan replied, "we may have a very fortuitous circumstance. His senior aide played an important role in the deception that led to the destruction of our laboratory."

"Even better, Great One. If we can extract information from such a source, we can more easily facilitate the minister's demise. I will make it my first priority to arrange for the detainment of the aide."

"That will not be necessary, Yaku. She is here in our custody, and we will soon discover what she knows."

67

TRAPPED

U.S. Embassy, Dubai City

Ten minutes had passed in the elevator vestibule. Xavier and Carlyle had remained crouched inside. The remaining Mongolian guard had made no attempt to disclose his location.

"There may be another way out of here," Carlyle whispered. "If memory serves correctly, there's an escape tunnel in the basement leading out to a side street." He motioned for Xavier to follow him.

They quietly slipped back down the stairs into the darkness of the lower level. Carlyle groped along the sidewall of the basement, looking for the access. The beam from the tiny flashlight reflected against the contours of stark concrete walls until a different sheen appeared—that of a metal door. Carlyle pushed against it, and the heavy door creaked open. The smell of stagnate air rushed to them.

"It's a short distance to the street level from here," Carlyle said as he hunched over to navigate the small tunnel.

Xavier followed closely behind, wondering as they traveled if the door at the other end was operable. Once they reached a set of short stairs, Xavier looked up to see what appeared to be a storm-cellar door with a bracing bar across it.

Carlyle tried the door, but it didn't budge. "Probably rusted solid," he muttered, looking around for something to jar it loose.

"Try this," Xavier said, handing him the knife he'd been carrying.

Carlyle pried it under the bar and applied steady pressure. The bar held fast. Just as he was ready to give up, there was a slight movement, and Xavier joined in the effort to twist it free. They pushed against it in an upward motion with their combined strength until the door flew open with a loud clang as it collapsed down against the outside metal framing.

The sunlight almost blinded them. It took a few moments to get their bearings.

Carlyle looked both ways down the street as he stepped up to the top stair. "It's clear," he said.

As Xavier started up the stairs, he heard a shot and watched helplessly as Carlyle went down. He cursed himself for not assuming the Mongolians would cover the exits.

"Harry, can you hear me?" Xavier asked, crouching back down under the cellar's door. He waited. There was no answer.

Xavier evaluated his situation. The shooter was surely in radio contact with the guard inside. Once the guard was aware of the situation, it would take him only minutes to find his way through the tunnel. Xavier knew they were trapped.

Peering out, he could barely see the building directly across the street, but judging by the direction of Carlyle's fall, the shooter was located on the roof of that building. Xavier knew that if he stayed put, he was a sitting duck—or a duck in a shooting gallery if he bolted from the cellar. He chose the latter, since dying in a dark, remote cellar would be much more ignominious.

When he heard the tapping of feet behind him, he realized that the guard was in the tunnel. It was now or never. His heart began to pound and adrenaline coursed wildly through his veins. Running laterally along the embassy building would make him an easy target, he knew, so he planned to run in a zigzag pattern toward the shooter's building.

But getting clear of the cellar would be the hardest part. With any luck, he might only get winged on his way across. He bolted out from under the cover of the cellar door and rolled into the sunlight. He spotted Carlyle's motionless body. He felt a momentary twinge of sorrow, but he quickly reengaged his self-preservation mode and scrambled to his feet.

Racing furiously toward the building, Xavier made himself as difficult a target as he could by dodging left and right. Once he was within a few feet of it, he hurled himself forward and braced for the impact. Just before his body smacked hard against the front of the building, a single shot rang out.

68

ESCAPE

R iggins was still located deep within his bunker beneath the CIA headquarters when he found a way to reconnect into Zangshe's network. After the virus had spread like a poisonous serpent throughout their data systems, the Chinese had established an alternate communication center. They were still in recovery mode and trying to restore some of their lost data when Riggins saw something startling on his screen. It was a report from the Chinese research scientist who had worked on the hybrid technology. The report indicated a successful replication of the original experiment. There was a description of and a timetable for the first actual use of the replicated hybrid. Riggins was certain that this was the game changer they had all feared, and he became determined to get a message to Xavier and Carlyle.

Although the continuing onslaught of sophisticated tracking cookies from the hacker had dissipated over the past few days, Riggins was still very concerned. He wondered if they'd found his basement domain. He double-checked his communication links: everything appeared normal. There were no obvious indications of the hacker's presence anywhere. Was it a coincidence that it had all stopped after his call to the director?

The answer to that question came swiftly and without warning.

The big screen in front of him was alive with activity. The secretary of state announced a federal mandate to pursue energy alternatives with several offshore investment companies. Some of the companies had already proposed resurrected solutions for the ongoing crisis to replace fossils fuels, including wind-driven turbines and solar and coal-fired power generation stations. Under the new mandate, the United States government authorized the dismantling of all regulation codes that restricted monopolistic dealings. It was a clear indication from the White House that whatever solution or solutions rose to the level of practicality, they would be permitted—or more appropriately stated, encouraged—regardless of their impact on the principles of open and free competition.

Is it an ominous sign of desperation or deception? Riggins wondered. *Maybe the White House is trying to get out in front of the leaks that are about to happen. An interesting tactic in which to announce negotiations with the Chinese. And one that might minimize my threat to the CIA director.*

As he pondered the implications, Riggins heard loud voices and boxes being thrown aside outside his locked storage gate. Looking up at his monitors, he confirmed its cause. He was about to crash his systems when he was startled by an image on the big screen.

But he was out of time. He hit the shutdown button that would permanently power down all of his systems, grabbed his computer tablet, and hurriedly climbed beneath his massive control station toward a section of raised floor panels. Lifting the panels, he quickly dropped below the floor and scurried through the three-foot-high compartment. When he reached the end, he turned abruptly to his right and continued along the far wall of the basement. Halfway down that portion of the passageway, he stopped and popped open a vertical duct vent.

Riggins grabbed a hold of the rope ladder he had installed inside the duct. Walking his way up the vent with the aide of the rope ladder, he climbed up into the small mechanical room on the first floor. Donning a mechanic's uniform that he had tucked neatly away up inside one of the dropped ceiling tiles, he attached his forged credentials, put on a baseball cap, and casually walked out the front door.

Getting caught once was enough. Riggins had learned that access into the CIA headquarters was extremely difficult. Exiting was far less involved, especially for temporary service personnel.

69

GOOD-BYE

Dubai City, U.A.E.

The impact of pummeling against the building's edifice knocked Xavier's breath away. He lay sprawled in a heap for a few interminable moments. When he finally caught his breath, he couldn't believe that he hadn't been shot. He looked back across the street surprised to see Carlyle still flat on his back but holding up his rifle.

From his knees, Xavier nodded toward the cellar. The guard in the tunnel must have stopped short of coming up when he'd heard the shot. Carlyle saw the signal and quickly got to his feet. The former Marine sniper waited patiently behind the closed cellar door.

When the Mongolian spotted Xavier across the street, he emerged to the top step to get a better shot. The butt of Carlyle's rifle caught him squarely in the windpipe, sending him choking as he fell backward down the cellar stairs. Carlyle pointed his rifle at the guard's thrashing body and pulled the trigger.

He turned around and quickly ran across the street toward Xavier. "You okay, Doc?" he asked as he held out his hand to help his friend up. "You looked like a kid crashing his bike into a wall," he added with a laugh.

Xavier grabbed on and rose slowly to his feet. "Thought you were dead, Harry," he said, gasping for air.

"So did he," Carlyle replied, pointing toward the rooftop. "Only way I could get a clear shot off—an old sniper's trick. I knew you wouldn't let yourself get trapped down there. Thanks for the diversion, Doc."

"Were you hit?" Xavier asked.

"Just grazed, nothing serious. But we need to book it out of here. No telling how many more of them are around," Carlyle said.

Xavier steadied himself on Carlyle's arm. "Good to see you alive and kicking. I didn't think it was possible for one shot to take you out."

"A skosh one way or the other and . . . we'd had a much different ending here," Carlyle said.

Xavier nodded. And he knew Carlyle was right: there probably were more Mongolians around. They were a killing team, and news of their failure would only rev up the troops. Xavier knew that he and Carlyle had to get away from this region—and quickly.

"Any thoughts as to where we go next?" he asked.

Carlyle was already on the move. "You were right, Doc. I need to contact Cheskin. He's our only hope at this point. When he learns about the facts surrounding the explosion in Jebel Ali and finds out that two of his agents were slaughtered, he'll be pissed. Hopefully, enough to come to his senses and listen to me. But I've got to do it in person."

"I agree. Riggins had indicated that someone compromised his communications system. No telling who's listening. But where and how do you plan to get with Cheskin?"

"There's only one place I'd feel safe doing it. The problem's getting there. But there's something I've got to do before I see Cheskin."

They reached the end of the street around the corner from the abandoned embassy. Both men looked warily in all directions for any signs of danger. Seeing none, they proceeded to Xavier's car, which they checked thoroughly for tampering. They weren't surprised to find a relatively crude explosive device wired to the ignition. The men quickly and deftly disconnected the appropriate wires, giving each other affirmative nods until the bomb had been successfully defused.

"It's clean," Carlyle said with confidence. "Let's head to the airport."

Xavier agreed, as he started the ignition. "But before you go through security, Harry, you might want to take a look in the mirror. You look like you've been through a war." Xavier was only half joking.

Harry took a peak at himself in the rearview mirror and chuckled, rubbing the several days of growth on his chin. "I'll clean up at the airport. I should probably patch up this scratch on my arm too."

Xavier looked over at Carlyle's blood-soaked shirt and smiled. "Ya think?"

Twenty minutes later, Xavier pulled up to the front of the terminal. It wasn't crowded. Departure flights were infrequent. And making any connections wasn't easy.

"Where to first, Harry?"

"I have some unfinished business to attend to before seeing Director Cheskin."

Xavier started to ask about the unfinished business but thought otherwise. "So this is where it ends . . . huh?"

"Whatever happens, it's been a real pleasure, Doc," Carlyle replied.

"Take care, Harry," Xavier said, extending his hand. "If I can contact Riggins, I'll brief him on your plans to meet with Cheskin and discuss the hybrid situation."

Carlyle smiled and shook Xavier's hand warmly. "You take care yourself. You're still a person of some interest."

"Will do," said Xavier, as he watched Carlyle walk into the terminal. Suddenly, he was overcome with foreboding. Maybe it was the lingering effects of the recent attacks. But there was a sense of finality that had accompanied Xavier's sudden prescience.

70

LECTURE

Dubai City, U.A.E.

There was little question that Dubai wasn't safe for Xavier. He
had given passing consideration to returning to Xiong Xian to
find a way to help Elena. Despite her tendency toward deception, he
felt obligated to her. She had helped him get into Zangshe. After
giving it more careful thought, he finally reconciled himself with the
fact that returning to China was nothing short of suicidal and that if
Elena were still alive, she'd find a way to help herself. She always did.

Sitting in the rental car not far from the airport, he felt as if he were
back where he had started in Quebec City—without a plan. He knew
that events were unfolding rapidly, and it was obvious from the recent
encounters that Zangshe wouldn't allow anything to thwart their
objectives. And it appeared that there was little he could do to change
that outcome. There seemed no chance of escaping the juggernaut the
Chinese had created.

But he had promised Carlyle that he'd communicate with Riggins.
For a man without a plan, it was a good place to start. Reaching inside
his pocket, he was pleased to find the tiny chipboard that he had taken
from the embassy's com-center in one piece after his collision with the

building. He removed the back of his PDA and extracted the network chip. In its place, he carefully slid in the chipboard from the embassy's server. He made some adjustments to accommodate the connection. Essentially, he was attempting to mask his device as the server. Although the GPS signature would show his precise position, it wouldn't identify him as the sender. Hopefully, if anyone were tracking his communications, it would buy him some time and might even keep Riggins out of trouble.

Xavier dialed the contact information Riggins had provided. Within seconds, the routing process had started. Riggins's number began ringing. It rang and rang. He was about to hang up when he heard the familiar voice.

"Who the hell is this?" Riggins answered breathlessly.

It worked! Xavier thought. "Sorry, Mr. Riggins, I needed to cover my tracks a bit."

"It's you," Riggins replied with relief. "No problem, Doctor. I was taken by surprise. The ID was a little strange."

"It's from an older server unit located in Dubai," Xavier said.

"Didn't realize any of that stuff still worked," Riggins replied.

"I'm not sure it does. But at least the network chip did. I swapped it into my PDA."

"Stealthy, Doctor . . . very stealthy. I'm impressed."

"What's your status, Mr. Riggins?"

"Not copasetic at all. My command center was broken into yesterday. I managed to escape out of the facility, and I'm . . ."

"Don't say anything else," Xavier interrupted, "as long as you're safe for now."

"Thanks for that. I'm not used to being on the run and out in the field, so to speak. Whoever the Agency's got hacking is very, very good. I couldn't find a workaround anywhere. And he found me."

"One of Cheskin's people?" Xavier asked.

"I assumed so. After I'd threatened to expose the Saudi agreement with the U.S. and demanded to meet with Cheskin alone, the hacker must've intensified his probes until they came knocking on my door yesterday."

Xavier's sharp intake of breath announced his disbelief. "You said *what* to Cheskin?"

"I thought it might get the heat off Agent Carlyle if I'd indicated that other people already knew the truth about the secret deals."

"Sounds as if your message got through, Mr. Riggins. But I'm not sure it changes anything for Harry. He's still very much a target of opportunity."

"Is he with you?"

"He's not here now. But I can tell you that he's okay and he'll contact you."

"I understand. Just glad to know he's still alright."

"When he calls, he'll want your help with Cheskin. The director needs to understand what's going on with the Chinese."

"That shouldn't be too difficult, if we can get his attention," Riggins replied.

"Leave that to Harry. He's got some new intel about the killings of two of his agent buddies as well the situation in Jebel Ali. That might rattle Cheskin's cage."

Absorbing the news about the agents, Riggins hesitated for a moment. "What's with you, Doctor?"

"Not sure yet. Things seem to be in Agent Carlyle's hands."

There was a pause.

"Excuse me for saying so," Riggins said, "but I think you're copping out. Agent Carlyle doesn't fully appreciate the impact of the hybrid technology . . . you do. And if this thing goes global and it's likely, aren't you going to be really bummed?"

"What are you talking about, Mr. Riggins?" Xavier asked with some annoyance.

"I saw something recently that scares the living shit out of me," Riggins began. "Based on the intel I'd hacked into, that Chinese cargo vessel is headed directly for the U.S . . . to the Port of New Orleans.

And it's not loaded with nuclear waste. The technical memo I saw outlined the results of Zangshe's successful attempt at replication of the hybrid and a description of their intent to test its effectiveness."

Xavier was stunned. He took a moment to process the information. *They've actually replicated it, and it's headed for the U.S.?*

"I guess I'm as disappointed as surprised," he finally said. "I'd hoped that my efforts in China had forestalled that eventuality. But the Chinese have found a way to insure that we won't interfere with their plans. This is the ultimate blackmail scenario. And you've uncovered it, Mr. Riggins."

"It's only logical that they would do this," Riggins replied. "And it's only logical that you're the best one equipped to respond. No offense, Doctor."

Carlyle was right about him, Xavier mused to himself. *The guy's irrepressible.* "Wait for Carlyle's call and help him in any way you can with Cheskin. I'll see what I can do about that vessel."

There was a brief pause. "There's something else. . . . Is it possible that one of your associates from QPR is working against us?" Riggins asked.

The question caught Xavier off guard. "Anyone who knew anything about the hybrid is dead. Why do you ask?"

"The hacker seemed well versed on the aspects of the hybrid technology. I copied the formulations that were used by Zangshe's scientist and tried to send them to you without identifying what they were. He blocked them and indicated that if I attempted to transmit any further hybrid data . . ." Riggins hesitated, ". . . great harm would come to someone that *you* care a great deal about."

Xavier was struck with horror. *Rachel!* his brain shouted.

71

ICE

Dubai City, U.A.E.

Parked back at Dubai airport, Xavier was fretfully mulling over Riggins's comment. *The Chinese must have a hacker inside the CIA. It's the only logical conclusion. Who else would know enough about the hybrid technology and me personally to make such a threat? Only Carlyle, Riggins, and Mac Cowan know my connection to Rachel.*

Xavier's mind was spinning with the possibilities of someone harming Rachel further, and he needed to know right then and there if she was okay. He knew he was taking a chance by making another call, but he *had* to know.

"Hey, Mac, what's Rachel's status?" Xavier asked when the private investigator answered the call.

"Everything's status quo," Mac assured him. "There haven't been any signs of improvement, but the doctor says she's hanging in there; she's a tough one. She's not giving up any time soon, Doc."

"I got some intel that someone may try to go after her. Please keep an extra close watch on things. And keep me posted," Xavier said, grabbing his duffle bag from the rental car. He headed toward the spacious but virtually empty terminal building.

"Will do, Doc. Heard from Carlyle lately?"

"Saw him recently," Xavier replied, hoping the short answer would assure Mac that Carlyle was alive and well.

"Tell him that some of his Agency friends here were asking about him," Cowan said.

I'll bet they were, he thought. Then he said aloud, "I'll let him know. Thanks again, Mac."

Xavier appreciated that the private investigator didn't ask him any specifics about his own status. He was glad to know that Rachel was safe, but for how long would she remain so, he wondered. He knew he didn't have much time to see this thing through. Getting to the cargo vessel wouldn't be easy much less trying to stop the hybrid device. And whoever the hacker was, he seemed to be very well informed and several steps ahead of Riggins.

Inside the terminal building, Xavier washed up and donned his spare set of clothes. Clearing security at Dubai was relatively routine since it had been downgraded over the years due to low activity.

The six-hour flight to London gave Xavier the opportunity to begin strategizing. He'd decided he would take a connecting flight to Miami. Once there, he would find a way to intercept the Chinese cargo vessel long before it reached the Port of New Orleans, somewhere in the deepest portions of the Gulf of Mexico.

The plane landed at Heathrow International Airport without event, but as Xavier expected, the security there unlike Dubai was very tight. As he attempted to make the connecting flight to Miami, he was checked and rechecked. Traveling one way with only a duffle bag and no luggage was an indicator to the profilers and made him a potential person of interest. For a while, he thought he might be detained. But finally, he was cleared to board.

ɞ

Xavier was near exhaustion after the recent events in Dubai and spent most of the five-hour flight to Miami trying to relax. But it hadn't occurred to him that there would be a surprise awaiting him when he landed. With their zero-tolerance policy, the Immigration and Customs Enforcement agents in Miami had meticulously scrutinized the flight manifest from Heathrow. Xavier's profile had looked suspicious, and before the plane even hit the tarmac, ICE agents were already in position to deploy onto the plane when it arrived at the gate. If it weren't for the annoyed flight attendants, Xavier would have been completely caught off guard.

⋐⋑

"I have a date tonight and I needed to be home on time," Xavier overheard one of the flight attendants complain to another member of the crew. "But apparently, ICE has other ideas. We'll be in a gate hold for a while until they check the plane."

"Say what it was for?" the other attendant asked with some worry apparent in her voice.

"Probably nothing. Looking for someone, I suppose," came the annoyed reply.

The second crewmember seemed a little taken aback by her coworker's selfishness. "I'd rather be safe than sorry."

Xavier instinctively knew the ICE was waiting for him, and he couldn't afford to be detained or arrested. Glancing around quickly, he made his decision.

Just before the pilot announced that the aircraft was making its final approach, he slipped back into the restroom immediately behind his rear-cabin seat.

He took out a small plastic lighter he had managed to hold on to since Dubai, knowing it might eventually come in handy. He gathered a wad of paper towels and dampened them, then lit the roll and dropped the smoldering mass into the waste receptacle. Sliding the locking mechanism closed behind him, he jammed the restroom door shut. He returned to his seat and waited.

It took only a few minutes for smoke to begin filling the small area.

The loud staccato blaring of the fire alarm sent all of the flight attendants scurrying into action. They tried to unlock the restroom door, but it wouldn't budge. Within five minutes, the smoke began to filter into the air-ventilation system and made its way into the main cabin. Not heavy, but enough to cause some concern among the passengers.

Xavier watched as the head flight attendant informed the flight deck of the situation through the intercom.

"Ladies and gentleman, may I have your attention," the captain said calmly. "It appears we have a minor emergency in the rear restroom, which requires us to perform an evacuation procedure. The aircraft will taxi to the closest off-ramp where the emergency door chutes will be deployed. Your flight crew will direct you to orderly disembark down the chutes. Emergency-response teams are waiting to assist you."

There was a collective murmur from the passengers as they looked nervously about trying to ascertain the whereabouts and seriousness of the incident. The flight crew did an expert job maintaining calm by assuring everyone that the plane would be on the ground within five minutes and that everything was under control.

The aircraft taxied to the nearest position immediately off the active runway, but it was the farthest point from the scheduled arrival gate. The chutes were deployed. The passengers were quickly loaded into several response vans and shuttled back to the main terminal. At the terminal, the passengers were directed to proceed to recover their carry-on baggage as well as their tagged luggage from baggage claim. Because of the on-board emergency, the airport authorities had attempted to set up a temporary area to question the passengers about the incident. But, in the melee caused by the hastily arranged logistics, most found their way through the customs checkpoint with their baggage and went on their way.

The ICE agents at the arrival gate were alerted to the emergency-landing procedure and had hurried back toward the main terminal. But, by then, Xavier had joined the throng and casually strolled through customs and disappeared into the milling crowds.

72

FAVOR

Miami River, Miami

Outside Miami International Airport, Xavier breathed a short sigh of relief. He knew there was no damage to the plane. The small fire in the trash receptacle had burned itself out by the time they had disengaged the locked door. And avoiding the clutches of ICE was essential if he was to finish his business. In contrast to the implications associated with the cargo vessel's destructive course, he considered the setting of a harmless fire a relatively minor infraction.

He hailed a cab and directed the Cuban driver to head for a location on the Miami River. Tucked away along one of the bending curves of the river was an old fishing marina. Many years ago, he had been involved in an undercover sting operation conducted in concert with the FBI's Miami office. Money from a Medellin Cartel drug operation located on the river had been used to finance an arms deal involving a terrorist sleeper cell in the Miami area.

Since most of the local agents were fairly well known, the head of the FBI's Miami office, Alex Veracruz, had asked Xavier for a favor. Xavier had been glad to oblige and posed as the owner of the marina.

His precarious role as a conduit between the river drug runners and the arms' dealers had led to the takedown of the sleeper cell.

After Veracruz had been seriously wounded on assignment in Cape Town, South Africa, almost ten years earlier, he had retired from the FBI. Fortunately for Xavier, Veracruz still lived in the Miami area, and it was time for his old friend to repay the favor. Xavier called him on the way to the marina. His PDA with the embassy chip had kept his anonymity secure so far.

"X-man, it's been a while," Veracruz said, upon hearing Xavier's voice. "I know you're not here on vacation."

"How'd you guess, Alex?"

"Maybe it had something to do with the global BOLO out on you."

Xavier had already suspected that a BOLO—*be on the lookout*—was sent to every worldwide-enforcement agency. Soon, there'd be no place safe to go. If the Chinese plot wasn't exposed, he could spend the rest of his life in a Federal penitentiary. "It's why I called, Alex. I need your help."

"I owe you, X, big time," said Veracruz. "But why in hell is everyone looking for your ass? Even my old buddies at the Bureau called to find out if I had any contact with you."

"It's complicated. Trust me when I tell you that the less you know the better."

"I know you well enough to appreciate the advice. But once I'm in, I'd like some understanding of the situation."

Xavier would have expected the same. "Meet me at the old marina, Alex. We'll talk."

Xavier's cab pulled up in front of a gray semi-dilapidated clapboard building. Covered with mildew and signs of termite infestation, the Feds had long since abandoned the marina after the sting operation.

Xavier paid the cabbie and walked around to the side of the marina's office.

There were several boats in the marina's yard resting in cradles and rotting in place. Xavier's eyes surveyed further back toward a large travel lift used to haul boats in and out of the water. Then he saw it. *It's still there*! he thought. *But would it work?* He moved closer and noticed that its propellers had been removed. Its imposing hull seemed in good shape. He grabbed a ladder and was about to climb up when he heard something behind him.

"You're not thinking of trying to use this old tub, are you?" Veracruz chuckled. Lean, with jet-black hair stylishly slicked back and wearing the latest in South Beach fashion, the Puerto Rican–born Veracruz looked like a rock star—hardly the image of a former head of an FBI office. But known for his toughness and covert skills, Veracruz had made a reputation within the Bureau as one of the most effective agents against terrorist sleeper cells.

"It crossed my mind," Xavier replied, smiling at his old friend. "It's good to see you, Alex. You're looking very sartorial as always."

"You know how it is, man. Down here in Miami, it's all about the look."

"You've always had that going for you. Anybody special in your life these days?"

Veracruz grinned. "They're all special, X, every one of them. How about you? I heard about your wife and daughter. Very sorry, man."

"Word travels," Xavier said.

"It's a relatively small world we operate in. And I try to keep in touch with the news. That's why I was so shocked when I saw the BOLO out on you. Tell me what's going on."

Xavier related the entire series of events leading up to his plans to somehow intercept and stop the Chinese vessel heading toward the U.S. It felt good to unload on someone he trusted implicitly. Veracruz listened with rapt attention, his eyes growing wider with each new piece of information. Xavier explained his concerns about causing an explosion and activating the hybrid too early, which ruled out the use of RPGs or any type of torpedo.

When Xavier finally finished the tale, the ex-FBI agent shook his head in amazement. "That's not an explanation, man. That's a fable. And you're expecting to stop a cargo vessel with that old piece of shit?" he said, pointing to the hulking remnants of the once drug-interdiction high-speed motor craft.

Xavier nodded. "I haven't filled in all the blanks. Got any ideas?"

Veracruz thought for a moment. "Given the time frame we're operating under, not many. But the first thing we'll need is a mechanic. And there's something that might work very well if I could get my hands on it. I'll make a few calls," he said.

"While you're doing that, Alex, I'll try to get a current fix on the location of the vessel," Xavier said.

Hoping the chip inside his PDA would continue to provide a measure of anonymity, he called Riggins.

"Hey, Doctor," Riggins answered. "Glad to hear from you. Haven't heard from Agent Carlyle yet. I've tried reaching out for him."

The news gave Xavier pause for a moment, then he asked, "What's your status?"

"I'm set up in temporary facilities. Don't have all the bells and whistles, but I can communicate."

"Be cautious, Mr. Riggins. They're closing the net. If we can't get Director Cheskin's attention, we won't have much time left."

"The White House has already moved to get ahead of the rumors about the agreements with the Saudis and Chinese," Riggins replied. "If there's any chance of convincing Cheskin otherwise, our job just got a whole lot harder."

Shit, he thought. *Carlyle might be walking straight into a hornet's nest.* "Were you able to keep track of the progress of the Chinese vessel?"

"I've tapped into the satellite link and got a new fix. It's approximately two hundred and forty miles almost due west of Miami, traveling at eighteen knots. At its current speed, I put the vessel in the vicinity of the Port of New Orleans in about two days."

"It's less time than I'd thought."

"Got a plan, Doctor?"

"Working on one as we speak. Can you chart out for me the deepest portion of the Gulf where the vessel's course is most likely to take it?" Xavier asked.

There was no response for a minute or so. Xavier figured that Riggins was accessing a map of the Gulf of Mexico.

"I'm guessing at what it is you intend to do," Riggins finally replied. "The deepest part of the Gulf is in the southwestern quadrant about two hundred miles off the southeast coast of Brownsville, Texas, in an area known as Sigsbee Deep. It's over fourteen thousand feet deep and the trough runs for nearly three hundred miles. But it won't work for what you probably have in mind. Sigsbee Deep is too far west of the vessel's projected path to be a factor. But there's another trough that runs quite a distance eastward off the Sigsbee. It's not nearly as deep, but it might serve your purpose. Here are the coordinates of the trough."

Xavier jotted down the longitude and latitude of the trough. "Thanks, Mr. Riggins."

"And there's a high probability that approximately one hundred miles of the trough would intersect with the vessel's direct course to New Orleans or approximately one hundred fifty miles due west of Sarasota, Florida," Riggins added.

Xavier did a quick calculation. They would have to get moving quickly. "Stay safe, and let me know what develops with Agent Carlyle and Director Cheskin.

"Will do, Doctor. If I can't get in contact with Agent Carlyle, I'm going to try a backdoor to Cheskin."

Xavier was about to caution Riggins against doing that when the line suddenly went dead. *Dammit,* he thought. *If he's not careful, he's going to get himself caught or worse.*

"Hey, X. Think I've got things arranged," Veracruz said, interrupting Xavier's concerns.

"We need to move quickly, Alex. We only have a day to get ready."

"Mechanic is on his way. The surprise packages will take a little longer . . . maybe tomorrow."

Xavier looked over at Veracruz. "It's tomorrow or never, Alex."

POSTURING

Xiong Xian, China

"We're aware of the situation in Jebel Ali. Our State Department is currently conducting its own investigation into the event," the agitated voice on the line said. "If we determine that you had any role in initiating the explosion, we will have little choice but to publicly condemn your actions. And you will be warned that any potential transgressions against the interests of the U.S. will be met with swift and severe repercussions."

Khan listened impatiently to his contact. "I assure you that what took place in the U.A.E. was a most unfortunate accident. I have no intention of challenging your sovereignty or threatening your interests. Furthermore, I will remind you that our arrangement clearly stipulates that you would not interfere with our activities in this hemisphere."

"There are always extenuating circumstances, Mr. Chairman. I hope that what is uncovered at Jebel Ali does not lead to the conclusion I've suggested or is in any way regarded as retribution for the accident at your laboratory."

"I grow weary of your veiled insinuations," Khan railed. "As you well know, your country is in dire need of the technology and energy solutions we have developed. Your own strategic oil reserves are quickly diminishing. I expect we can work together toward a successful partnership."

"Successful partnerships are built on trust. I'm *hopeful* that remains possible," the contact said, hanging up.

Khan stared across his desk at Yakubla. "There is not much time remaining," he said. "Once the official report concerning the cause of the event at Jebel Ali is made public, there will no longer be any reason to coddle to the West. But in the meantime, the impact of the damage assessment will create so much distraction and concern that the final stage of our plan can proceed without notice."

"Everything is on schedule, Great One," Yakubla assured him. "The cargo vessel should arrive at the port's holding zone within three days. The captain was informed of his orders. Based upon the ongoing IMA investigation of the incident in the Adriatic with the Italian Navy and the implications of sanctions, I seriously doubt that anyone would dare to intercept the vessel and interfere with your plan."

Khan sat back in his leather chair with a smile twitching on his lips. Once all of his plans had been carried out, *he* would be the most powerful man in the world. He would lead his country and the countries that bowed to him to new heights, and it would be the dawn of a glorious new era. His namesake would shine praise on him from the eternal blue heavens.

PERSPECTIVE

Langley, Virginia

CIA Director John Cheskin was at wit's end. Not only was his agency in full-search mode for one of its most senior agents and his accomplices, but he was also being hounded by the State Department over the document leaks. On top of that, there was the ongoing investigation of the illegal stoppage and boarding of the Chinese cargo vessel in the Mediterranean. Apparently, one of the perpetrators had testified in front of the Italian General Magistrate that a former CIA operative was also implicated. Finally, Cheskin had received a directive by his contact in the State Department to investigate the facts surrounding the Jebel Ali incident. The director was in desperate need of a good day, but the bad news just kept on coming.

"Director, I'm sorry to say we were unable to contain Agent's Carlyle's IT guy."

"What do you mean, 'unable to contain him'?" Cheskin barked at his deputy director—a recent political appointment he had been forced to accept.

"He was able to slip through security. We believe he used a disguise to exit the main checkpoint."

"This is the goddamn CIA headquarters!" Cheskin bellowed. "Don't you think we should be able to control our own premises?"

"I don't know what to say, Director. We traced his escape route from the basement to a small mechanical room on the first floor. He must've had duplicate credentials hidden somewhere . . . most likely that of a service personnel."

Cheskin held his head in his hands. "And how can we expect to track down Agent Carlyle when we can't even contain a low-level IT geek?"

The CIA deputy director was speechless.

"Do you at least have some news about the QPR scientist?" the frustrated Cheskin asked.

"We believe he was onboard a flight from Heathrow to Miami. ICE was about to pick him up when the plane's captain declared an emergency landing. In the melee that followed, ICE lost him."

Cheskin got up from his chair and walked around to the front of his desk. He sat down on the front edge of it to face his subordinate, up close and personal. "I know your old man's a high-ranking member of the Senate Armed Services Committee, but if you don't bring me some results in the next twenty-four hours, you *will* be looking for a new career, Deputy."

The deputy director hastily exited. As Cheskin was about to close the door to his office, he caught a glimpse of the expression on his assistant's face. "Sergeant Strong, come in here, please," Cheskin said.

"Sir," the grizzled twenty-five-year veteran of the Marine Corps smartly replied.

"I know you see and hear what's going on around here," Cheskin said. "Have any perspectives you'd like to share?"

"Permission to speak freely, sir."

Cheskin nodded.

"You're burning valuable resources chasing around for the wrong guy. Agent Carlyle's one of the best and smartest assets the Agency has. You need to reassess you're situation, sir. The source of all this commotion's coming from the White House, more specifically from the State Department."

Cheskin folded his arms across his chest. "No shit, Sergeant. Tell me something I don't know."

"The two agents in Dubai haven't reported in for several days. And I just received a call from Agent Carlyle's IT guy—name of Riggins. He wants to meet with you. He said it's very important. I'd highly recommend it . . . sir."

CRAFT

Miami River, Florida

Veracruz's mechanic had spent the past few hours crawling around inside the bowels of the huge engine compartment of the high-speed offshore craft. Designed by a world-renowned naval architect, the speedboat was more than seventy-feet long and built entirely of Kevlar-laminated material. It was not only extremely durable but also virtually bulletproof. And because of its unique stepped-hull configuration, the boat was capable of maintaining speeds in excess of fifty knots even in rough sea conditions. Its highly specialized surface-drive propulsion system powered it effortlessly over the water, giving the feeling of gliding on a cushion of air.

Much smaller but far more maneuverable than a Coast Guard cutter, the high-speed craft was extensively and successfully used by the Miami FBI to apprehend all manner of water-based conveyances. Having extended range, there was nothing it couldn't eventually outrun. But there was one big problem now—actually getting it *to* run.

"It's not as bad as I'd thought, Agent Veracruz," the burly mechanic told him. "Although most of the wiring's shot and the fuel lines have completely disintegrated, the engine block was pickled correctly. I think it'll be okay. After I rewire the ignition into the new battery banks, I'll do a compression check to see what's going on inside. Assuming we don't need any major engine parts, I think I can have it in fairly good shape soon. But we need to find the propellers and a shit load of clean diesel fuel."

"I'll scout around for the props," Veracruz replied. "They've got to be here somewhere. But getting that much diesel fuel is another issue."

Xavier heard the discussion between Veracruz and the mechanic. "There's a storage area in the rear of the main facility behind the travel lift. Let's take a look for those props," he suggested.

Both men rummaged through the morass of old scrap metal and engine parts strewn about in large piles throughout the storage area. What they were looking for should have been fairly easy to find. The propellers were almost three feet in diameter and weighed almost three hundred pounds apiece. But nothing fitting that description was in sight.

"It doesn't look good, X. And without them, we're obviously screwed."

"It makes little sense that someone would haul them off," Xavier said. "The props were expensive, but they were custom-made for one particular craft. And they would be of no value to anyone else," he said, as he moved toward the rear door. He opened it and stepped outside to look around in the overgrown brush. As he turned to go back inside, he noticed two slightly raised mounds not too far from the rear door.

"Over here, Alex. Give me a hand," Xavier said, looking for something to use for digging.

Xavier found an old shovel. As he removed the top layers of soil, the tarnished bronze finish of the large props appeared. Veracruz and the mechanic joined him, and the three men quickly cleared away the loosely attached underbrush to fully expose the props.

It seemed odd to Xavier that someone would have made the effort to carry the heavy parts outside and partially bury them behind the storage area. He thought about this as he, Veracruz, and the mechanic began hoisting up the propellers.

Xavier saw it first . . . something had been buried underneath the propellers. They lowered the props back down away from the mound.

"Look at this, Alex," Xavier said, tugging at the corner of a large plastic garbage bag.

Together they grabbed onto the plastic bag and pulled it out of the hole.

Tentatively, Xavier opened the bag and stepped back. "It's human remains," he said gravely. "And there's another one."

Stunned, Veracruz followed Xavier's line of sight toward another plastic bag about three feet away.

It took a few minutes for the impact of what they'd found to register.

"I have a good idea who these two were," Veracruz finally said. "Do you remember the two cartel members we captured and who turned state's evidence?"

Xavier nodded and asked, "Didn't they go into witness pro - tection?"

Veracruz nodded. "Yeah, and they went missing a short time after- ward. I guess we've found them. I'll have the lab confirm the remains."

"Ballsy . . . bringing them back here," Xavier said.

"Typical cartel way of dispensing their brand of justice," Veracruz replied.

"Let's get these props over to the boat," Xavier said, "and hope we don't find any more bodies."

Once the three men had finished laboring to affix the heavy pro- pellers to the shafts at the rear of the boat, the mechanic jumped back onboard to continue with his evaluations. Minutes later, the roll of tires approaching got Veracruz's attention. "It's the surprise packages," he said with a grin.

Like a kid in a candy store, Veracruz helped unload the pickup truck and sent the driver on his way. "He's one of my guys. I think he still believes that my retirement was the ultimate cover story. And I had to call in some serious markers for these," Veracruz gloated, putting on the attached insulated gloves and pulling out one of the two round sealed plastic canisters from a large chest of dry ice. It was about the size of a large round loaf of San Francisco sourdough bread.

"What've you got there?" Xavier asked, looking more closely at the canister.

"You said you wanted something failsafe to use against the cargo vessel."

"And these two things will do it?"

"Actually, X, one of them would do the job, but just in case, two will be that much better. And I know you'll dig the science behind how they work. But we'll need to keep them cold."

"I can't wait to hear that," Xavier said, noticing several gear bags left behind by the pickup truck. "More goodies?"

"Navigation charts, a couple of assault weapons, flare guns, satphone, and scuba gear," Veracruz said, unzipping the waterproof duffle bags. "Everything a well-equipped interdiction boat needs."

"Let's hope we have one that works," Xavier said, as they walked back toward the maintenance area. "By the way, what about the diesel fuel?"

"I'm working on that too, X. There's a local guy who used a barge to supply diesel fuel for the big luxury yachts. Unfortunately, his business has all but dried up. But he owes me."

"Who doesn't in this town, Alex?"

"My ex-wife," he chuckled. "And she's remarried to the fuel-barge guy."

"Sounds like you should owe him."

"You never met my ex-wife, X. She's a keeper. But I managed to screw that up."

"Takes a lot to admit that. She must be something special," Xavier said, thinking again about Rachel.

"And *beaucoup* rich too—daughter of the Bacardi Rum family."

"It must be hard being you, Alex. At least you have a sense of humor about it," Xavier quipped.

"It's one of my endearing qualities. And it keeps me humble," the former agent replied, winking at Xavier.

"Let's see how the mechanic is coming along," Xavier said, looking at his heirloom watch, amazed that the thing was still ticking after all he'd been through. "We've got less than twelve hours to make the rendezvous point with the cargo vessel. And besides, I don't want to hang around here any longer than necessary. Although I've covered my tracks pretty well, that BOLO notice casts a large net."

"I know, X. I'm worried too that some of my agency buddies here in Miami might decide to tail me. They know how tight you and I were."

Xavier nodded his acknowledgment as both men climbed up the ladder and stood over the open engine compartment. He and Veracruz watched as the mechanic, sweating profusely, finished hooking up his computer tablet to several engine control points.

With the new wiring in place and a primer of diesel fuel in the cylinders, the mechanic tried cranking the massive engines. He didn't need to start them, only turn them over for a compression reading. After several attempts, he studied the information from the hardwire connection to his computer tablet. He looked up at Xavier and Veracruz with his thumbs up. "She'll be good to go."

Several hours later, a fuel barge pulled up alongside the dock where the travel lift had deposited the high-speed craft. Veracruz jumped onboard and greeted the barge owner warmly. After a few minutes, two helpers came topside to begin the fueling process.

Meanwhile, the mechanic had finished rewiring the radar unit sitting atop the arch. "This unit's well beyond its useful life. But it's working for now," he said, looking over at Xavier.

"Hopefully, it'll last a bit longer," Xavier said, watching as the fuel barge's pumps filled the craft's two huge fuel tanks. "How much burn time do you estimate we have when full?" he asked.

The mechanic hit some keys on his computer tablet. "Depends, of course, on your speed. But I'd say you'd have an approximate range of five hundred nautical miles at maximum cruise speed," he replied. "On second thought, the engines aren't tweaked, so maybe a little less than that."

Enough to get us out there, but more than likely only halfway back to the closest point of land, Xavier mused.

76

CHAMELION

Xiong Xian, China

E lena Dupre was sitting pensively in front of Khan's massive desk feeling somewhat uneasy but confident she could bluff her way through any interrogation. She had not heard anything from the minister. After the alarm had sounded in the research laboratory and all employees had been instructed to return to their offices, Elena had found her way to Zangshe's liaison officer. She'd indicated to him that her associate, whom she had thought was a technical advisor for the ministry, was in fact responsible for the damage inflicted on the laboratory. The liaison officer forwarded his report of her accounting of the events to the chairman's office. In part, the report read:

> I was instructed by the Minster of Technology to initiate an independent investigation of Zangshe's nuclear-waste-storage practices. As part of the investigation, I was assigned the technical advisor and directed to have him accompany me on the visit. After we had cleared the security gate, the advisor forced me to cooperate with him with threat of death. When we were led to the underground tunnel, I managed to escape by finding an exit ladder up and out of the blast tunnel. And I am most sorry

for the damage and loss of life caused and wish to convey the Ministry's sincerest apologies for the breach in our security process.

Khan had reviewed the liaison officer's report and had requested that she be brought to his office for further questioning.

"You have told us quite an interesting story, Ms. Dupre. If I am to believe your account of the events, you are entirely innocent of the actions that occurred," he stated flatly.

"I was duped, Mr. Chairman. And by a very experienced operative," Elena replied with conviction.

"I fully expect that you will identify the operative," Khan said in answer, apparently buying Elena's story. "However, I am most curious about something else. Is it possible that your own minister was involved in the plot against Zangshe?"

Elena hesitated. "I'm not certain I understand the meaning of your question."

"I think you do, Ms. Dupre. It is no secret that your minister has declared his intentions to shut down Zangshe's operations. Why should I not believe that this was part of his plan?"

"He is someone who follows the rules," Elena replied, crossing her leg. "I can assure you that he would not condone such activity. It is why he launched the investigation and sent me here. He believes he can force you to comply with INA guidelines and clean up your waste-storage problem."

"I can appreciate your loyalty, Ms. Dupre. And it makes perfect sense that you would defend his motives. However, your entire story is either an elaborate fabrication or you are ignorant of the role you were asked to play. However, you appear far from ignorant."

Sensing a trap, Elena's stomach tightened. "You seem to have other information that puts me at some disadvantage, Mr. Chairman."

Khan smiled. Elena thought it was meant to put her at ease, but she found it disquieting. Still, she didn't let on.

"You are most clever, Ms. Dupre," Khan said with obvious admiration. "I can see why Minister Chek employs you. Unfortunately for you, your own minister has disavowed any knowledge of your visit here."

It was unexpected—the response from the minister to Khan, if it had actually happened. Elena tried to reason through the situation. But there was an element of logic involved, if the minister had been confronted by the specter of a scandal. If that was the case, she had but one option.

"What is it that you wish for me to say, Mr. Chairman?" she asked.

"If I choose to believe your story, Ms. Dupre, it is clear that your minister has abandoned you. On the other hand, if I choose to believe him, then your actions here will be severely punished."

Khan smiled again. This time, Elena knew it was not to put her at ease. She stared into the tyrannical despot's brooding eyes. "Then you leave me little choice. I will cooperate in any way you desire."

77

DEVICES

Miami River, Florida

Eighteen hours had passed since Riggins's last satellite fix on the cargo vessel. The cargo vessel was already through the Straits of Florida, around the Florida Keys, and heading northwesterly toward New Orleans. If Xavier intended to intercept it in the trough area described by Riggins, they would have to leave very soon. Even considering the superior speed of the FBI craft, the closing distance would put the vessel's location close to the outer edge of the deep trough.

Veracruz had provisioned the craft with enough food and libations for a week. They wouldn't need it. But Xavier had decided to humor him. "Think we'll have enough time to eat and drink all that, Alex?"

"First of all, I'm not a boat person," Veracruz replied. "I hate the notion of being that far off shore. And there are two things that calm my nerves . . . sex and food. Unless I'm mistaken, our danger quotient will be maxed out. And believe me, X, you don't want me freaking out out there."

Xavier grinned. "This is coming from a guy who brought down some of the most dangerous terrorist sleeper cells in FBI history."

"All of that was done on good ole terra firma, not somewhere in the deep clutches of the Gulf of Mexico," Veracruz replied in good humor.

"Well, you've got seven hours to chow down before we hit the target zone," Xavier said, as he turned on the ignition switches, bringing the turbo-injected, high-performance diesel engines rumbling to life.

The mechanic checked the gauges. "They look pretty good. Watch your fuel consumption. If it jumps up suddenly, throttle back some. It may take a while for the carbon to burn out of the injectors," he said, hopping off the craft and giving them a high sign.

With the dock lines freed, Xavier eased onto the throttles. As the sun began to rise, the big speedboat pulled slowly away. The river meandered for about two miles before it widened into open water at its mouth. Xavier had to bridle in the horsepower for the twenty-minute trip down through the busy river traffic to Brickell Key and the Biscayne Bay.

Once in the Bay, he turned due south and leaned on the throttles. There was a momentary lull as the engines spooled up and the craft dragged listlessly through the water. Then, in the next moment, as if by Neptune's hand, the hull was lifted out of the water, breaking the powerful suction. The high-pitched sound of the whining props churning up tons of white lather launched the one-of-a-kind craft into a frenzied pace as it screamed over the tops of the bay's light chop.

Xavier and Veracruz held on as the speedometer climbed to fifty knots. Within minutes, the unique hull design of the craft had created a cushion of air between the seas. There was no sensation of bouncing or bucking against the waves. Xavier set the autopilot for a direct course down through Hawk's Channel to Key West. It would take two hours to get to the Straits of Florida and into the Gulf of Mexico.

Veracruz had already begun feasting on a breakfast of Cuban sandwiches and fried plantains.

Watching his friend devour the food, Xavier shook his head. "Before you pass out, Alex, I'd be interested to know how those devices in the canisters work."

Veracruz smiled. "I thought you'd never ask," he mumbled, choking down his food. "They were initially developed by the Mossad for use against Iranian ships in the Persian Gulf. And more recently, the Coast Guard has used them to sink retired Navy vessels for artificial-reef protection. The exterior of the device is shaped like a clamshell and has a protective coating covered with a turpentine resin. It's a very powerful corrosive mechanism that employs a waterproof phosphorus fuse. When the phosphorus erodes the device's protective coating, it allows the turpentine residue to mix with a highly concentrated form of nitric-acid solution. A violent chemical reaction results that rapidly bores through the metal of the ship's hull. Within a very short while, it'll disintegrate a twenty to thirty foot section of the hull before extinguishing. And without the slightest explosive impact or warning and with no risk of countermeasures."

Xavier frowned. "I understand now why they need to stay iced. High concentrations of nitric acid can be a bit unstable otherwise. How do you activate it?" he asked curiously.

"That's the best part of the ingenious device," Veracruz said, grabbing a bottle of water to wash down his feast. "Depress a button on top of the device, and it activates an electromagnet that locks the device against the ship's hull."

"That's it. Nothing else?" Xavier asked.

"The Mossad doesn't leave anything to chance," Veracruz replied. "Radio-frequency signals could be jammed. This is old technology . . . simple but effective application of electrolysis. There is only one button. The electromagnet generates a small but steady charge that activates the fusing mechanism of the clamshell and initiates the entire chain reaction."

"Electrolysis!" Xavier said. "I'm very impressed. Now, all we need to do is to get close enough to deploy them."

"That's why I'm planning to eat all the way there," Veracruz smiled, hoisting another sandwich to his mouth.

78

HARBINGER

Gulf of Mexico

On board the Chinese cargo vessel, the captain and his skeleton crew of six were twenty-four hours from their final destination. With only four hundred fifty miles left to cover, the vessel's speed was slowed to fifteen knots to conserve fuel. Driven by twin screws and fueled with crude oil, the older-type single-hulled vessel had made many successful voyages. And after more than two weeks of sailing, the captain had promised a small celebration to mark their last evening at sea.

The sojourn from the Port of Tianjin was uneventful. And the cargo vessel had already received its preliminary clearance to enter the security holding area lying less than a mile outside the Port of New Orleans. Although the vessel's manifest was not entirely accurate, the captain was confidently reassured by Zangshe's headquarter staff that he would not encounter any difficulties whatsoever from the U.S. authorities.

"Make certain that the inner cargo bay is welded closed," the captain said to his first mate. "When we reach the holding area and the authorities from the U.S. come onboard to inspect our manifest, I will inform them that we have had some leakage in our watertight compartments. And we will need repairs to be made at the nearest docking facilities."

The first mate looked confused. "Yes, Captain. But when we arrive at the docking facilities and they find no leakage, there may be more questions. We have no such cargo as listed on the manifest."

The captain stared at his first mate. "By that time, I can assure you, our company will have made arrangements that will clearly explain our situation," the captain replied calmly, not wanting to cause anxiety among his small crew.

But even the captain was oblivious to the potential for the catastrophic consequences of his future actions. He was instructed merely to dock the cargo vessel and await further instructions from Zangshe. And he was completely unaware of the small containment enclosure holding the replicated nuclear hybrid that had been strategically affixed to the inner side of the cargo vessel's main fuel tank.

79

INSIGHT

Langley, Virginia

The State Department informed Director Cheskin that he was required to testify at an upcoming hearing related to the Italian cargo-vessel incident. It was requested that he bring all pertinent information on a covert operative known as X-man. The problem was that he had no such intel or any idea where to find the operative. Members of covert teams often disappeared from the Agency's radar screen, sometimes permanently, leaving little traces of their existence.

But the State Department was unrelenting. They had agreed with the international tribunal and the Italian government's investigation into the illegal stoppage and boarding of the Chinese cargo vessel to provide whatever assistance necessary to determine the responsible parties. Cheskin was caught between a rock and a hard place.

On the verge of the Senate hearing over the Mediterranean incident, the Agency was in upheaval. The recent high-level investigations of one of its senior agents as well as a member of the IT department had spread uncertainty and paranoia throughout the Agency's rank and file.

But despite the constant pressures being applied to the Agency,

Cheskin began to have serious doubts over the nature of the arrangements between the State Department and the Saudi government. Too many things didn't add up. His own inquiries into the large buildup of mercenary forces along the Persian Gulf had pointed toward the involvement of the Iranians. When he had raised the issue in his briefing sessions on Capitol Hill, he was told that it was not an item of concern. And then, there was the intel from the sat-images he had received from SATCOM, clearly showing the daily arrival of Chinese cargo vessels at the Port of Ad Damman. The directive he had received from the White House's general counsel to put a blanket of secrecy over any dealings with the Saudis was the final straw. He had decided to follow up on his Marine assistant's recommendation.

"Sergeant Strong, arrange a meeting with Carlyle's technical guy. Let's find out what he knows," Cheskin said.

Strong nodded. "Right away, sir. And I've just commandeered a report from the INA regarding their preliminary findings in the Jebel Ali explosion. Here it is," Strong said, handing Cheskin the file.

"I hesitate to ask how you *commandeered* this, Sergeant. Suffice to say, you seem to be the only one providing me any reliable intel."

"It's a Marine thing, sir. We have our ways," Strong replied with a smile, as he saluted and returned to his desk.

Cheskin opened the file. Somehow he wasn't surprised. Carlyle had been right after all . . . once again.

80

ODDS

Key West, Florida

The high-speed craft kicked up a huge waterspout behind its props as it skimmed by the outer marker for Key West and into the Gulf of Mexico. Approximately five hours behind the cargo vessel, they were making up ground quickly.

But the current weather report on the VHF radio was soon to change things. There was a quick-developing and fast-moving tropical storm that had come up through the Caribbean Sea. It was already around the western tip of Cuba, and its current track had it heading their way. Xavier knew that their ride was about to get a little bumpy.

"Better stow the gear down below, Alex. We have about an hour of clear weather before we get kicked in the ass."

"Just what we need. Something else to add to the mix," Veracruz muttered.

"It might actually work in our favor," Xavier said, studying the radar screen. "If we time it right, the weather may act as some cover for us. Look at where the storm's coming from," he said, pointing to the screen. "See that mass of green images, its clutter from the storm clouds. When we turn northwest we'll intersect the storm's track and it'll be directly behind us. And the cargo-vessel's radar won't be able to see us clearly coming up from their stern because of all that clutter."

"Leave it to you, X, to find a bright spot in a storm," Veracruz cracked.

"Yeah, but the high waves and wind should make for an interesting situation trying to maneuver close enough to the vessel's hull to affix those devices," Xavier replied.

"On second thought, maybe we should let the storm pass, X," Veracruz suggested with a hopeful tone.

"We don't have that luxury, Alex. If we wait too long we won't have enough fuel to reach the cargo vessel. And if that happens, there's a good chance the nuclear hybrid could be detonated inside the Port of New Orleans. *Sixty percent* of all U.S. shipping would be disrupted, not to mention the extensive damage to one of the world's largest harvesting areas of seafood. Remember the target at Jebel Ali? There's a brand-new desalination plant in operation at the mouth of the Mississippi River. More than fifty million people could be affected."

"Okay . . . okay. I get the message. We're going to do this thing come hell or tropical storm—maybe both."

"Let's be positive," Xavier said. "The Chinese won't expect us in the midst of a storm. We probably won't have to deal with small arms fire or worse."

"That maybe true, but being crushed by a heaving cargo vessel's hull is not on my bucket list either," Veracruz said, still munching on the snacks he'd packed.

"I've been thinking about that as well. And you're not going to like my plan," Xavier warned.

"And the beat goes on. Tell me what more excitement I can look forward to," Veracruz said with much more levity than he felt.

Xavier knew that they had maybe a fifty percent chance of pulling off a successful rendezvous. Depending on the size of the storm waves, they could risk being sucked under the vessel's hull as it rode the action of the waves. Even the massive Chinese cargo vessel would experience substantial rolling and lifting motion in the storm. As a consequence, it would require them to maneuver their craft close but not in contact with with the vessel's hull.

"We're going to have to use the craft's dinghy to get close enough," Xavier said, pointing to the bow where a gray hard-bottom auxiliary was mounted. "Hopefully, its still floats," he added.

Veracruz scrunched up his face. "Jesus, X, the degree of difficulty keeps increasing exponentially. How's your idea going to work?" he asked, before chugging down another bottle of water.

"We'll tie off the dinghy against the side of the craft's hull and pull alongside the cargo vessel. The dinghy will act as a large fender and hopefully, buffer us from some of the actions of the vessel's hull. That's the theory anyway," Xavier said, shooting the retired agent a quick grin. "But it could work."

Veracruz's eyes widened. "Let me understand what you have in mind. You're planning to put an even smaller boat possibly under many tons of crushing steel?"

"I'm not going kid you, Alex. There's better than a fifty-fifty shot of that happening. Except that, with some careful maneuvering of the craft, we might be able to avoid disaster."

Veracruz didn't respond for several moments. "And I guess it'll be me in that little boat," he said with resignation. "After all, if I tried driving the craft, we'd both end up as fish food."

JUGGERNAUT

Xiong Xian, China

"Great One, all is well in Ad Damman," Yakubla said, taking a seat across from the chairman once he'd been directed to do so. "The construction of the fuel-processing center is nearly completed. And cargo vessels arrive every day to fill the new waste-storage areas. Within the month, we can turn over the operations to the AET Corporation."

Khan nodded his head slowly, taking in the information, and tugged at his long braid. "I have had recent discussions with AET's CEO, and he is concerned by the wavering of the U.S. State Department. He has indicated that informal inquiries were made regarding the nature of our arrangements with the Saudis and the U.S. And he would prefer to wait until all such conversations have run their course," he said with grave displeasure.

"How long will that be, Great One?" Yakubla asked, well aware that any delay would jeopardize their plans and Khan's fury would be unforgiving and dangerous.

"Too long, Yaku. I have reminded him that time is not in our favor. The impact of Jebel Ali will be at its height soon and will only serve our interests if we proceed as planned. Once the U.S. becomes fully cognizant of our intentions, they may move to stifle our initiatives."

"Then it is imperative that we continue with our plan to dock our vessel in the targeted location. The captain has reported that his clearances were approved and that he awaits further instructions," Yakubla said.

Khan got up from his desk and started to pace. "Once we announce our threat, there will be an immediate reaction from the U.S. authorities. Unfortunately for them, there will be little they can do to neutralize it. It is at that moment that we will force them to accept our terms. If they do not, we will demonstrate our resolve."

Yakubla sat quietly.

"I am interested in your thoughts, as always, Yaku," Khan said, turning toward his friend.

"I agree with your assessment of the situation in the U.S., Great One," Yakubla said. "However, I am troubled by our decision not to silence the QPR scientist when we had located his whereabouts in Quebec."

"Tell me what concerns that warrior's mind of yours," Khan said with true curiosity.

"He is most resourceful and has caused us serious problems. Although he led us to the agent in Dubai, the one you believed can harm us most with the U.S authorities, we were once again unsuccessful in our attempts to silence him as well as the agent."

Not revealing his disappointment in Yakubla's performance in order to keep his friend confident for the days ahead, Khan nodded and said, "This scientist appears to be somewhat like you, Yaku. Keeping him alive served an important purpose. And, now that he has escaped once again, we can use that to our advantage. He has most certainly alerted others to the hybrid's capabilities, and with his con - firmation of the superparticle's power, our threat becomes even more convincing."

Yakubla nodded in understanding, and Khan continued, "But I am confident that you will prevail as always. No one can escape your reach for very long."

"Your confidence is appreciated, Great One," Yaku replied. "But I have very uneasy feelings about the scientist. The man is most unusual."

"As are you, Yaku," Khan replied with a nod of his head, dismissing Yakubla's concern.

Yakubla returned the gesture. "On another matter, Great One, what is that you wish me to do about Minister Chek?"

"The minister's time is coming to an end, Yaku. I have persuaded his senior aide to cooperate with us against him. Ms. Dupre is preparing documentation that will clearly implicate Minister Chek's sanctioning of his representatives' visit and their intent to attack our research laboratory in his efforts to disrupt our operations."

"I am not certain I understand how that will help our cause, Great One."

Khan smiled knowingly. "I have planned to hold a press conference with the senior aide to disclose the documentation. Surely, the premier will not want the embarrassment of one of his most highly regarded ministers exposed as the one who caused such an atrocity upon a private Chinese company."

It was Yakubla's turn to smile. "A most effective argument. And one that is certain to bring down Minister Chek."

"There is one more aspect of the report," Khan added with some uncharacteristic glee.

Yakubla looked at him expectantly.

"Ms. Dupre's report will also disclose the involvement of the American CIA as a cooperating partner with Minister Chek in the attack against our facility. It will be another reason for the premier to exercise his diplomatic outrage with the U.S. State Department."

82

INTEL

Langley, Virginia

"Mr. Riggins, you're very resourceful," Cheskin said as soon as the call connected. "Somehow you've managed to elude my agents again and again. I understand that you have something to show me . . . some proof of your assertions."

Riggins responded, "Yes, Director, I do have the proof. But as I told Sergeant Strong, I need your assurance that if we meet you won't have me arrested."

"Have you committed any Federal offense, Mr. Riggins?" Cheskin asked.

Riggins paused, then said truthfully, "Not recently, Director. But I may be about to. Unless you agree to my terms, I'll have no choice but to release confidential documents to the press."

"You're willing to risk incurring the full wrath of this agency?"

"I am . . . especially when the Agency is misguided and mis - informed."

Cheskin paused, then let out a sigh. "If I agree to your terms, I'll insist that you give me *everything* you have, including any information concerning Agent Carlyle's whereabouts."

"I will bring all the information you need to see with me," Riggins replied. "As for the latter, I have lost total contact with Agent Carlyle. He has not responded to any of my messages." His concern for the agent was apparent in his tone.

"Hmmm," Cheskin murmured thoughtfully. "Are you aware of any circumstances that might have led to his disappearance?"

"The most recent information I have is that he wanted to meet with you to convince you of the Chinese corporation's plot to sabotage the agreements between the Saudis and the U.S."

"I already know about the Chinese's complicity at Jebel Ali. Agent Carlyle was right about their motivations."

"That's only part of what he was going to tell you."

"And you know the rest?" Cheskin asked.

"Most of it."

"Is it something I should be aware of now, Mr. Riggins?" Cheskin said. "We already know about the nuclear-waste storage site in Saudi Arabia. And that's a problem more specifically for the Saudis, not us. The Chinese explosion at Jebel Ali will be fully investigated by the INA, and they will be held accountable. What else is of such importance that Agent Carlyle's life's in danger or the cause of his disappearance?"

Riggins hesitated. "Your agents in Dubai were killed, Director. The Chinese don't want us to know what their real intentions are."

"Oh, no," Cheskin uttered. It was what he had feared. "But what is it that the Chinese don't want us to know about, Mr. Riggins?"

"It has to do with another cargo vessel . . . the one headed to the U.S.," Riggins told him.

Cheskin was momentarily stunned, then asked, "The Chinese have sent a cargo vessel to the U.S., similar to the one they had sent to the UAE?"

"No, Director," replied Riggins. "This one's *very* different. It's *far* more deadly. . . . And it's almost here."

Silence.

"Director, are you still on the line?"

"I'm here, Mr. Riggins," Cheskin finally said. "I suppose you have the proof of this."

"I discovered this plan recently. I hacked into the Chinese company's server. And no thanks to *your* hacker, it took me longer than necessary to get the intel."

"Can you tell me where it is now—the cargo vessel?" Cheskin asked, his concern growing into dread.

"The last sat-fix puts it past the Straits of Florida and heading in a slight northwesterly direction."

"Do you know its destination?"

"The Port of New Orleans," Riggins replied.

"Ah, shit," Cheskin uttered. "I'd like to see that intercepted Chinese intel, Mr. Riggins. Where can we meet?"

"There's a Starbucks café at Union Station in D.C. See you there in an hour."

"Will do," Cheskin replied. "And, for the record, Mr. Riggins, the Agency wasn't hacking into any of your systems."

83

NATURE

Gulf of Mexico

Xavier saw the squall line approaching off the port side of the boat. According to the radio reports, the tropical storm had grown in intensity and was nearing category-one hurricane status. Its current track put it on an intersecting course with the small FBI craft. The sea roiled as the winds whipped at the crests of the waves, sending plumes of saltwater twenty feet high. Everything was secured on deck as the men braced for the storm's full impact.

As the squall line passed over the craft, sheets of heavy rain reduced the visibility to near zero. The high-speed craft continued its acceleration directly into the abyss. Xavier stared at the radar screen in front of him. From the oncoming expansive mass of green clutter on the screen, he knew they were about to hit the leading edge of the raging storm system. It looked like a huge monster bearing down on them, and they were heading straight into its mouth.

Common sense dictated that they should have turned around and high-tailed it in the opposite direction. Xavier's survival instincts were screaming for him to do so. It took every ounce of his resolve to stay the course. They were on a collision path toward a terrifying force of nature—one of the most powerful phenomena on earth.

Xavier had carefully studied the direction and approximate speed of the storm. It was traveling slightly slower than the craft at about thirty-five miles per hour. His plan was to continue to run more north-westerly, hoping to travel parallel with the storm system and avoid its direct punch. But the system had shifted dramatically eastward, blocking their escape and descending directly on them. Based on its image, the system was over one hundred miles in diameter, covering the entire radar screen at maximum scan.

"You better tighten your life jacket," Xavier said to Veracruz. "This is going to get very ugly."

"No shit," Veracruz uttered, fumbling with the tie straps of the vest. "Any reasonable person could've seen that."

"And you'd call us reasonable people?" Xavier quipped, trying to keep the mood light, knowing it was but a feint attempt. "The good news is that we only have a couple of hours to rough this out. Then, we'll be able to outrun the leading edge of the storm to the north. The bad news is that we have a couple of hours to survive it."

Veracruz just shook his head. "After all the things I've been through, I'm likely to die out here with a stinking life jacket on."

Xavier smiled and was about to reply when a blast of wind knocked the craft sideways almost capsizing it. He struggled to control the action of the craft, but the force of the wind and the water against its rudder prevented him. Instead, the craft began nosing under on its starboard side. The fast-turning props screamed as they were forced out of the water from the listing angle of hull. Xavier pulled back on the throttles and turned slightly eastward with the storm's surge. The craft immediately gained enough purchase under its hull to level off.

They were now heading in the same direction as the storm and away from their course. But what followed was even more frightening than the near capsizing. Looking back, Xavier's eyes widened in horror. An enormous wall of water was fast approaching. He started to shout to Veracruz when the giant wave hit them.

313

84

MESSAGE

Gulf of Mexico

The captain of the cargo vessel received an alert from his navigator concerning the increasing strength of the storm. The powerful radar system and weather instrumentation helped the navigator plot the storm's advance.

"The center of the storm's circulation appears to be better organized. It is nearing hurricane strength," the navigator told the captain. "But it should not affect us directly. It has shifted more easterly, and we should only experience some wind gusts and higher sea conditions from the outer bands."

The captain peered at the color-enhanced radar screen. "It looks like there may be some severe thunderstorm cells from all that clutter. Hold your course for now and inform me if the conditions change," he said, turning to leave the bridge to head for his quarters.

"Captain, please wait. I received an e-mail communiqué from Zangshe headquarters a few minutes ago," the navigator told him, "I have printed it out for you," he said, handing him the copy.

The captain read the message.

Proceed as planned to the port's repair docks and immediately request that a fuel barge replenish your tanks. Further instructions will follow once you are inside the port.

At first glance, the captain assumed everything was in order. Although he had no idea why his cargo vessel had been directed to the U.S. in the first place, he had been assured it was a most important assignment. A bonus would be awaiting him upon his return. But as he thought more about the short communiqué, he realized that the instruction to request immediate refueling was highly unusual. In his many years as captain, he had never needed to be directed to refuel his vessel. It was standard procedure to do so and most typically occurred immediately preceding departure from a port for the next leg of a trip.

85

TROUBLE

Gulf of Mexico

The stern of the craft rose high in the air as the giant wave roared over them. Xavier caught a glimpse of Veracruz seated across from him. Sheer terror distorted the former agent's face. He knew there would be a similar expression on his own face.

The water's force pushed the craft violently downward into the base of the wave, in a pitch-poling effect, like somersaulting, as the bow dug in, trying to force the stern over. Tons of water cascaded over the beleaguered craft as it slid further down toward the bottom of the wave's trough. There was nothing they could do but hold on and wait.

As everything darkened around him, Xavier felt himself being jammed against the helm. He could barely move. Reflexively, he reached his hand toward the throttles and pushed them full forward. The craft shuddered under the weight of the water. Xavier heard the engines revving past their redline. The props clawed for traction against the almost vertical side of the massive wave.

Strangely, the bow lifted ever so slightly, tilting the hull backward and giving the props a chance to embed the blades. With a sudden thrust, the craft bolted upright. Xavier was thrown back into his seat as the stern buried itself against the falling wave. There was a jarring motion as they accelerated out of the bottom of a rogue wave's trough and up onto the back of a smaller one ahead. Xavier eased off on the power and guided the craft out of the clutches of the killer wave. He allowed himself to breathe a sigh of relief. He looked across at Veracruz and was glad to see that his friend was still in one piece.

For the next hour and a half, Xavier repeated the process of accelerating up the back of the swelling waves and easing off while surfing down their faces. Soon, the craft gradually began to outpace the storm's progress. Xavier guesstimated that they were almost sixty miles east of their original course and approximately two hundred miles from the cargo vessel. Looking at the radar screen and assuming that the storm track remained constant, Xavier determined that they should reach the storm's northeastern outer band in fewer than thirty minutes. Once there, they could turn northwesterly again to pursue the cargo vessel, which was still not visible on the radar screen.

"You okay," Xavier asked Veracruz.

The former FBI agent had his head buried between his knees. "If I don't lift my head, I'm fine. My stomach is up around my throat, and I'm real close to losing those Cuban sandwiches."

"That's not too bad, considering," Xavier said, with a slight smile. "We should be getting into smoother water soon, Alex. Hang in there."

The center of the storm was almost sixty-five miles off their port stern when Xavier finally turned toward the direction of the cargo vessel. He punched the throttles full forward and checked the fuel gauges. They had about five hours of fuel remaining. If the cargo vessel had maintained its cruising speed of eighteen knots, it would put them about one hundred fifty miles dead ahead, or three to four hours of fuel burn time.

A flash caught Xavier's attention. He looked down. A red warning light had suddenly appeared on the craft's instrument panel.

86

ASSERTIONS

Langley, Virginia

"Director Cheskin, your request for assistance from the FBI and the Coast Guard is out of order," Secretary of State Marlin Baskin said into his cell phone. "Your assertions about the Chinese cargo vessel are baseless. Besides, as you are well aware, we're already currently embroiled in an international investigation involving illegal activity against another Chinese vessel from the same company. I'm not about to authorize any action that would further heighten tensions between our two countries."

"Mr. Secretary, I have proof of the intelligence regarding the vessel's cargo and its destination. Furthermore, there is a connection between the recent explosion in Jebel Ali and the Chinese plans for their vessel heading toward us."

"What proof do you have, Director?"

"We were able to intercept a confidential message from the Chinese company's server that details their intentions to position a nuclear device of some sort within striking distance of one of our most strategic ports."

Baskin cleared his throat. "I'm not going to ask how you're able to procure that information. But if it's accurate, I'm interested in hearing your opinion on why the Chinese would take such precipitous action."

"I thought you might be able to shed light on that question, Mr. Secretary. I'm not privy to the discussions regarding the nature of the existing agreements between our country and the Chinese. Or for that matter, the current White House's policy on its laissez-faire posture in the Middle East."

"And you think those issues are related to what you've contended?"

"Don't you, Mr. Secretary?"

"Your impertinence is not lost on me, Director. If you have something to say . . . say it."

"I believe the Chinese have no intentions of honoring anything you've agreed to with them. Based upon their activities in the Middle East, especially the recent killings of two of my agents, they appear determined to impose their will on us—*whatever* that entails."

"You're painting the situation with a very broad and dangerous brush, Director. If your suspicions are wrong, we will have a major international crisis on our hands."

"And if I'm right?" Cheskin asserted.

There was a brief pause, then Baskin said, "Before I'm persuaded to act in support of your request to interdict the cargo vessel, I'll need to verify that your intel is completely incontrovertible. Please send the report to my attention by special carrier."

"There's little time for that, Mr. Secretary. I have reliable intel that the vessel is very close to its destination. We'll need to act immediately if we're to prevent the vessel from entering our security perimeters," the director warned.

"Then get me your intel quickly, Director. And in the meantime, I'm directing you to stand down pending further notification from my office," Baskin replied, ending the call.

"Goddammit," Cheskin spat out when he realized he'd been dismissed. "Sergeant Strong, have my car meet me downstairs. I need to get to downtown D.C. quickly," he said, hurrying out of his office.

"Director, I just received a call. The connection was poor, and then we got cut off," Strong said. "I'm pretty sure it was Agent Carlyle."

87

DILEMMA

Gulf of Mexico

The craft's warning light indicated a bilge alarm, which meant that either the bilge pumps weren't working or there was a leak substantial enough to overwhelm the pumps. If the pumps malfunctioned, the buildup of cooling water from the shaft log that drove the propellers would begin to fill the bilge, causing some minor issues. A leak, on the other hand, was a much more immediate problem.

Veracruz tended the helm while Xavier checked out the situation. Making his way into the engine compartment and down toward the bilge area, he saw the water flowing in steadily. Right away he knew it wasn't a bad pump. The craft had sprung a leak. Near the stern where the propellers shafts exited the transom, there was a half-inch crack in the Kevlar laminate. Apparently, the twisting and torquing during the rogue waves' onslaught had overstressed the craft. The vibration of the shafts from the propellers seemed to be exacerbating the problem. Slowing the craft down substantially would help to minimize the leak and allow the pumps to keep up with the flow, but this wasn't a favorable option.

"We definitely have a leak," Xavier said, returning to the deck. "It means we'll have limited time to overtake the cargo vessel before the bilge is completely flooded."

"What then?" Veracruz asked.

"Once we slow down, things get better. If we can get to the cargo vessel and do our business, there's a chance the pumps can keep up with the water and we can limp home."

"Otherwise?"

Xavier looked at this friend. "Otherwise, we sink trying to get there."

Veracruz thought for a moment. "What choice do we have? We've come this far, X, let's give it a shot."

"Glad we agree, Alex. I didn't want to have to force you to swim to shore," Xavier quipped.

Veracruz smiled. "That wouldn't have happened. I can't swim a stroke."

Xavier shot his friend a crooked smile. There was little more he could do about the leak. Instead, he turned his attention to the old radar unit. The images were a bit fuzzy, but he knew the cargo vessel was still slightly out of range. Besides, when an image that size popped up on the screen, there would be no mistaking its presence. His concern was that the cargo vessel's radar technology was much more sophisticated than theirs and had already detected them. If so, their craft probably hadn't elicited any scrutiny yet. And since the storm's outer bands were moving northeasterly, there might still be a chance of motoring up behind the cargo vessel without causing alarm. At least that remained Xavier's hope. But for now, the urgency had shifted from being identified to simply staying afloat.

With that in mind, Xavier set the throttles to seventy-five percent power. His analytical mind had already calculated the probability of covering the distance to the cargo vessel before the leaking water enveloped them. Based upon what he saw below, he had estimated that it would be very close . . . maybe too close.

88

CRUSADE

Beijing, China

It was early morning in China's capital city. Minister Chek was in his office well before sunrise. He had been preparing for this day for a very long time, and he greeted it with much anticipation. When he was a very small boy, his family's village had been ravaged by the effects of nuclear waste from Zangshe's mining operations. His grand-mother—his only surviving relative—had managed to get them to safety, sparing them the quick but painful death the rest of his family had suffered. Once Chek was old enough to understand what had hap-pened, he had sworn an oath of retribution against Zangshe and its principles.

Under his constant pressure, the INA had finally pushed aside Zangshe's appeal process. Instead, the regulatory agency had announced their intentions to begin a series of extensive site inspections designed to ascertain the extent and severity of the alleged abuses perpetrated by Zangshe.

According to Chek, who had gathered volumes of evidence against the mega-enterprise, as many as two hundred thousand people had died or were terminally sickened by the long-term and mindless disregard for human life. From the poisonous leaching into the aquifers under the Taihung Mountains where its operations were located, to its careless handling procedures in the working mines, Zangshe had constantly ignored and scoffed at the increasing complaints and notifications from the surrounding community governing officials. Even the national government had turned a blind eye toward the ongoing catastrophe.

But finally, Chek had focused the attention of the INA on the dire situation. His earlier public campaign and clever manipulations of the press to embarrass the regulatory agency into action had proved effective. Chek had even managed to use the accident at Zangshe's laboratory against the company. He blamed the explosion and the resulting deaths of more than two hundred workers on Zangshe's lack of effective safety measures and disregard for effective venting of the uranium-mine gases. Chek's claims became an overnight international story.

The real facts didn't matter. The INA had no choice but to set aside the legal challenges from Zangshe's attorneys and begin the site inspections in earnest.

With that underway, Chek had completed the next step in his quest to make good the promise to avenge his family and his decimated village. He knew it would never be possible to punish Zangshe enough for its heinous crimes, but he had made it his lifelong crusade to try.

Events were aligning in Chek's future that were completely out of his control but would dramatically impact the outcome of his quest against Zangshe. Events that even the thoroughly prepared Chek could have never imagined.

89

HACKER

Union Station, Washington D.C.

R iggins located himself inside the Starbucks café, facing the window toward the main shopping area. Union Station was a heavily trafficked tourist destination. It was a very public place to meet with a number of egress opportunities if the situation with Director Cheskin went sour.

But Riggins's main concern centered on his recent discovery of the hacker's identity. After Cheskin's comment that the hacker didn't belong to the Agency, Riggins had investigated further and followed his suspicions that the hacker was somehow connected to QPR. His suspicions were correct. Although he had attempted to route his communications through several switching hubs, he also had to assume that the hacker knew of his meeting with Cheskin. On top of that, it was highly probable that the Chinese were now aware that he had knowledge about the hybrid and its destination. Given their propensity for eliminating loose ends, he had become a likely target.

All of this gave Riggins a strange sense of excitement, and for a moment he fancied himself a true agent, like Carlyle and the others. There he was, the bearer of top-secret information about to meet with the Director of the CIA. The adrenaline that coursed through his veins gave him an unfamiliar high. This was a very different experience from chasing down hackers . . . and being one. Oddly, after all his years in the CIA, he felt as if he finally belonged and was actually valued. As he contemplated the situation further, his mind began calculating the odds that someone had followed him to Starbucks.

A sudden stabbing pain in his chest stopped all of his mind's chatter. Instead, he was flooded with another kind of sensation. He hadn't seen or heard anything. But the impact of the bullet had immediately sent his body into shock. He looked down and saw to his dismay blood spreading across his shirt, disfiguring the image of the imprinted Superman logo. Light-headed and moving as if in a dream, he edged out of the booth and stumbled toward the rear exit. The small, milling crowd that had gathered inside the café barely took notice of him. Since no window was broken, Riggins realized that the shooter had to be in the crowd. He knew he had to get outside. As he tried to hurry his step, his feet grew heavy. Consciousness was quickly ebbing away.

Riggins fell against the rear door of the café. It swung open abruptly, causing him to tumble out awkwardly onto the sidewalk. He heard footsteps closely behind him. In desperation, he tried to get up and even thought of running, but his legs collapsed under him. A cold darkness overcame him as he lay facedown beside a trash receptacle. His prodigious mind still functioning, he thought it ironic to die in the shadows of city waste. The last thing he was aware of was the sound of a gun cocking and a strong hand on the back of his shoulder.

90

RENDEZVOUS

Gulf of Mexico

The weather had improved only slightly as heavy rain bands continued to pound at the craft as it sped toward the cargo vessel. Large swells extended outward from the storm's center for over one hundred miles. The visibility was reduced to less than a few yards past the craft's bow. The radar screen was filled with green clutter behind them, and the image of the cargo vessel loomed up ominously each time the craft rose onto the top of another large swell.

Xavier had kept a close eye on the bilge alarm. For the past two hours, the light had flickered on and off, indicating that the pumps were barely able to keep up with the leak. They were only thirty miles to the stern of the cargo vessel and the alarm light was now more on than off. *It's going to be damn close,* he thought, as he looked over at the snoozing Veracruz. Between the seasickness and constant smell of diesel oil mixing with the bilge water, his friend had decided that sleeping might ease his discomfort.

He estimated that the cargo vessel had slowed somewhat, probably due to the large swells. Over the next hour, Xavier studied the size and direction of the swell action in relationship to the position of the cargo vessel. He began to feel more confident that they could pull alongside the vessel and ride the large waves without being crushed. Fortunately, there would be almost no side-to-side motion causing the vessel to yaw and rise dangerously above them.

The question still remained: could they approach without being detected? There was extremely heavy clutter on the radar behind them. Would the cargo vessel's radar be affected similarly? They were approximately five miles from the vessel when Xavier's VHF radio came to life.

"Port security, port security, this is Chinese cargo vessel, *Chen Yuan* calling, over," a voice in broken English said.

Xavier froze. He waited for the response.

"This is port security, go ahead vessel *Chen Yuan,* over," came back the reply.

"We are advising you that due to weather conditions, our arrival into your security holding zone will be delayed, over."

"Roger, vessel *Chen Yuan,* when you are within two miles of the outer marker we will dispatch a pilot boat to assist you, over."

"Thank you. This is vessel *Chen Yuan,* over and out."

Xavier breathed a sigh of relief. Maybe they hadn't been spotted or maybe they'd been ignored in the wake of the storm. Oftentimes, smaller vessels followed larger ones to safety. In any instance, at least the vessel had clearly identified itself. He was almost certain it had to be the Chinese vessel based on the course heading and location. But it was positive confirmation.

"Alex . . . Alex," Xavier called over toward Veracruz to wake his friend.

"Unfortunately, I'm awake," Veracruz grunted. "Tell me we're back in Miami, X."

"Not quite, but we're almost to the cargo vessel. We need to get the gear and the auxiliary dinghy ready. It's about a mile or so until the fun begins."

Xavier knew that getting the small dinghy in the water wasn't easy in the huge swells. But he didn't want to wait until the last minute and have a hitch. "I'm going to lower the dinghy into the water and trail it behind us until we get up to the vessel," he said. "Take the helm, Alex."

It took some doing, but Xavier managed to lower the dinghy in the water with the craft's small hoist. He attached a long line to it and tied it off the stern cleat of the craft. The little boat bobbed steadily behind them.

When Xavier returned to take the helm, Veracruz went below to get the gear bag. It wasn't long before he emerged with the bag, but he looked ready to keel over.

"Are you going to be okay?" Xavier asked, commenting on his friend's sickly pallor.

"Probably not, but how much worse can it get?" Veracruz quipped, ever ready with good humor.

Xavier shot him an amused glance, just as an enormous rumble erupted, vibrating the craft like a quake. Xavier looked at the radar screen. It showed that they were right on top of the vessel. The vibration dissipated as a swell came between them and the vessel.

"Shit! Sorry I said that!" Veracruz yelled, still with a hint of humor despite the situation.

With the visibility very poor, it was an eerie feeling to be so close and not be able to see anything. But they could hear the sound of the huge vessel as it plowed through the seas. Along the hull of the speedboat was a remnant foam trail from the vessel's huge wake. This told them they were right off its stern.

The swells appeared to have grown longer and less steep. Xavier peered through the battering rain, searching for the outline of the vessel. He eased off on the throttles to try to gauge the speed of the lurking ship. The small craft rose once more on the back of a long swell. The bilge alarm had been steadily red for a while. With anxiety etched on their faces, both men peered into the darkness. Then, all of a sudden, the hulking outline of the enormous vessel appeared directly in front of them as if out of nowhere. And it was a whole lot bigger than either of them had ever imagined.

91

RESCUE

Union Station, Washington D.C.

The bullet had entered through the left side of Riggins's chest, but there was no exit wound in back—the bullet was lodged in his body. Cheskin tucked his gun away and dropped to the ground to try to resuscitate the techie.

He had entered the coffee shop just as Riggins had been shot. He had watched in amazement as Riggins stood up and stumbled toward the rear door with the shooter on his tail. Cheskin had quickly sprung into action from across the café and followed the shooter and his prey outside. Cheskin's driver had followed close behind.

Aware that he was being followed, the shooter turned left once outside the door and headed into an alley that ran along the back of the mall. Cheskin directed his driver to give chase while he attended to Riggins.

"Call 911!" he yelled to a passerby who stopped to help and had immediately complied.

Riggins's pulse was weak and he wasn't breathing. Cheskin tried to stem the bleeding with direct pressure, but the wound was gushing too quickly. The situation seemed dire, but when the paramedics arrived on the scene within minutes of the pedestrian's call, Cheskin felt the stirrings of hope. The EMTs stabilized the unconscious techie long enough to load him into the ambulance and quickly whisked him off to the hospital.

Cheskin's driver came bounding back from around the corner of the alley. He had lost sight of the shooter in a crowd.

"Let's go," Cheskin said. "We need to follow that ambulance to the hospital."

"Make sure that nobody tries anything here," Cheskin said to his agent when the two men got out of the car in the front of the emergency room. "Have several agents posted outside this area," he instructed before bolting through the entrance to the ER.

Cheskin knew that without Riggins's information, he had no chance of making his case with the Secretary of State. As he rushed passed hospital security flashing his credentials, he recalled that the shooter was of average height. He had called into the D.C Metro Police to be on the lookout for anyone suspicious in and around the Union Station area wearing a ski cap, gray sweatshirt, and jeans—not very distinctive, and more than likely a pro who had already blended into the crowded station's traffic.

Cheskin found the emergency doctor attending to Riggins and introduced himself. The doctor had just come out of the triage room where Riggins had been taken.

"We've stabilized him for the moment, Director Cheskin. I can't give you any more details at the moment. We really won't know anything further until he's in surgery. We'll keep you posted," the ER doctor said, heading quickly into another room.

Cheskin stopped at the emergency desk. "One of my people was just admitted and I need to know when he's headed into surgery."

The desk nurse looked up slowly and peered at him over her glasses. "And who might you be?" she asked impertinently.

"I'm Director of the CIA and I'd appreciate your cooperation."

"And I'd appreciate your backing off. As you can see we're very busy with multiple emergencies," she said, putting her head back down.

"Listen to me," Cheskin urged. "I understand your situation, but try to understand mine. I've got a seriously wounded agent with vital information that could avert a major disaster."

The nurse stared back at Cheskin. "I'm finishing up a twenty-four-hour shift and in the midst of dealing with a terrible bus accident. I'd say I have a major disaster of my own right here. Now director, *please* back off until I have time."

Cheskin banged his fisted hand on the countertop. "Who's in charge here," he bellowed.

"That would be me," a diminutive male nurse replied as he approached from down the hall. "How can I help you?"

Cheskin tried to reign in his temper. "I'd like to know when my agent is going into surgery."

"I just left the room and he's heading up for surgery as we speak, Director Cheskin," he said, looking down at Cheskin's ID. Handing him a plastic bag that contained a bloodstained file, he added, "Here, you may find this of some interest. It was tucked inside his jacket. We found it after it was cut off him. I don't know how much of it you'll be able to read. It seems to have gotten in the way of the bullet."

92

INFLICTION

Gulf of Mexico

In the waning hours of late afternoon, Xavier had finally maneuvered the craft to within several hundred feet of the hulking vessel. As soon as it was on the same swell as the vessel, it became easier to judge the speed and angle of approach. He directed Veracruz to bring the dinghy alongside the craft and to tie it off tightly against its port side.

"Okay, Alex, moment of truth. I'm going to move as close to the centerline of the vessel as possible . . . where the movement between the two hulls is minimized and the damage can be maximized. As soon as that happens, I want you to affix the devices."

Veracruz fumbled with the insulated gloves in the ice chest for the clamshell objects. "It won't take long, X. Once I arm each one, they'll be so attracted to that steel hull they'll practically fly out of my hands."

Xavier managed a smile. "You'll have to gauge the distance, Alex. Just try to keep as much of your body inside the dinghy's hard rubber hull as possible. Let it absorb the impact of any rubbing."

With a nod, Veracruz eased himself over the craft's side into the dinghy. Xavier carefully eyed the closing distance between the vessel's massive steel hull and the craft's much smaller Kevlar mass. As he edged closer inch by inch, he felt the effects of the vessel's wake pulling and pushing at the craft. The sheer power of the vessel vibrated the craft's hull like a toy boat, making it difficult for him to hold his line. He kept his eye focused on one location on the hull much like an air-craft-carrier pilot looks for one spot to land on. Ignoring the staggering volume of steel towering over them, Xavier skillfully manipulated the craft to within six feet of the vessel. It was as close as he dared.

"Do it now, Alex!" he shouted above the din of the vessel's rum-bling vibrations.

Veracruz carefully handled the clamshell devices. He placed one of them beside him in the dinghy as he armed the first device. With down-ward force on the pressure switch, Veracruz actuated the chain-reac-tion-driven device. A faint vibration assured him that the process had been initiated. He waited patiently for the dinghy to move closer to the cargo vessel's hull with the swells' action. The sound of the water rush-ing furiously past the massive ship was disconcerting. As the two ves-sels moved in a heaving motion to within a foot and half of one another, he quickly reached across and snapped the first device in place. The instant he attached the clamshell device, it began its task. Small whiffs of chemical smoke followed by an acrid smell indicted that the nitric acid had been activated by the ignited turpentine film covering the entire outside of the clamshell. Wasting little time, Vera-cruz signaled to Xavier to move the craft forward, and he repeated the process with the second device, placing it approximately twenty feet away from the first one. Just as he finished getting the second one snapped into place, the distance between the vessel and the dinghy's hull suddenly closed, knocking him backward and onto the floor of the dinghy. He howled in pain.

Xavier immediately steered the craft a safe distance away from the vessel. He rushed to the dinghy to assist Veracruz, whose right arm had been crushed by the impact. Xavier quickly ascertained that his friend had suffered a compound fracture—his ulna bone was protruding from the skin. Xavier leaned over to help him.

"Alex, can you get into the craft?" he asked.

Veracruz was a tough guy. "I've got a broken flipper, X, but my legs are fine," he replied with an agonized grimace, as he slowly rolled over the side and into the craft.

He seemed capable of dealing with the pain, but Xavier knew that shock would be setting in soon. He had to set the arm and bandage it. "Let's get that arm attended to, Alex. There's got to be a first-aid kit around somewhere," he said.

As the craft dropped back from the stern of the vessel, Xavier noticed that several crewmembers had gathered along the rail of the vessel and were looking down at them. In the pelting rain, it was hard to make out any distinguishing features. But the sound of pinging spits in the water nearby clearly indicated their intentions. Apparently, they had tried to observe the actions of the craft from directly above, but were unable to see anything until the craft had drifted back away from their vessel. If things went as planned, they would soon learn what had transpired.

Xavier had essentially stopped their forward motion and allowed the cargo vessel to steam away from them. Within minutes, the vessel had moved several hundred yards away and out of gunshot range. The craft sat still in the water. Xavier was hoping to give the pumps time to expel some of the water from the bilge. But already, they began listing to one side.

He helped Veracruz with the injury. Between the two of them, they were able to set his fractured arm and apply a crude bandage to the wound. His friend was clearly in pain and would need medical assistance soon. The GPS coordinates showed that they were approximately one hundred ten miles due west of Sarasota, Florida—too far for their remaining fuel and definitely too far for their sinking boat. Xavier had only one option left.

"Alex, I'm going to call in our position to the Coast Guard."

Veracruz nodded and smiled weakly. "How much time's passed since we put the device on the vessel?" he asked.

Xavier checked his watch. The old chronometer was still ticking despite the elements. "Almost twenty minutes."

"It shouldn't be long now," Veracruz said. "Their bilge alarms should be going off shortly."

Xavier and Veracruz watched as the enormous ship continued to press forward away from them, the crew unaware of its soon-to-be mortally wounded hull.

93

ORDERS

Gulf of Mexico

The captain of the cargo vessel was resting comfortably when the
first mate knocked at his cabin door.

"Captain . . . Captain. I must speak with you. There was a slight
incident with a small pleasure craft."

The captain opened his door. "What is the incident about?"

"We had been observing the craft following us for some time,"
the first mate replied. "It appeared to be running from the storm and
staying in range of our vessel, possibly for assistance. But per your
instructions, we did not make radio contact with them. About thirty
minutes ago they pulled alongside and appeared to be attempting to
board the vessel. We were successful in chasing them away. I thought
you should be—" The first mate was interrupted by the shrill sound
of an alarm.

The two men rushed to the bridge. When they arrived, the ship's
engineer was busily trying to assess the reason for the alarm.

"What is happening?" the captain asked.

"There was a breach in the hull of the vessel, sir. It appears we may
have struck something from the storm. But the watertight compartments

should contain the flooding and the alarm should reset itself," the engineer replied calmly.

The captain and first mate anxiously watched the alarm board. Shortly, as the engineer had indicated, the alarm turned off and the panel returned to normal status.

ଔ

The phosphorus fusing initiated the reaction between the turpentine and nitric acid inside the clamshells. The resultant mixture became violently voracious. The outer skin of the hull was merely an appetizer. Once the ravenous concoctions from both clamshell devices had fully dispersed, fifty feet of the ship's hull were devoured like a full-course meal.

ଔ

The captain turned to the first mate. "We will need to radio our situation to the U.S. authorities. As soon as we are safely at anchor, we will need to have an assessment made of the damage to our hull."

"Aye, Captain. I will transmit our situation immediately," the first mate said, as he turned for the radio room.

The sound of the alarm bellowing again startled everyone, most especially the engineer.

"It cannot be!" he exclaimed, staring incredulously at his computer screen. "Apparently, the hull has suffered massive damage. Seawater is pouring in at the rate of over twenty thousand gallons per minute and increasing," he said, looking up at the captain. "The watertight compartments cannot contain the pressure and our pumps will soon be overwhelmed, sir. We need to consider abandoning the vessel."

The captain was dumbfounded. Never in his worst imaginings did he ever think this possible. This vessel was the top of its line, safest of all cargo transports. It was the lion of the seas. And now it was about to be swallowed up in a matter of moments by some mysterious occurrence.

"I must contact Zangshe headquarters immediately. Get me a connection on the sat-link," the captain yelled.

Within moments, the contact had been made. "Taiji, I regret to inform you that our vessel has suffered most serious damage apparently from the severe storm. Our hull has been critically breached, and we are taking on too much water to sustain floatation. I am about to issue a mayday command and abandon ship."

There was a slight delay in response. "You are most certain of your condition, Captain?" Yakubla asked.

"There is no doubt of our circumstances, Taiji. We are already beginning to list uncontrollably."

"I must order you not to issue the mayday notice," Yakubla said sternly. "Instead you are directed to ask the engineer to give you the remote device he has in his possession."

"But Taiji, we will need to notify the authorities soon if we are to be rescued."

"That will not be necessary, Captain. Your loyalty and sacrifice are greatly admired and appreciated by Zangshe."

"What is it that you are requesting, Taiji?"

"You will activate the remote device and press the detonator. There must be no trace left of the ship to be found if salvaged."

"Taiji, we are in waters more than two thousand feet deep . . . surely a fitting graveyard for the vessel."

"I will not say it again, Captain. Do as you have been ordered or your family will suffer the consequences of your failure," Yakubla barked and ended the connection.

The captain's expression froze with terror. He looked down at the engineer. "You are holding something for me?"

"Aye, Captain," he replied, handing him a small remote. "I was instructed not to say anything about this until we had docked in port. I am sorry for the deception."

The captain nodded his head slowly. "Apparently, we have all been deceived. Make provisions to get everyone off the vessel immediately," he said.

"It seems to make little sense to use the remote detonator, Captain. The vessel will shortly find its way to the bottom on its own," the engineer said.

"I have my orders. And now you have yours," the captain said, settling down in complete despair into the captain's chair at the helm.

94

ENERGY

Gulf of Mexico

Thirty minutes later, Xavier watched as the cargo vessel moved almost five miles away from their drifting and badly listing craft. The weather had improved considerably as the storm front had finally moved past them. He was able to follow the vessel's progress up and down the large swells through his binoculars. It was obvious that it had slowed considerably, most likely in response to the bilge alarms. He looked at his watch. The Coast Guard had already dispatched a rescue helicopter. It would be on location in less than an hour. By that time, most of the vestiges of the wounded cargo vessel would have disappeared.

"Shouldn't be long now, X," Veracruz said, following the vessel's movements along with Xavier.

"How's the arm, Alex?"

"Not bad enough to keep me from watching this," he said, as a fiery explosion from the vessel surprised both of them. "What the hell?!" he shouted.

Xavier refocused his binoculars and zoomed in more closely on the vessel. The entire rear section of the ship was ablaze. "They've detonated the fuel tanks," he said hesitantly, noticing that the vessel's position had already changed dramatically. It was slipping stern first quickly into the sea.

"Why would they do that?" Veracruz asked with curiosity and concern.

Xavier continued to peer through his binoculars. "They don't want to leave any evidence. It'll look like an accident from the storm. And more than likely, give them the opportunity to try this again," he replied, putting the binoculars down and looking over at Veracruz with a sense of some pessimism.

༄

The explosion in the fuel tanks of the nearly submerged cargo ship blew apart the hybrid's containment enclosure. Once exposed to the oxygen-rich environment of the enormous cargo hold, the hybrid expanded rapidly, absorbing the full force of the explosion. The resultant nuclear reaction triggered a release of energy so incredibly powerful that it completely obliterated the vessel. Within nanoseconds every scrap of material binding the vessel together had vaporized. Absolutely nothing remained except for the now fully developed hybrid. It had reformed its molecular structure within the enormous mushroom cloud that had menacingly gathered above the surface of the water, where the vessel had stood only moments prior. In a series of continuing nuclear interactions, the hybrid reabsorbed each subsequent release of energy from its *own* explosions and repeated the process until every last molecule of energy was dissipated.

Most of the impact of the energy release was directed downward into the depths of the Gulf. But shock waves from the initial explosion had traveled through the water. The small FBI craft, now almost eight miles away, was shaken so hard that it cracked apart, hurtling Xavier and Veracruz into the water.

༄

"Are you okay Alex," Xavier asked, grabbing onto a section of the craft's broken hull.

"That was impressive as hell. What was it?" Veracruz replied, floundering in the water and trying to hold on to the hull with his good arm.

"The fuel-tank explosion set off the nuclear hybrid. Had it not been for the fact that it occurred out here in the Gulf, the impact would have, in all likelihood, destroyed the entire port area," Xavier replied. "I wasn't certain what to expect from the hybrid's reaction. But from what we just witnessed, it is even more powerful and dangerous than I had suspected. If we can't wrest the formulation of the hybrid from the Chinese, we may be facing more of these incidents under much different circumstances and more exposed venues."

"This is about exposed as I can be, X," said Veracruz struggling to stay afloat.

Xavier treaded water over to his friend and helped him get a tighten grasp on the section of broken hull. "I'll make certain you get back safely to Miami, Alex. And fortunately, I believe that most of the devastating effects from the hybrid have been contained . . . for now.

The men were unaware that the force of the energy released from the hybrid had been felt many, many miles away. The Coast Guard pilots had been honing in on the emergency transponder signal from the craft's emergency position-indicating radio beacon, which Xavier had initiated. The Coast Guard pilots had already identified the image of the cargo vessel clearly on their radar screen when they had departed from their base in Sarasota. But its inexplicable disappearance from their radar in the past ten minutes puzzled them. As they drew closer to the target area, the pilots watched with concern the series of explosions occurring out on the horizon directly above the area where they had first identified the vessel's position.

"I've only seen pictures of that effect," Commander Rob Mullins said. "If I didn't know better, I'd say it looks like some sort of atomic test."

"There's nothing on the NOTAMs indicating any type of test," the copilot replied, referring to the federally issued notices to all mariners.

"I wouldn't have thought so. Those tests are not scheduled until later this year over near the Sigsbee's trough," Mullins said. "But take a look at that," he stated, pointing below.

An energy wave was traveling over the remnants of the storm swells. It had formed at the point of the explosion, traveling at a speed of four hundred miles per hour, moving quickly past them on its way toward the shoreline. The energy from the explosions had generated a tsunami that was destined to cause substantial damage along the west coast of Florida, which was already being hammered by the tropical storm.

"Call it in," Mullins said to his copilot. "They won't have much time to react along the shoreline. Let's get our two stranded mariners and take a look around for any survivors of that cargo vessel. We'll need to get back to base immediately. They're going to need our help."

95

PROOF

Washington, D.C.

Cheskin waited anxiously for a report from Riggins's attending surgeon. When the doctor approached him not very long after they had taken Riggins in for surgery, Cheskin knew from his dour expression that it was not good news.

"We've done everything possible for your guy, Director. But there was substantial damage to his lung and coronary arteries. He's lost a tremendous amount of blood and remains on life support in critical condition. It is unlikely he'll survive through the evening. Does he have any next of kin to notify?"

"He doesn't," Cheskin replied. "I had Langley check into his records. Seems the guy had been an orphan and was all alone."

The doctor paused respectfully for a moment, then added, "You might be interested to know that the bullet seemed to have been made entirely of plastic and shredded apart on impact. That's what caused the massive hemorrhaging."

So the shooter was a pro, Cheskin thought to himself. "I appreciate that information, doctor. I will want to see the autopsy report of course. And the remaining fragments of the bullet will be required for evidence."

"Of course," the doctor replied, shaking the director's hand, and the two parted ways.

Cheskin met up with his driver, and the two headed back to the car.

"Where to, Director?" the agent asked.

"Back to the office," he replied.

With furrowed brows, the director began going over the details. He was familiar with the type of weapon that had been used to shoot Riggins. It was common among terrorists, who found them much less likely to be detected by airport security. He fished his phone out of his pocket and dialed the deputy director.

"I want *every* suspected sleeper cell in D.C. investigated immediately for any involvement in the shooting at Union Station today," Cheskin said firmly when the deputy director answered.

"We've already looked into the technical assistant's history as directed, and, as you know, we have limited resources, Director. What about the ongoing search for Agent Carlyle and the investigation of the Jebel Ali incident? We have all of our people on that."

Cheskin huffed, then barked out, "Suspend those assignments and call the FBI. Have our agents work with them to get to the bottom of this immediately!"

"Understood," the deputy director said, and the call ended. Cheskin turned his attention to the bloodied file that had been taken from Riggins's jacket. He slipped on a pair of evidence-handling gloves and lifted the file out of the protective plastic sleeve in which it had been placed. The doctor was right about the file being difficult to read. The blood-soaked pages had ragged tears from the plastic fragments. He could identify the source of the information from the top of the first page. It was in Mandarin, but Riggins's notes alongside clearly identified that it was from a Zangshe computer server located in Xiong Xian, China. Several of the following pages had complete sections missing from the tattered report. As his eyes skimmed through the readable portions of the file, he stopped at one place and a faint smile emerged.

"Turn the car around," he said to his driver. "Let's get over to the White House."

96

NEWS

Xiong Xian, China

"We have encountered some unexpected bad luck, Great One," Yakubla said, as he entered Khan's office. "The cargo vessel carrying the hybrid was caught in a tropical storm and sustained crippling damage. I directed the captain to detonate the vessel to eliminate any trace of the hybrid."

Khan grabbed at his braided knot and stood up from his desk. "This is a most unfortunate turn of events," he seethed thunderously, the veins of his neck protruding. "How is it that our strong vessel succumbed to the ravages of a *tropical* storm?" he railed, approaching Yakubla. "Do you not find that unusual?"

There was a faint twitch at the corner of Yakubla's eye in the face of Khan's rant. "I did, Great One. I questioned the captain, specifically, to find out if his conditions were dire. He confirmed that the vessel had somehow suffered critical damage to the hull and that it was indeed sinking."

Khan turned his back to his second in command. "I am unfamiliar with the force of any storm that could cause such damage to one of our vessels. The captain must have been negligent." Khan couldn't fathom that he wouldn't prevail in the end, even with this major set-back. He turned to Yakubla, his composure regained. "But you have done the right thing, Yaku. We cannot have any evidence that would reveal our intentions before we have had time to replace the threat. And we *will* replace the threat, Yaku."

"We are working to restore all of QPR's specifications regarding the hybrid's formulation. Dr. Liang has assured me that he should have most of the data recovery completed within a short time from now," Yakubla assured him.

"We must begin the replication process very soon," Khan replied. "However, it seems we will be gaining some leeway in our timetable since the threats from Minister Chek will soon be neutralized."

Yakubla nodded. "On that matter, I have received information from our sources that important news concerning very significant changes in the national government will be released shortly."

Khan smirked. "Our plan to expose Minister Chek's role in the horrific bombing of our laboratory must have had exceedingly good results," he said. "I look forward to being able to deal with our nuclear-waste problems and the INA on my terms once the announcement of Chek's removal from office is made public."

97

PROTOCOL

Sarasota, Florida

Xavier and Veracruz were plucked from the waters of the Gulf of Mexico by the Coast Guard chopper. The search for surviving crewmembers from the cargo vessel proved fruitless. Apparently, they had all perished in the explosions.

"What were you doing out here in the storm?" Commander Mullins asked Xavier.

Xavier hesitated. He realized that his story wouldn't take long to check out. The BOLO out on him would soon verify his identify. But for Veracruz's sake, he didn't want to discuss the matter with the Coast Guard without first getting promises of immunity for his friend from the CIA and Cheskin. "It's a matter of national security, Commander. You'll need to contact the CIA at Langley. Ask for Director Cheskin."

At the mention of national security and the specific reference to the director of the CIA, Mullins decided it was definitely above his pay grade to question any further. "We'll have an ambulance ready to take your friend to the hospital for treatment. And I'll call your request into base command," he said to Xavier.

Xavier nodded. "Thanks, Commander," he said, shooting a glance at Veracruz, who was in no condition to undergo questioning. The call to Cheskin would be interesting. But he had little doubt that the CIA would provide the release to get him back to Langley. And getting immunity for Veracruz wouldn't be difficult. He had a lot of information chips to cash in and saving his friend's pension was more than worthwhile.

The chopper landed in the midst of strong winds. The back end of the tropical storm system had settled onto Sarasota and was pounding its shoreline. But that paled in comparison to the damage inflicted by the huge tidal wave, which had hit thirty minutes earlier. The entire coastline from the Florida Keys to Tampa had suffered major inland flooding and substantial building damage.

Xavier's request to contact the CIA had already been made. The ambulance was ready on the tarmac to take Veracruz straight to the hospital. In the meantime, Commander Mullins had been requested to assist in an emergency evacuation and was awaiting the fuel truck for his chopper. Xavier hopped off and was greeted by a Coast Guard officer who escorted him to base command.

"I understand you've requested us to contact the CIA on your behalf," Rear Admiral Peter Hansen said to Xavier.

"Director John Cheskin to be more specific, sir."

"Since you're here, mind telling me what this is all about?"

"As I indicated to your pilot, sir, it's a matter of national security."

"I've got a tropical storm on my doorstep, rogue tidal-wave damage, and a cargo vessel that mysteriously sank underneath a mushroom cloud in my watch area. I'm a bit short on patience, and I'd like an explanation as to what the hell you were doing out there," Hansen replied irately.

"I don't know what you want to hear, Admiral. The best I can do is tell you to contact the CIA."

Hansen stared long and hard at Xavier. "My men risk their lives to save your bacon, and you give some cockamamie excuse."

"Sorry about the situation, sir. And frankly, I'd be pissed too if I were in your shoes," Xavier replied apologetically.

Hansen nodded as if in resignation. "Get me the director of the CIA, Ensign," he yelled to his adjutant.

The line in Hansen's office buzzed. He picked it up.

"Director Cheskin's office," Sergeant Strong answered.

"This is Rear Admiral Hansen from the U.S. Coast Guard Saratoga Station in Florida. May I speak to Director Cheskin?"

"He's currently unavailable, Admiral. Can I help you, sir?" Strong asked.

"There's a Dr. Xavier here who has requested that the director of the CIA be contacted."

"I can vouch for him. And I'm certain the director would like to speak with you. I can route your call directly to his cell."

A few moments elapsed as Strong connected the call. "This is John Cheskin. Who am I speaking with?"

"This is Admiral Peter Hansen, U.S. Coast Guard, sir. We have a Dr. Xavier in our custody. He was rescued by one of our choppers in the Gulf of Mexico today and claims that he was involved in a matter of national security. He said that you were to be contacted for any explanations."

"That's affirmative, Admiral. Can I impose on you to have one of your jets fly him to Langley immediately?"

Hansen hesitated briefly. "I can arrange for that, Director."

"May I speak with him, Admiral?"

"Certainly," he replied. "But before I do that, is there anything you want to tell me regarding the situation that my pilots observed?"

"I'm not certain what they had observed, Admiral," Cheskin replied.

"A cargo vessel vanished off their radar in a matter of seconds, and they witnessed what appeared to be a nuclear explosion."

"I'm sorry, Admiral, I'm not certain what I can tell you until I've had a chance to hear Dr. Xavier's account of the events. But from the brief information you've just related to me, it would appear that the cargo vessel may have suffered some type of catastrophic failure as a result of the storm."

Hansen paused for a few moments. "I gather I won't be hearing details from you anytime soon, Director."

"I appreciate your understanding of the circumstances, Admiral. May I speak with Dr. Xavier?" Cheskin asked calmly.

Hansen handed the phone across his desk.

"Director Cheskin," Xavier said.

"Dr. Xavier," Cheskin said, letting out a sigh. "You're a very hard man to catch up with. I gather you have some information for me regarding the cargo vessel. It can't be coincidental that you're in the Gulf at the same exact time as the Chinese vessel."

"Your assumption is correct, sir," Xavier replied respectfully.

"You don't need to say much on your end, Doctor. I already know about Mr. Riggins's confirming intel regarding the cargo vessel and its cargo. Did you have contact with the cargo vessel?"

"Yes, sir."

"Is the cargo secured?" Cheskin asked tentatively.

"In a manner of speaking."

"Do we have an imminent threat?"

"Not anymore."

"So we're safe then?"

"For the time being, sir."

98

RECOGNITION

Langley, Virginia

C heskin took Riggins's proof of intel to the United States' Attorney General, and it set off a firestorm of activity in the White House. Although somewhat incomplete, the information in the bloodied file was confirmation enough that the Chinese corporation had no intention of honoring their agreement with the U.S. And based upon the information in the file, the actions that had been taken to interdict the cargo vessel were deemed justifiable. But the report from the Coast Guard and Cheskin's brief conversation with Xavier had left much to speculation.

The Coast Guard jet had Xavier in Cheskin's office within ninety minutes of their call. Although he had been given a change of clothes, Xavier still looked as if he'd been through hell and back. He gladly sipped the coffee the director's assistant had given him the moment he sat down across from Cheskin.

"Dr. Xavier, I have to say that this entire matter leaves me wondering who you really are and how you got mixed up in this situation," Cheskin said, rubbing his neck.

"It was Agent Carlyle who initially contacted me at QPR with questions regarding a research agreement with the Saudis and its possible connection to problems in the Middle East. From that point on, it seemed I became an unwitting participant in the events that followed."

"You don't expect me to believe that you didn't know what was going on."

Xavier frowned. "Not entirely. But the circumstances dictated my involvement. Friends of mine were threatened, even killed, over a serious mistake in judgment I'd made. It wasn't hard to be drawn into the mix so to speak. I'll always regret that it costs the lives of so many people."

Cheskin didn't respond immediately. He slowly picked up a file and handed it to Xavier. "You might take some comfort from this. As a result of your involvement and Agent Carlyle's dogged determination, the agreements with the Saudis and the Chinese are now under full Senate review. It seems that our Secretary of State had very strong incentives to sponsor the arrangements among the parties. He owned substantial shares of stock in Alternate Energy Technology Corporation, which you might know is a subsidiary of Zangshe Inc.

"And it was the secretary who brokered the final agreements with both countries under the aegis of the new International Economic Development Act, which required limited executive review. Unfortunately, as it turned out, the president was not made aware of the details of either agreement. The secretary's role in this matter along with others is currently being investigated on charges stemming from official misconduct to treason for the release of confidential information compromising our national security."

Xavier quickly perused the file; he stopped and looked at Cheskin. "I have to say that your Mr. Riggins is largely responsible for uncovering most of the information that led us to this point. His uncompromising principles and loyalty to the Agency should receive the highest commendations."

Cheskin smiled. "I've only recently become aware of the efforts he had made to document and expose the facts. His ability to somehow intercept vital intel from the Chinese, including the details about the nuclear threat, may have saved millions of lives. His contribution to his country will always be remembered here in the Agency."

Xavier wasn't certain, but Cheskin's remarks about Riggins sounded more like a eulogy. "Where is Mr. Riggins?" he asked slowly.

Cheskin dropped his head slightly. "I'm sorry to say that he passed away late last evening from wounds that he'd received trying to get his report to me."

There was an interminable silence between the two men, as deep sadness crept through every cell of Xavier's body. He hoped his ears had betrayed him, but he knew in his heart that the terrible news was true. *Riggins dead? That crazy, brilliant techie. I told him to watch his ass more carefully,* he reflected with a mixture of anger and remorse. "Who killed him?" he finally asked.

"We think it was someone connected to a local sleeper cell. The weapon used was one that they've employed in the past. I've got most of my agents and half the FBI in D.C. scouring for every lead."

"With all due respect, Director, I doubt it's a terrorist hit—only made to look that way," he said. The director took obvious note of his comment. Xavier added with a sigh, "I'm deeply saddened by the death of Mr. Riggins. I'd developed great respect for him over this matter and considered him a good ally . . . and friend. He'll be deeply missed."

"He will indeed," Cheskin agreed. "What will you do now, Dr. Xavier?"

Xavier's mind was cluttered with varying emotions, all conflicting and congealing. "I haven't thought about it much," he replied truthfully. "But I'd like to make certain that former agent Veracruz is not implicated in any way over the incident with the cargo vessel. Beyond that, I'm not sure what I'll do. Once I'm back home in Black Hills, I'll decide on what's next in my life."

"In regards to Veracruz, I'm not certain what your concern is," Cheskin replied matter-of-factly. "The Coast Guard report clearly indicates an accidental sinking of the cargo vessel, most likely the result of the storm."

Xavier forced a grin. "Convenient, that storm, but not something I'd planned on."

"Speaking of which, how *did* you manage to stop the Chinese vessel?"

"It was basic chemistry, Director. A little electrolysis under the right conditions can make a helluva hole," Xavier replied.

"Whatever it was, the country and this agency owe you a debt of enormous gratitude," Cheskin said. "If you ever decide to come back, there's a job waiting for you. We could use your talents."

"Thanks, Director. But I think that part of my life is finally over. What's the news on Agent Carlyle?'

Cheskin shook his head. "Unfortunately, he's completely off the grid. The last thing we know is that he took a flight out of Dubai to Riyadh and then on to Hong Kong. He may have made an attempt to contact me, but the call failed. Since then, we've heard nothing."

Riyadh, Hong Kong?! What was he up to? Xavier wondered. "I hope he's safe. But I had a bad feeling when I left him in Dubai."

"I've put the word out that he's a very valuable asset and we want him back here in one piece. I trust he'll get through to us somehow if he's still alive," Cheskin replied sincerely.

He had already lost Riggins, and so it was even harder for Xavier to believe that Harry could be gone as well. Nevertheless, he knew that between the Saudis and the Chinese, Carlyle was a marked man. "If you do hear from him, I'd like to know, Director."

Cheskin nodded. "Leave a contact number with Sergeant Strong, Doctor," he said, as both men stood up and shook hands.

"On behalf of the country, I want to thank you again for what you did," Cheskin said. "Oh . . . incidentally, Mr. Riggins had left this for you—a name he thought might be of interest to you," he said, handing Xavier a slightly tattered and bloodstained piece of paper folded in quarters enclosed in a small plastic sleeve. "I was able to recover it from part of the file that was found on him."

Xavier had seen plenty of blood before, but seeing Riggins's blood made him pause. He placed the sleeve in his pocket. It was a painful reminder of the whole affair.

"Thanks, Director," he replied solemnly, walking out of the office with a heavy heart.

99

FATE

Beijing, China

Minister Chek was in the midst of discussing the formalities of the Zangshe site inspections with a few members of the INA when his assistant interrupted with a knock at the conference room door. She motioned for him to join her in the hall.

Once they were in private, she bowed and said with an apologetic tone, "Mr. Minister, the National People's Congress has summoned you. They have directed that you appear *immediately.*" She stressed the last word more so than she probably had to.

Chek was at first surprised, then concerned that his independent behavior may have finally reached the boiling point. Over the past ten years, he had been highly regarded for his acumen in technology, but he had become a target of criticism for advancing the welfare of the common people. Although he enjoyed the support of the premier, his views were not widely popular, especially among the elitist within the Communist Party hierarchy. He wondered with apprehension if his day of reckoning had arrived.

He returned to the conference room and quickly adjourned the meeting without explanation. Then, without further preparations, he

walked from the ministry offices to the large and imposing main building where the Chinese Politburo Standing Committee of the National
People's Party was located. Chek had made several presentations there
in the past and knew the workings of the building quite well. When he
arrived at the main reception desk, he assumed he would be directed to
one of the large hearing rooms to appear before the Politburo's panel.
Instead, he was escorted past the hearing room and upstairs toward
the offices of the premier.

A strong feeling of uneasiness came over him—a feeling he was
unaccustomed to. His bravado and courage under fire had always been
his hallmark among his peers as well as his superiors. But to be summoned by the National Party Congress was never regarded as a positive request. Even he began to doubt the outcome of his future, now
apparently in the hands of the Politburo.

Chek was quickly ushered into an anteroom outside the main office
complex. Expecting to be instructed to wait, he looked around for seat-
ing. But the escort, instead, led him through the large carved door and
directly into the cavernous offices of the National People's Congress.

"Minister Chek," the Secretary of the Politburo greeted him. "I am
pleased you have come so quickly. There is a matter of grave concern
we wish to discuss with you. Is there something we can get for you? A
refreshment maybe?"

The offer was unexpected. Chek bowed politely. "Thank you, but I
am quite fine," he replied, gazing in awe at the dimensions and scale of
the space. The room was adorned with early-century Chinese carvings
and sculptures reflective of the many periods of Chinese rule and domination over vast regions of the Asian continent.

Chek observed that seated around the enormous oval-shaped table
and surrounding the secretary were several people he did not recognize. He was directed to sit at the opposite end of the table facing the
secretary.

"In that instance, we would like to begin," the secretary continued.
"As you are aware, Minister Chek, we have followed your progress in

the party with much interest. You have demonstrated a certain independent manner and have made some rather controversial decisions on matters of public policy. Your inclinations toward the rights of the common worker have not set well with some in our government. And a few of your actions have even garnered international attention. It is partially the reason that we have summoned you here today. There is an event that has arisen of very serious consequences. One in which your character and strength will surely be tested."

Chek was completely and utterly clueless as to the manner and meaning of the meeting. It was abundantly clear to him that whatever was about to happen would be well documented for the premier's review. He believed at that moment that his beloved grandmother's vision of his future was misguided. She had predicted great things for him. She foresaw his triumph over many tribulations and his place as an important person in China's history. She had been correct about so many things. But now, he thought, that all of it had amounted to little more than a grandmother's fervent wish for her only grandson.

"Minster Chek, it is with great awareness of our current role in the world as a leader that necessitates we make the right decision for our country. We had entrusted you with the responsibility of an important ministry position. One in which the highest degree of integrity and devotion to the betterment of our culture was vested. And most consistently, you have demonstrated the willingness to ignore certain restrictions and proceed under your own guidance," the secretary paused, and Chek fought the urge to shift in his chair. "We have summoned you here today," the secretary began again, "to request your continued leadership and your example of modern enlightened initiative in the capacity . . . as our new premier. As you know, Premier Wei has been ill for sometime now and is incapable of continuing in his current position."

Chek was completely overwhelmed by the announcement. For the first time in his life, his tongue was silent. He could do little but muster a short bow.

The secretary continued. "I know this may be rather shocking news to you, Minister Chek. But, although you are relatively young in years, your behavior and demeanor have demonstrated a wise and thoughtful manner. Most everyone here in the ruling party structure is convinced of your superior qualifications. Premier Wei has always thought of you as his protégé and has given us his blessings on this decision. I trust you will embrace it as you have everything else requested of you."

Again, Chek bowed, deeply this time, and cleared his throat. "I am most honored you have entrusted me with your faith. I have great love for our culture and the Chinese people. Our role in the world today will be judged by how we govern our immense population. More importantly, we will be challenged by the demands of a world struggling to survive its own excesses. I welcome the opportunity to lead our country toward better and more humane solutions and gratefully accept the responsibility of premier."

100

RECKONING

Black Hills, South Dakota

Xavier phoned Veracruz as he headed toward his gate for his flight back to Black Hills. He wanted to check on the progress of his friend's arm and to inform him about his meeting with Director Cheskin.

"You'll be pleased to know, Alex, that we had nothing to do with the sinking of the cargo vessel. It seems that the Coast Guard had officially reported the incident as an accident of the storm. In any case, I hope your arm's better and you can soon get back to enjoying the many fruits of your South Florida lifestyle."

"Thanks, buddy. But the rest of me works just fine," Veracruz chuckled. "It was real . . . I mean the whole adventure. Glad everything turned out okay. If you're down this way again, let's plan on doing something a bit more relaxing and definitely on dry land. Stay in touch."

Xavier smiled. "I'll let you pick the activity next time. But for now it's back home to South Dakota. There's a lady there I'm praying recovers enough for you to meet one day. Many thanks again, Alex," he said. He stopped briefly at the newsstand to pick up a copy of the *Wall*

Street Journal. Glancing down the front page, his face glowed with a wide smile.

The headlines read:

NEW GOVERNMENT IN CHINA BEGINS ITS REFORMS
WITH CRACKDOWN ON ALL INHUMANE TREATMENT OF WORKERS

In the body of the story, the new ruling party, headed by its recently appointed Premier Yao Chek, had initiated new guidelines for the equitable treatment of all workers in the Chinese economy. Furthermore, all industries that didn't comply with strict regulations for safe working environments would be severely penalized.

But that wasn't what had gotten Xavier's attention. In the second paragraph, in bold type, was a related story:

The former chairman of Zangshe Inc., Kongi Khan, has been arrested by the People's Liberation Army. Khan has been cited for his role in the egregious manner in which his company has fostered and continued the harmful nuclear-waste storage practices that has led to the deaths of countless hundreds of thousands of local Chinese villagers and workers. In another move that portrayed the new Chinese regime's intolerance of such abuses, all assets of Zangshe, including its current mining operation, have been nationalized. Proceeds from the profits derived from ongoing operations as well as from the cache of assets will go toward a fund established to compensate families who have lost members due to various forms of radiation poisoning.

How damn fitting, Xavier thought. *There's some justice in the world after all.*

Xavier's flight had landed in Black Hills a little after midnight. He grabbed his carry-on bag and headed for the taxi stand. Since there was no curfew for visiting critically ill patients, he had the cabbie drop him off at the hospital.

After checking in with the front desk, Xavier made his way to Rachel's room. It was dark except for the glow of the life-support machines. Xavier bent over and stroked her once silky hair. He was shocked at how much her condition had deteriorated over the past weeks. Her normally healthy complexion and skin tone had diminished to a sickly pallor. The machines pumped incessantly, keeping her lungs breathing and blood flowing.

The entire sequence of horrible events came rushing back to him. The sight of her lying on the rail car floor, his cradling of her body, and the urgency in the hospital was almost too much. He sat down beside her bed with his head in hands and wept.

It wasn't the first time he had done so, but it was the first time he had truly come to grips with the reality of her situation. And he longed for her to be well, to be able to hold her and to start a new life with her by his side.

He reached out and squeezed her hand. The hours passed as he held her nearly lifeless hand in his own. The night nurse had come by to change her medical gown and bedding. She nodded to him and left. He moved closer to her again and said a prayer. Something he hadn't done in earnest in years. As he gazed out her hospital window at the moonless black sky, he thought he felt her hand twitch. *Probably an involuntary muscle reaction,* he thought. Then it happened again. His own heart skipped a beat. He tried to keep his hope from getting the better of him. Could this be a good sign or was it part of her condition? But it continued occurring. He waited until morning to talk with the doctor.

Xavier explained what had happened during the night. The doctor listened attentively.

"Dr. Xavier, your friend has suffered a very traumatic injury. Some involuntary movements are to be expected. I wouldn't get my hopes up too much. If it continues and there appears to be a pattern to them, we'll try to evaluate the situation more carefully."

"I prefer to remain hopeful. She's a fighter with an indomitable spirit," Xavier replied.

"I'm glad you feel that way. She needs that kind of support," the doctor said, patting him reassuringly on the shoulder.

With a renewed sense of optimism, Xavier left the hospital to go home and change his clothes. With no other plans, he decided to spend all of his time with Rachel until she recovered. He had owed her that much and more.

Returning to his house, Xavier noticed that hardly anything had changed—except for the mail that had piled up on his kitchen table. Apparently Mac Cowen had been collecting it during his absence. As Xavier casually went through the stack of mostly garbage mail, he was reminded of the folded piece of paper that Cheskin had handed him, which he had forgotten in the aftermath of everything that had happened.

He shook the paper out of the plastic sleeve and unfolded it. Much of it had been rendered illegible by the bloodstains, but he was able to make out several paragraphs in Mandarin. Riggins had attempted to translate them. He had gotten most of it correct.

The Chinese contact at QPR was a scientist. But Xavier was momentarily confused. They had already deduced that Elliot Winston was the contact. Why would the techie go to the trouble of reconfirming that fact? But as Xavier transcribed further, it was clear there was a different name, indicating that someone else was the contact and the hacker . . . the one who had harassed and finally targeted and killed his friend. Riggins had translated it as *Gordon Hairston,* but Xavier knew that Western names in Mandarin didn't exactly translate. That's when he realized, to his utter horror, who the QPR conspirator was— Gunter Hammerstein!

At that moment, Xavier felt as if someone had dropped a hammer on him. He had wrongly accused Elliot Winston of betraying everyone and conniving with the Chinese. All the time it was Hammerstein. It was the Austrian who had transmitted the hybrid data to Zangshe and had him set up to be killed at the general store. In the end, it was Hammerstein who was ultimately responsible for everyone's misery, including the attack on Rachel and Riggins's death—and most probably the death of his wife and daughter too.

It all made tragic sense when he thought about Hammerstein's unlimited access to QPR's research, including Winston's encrypted files, and his unparalleled computer skills. Riggins's skills had been beyond very good, but he had still been no match for the Austrian's unrivaled genius in the cyberworld. The facts that Hammerstein was married to Khan's sister and had taught at the University of Beijing where they had met were buried deep behind a secured Chinese firewall. It was Riggins who had put it all together—albeit to his final detriment.

Xavier vowed somehow, someway, to find Hammerstein and make him pay dearly with his life. His head was spinning with rage and mind-numbing revenge when his PDA chimed.

"Dr. Xavier, this is Dr. Wilson at the hospital. After you'd left this morning, Ms. Sinclair began showing some signs of consciousness. I'm not sure yet what it all means, but I think you should come back to the hospital as soon as possible."

Xavier tucked his anger away for another time. "I'll be right there!" he said with enthusiasm. *Maybe I'll get her back,* he thought hopefully. *I need her now more than ever.*

Outside, his Jaguar was waiting for him. It had been fully repaired and looked like new—vintage new. He plucked a note from the windshield. It read, *I took care of both of your girls while you were away.* —Mac

Xavier smiled, and ran his hand along the smooth finish. *Life has a way of coming full circle,* he thought to himself, as he climbed in and accelerated the powerful roadster through the winding turns along the ridge road down toward the hospital . . . and Rachel.

EPILOGUE

Shortly following the nationalization of Zangshe Inc., the INA had issued its findings in the investigation of the Jebel Ali explosion. It was determined that Zangshe had purposefully initiated the destruction of its vessel, which had caused a nuclear-waste catastrophe of devastating proportions. The new Chinese regime had immediately acknowledged its liability and agreed to pay reparations to the government of the U.A.E. for the extensive cleanup process and the construction of a newly relocated desalination plant.

An international tribunal had also determined that the egregious Jebel Ali charges leveled at Zangshe's former chairman had constituted war crimes.

After an extended trial lasting almost nine months in which Khan vehemently denied all allegations and had attempted to bribe every member of the tribunal, a verdict was handed down to the Chinese Supreme People's Court for final disposition. Kongi Khan was eventually found guilty on all charges. In addition, under the auspices of the new premier, Khan was further found guilty of reckless disregard for human life resulting in the deaths of countless thousands of Chinese people, including the new premier's family. And in a most unprecedented motion, Premier Chek personally signed the final order of the courts and recommended the maximum penalty for punishment. On a cold, blustery day, Khan was led manacled into an old abandoned mineshaft. Wearing the clothes of a common worker, his head shaved clean, Khan was executed by a Chinese firing squad.

Amidst the wake of happenings surrounding the new Chinese premier and the downfall of Khan, there was another less-publicized development on the international economic front. The nuclear-fuel production facility that had been constructed on seized Saudi Arabian territory, as well as the nearly 10 million metric tons of nuclear-waste material in the newly designed storage areas, were all turned over to the Saudi government. And in return for the U.S.'s assistance in helping to secure certain Zangshe assets from China, the Saudi government agreed to enter into a long-term energy alliance with the U.S.

With the blessings of the new secretary of state and the full support of the U.S. Administration, the chairman of the restructured AET Corporation, Andrew Wyncroft, had negotiated a joint venture with the Saudi government for the development of an entirely new form of energy system. Coupled with the nuclear-conversion engine design, the encapsulated-uranium fuel would create worldwide market opportunities and help lead the Saudi royal family back to prominence. Princess Almira bin Razul was named the president of the newly formed joint-venture entity and had finally proven her father right that she would be the one to restore the royal family back to prominence.

After the arrest of former chairman Khan, his closet friend and fellow Mongolian escaped the clutches of the Peoples Liberation Army. Gansukh Yakubla had taken refuge at a secluded resort owned by him in Hong Kong. His own massive investments would afford him the most opulent of lifestyles for the rest of his life. He lived as if he hadn't a care in the world, totally unaware of Princess Almira's agreement to provide valuable intel to the director of the CIA as part of the new American-Saudi energy alliance.

Cheskin, however, wasn't the first person to receive the valuable intel from the princess. There was another who had obtained it earlier and under different circumstances. When he had returned to the royal palace, he had confronted the princess about her deceptions and liaisons with the Chinese. Threatening to complicate her negotiating status with the U.S. authorities, she had reluctantly agreed to give him her Chinese contact in Saudi Arabia. She had told him about the suspected whereabouts of the one who had orchestrated the Jebel Ali explosion, the attempts on his life, and the murders of his friends.

ॐ

On an overcast morning in the bustling downtown center of Hong Kong, Yakubla had decided to enjoy the day with one of his many concubines and had given his bodyguards the day off. His brand-new bulletproof Rolls Royce had pulled up in the front of the world-class Mandarin Oriental Hotel. With the aplomb of a dignitary, Yakubla exited the rear door of his car and walked arrogantly toward the grand lobby entrance.

From across the square, on a nondescript building rooftop, a lone gunman had waited patiently. After following a trail of leads, he had received a tip from a local contact that his target would be making an appearance at this location. Sighting his sniper weapon and staying motionless without the hint of breathing, he took dead aim at the big Mongolian. With a deft squeeze of the trigger, the high-powered projectile exploded from the barrel and struck the right arm of Yakubla, severing it. The next round, fired in quick succession, severed his left arm. As Yakubla screamed out in agony, the sniper let go another round, which tore a three-inch hole in his back. Still conscious, the final bullet struck the base of Yakubla's head with such force and angle that it blew it clean off his neck.

The sniper efficiently packed up his weapon and went downstairs to join the hysterical throng that had gathered. He calmly walked over to the Mongolian's mutilated body and threw down two Marine-sniper insignias.

Looking out over the Champs-Elysees from her stylish apartment, Elena Dupre contemplated the events that had recently transpired. In the course of the melee that had ensued following the PLA's arrest of Zangshe Inc.'s chairman, she was able to slip through unnoticed. Within a few days, she had safely made her way out of China and back to France. In the time preceding the announcement of Minister Chek's appointment, Elena was able to gather valuable intel about the extent of Zangshe's nuclear operations. Most of it, she had already passed along to her agency contact. But one tidbit of information was important to only one special person. And that person would be very interested in knowing the whereabouts of the hacker and the conspirator from QPR.

She opened a file in her computer tablet, paused reflectively for a few moments, and smiled. With a gentle touch from her strong nimble fingers, she slowly pressed the key function. A parting intel message was sent to a former close friend and fellow operative.

ACKNOWLEDGMENTS

A debt of gratitude to Dr. Nikola Stojsin for his intellectual guidance and tireless efforts in discussing technical concepts and reviewing early, not-ready-for-prime-time manuscripts.

To Colonel T.J. Segura, Major Spence Cyzmanski, and Master Sergeant Mac Grady for valuable insights.

To my many affiliations at Bell Labs Research for perspectives gained.

To my friends at the FBI and CIA whose dedication and personas provided inspiration. You know who you are.

To my dear friend Albert Gencarella for his candid comments and encouragement.

To David Hammond, Mark Blackburn, Robin Jay, Barry Weiss, and all my colleagues at Horizon Publishing for their constant support and professionalism.

To my editor, Carol Rosenberg, for helping to get me past the finish line. And to her husband and business partner, Gary Rosenberg, for his artistic talent.

And finally to my best friend and beautiful wife, Jayne, for her patience, faith in me, and constructive criticisms. Her "I need a good book to read, why don't you write me one?" remark, was the initial catalyst. All my love.

ABOUT THE AUTHOR

Geoff Hammond is a successful entrepreneur. Although he's been writing for many years, *The Last Khan* is his first novel. Inexplicably, his extensive treatises related to business ventures and strategic misadventures somehow became the precursors for this seemingly ripped-from-the-headlines fictitious work. He and his wife, Jayne, divide their time between the pristine beaches of South Florida and the gentle, rolling hills of Tennessee.